LIGHTNING STRIKES TWICE

DALE M. NELSON

Copyright © 2025 by Dale M. Nelson.

All rights reserved.

No part of this book may be reproduced in any form or by any electronic or mechanical means, including information storage and retrieval systems, without written permission from the author, except for the use of brief quotations in a book review.

Severn River Publishing
www.SevernRiverBooks.com

This is a work of fiction. Names, characters, businesses, places, events and incidents are either the products of the author's imagination or used in a fictitious manner. Any resemblance to actual persons, living or dead, or actual events is purely coincidental.

ISBN: 978-1-64875-650-4 (Paperback)

ALSO BY DALE M. NELSON

The Gage Files

No Prayers for the Dying

One Bullet Away

Lightning Strikes Twice

Even Gods Bleed

With Andrew Watts

Agent of Influence

A Future Spy

Tournament of Shadows

All Secrets Die

Never miss a new release! Sign up for the reader list at

severnriverbooks.com

"...we are all underground men making the brief transit from darkness to darkness."
—Ross Macdonald

"In war, truth is the first casualty."
—Aeschylus

1

I trudged into my office at the crack of two and ordered a drink.

By "office," I mean the Santa Monica tiki bar where I conduct most of my affairs. I'd just abandoned a case when I'd realized what the client was really after was some light industrial espionage packaged as research for a wrongful termination suit. I figured out what was going on before I'd broken any laws, but the client didn't appreciate when I'd called him out, and now I wasn't getting paid.

So, it seemed like a good time to drop by Cosmic Ray's and figure out my next move.

I was enough of a fixture here that they eventually named a drink after me. I'm forbidden from disclosing exactly what's in "Gage's Grog," but three of them in a row will put me on the floor. Ask me how I know.

The drink order wasn't so much an exchange of words as much as it was Ray seeing the look on my face and interpreting the need. About five minutes later, Carrie, one of the semiprofessional surfers who rounded out waking hours with shifts at the bar, set the tiki glass in front of me with its scowling tribal masks. "Smile, Matt, you're scaring the tourists," she said.

Whatever.

I needed that job. It'd been a slow and agonizing couple of months since Miami, and I was running out of things to take my mind off what I'd done there. I was also hoping this case would have been a bridge into more corporate security work. Anything steadier than this. Overproof rum and neon juices chipped away at my mood but didn't markedly improve it. It wasn't just being lied to. It was more that this asshole genuinely thought that hiring me to steal from his ex-employer was a legitimate way to advance his career. And that it was okay to make me complicit in the act.

Also, there was no other work in the pipeline.

Well, at least I had enough in my pocket to pay for the drink.

Wait...did I?

Shit.

My phone rang, and Jennie's face appeared on the screen. I used a picture of her looking out over the water at sunset. It was a candid shot, capturing a nice moment. For some reason, Jennie was angry I didn't use her official portrait. Like anyone else is going to see my phone.

"Hey," I said.

It could've been my mood or it could've been the alcohol adding some fuzz to my voice; she responded with asking me what was wrong.

"Nothing," I told her. "Just a shit day. What's up?"

Jennie was the reason I'd moved to LA in the first place. Well, maybe not all of it, but the scale tilted heavily in her favor.

Our relationship is complicated. At least, for me. We never broke up all those years ago, in that she never said the words and I certainly didn't. The thing just faded into the background until it wasn't anymore, so I never got the benefit of closure. She, apparently, didn't need it. We were like the Koreas, with the occasional hook-up. Armistice with benefits.

"I need to talk to you. Where are you?"

"I'm at the office," I said, and swirled the remnants of my drink, hoping she couldn't hear the ice crack.

"How soon can you get home?"

"Why not just come here?"

"I'm not...Matt, this is serious. I need to see you, right now."

My senses weren't deadened enough that I couldn't detect the concern in her voice.

"Okay," I said. "I can be home in five minutes. My car is here, though. I can come to your place. It's not a big deal."

"No, it's got to be yours."

I rented one floor of a split-level, midcentury home a few blocks from the beach. My landlord was a nice guy, if a little usurious. Whereas Jennie had a fortieth floor, corner-view condo in the Fashion District. I much preferred meetings at her place. It wasn't typical digs for an investigative journalist, but she'd been part of a team that broke the Panama Papers about ten years ago, for which she'd earned a Pulitzer Prize and a book deal, hence the luxury condo.

"Can you tell me what's going on, at least?"

"Not over the phone," she said.

I slid out of the booth, hoping I still had my sea legs, and made for the door.

"Matt," Carrie called after me.

Right. The check.

"Put it on my tab," I said.

"Seriously, for like the eightieth time. We. Do. Not. Have. Tabs. And if we did, yours would be seriously overdrawn." She put her hands on her hips and cocked them to one side, which is the universal gesture shared by all women that can best be interpreted as, "I've exceeded the amount of shit I signed up to take today."

The patron saint of itinerant private detectives chose that moment to smile upon me, because there was a crumpled twenty in my pocket. I gave that to Carrie and asked for no change.

Turned out, that would be the last run of good luck I'd see for a while.

On a good day, it was forty-one minutes from Jennie's condo to my place, and there were no good days in LA. However, she arrived ten minutes after I did, so she must have been on the move when she called. Jennie was tall, lithe, and possessed of a kind of elegance that could not be taught. Her blond hair was streaked through with natural highlights, and I'd go to my grave swearing her eyes were blue-green.

She breezed past me when I opened the door, leaving only a whisper of her perfume. There was no hug. "So, now will you tell me what's going on?"

Jennie stopped midway into my living room and turned on her heel.

"This is the only place in LA County that I am absolutely certain is free from electronic surveillance," she said.

One of the biggest challenges for the security inclined is society's reliance on wireless connectivity for everything. It's harder to find wired devices, so I've had to become something of an audiophile. You'd be amazed at how easy it is to turn a Bluetooth or Wi-Fi device into a microphone. Thankfully, my landlord was cool about my wiring the place for surround sound, with speakers conveniently placed right near the windows. I put music on to muffle the sound of our conversation and make it harder to record the vibrations on the windows. Yes, I do periodically sweep my home and my Land Rover for bugs.

"You know about my reporting on Russia, right?" Jennie asked from her seat on my couch. I sank into the love seat next to her.

Jennie was an investigative reporter, with most of her work through the Orpheus Foundation, a Brussels-based collective of journalists specializing in exposing governmental corruption and transnational crime. However, they went after the Russian Federation with a particular vengeance.

"Well, I remember that your work with the Panama Papers kicked off a whole series of stories on where Russian oligarchs were hiding their money. Memory serves, more than a couple European governments and multinationals weren't happy to find that out. Is that what this is about? You aren't worried about the Russians, are you?" The Russian Federation had a bad habit of silencing their own journalists, though I'd never heard of them going after one from the West.

"Yes, no. Not exactly," she said. "I think it's the FBI."

"Wait, what?"

"It started about six months ago. You were busy with the Miami thing, and I didn't want to bother you. You remember the series I was working on about Havana Syndrome, right?" Jennie said, and I nodded. "I released the most recent story last March, and a couple of FBI agents came to visit me shortly after. They claimed I'd received national security information and demanded I turn over my source. When I told them to go to hell, they got a judge to order me to give up the source. Which, obviously, I won't do. I don't know that they tapped my phone. We've got our lawyers looking into it, but the Justice Department is claiming their national security bullshit and won't disclose whether they are or not."

That explained wanting to meet at my house.

An ugly sensation crashed through my stomach like a bitter tide, and I was already regretting the lava drink I'd had for lunch.

"Havana Syndrome," or what the government officially called "Anomalous Health Incidents," was the term given to describe a spectrum of debilitating symptoms suffered by CIA and State Department officers, even some family members, at overseas postings. The effects included intense pain and pressure in the head, often with sensations of heat, extreme disorientation, vertigo, and nausea. These were almost always accompanied by a metallic ringing or chirping sound. Because the first instances were reported shortly after the US reopened its embassy in Cuba, it became known as Havana Syndrome.

I knew about it all too well.

Initially, we wondered if the Cuban intelligence service, the DGI, had an electromagnetic or sonic weapon they used to target our spies and diplomats. The Cubans couldn't have built something like that on their own. They didn't really have the knowhow, and decades of crippling sanctions had all but ruled out the presence of any domestically created advanced technology. The incidents' timing further undercut that theory. If you're Cuba, why undermine the thawing of US-Cuban relations and risk eliminating sanctions by attacking the Americans?

Their one-time patrons, Russia, on the other hand, could absolutely do it.

The incidents mysteriously stopped in 2021. A year later, the Office of the Director of National Intelligence said that they'd just concluded an "exhaustive multiyear study" conducted by an external panel of experts who'd concluded that these Anomalous Health Incidents were the result of, what they termed, "mass psychogenic illness" caused by "acute stress."

I didn't buy that for a second. Sounded like Jennie didn't either.

"It's no secret that many within government speculated the Russians were behind this," Jennie said.

"Well, even if the Cubans were responsible for the incidents in Havana, they could never have developed it themselves. Fidel Castro was still alive when we reestablished diplomatic relations. The DGI was also intensely loyal to him, perhaps more so than they were to the country. There was a theory that Fidel wanted to undermine the diplomatic thaw and perhaps the Russians gave him a tool to do it."

"I have a source. He's a diplomat stationed in Europe. He has a contact, a Russian national, who says they can confirm their security services are responsible for these attacks. He offered to introduce us, says the guy is willing to talk. I was hoping you could meet him and vet him to see if he's telling the truth."

"I don't know, Jen."

"You told me before you thought the Russians were involved, if not overtly responsible," she said.

"This isn't really what I do."

"Matt, you have a hell of a lot more experience at telling if people are worth the information they claim to have than you do cracking cases."

"This is complicated for me, for a number of reasons. First, I'm not sure I want to get in between you and the FBI. I just got those guys off my back. I have my PI license now, which they'd blocked me from getting. Russian intelligence also knows my true identity. Not sure it's a great idea poking that bear."

That wasn't all, though.

Havana Syndrome was personal for me. I'd been in Cuba on an op once, and my partner was hit by whatever it was. The Agency brass didn't believe his account, and I went to bat for him. They accused him of malingering. It turned out to be a common refrain for those suffering from AHI. Agency leadership would deny the incidents, downplay the symptoms, and accuse those suffering of dodging work.

It was little more than institutionalized gaslighting.

My friend had been badly hurt, but no one took it seriously. Maybe it was because there was no "evidence." I don't know. I'd already earned a reputation at Langley for having sharp elbows in narrow hallways. My loud and persistent advocating for Dylan and the increasing number of victims did nothing but hone my inclination toward windmill tilting. I burned a lot of bridges trying to get people to pay attention. Later, when I needed the political support to bail me out of my own shitstorm, the help wasn't there.

It was viscerally painful and humiliating, and I didn't want to relive any of that.

Most of all, I didn't want to potentially expose more survivors—some of whom I knew well—only to have them endure the pain of false hopes smashed against the rocks. Call me cynical, but I didn't see a news story reversing bureaucratic opinion. What good was tearing open old wounds? The Director of National Intelligence issued a final report and could back their conclusion up with thousands of pages of research and expert testimony.

Jennie wanted me to talk to a guy.

I didn't say any of this to her. In her mind, this would be all the validation she needed. Instead, I told her, "I'm sorry, I can't get involved. I have reasons for that, and I want you to respect them."

"I'm not asking you to get involved, Matt. All I want you to do is talk to my source. Agree to meet their contact. If he seems legit, tell me, and I'll take it from there."

"Why can't your contact just do that?"

"Because he's not you. He's an economist. You already know that the Russians have come after the Foundation more than once. I just want your read on this guy that he knows what he's talking about and that this isn't some attempt at getting inside."

I could appreciate that. The Orpheus Foundation had made a powerful and unforgiving enemy of the Kremlin over the years and needed to constantly stay vigilant for reprisal.

"That's the other thing," I said.

"What other thing?"

"Your whistleblower. The State Department has an official channel for that. First of all, they shouldn't be talking with a Russian citizen about this shit. I'm assuming this person is still overseas? They need to report that to their Regional Security Officer."

"They've tried official channels. No one is listening."

"That doesn't mean it's okay to go to the press."

"Whose side are you on, Matt?"

"Some things aren't easily distilled into 'sides,' Jen. Someone doesn't get the answer they like, so they leak it to the press?"

"That's not what this is."

"Well, I can tell you that the ratio of Edward Snowdens to Mark Felts is about a thousand to one."

It was fair to say that in most of my career, I'd maintained, at best, a casual relationship with the rules. One area where I absolutely did not bend was with leaking information to the press. I think Felt did the right thing, because he had absolutely no other recourse. You figure out the president violated the law, there are perilously few options. Especially when that president was Richard Nixon. And, he gave Woodward and Bernstein clues. They had to figure it out. Despite all that, Felt still agonized over the decision. I was sure that Jennie's source had multiple official avenues they hadn't pursued.

Jennie leaned forward, closing the distance between us.

"Matt, I brought some of my backgrounding. Please look at that tonight. If you're still not convinced it's worth pursuing, I won't ask again." Jennie reached into her bag and pulled out a thumb drive and a slip of paper. "It's encrypted. Here's the passphrase."

That, in and of itself, was something. Jennie normally acted like my security precautions verged on paranoia. The fact that she was following them spoke volumes. She was genuinely scared about something.

I took the drive.

"I'll have a look and let you know," I said.

Jennie stood.

"Not being believed is an awful feeling. I thought you'd…I don't know, your reaction surprised me."

"I have very little to hold onto right now. Please understand why I don't want to risk what little I've got."

"You are the only person I trust with this."

Jennie touched my shoulder, though I couldn't interpret the gesture. She left. I fired up my laptop, accessed her information, and started skimming it to get a sense of what I was looking at. Then, I decided that I'd need to make some phone calls.

If I have a character flaw…and mind you, I said *if*, it's that I can't say no to her.

2

Jennie's research was, as always, thorough and compelling.

There were some fifteen hundred documented instances of Havana Syndrome since 2016. By 2017, there were cases reported at our embassies in Moscow, Taiwan, China, Colombia, Vietnam, and several former Soviet republics. More concerning were the incidents reported in allied nations, Australia and the United Kingdom, and one instance against Canadian diplomats on a delegation to Pittsburgh. The staff at Vienna Station reported multiple instances; some were so severe it required the emergency medevac of multiple personnel. Eventually, Langley sacked the Chief of Station over it.

Most troubling, perhaps, was the attack against a US national security staffer on the White House grounds.

In the first days, before the government knew what was happening, they referred some victims to a neurologist at the University of Pennsylvania. A 2018 research panel sponsored by Penn published a report in the *Journal of the American Medical Association* concluding that the affected Havana personnel suffered brain injuries. A subsequent report from a different group of scientists concluded these injuries were consistent with the effects of electromagnetic exposure, specifically radio frequency or microwave.

Then, conflicting studies started appearing. One suggested that "psychological distress" could also cause the reported symptoms. Another assessed the ringing or buzzing sound commonly associated with the cases was actually caused by, of all things, the Indian short-tailed cricket.

I followed a seeming point/counterpoint with the research. One group would issue a study suggesting the cause was some form of directed energy, and another would appear arguing the opposite. One weapons expert would state in an interview that the effects could only be attributed to a weapon. Another would argue later it couldn't possibly be. Looking at it in the aggregate, it seemed like two sides of something plinking each other from the shadows.

Jennie's research noted that symptoms varied across the different locations. Some of the effects in Guangzhou were different than those reported in Vienna, as an example. The Intelligence Community said that proved their argument this couldn't be the result of a weapon. Jennie asked a question here: *Does this suggest different weapons?*

Jennie's research did not include any information from the State Department source or their Russian contact. She and I communicated periodically that night over Signal, an encrypted messaging app, and she explained that she wasn't letting that information out of her sight until she knew I was on board.

Without that, it was hard for me to evaluate whether I should proceed. Eventually, Jennie relented and said I could come over and see it. I said I would when I got back. I told her that I needed to speak to some people, and those conversations had to be in person. Jennie said the Foundation would cover my travel, as they always did.

Before it got too late in the evening, I called Dylan West.

There was a conversation we needed to have, and I wouldn't do it over the phone.

After he confirmed it was okay for me to come talk to him, I booked a flight the next morning for Santa Fe.

Like me, Dylan had joined the CIA following 9/11 out of a patriotic need to do *something*. We'd joined the Clandestine Service at the same time, though it wasn't until our posting in Nate McKellar's unacknowledged dirty tricks squad that we became close friends. Our unit was created to go after the dangerously powerful and chronically unaccountable. The Russian oligarchs whose dark money moved whole economies, the terrorist financiers, and the people who sold arms to terrible people so they could finance overthrowing governments they didn't like. We went after the worst of humanity in operations that our government would flat-out deny existed if we were caught.

That was what brought us to Havana in 2017. Following the first instances of Havana Syndrome, the Secretary of State announced we would be closing the embassy indefinitely. That also meant the CIA station inside it. Dylan and I entered Cuba under a commercial cover with the mission of seeing what the Cuban DGI and Russian operatives on the island would do in our absence. Would they try to infiltrate the embassy or our station? Would they go after our network of assets? Turns out, all of the above. We caught the Russians trying to break into the embassy and stopped them. Then framed them for some actions we knew would force the Cuban government to expel them.

One night in his hotel room, Dylan felt a wave of heat hit him, followed by an intense ringing or buzzing sound. Then came the pressure. He told me he felt like his head was in a vise grip. Alerted to similar reports from Agency officers stationed there, Dylan immediately knew the same thing was happening to him. He rolled out of bed and moved into another part of the room, feeling a brief sensation of relief, until he got hit again, only it was more intense now. Whatever it was, it followed him. Dylan scrambled to the bathroom, getting there just in time to throw up. Then, it hit him a third time. Dylan stumbled into the hallway and came to look for me.

As soon as he made it to the hallway, the pressure, the noise, it all stopped. He'd stay nauseated and disoriented for some time.

Why hadn't the same thing happened to me? Because I was in a new room and whatever person at the hotel on the DGI payroll hadn't had time to report the change. The toilet in my original hotel room had broken, and when they said they couldn't get a plumber for a few days, I asked for a new room and greased the gears with some currency. I'd only just moved my things when Dylan practically collapsed in my doorway.

The next day, it was clear he needed medical attention. I notified Nate of what happened, terminated the mission early, and flew home on the first available flight. That's when Dylan's real nightmare began.

The administration at the time publicly blamed the Cuban government for Havana Syndrome. The Agency's official position, however, was that it was something else. Not only that, they were adamant in their denial that it was a weapon.

We still believed our covers were good. We were just Americans in Cuba, and that made us targets.

Dylan was never the same after Havana.

He had trouble focusing, it took him hours to compose a single cable, and the finished product was often incomprehensible. We couldn't put him back in the field, not until he'd fully recovered. Nate tried to keep him on the team as a support officer, but even that proved to be too much. Reluctantly, Nate had to let him go, and Dylan was reassigned to another section in the Clandestine Service. Dylan bounced between headquarters jobs, each with successively worse performance reviews. In an effort to get him back into the field, headquarters assigned him to a fairly easy job at our station in Panama. Dylan lasted a year. His supervisor said he was lazy, incompetent, and couldn't handle the most rudimentary tasks. They curtailed his tour—a veritable death sentence in the Clandestine Service—and sent him home. This coming from one of the most capable and courageous operations officers I'd ever known.

He wasn't "lazy." He couldn't focus.

Dylan quit the Agency shortly thereafter.

All that time, I'd lobbied on his behalf, even barking at the senior intelligence staff about what happened in Havana.

After he quit the Agency, Dylan and his wife relocated to Santa Fe, where she had family, and they focused on raising their two kids. Dylan was working now. He'd connected with a few other victims and formed an organization to lobby on behalf of the fifteen hundred documented sufferers.

Given all that, you might be wondering why I wasn't barreling into this case at full tilt.

I'd never believed that it was any of the things the government tried to pass off as truth—faulty HVAC, mass hysteria, or goddamned Indian crickets. Christ, we'd known the Russians were working on directed energy weapons since the Cold War. Since the beginning, there had been several government officials who'd gone on record to say they believed this was the result of a weapon and our people were deliberately targeted. Many independent experts said the same, either in testimony or in the press.

But, officially, two successive presidential administrations—wildly opposed to each other—weren't buying it.

With such vociferous denial, I had to wonder if maybe *we'd* gotten it wrong.

I mean, I know what I saw. And I believed Dylan completely. In my darker moments, I wondered if we were in the minority.

The Orpheus Foundation wasn't the only outfit looking into it. *The New York Times*, *The Washington Post*, *The Atlantic*, *Vice News*, along with European outlets *The Guardian* and *The Insider*, all investigated Havana Syndrome. Many of them concluded, as I had, that it seemed at least likely these were intentional attacks by a foreign actor. Despite that reporting, the United States government remained steadfast in its denials.

Given all that, what good did Jennie think we could accomplish here?

That question was on my mind as I pulled up to Dylan's house, gravel crunching under my rental's tires. The home was tucked into a quiet neighborhood in the green foothills on Santa Fe's east side.

We hadn't spoken much since he'd gotten out and even less since I did. I knew Agency connections were hard for him, brought back some memories he'd rather forget. It reminded him that the organization that he'd faithfully served, had sacrificed his health and his future for, had turned its back on him.

Dylan contacted me, though, after I'd gotten booted and said not to let the bastards get me down. He also said he didn't believe what he heard, that he knew me better than that.

Sometimes, you just want to be believed and know someone is in your corner.

Dylan greeted me with a hug and showed me into his home. It was a nice place, single-story in a strong desert southwest vibe. It was new construction. Word was there was a quiet settlement between the Agency and some of the victims, though not all of them. He'd gotten something from them and chose to fight on anyway. Dylan offered me a coffee, and we moved to a living room that had a floor-to-ceiling view of the mountains beyond. My friend had put about twenty pounds on since I'd seen him last. Brown hair, shot with a little gray, and he'd grown a beard, which he kept neat. Dylan had been an avid cyclist and mountain biker when I'd known him. I suspected that was done. We caught up for a while, I shared some of the highlights of my first couple years as a private detective, my work with Orpheus. He told me about his kids, his family, and the work he'd done for the advocacy group he helped start. Dylan seemed like he was in a good place.

Sometimes you can't find peace, but maybe you can find acceptance.

"How are you doing? I mean, really doing?" I asked.

"I have good days and bad ones. Seems like a common refrain among the victims. I can work, now, at least. Took a long time to relearn how to concentrate. I get tired easily. I meditate, do yoga, take a lot of walks. Don't know if any of it helps, but it feels like I'm doing *something*. Advocacy gives me purpose, which is important. I've testified a few times before Congress," Dylan paused and lifted his coffee. "We lost someone recently, Terry Asher. He was an ops guy, like us. Came up a little after we did. Hard charger. His whole identity was being a spook, took it hard when they yanked it away from him. Then, the Agency denying it even existed was more than he decided he wanted to handle. Don't know what else was going on with him. I don't think he'll be the last either."

"Why do you say that?"

"We, the group of us, started looking at veteran suicides after Asher died. There are studies that correlate traumatic brain injury with an increase in suicide rate. And, for a lot of us, this is all we knew. Then to be called a liar. That's a shitty pill, man. We're starting to see other things too, like cancer. We're talking with some medical research groups now. They're trying to figure out if there's a correlation between Havana Syndrome and neurologic conditions like Alzheimer's or Parkinson's."

Before flying out here, I'd told Dylan why I wanted to see him, what Jennie wanted me to do. I didn't want him to feel blindsided when I asked him questions.

"So, you must have spoken to a few hundred other victims at this point, yeah?" I asked.

"Between our guys and State, plus the handful of DoD personnel who have come forward—military attachés, mostly—yeah. I'll say this, Matt, you and I have both been trained to tell when people are being deceptive. Of all the people I've met, only one did I think was making it up. I checked him out. He got kicked out because he was a bad intel officer and was looking for a way to get the Agency back."

"Everyone believes these were intentional acts?"

"I think a lot of people don't know what to believe. I'd say most of the spooks think it was a weapon. There just isn't a plausible explanation for it to be anything else. Crickets and faulty air conditioning? I mean, come on. One thing we all agree on is that the mass psychosis thing is bullshit and insulting."

"The thing that always struck me was you saying that it *followed* you around the room. When I had to testify at your board hearing, that was the point I kept harping on. That you physically moved, it stopped, and then it happened again."

Dylan's jaw tightened, and he went somewhere else for a time. Wherever he went, I let him be.

"Yeah. You know, it happens once, it's a fluke. Three, four times, that's a pattern. This has come up a few times among some of us. Especially people that reported it happening in a room with an exterior window." Dylan shook his head. "I don't want to get us sidetracked, Matt, but you can't know how much I appreciate you going to bat for me. To go through this, and have them call me a liar." Dylan's voice caught in his throat. "I know you caught some hell for it. All we want is to be believed."

I remember thinking the same thing at that board. They actually told me, "If you weren't in the room when it happened, how could you know?"

"I guess that's what this is about," I said. "My client has done a lot of reporting on this."

Dylan nodded. "Yeah, I've read her stuff. Most of us have."

"I need to be careful with how much I share, here, but she's got a source who claims they can prove Russian culpability. She's hired me to vet their information. If she's right, it could blow this open."

"What's the problem?"

"I didn't want to do this without talking to you first. There is going to be some blowback."

"What do I have left that they can take?" Dylan asked.

"The Intelligence Community's report is out and is public record. If she proves them wrong, the only conclusion left is that there was a cover-up. That has consequences. But there's implications for you, too. Your group is making headway, slowly. Maybe it's not recognition, but there's talk Congress might grant you medical benefits. Like they've done with Agent Orange and burn pits. If Jennie swings too hard and misses, especially if her argument is based on a cover-up, the Intelligence Community is going to circle the wagons. They'll pull out of any potential settlement to prove they're right. That opens up a lot of fresh hell for a lot of people."

I didn't share my other concern, which was that I worried about the source. It wasn't believable that this person's first course of action was to go to a reporter. If they really did have information, they'd run it up official channels first. Jennie would be their last resort. There might be a good reason no one acted on it. Or, like I'd told her, that person got told no and took matters into their own hands. Or, what if her source was wrong? What if they were duped by a Russian intelligence service?

"Normally, my job is to speak for other people. I won't do that here. You're right about the risk, Matt. I can't tell you whether or not she should do this, and I can't give you permission. I don't want you to do this out of some obligation to me. And I don't want you to *not* do it because you're scared of what would happen."

"You know you just covered all the bases, right," I said dryly.

"I trust your judgment. If the facts are there, I know you'll do something with it. If they aren't..." He chuckled. "Well, I'd hate to be the guy that wasted your time. Look, most of us can't get into the field anymore to do what you do. The fact that you'd even be willing means a lot to a lot of people. I heard about that thing with the Chinese last year."

"You've been talking with Nate?" I asked.

"He checks in from time to time, and yes, he told me what you did. The point is, I know the kind of case officer you were, and I can only imagine you're the same way as a detective."

"Yeah, but even if we prove it was a weapon, so what? The Agency isn't going to change their position."

"Probably not. Matt, there's no VA for broken spies. We've got nowhere to go. If this was intentional and you can prove it, that helps our case with Congress. If you check it out and prove it's bullshit, that has value too. The last thing this group needs is disinformation and false hope. The last thing we'd need is the IC to get ahold of some false prophet, prove him wrong, and say, 'See, we told you so.'"

Dylan walked a fine line and did it skillfully.

He knew what our relationship meant to me and the guilt I felt over coming out of that mission clean. He wouldn't play on that. Nor would he use his position as the head of a survivors' group to convince me to do it.

"When's the last time you spoke to Nate?" Dylan asked. I suspected he already knew the answer.

"It's been a while. That case, it cost him his job," I said.

"The decision he made cost him his job. Nate is pretty clear-eyed about that. He doesn't blame you. For whatever it's worth, Nate was senior intelligence service. He knew the brass, hell, he *was* the brass. It might be worth talking to him."

"I'll think about it," I said.

As much as I wanted to stay and catch up with my friend, I had a plane to catch. There was one other person I needed to speak to. Dylan walked me to my car.

"Please give Charlotte my best and tell her I'm sorry I missed her."

"Shit, she still doesn't forgive you for Athens. I'm not telling her you were even in the state."

Dylan held the deadpan as long as he could before we both broke into a much needed laugh. We embraced, and then I made for the car. "I'll let you know what I decide, and I promise I'll come visit soon."

Dylan said, "Be careful, Matt. There's people on both sides of this who don't want to see rocks kicked over."

My plane touched down at Reagan National. I rented a car and texted the person I was here to meet. I'd burned the entire day flying, and it was now the height of DC's rush hour. I could be sitting in traffic for an hour or better, just to crawl a couple miles. Thankfully, the person I was here to meet worked at the Pentagon, which was barely two miles from DCA.

My phone rang as I pulled out of the airport. Not the person I'd flown here to see, but a friend returning a call.

"Good evening, Special Agent Danzig," I said.

"I figured it was only a matter of time."

"Thanks for calling me back. I'm about to step into a meeting, but can I ping you when I'm back in California tomorrow? I'd be happy to pop up to San Francisco and meet you."

"Actually, I'm back in DC now. I just transferred about a week ago. New assignment and it happened kind of fast, sorry I didn't get a chance to tell you. Why, where are you now?"

"Uhhh, leaving Reagan."

"That probably means you're deeper into this thing than is good for you."

3

Danzig and I agreed to meet up later that night. She knew about my connection to the Orpheus Foundation, so it wasn't hard to guess why she thought I was in over my head. Also, she knew me well enough by now that sentiment usually wasn't without merit.

My contact texted me back with a location at the Pentagon City Mall.

That had been an awkward conversation.

When I'd first met Colonel Rick Hicks five years ago, then a lieutenant colonel, I'd been an active Clandestine Service officer and he'd only known me by a cover identity. Hicks was an Army military intelligence officer appointed by the Defense Department to investigate Havana Syndrome cases. DoD has personnel stationed at US embassies, and each embassy is also guarded by a detachment of US Marines. So, DoD has a vested interest in someone potentially targeting embassies, and they'd always taken a harder line on this than the Agency had. An acting Secretary of Defense even stated the intent for their investigation was to get "the government off their asses."

There are few places hotter and more humid than DC in the summer. Those places are all in Southeast Asia.

I peeled myself out of my rental car and headed into Pentagon City, a sprawling complex of shopping, restaurants, and condos a short distance from the world's largest office building and the Potomac River. I found Rick in civilian clothes, nursing a bottle of water. He stood when I approached. Rick was average height and had enough muscle on his frame to not be considered lanky. Ice-blue eyes and graying hair.

"Nice to meet you...Matt," he said with a wry smile.

"Good seeing you again, Rick. Thanks for making the time."

"So, you're a private eye now?"

When I'd reached out on the phone, I'd been cagey about why I wanted to see him, just that I had a case he might be of some help on.

"That's right. My client is a reporter. I do contract work for her outfit from time to time, freelance investigation or security. You'd be surprised at the lengths some groups will take to hide things."

Rick laughed, as if it were an inside joke. I hadn't meant the quip to frame our conversation, though I guess that's exactly what it did.

One point for Freud.

"Since you were completely evasive on the phone, any hint as to what this is about?" Rick said, a mischievous light in his eye.

"My client is investigating Havana Syndrome."

That mirthful light in Rick's eyes iced over fast.

"Let me stop you," he said. "I am no longer involved in the AHI investigation."

I noted he used the government's official term, Anomalous Health Incidents, and tried not to read too much into it.

"You were, though. I never saw the final report, but I—"

"That's because there wasn't one. I spent two years on that project. We were about a month away from presenting our findings, and orders came down the chain to cancel it."

Rick had been with the Defense Intelligence Agency at the time. In addition to being one of the twenty-six organizations composing the Intelligence Community, the DIA managed the defense attaché program. Defense attachés were senior military officers assigned to American embassies and, officially, acted as liaisons to their host nation counterparts. They also acted as an integral part of military intelligence and special operations in those countries. After Havana Syndrome cases appeared at multiple locations across the world, with no common denominator, DIA empaneled then Lieutenant Colonel Rick Hicks to lead a comprehensive assessment into its potential causes. He'd interviewed me, and several other members of the Clandestine Service, as a part of that.

"You were ordered to kill the investigation?"

"Yep. Was told to turn all my work in and not to ask questions. Far as I know, it's in a vault somewhere. Or a burn bag."

"My client thinks there is new evidence that suggests a foreign actor's culpability. Can I ask you some questions?"

"I'm not comfortable talking about this, Matt."

"Who is going to know?"

"Isn't that the point?"

"I won't tell anyone I spoke to you. This is just for my own research."

"I don't understand."

"Because, I haven't decided to take the case yet. I've got my experiences and my opinion, but that's limited to one event. I don't buy the 'mass hysteria' explanation. However, I find it hard to believe that the IC could find a hundred medical experts to testify in writing that this is a psychological effect. The National Institutes of Health also shot down the idea of a weapon."

"So why does your client think there's something to it?"

"A new source. Allegedly, someone with direct knowledge. Like I said, I have some doubts, so I wanted to talk to you and see what your conclusions were. You struck me as being an unbiased investigator, so your opinion is valuable to me. I have some personal reasons to take this on, and some professional ones for leaving it alone."

Hicks considered that.

"Look, man, all I can tell you is where my team's research pointed us. We conducted hundreds of interviews—victims, medical personnel. CIA, State, and DoD headquarters staffs that took the reports. We spoke with independent medical experts, physicists, and even some weapons experts."

Rick's words trailed off, and he looked around. It was a subconscious tic, and usually meant the subject was about to say something they shouldn't.

"I could never prove there was a weapon. There were clues, sure, but to use a tired phrase that might be a little too on the nose, there was no smoking gun."

"What were some of the clues?"

"Your partner wasn't the only one who reported feeling effects, moving to a different location in proximity, say another room in an apartment, and then feeling the effects again."

"Like they were being followed."

"Like they were being targeted," he said. "We couldn't account for that. And there was no environmental common denominator that we could find."

"Do you know why they killed your investigation?"

Rick shrugged. "New administration, new priorities. This is four years old, mind you. I was told that the new Secretary of Defense didn't consider it a priority and wanted us to shut it down."

"They wouldn't even let you present your findings?"

"Nope," he said.

"What level of confidence would you give it that a foreign actor was involved?"

"And this doesn't make it into your friend's story? Not as deep background, or whatever they call it?"

"No. I won't even tell her I spoke to you."

"No other explanation made any sense. Also, when the government doesn't care about something, they just let it go until it dies. They only shut things down hard when they want it gone."

Rick and I finished shortly after. I thanked him for his time, mindful about keeping him too long from his evening commute. I went in the opposite direction, heading into the District.

Off the Record, the "DC-famous" bar in the Hay-Adams hotel, is billed as "the place to be seen and not heard." Red walls, mahogany trim, a gilded fireplace, and portraits of the city's elite, past and present. There's an unwritten, understood, and inviolate code among patrons that you don't tell anyone about who you saw there and you make a point not to overhear anything.

Danzig arrived before me and was standing near the bar.

Our relationship had gotten off to a rocky start. I'd already had a bad reputation with the Bureau, owing to some...complications with my exit from the Agency. Long story short, Danzig thought I was playing for the other team when we first met. However, we eventually found a way to work together and rolled up a Chinese espionage ring. It was Danzig who got my record cleared so that I could get my PI license and even apologized for the Bureau blackballing me. She'd been a valuable resource for me on several cases, and I'd done some freelance surveillance and even undercover work once in return. More importantly, she was a good friend.

I maneuvered through the crowd and slid up next to her at the end of the bar. She was working and so was drinking a club soda. I was also working, which was why I ordered a martini.

"It's good to see you, Matt," she said.

"Yeah, you too. So, how'd you end up back here?" Her last gig was a kind of flying squad for counterintelligence in Silicon Valley.

"It's a desk job," she said at length. "Before I got into CI, my specialty was gem smuggling, so this is a kind of policy job in that space."

"That sounds...fun."

"Fucking shoot me." She made eye contact with the bartender and just pointed at my drink.

"The job. I'm a street cop. I get that there's a certain amount of headquarters time that you have to do. You got to know how the system works, right? Staff jobs are a stepping stone to something else. I just don't want to leave the field."

"I stayed operational my whole career, and it cost me."

"How do you mean?"

"When it came to needing the kinds of political connections you make from headquarters gigs, I didn't have them."

"And you're a natural bridge burner," she said. The bartender deposited a martini in front of her.

"Fair," I said.

Danzig, smiling, said, "We know our own."

"Well, here's to that," I said, and lifted my drink to toast her.

"How are you doing?"

"Fine, why?" I said.

"I talked to Michelle Silvestri after your case in Miami. She said you had it pretty rough."

"I'm fine," I repeated. I had to kill a man to protect a kid. I still saw his face every night when I slept.

"You've been here five minutes and that drink is almost gone. 'Fine' people don't gulp martinis."

"It's hot outside, and they didn't give me a water back," I said.

"I've had to use my service weapon in the line of duty, Matt. That puts me in the minority of active agents. There's mandatory counseling after that. It helped."

"I said that I was fine, so can we please drop it."

"I'm just saying you don't have to do this alone."

"Do what?" I asked, perhaps with a little more edge than I'd intended.

Danzig set her drink on the bar, framed by her hands. "If you need a friend, Matt, someone that understands, I'm here for you. If you don't want to talk, I will respect that and not ask again."

"Thank you. Truly. And please don't ask again," I said.

Danzig, still staring at the glass in front of her, said, "Now that that's out of the way, what in the hell are you doing with Jennie Burkhardt?"

That was supposed to be *my* line.

"That's what I wanted to talk to you about. I wanted to know—"

"Your girlfriend is about to violate about a dozen national security statutes."

"She's not...I don't think that's what this is."

"When she's cultivating sources and soliciting information, it is." Danzig rotated her torso to face me. "A United States Attorney is preparing to charge her with espionage, Matt. The agent in charge of this case reached out to me because I know you. They assume you're involved because of your relationship with Burkhardt."

"I do also conduct investigations from time to time. I—"

Danzig cut me off.

"Let me tell you how this plays out in court. Burkhardt is going to be accused of cultivating assets within the United States government for the purpose of accessing classified information. Where do you think they'll say she learned how to do that?"

"She's a reporter. That's her *job*, Katrina. And she didn't 'solicit information.' She's got a whistleblower who reached out to *her*."

"That's not what our information tells us."

"Well, maybe your information is wrong."

"I don't think so."

"Look around you," I said, gesturing to the bar. "Some flavor of this situation is probably happening at three tables in this bar. Hell, the House Foreign Affairs Committee chair is meeting with a *Post* reporter right over there."

"The difference is the congressman is not passing classified information to the *Post*."

"I mean, it's Congress, so..."

"This is serious, Matt. Burkhardt solicited information from a government official. They did not volunteer it. We have no record of a whistleblower complaint."

Unfortunately, I couldn't refute that. Though, absence of a thing wasn't necessarily proof that it didn't exist. And the fact that there was no official record didn't mean Jennie solicited information.

"Matt, I appreciate how this probably looks to you. And, believe me, I respect the press's responsibility to hold agencies accountable. But there is a clear difference between investigative journalism and trolling for secrets, lighting fires, and pointing at the smoke."

"Tell me this isn't just another attempt to control the narrative? To save the government from the embarrassment of the public learning they're falling down on the job," I said.

"You really think that's what this is about?"

"Are you telling me it isn't? Do you even know what Jennie is investigating? They organized facts to fit a conclusion, to tell the story they want to tell. Why is that? What are they hiding this time?"

"For Christ's sake, Matt, everything isn't a conspiracy. Also, the government isn't the villain in every story all the time. You are deeply cynical and incredibly jaded—and not without merit—but maybe that's clouding your judgment, just a little. And maybe Jennie Burkhardt knows that too, and is using it to her advantage."

That was too far.

As an almost feral reaction, I stepped back from the bar and turned to leave.

"Matt," Danzig said, reaching out to grab me by the arm. "If Burkhardt walks away from this now, the Justice Department will drop the charges. If not, she's going to get prosecuted. I don't need to tell you what the conviction rate is on federal cases. They will bring you down with her."

"I haven't even taken the case yet."

"Then do yourself a favor, and don't. You just got your life back, you're doing good work, valuable work. If you can't walk her back from the ledge, it doesn't mean you have to jump off it with her."

"One of us is going to regret this conversation," I said, and dropped a pair of twenties on the bar. "Give him the change." I shouldered my way toward the door. I was about ten feet from her when Danzig called after me.

I turned.

She held up the money I'd left on the counter. "You're ten bucks short," she said.

Twenty-five-dollar martinis. This fucking town.

4

There was a late flight to LAX out of Dulles, which got me back home at nine. I could just make it. I messaged Jennie over Signal, told her that I'd be back tonight and that we needed to talk.

The trip convinced me that the government wanted any investigation into Havana Syndrome shut down immediately, and with force.

The key question was why.

Which was a little different than the question my client hired me to answer.

Jennie met me at the airport. It was a full hour from when I'd landed to when I finally got to the exit, because even with everything closed, LAX finds a way to be less efficient than most of the developing world. I'd managed a few hours of sleep on the plane, so at least I had enough juice to make it through debriefing Jennie.

What Danzig warned me about rattled me to my core.

Worse, I didn't have the first inkling on how to bring that up with Jennie.

I'd known Jennie for almost thirty years. She was a relentless and gifted seeker of truths, but she also believed deeply in her profession, in the importance of its function in society. Jennie was the first to go after reporters who let their own biases get between themselves and the facts.

Jennie even campaigned fervently, if unsuccessfully, for an official canon of ethics, not unlike the Hippocratic oath. I'd never known her moral compass to steer her wrong.

She was a lot like Katrina Danzig, and under other circumstances, I think those two would be fast friends.

During the drive to my house, I filled Jennie in on my talk with Dylan. I didn't mention my conversation with Rick Hicks, out of respect for what he'd revealed. The specter of that contentious dialogue with Danzig loomed large in my thoughts, but I didn't bring it up.

When we got to my place, I put some jazz on the stereo, not loud enough to wake the neighbors but enough to put Jennie at ease that we wouldn't be listened to. At least now I understood the source of her paranoia.

In truth, I'd made my mind up after talking with Dylan. The flight to DC was truly to try to talk myself out of it, a chance to prove the negative. Rick convinced me to keep going.

"I'll go meet your source and vet his contact. Where am I headed?"

"Lithuania. His name is Charlie Auer. He's an economic officer at the embassy in Vilnius. He's currently helping the Lithuanian government with their smuggling problem, which is how he came to know this Russian." I knew a little about that from my time in the Agency. As sanctions ramped up on Belarus for their horrendous human rights record and continued close ties to the Russian Federation, they'd taken to smuggling and black marketeering to make up the difference. The Lithuanians had to close four of five border crossings with Belarus to get a handle on it.

"How did you first get connected with him?"

"Charlie reached out to me," she said. "He said he'd followed my reporting on Havana Syndrome, was frustrated that the government wasn't doing enough. Told me he'd had colleagues, some good friends, that suffered from it and he wanted to help them." The last reported case was about four years ago, so it stood to reason that Mr. Auer was at least midcareer. I'd been worried this Auer was an impulsive, first-tour kid, fresh out of grad school, who got an answer he didn't like and decided to take matters into his own hands.

"How did you—"

"He sent me pictures of himself inside and outside the embassy, also included a shot of his State Department ID. I know how to validate a source, Matt."

"Right. Okay, so the plan is that I fly to Lithuania and meet with Mr. Auer. He will introduce me to this Russian businessman? I talk to him, feel him out, and verify that he's worth talking to and that he's not a plant."

"The Russian's name is Grigori Fedorov. He's actually a dual Russian-Swiss citizen. He works for a company called Infinitechologie. Berlin-based, but they've got an office in Zürich, and he travels to Vilnius often. The Lithuanians have been trying to leapfrog their economy, so they've invested heavily in the tech sector. They've also got a lot of Belarusian refugees looking for work, wanting to learn software, that sort of thing."

"How exactly did Auer make the Havana Syndrome connection?"

"This is the other thing I wanted you to pressure test. The story goes that Auer met Fedorov in Vilnius, while Fedorov was there on business. This was about six months ago. They met on a few other occasions. Auer said that part of his portfolio is economic security, so he was concerned that Fedorov was trying to pump him for information. Then, after about three months of this, Fedorov asked how he could get asylum in the US." This was the part where alarm bells started going off in my head. Jennie continued, "Auer told him visas for Russians were restricted now, so he'd need a compelling reason for it. That's when Fedorov told him that the Russian government pressured him to use his position to acquire Western defense technology. Fedorov said at first he thought it was for radars or something."

"Did he say, specifically, that it was for a weapon?"

"No. So, Auer takes this to his superiors at State, and they told him to break off contact immediately. Said they were worried Fedorov could be Russian intelligence trying to recruit him." The gently ringing alarm bells in my head were now a full-on air raid siren. Grab a helmet and get under a desk, because shit is incoming.

"I guess he didn't take their advice. Did Auer say if he reported his contacts with Fedorov to the local CIA station, or to the Regional Security Officer?" Most of the time, the State guys didn't know who the CIA people were, except the station chief, who was in a declared role and not undercover. But sometimes they figured it out.

"I did ask him if he talked to the Agency, and he told me they weren't interested. He didn't say anything about raising this with security."

Something for me to dig into further.

"Jen, I've asked you this before, but if I'm going to take this on, I have to know. You have not, to your knowledge, received any classified information? Maybe something that a different source passed to you?"

"No," she said, incredulous.

"I'm sure there are sources you haven't told me about."

"Matt, I said I hadn't. I want this story, but I'm not breaking the law to get it." Jennie was earnest, not offended, in her denial. I believed her.

I stood, barely steady on my feet, desperately in need of sleep.

Jennie stood and wrapped me gently in an embrace, staying there a heartbeat longer than necessary for just "goodbye." When she released me, she asked, "What about your FBI friend? The one you worked with on the spy ring? Danzig, was it?"

"What about her?"

"Oh, just wondering if it's worth reaching out to her. I thought since you're friends, she might be able to help with these assholes that are harassing me."

That conversation is not going to go the way you want.

"Probably not right to get her involved. I don't want to trade on our friendship."

"Of course, of course. Just asking."

"Let me see what I find out in Vilnius and then see if it's the right time to talk to Katrina."

"That's fair. Good night, Matty. Get some sleep." Jennie smiled at me and left.

During the Cold War, CIA learned some hard lessons about operating in denied areas. We canonized those as "Moscow Rules." Chief among them, always assume you are being watched. Danzig knew I was on this case almost as soon as I did. While it was not a hard leap to conclude that I would be the person Jennie Burkhardt would turn to, it certainly added a point in the column of the FBI spying on her.

Good to remember Rule Number Four: *Do not look back. You are never completely alone.*

Two days later, I left for Lithuania knowing that I did not have the full story. From anyone. My main goal was to keep Jennie out of federal prison. She couldn't write a story if she was behind bars. I also had a responsibility to her, if not the victims, to make sure this was done above board. We weren't stealing secrets to crack this. While I believed Jennie was being honest with me, I also needed to confirm her source was playing straight with her.

One of the many things that didn't make sense to me was how Charlie Auer constituted Jennie soliciting classified information? If Auer never told his superiors what Fedorov allegedly knew, how did that information become classified? Jennie assumed Auer was being completely honest and transparent with her. That may not be the case. And he had told his superiors about the contact. That should have triggered a series of actions with the local CIA station and others.

That was different than Jennie receiving classified information, which was what the FBI was alleging. But it could explain why the FBI was involved.

Again, another thing that didn't add up.

I called Danzig before I left to apologize for losing my cool at the bar. She said she understood and reminded me to be careful. She told me: "If you really care about Burkhardt, talk her out of this."

I said I'd be out of touch for a few days and would contact her when I could.

The first leg was Los Angeles to Brussels so that I could check in at the Foundation's headquarters. If I was going to be working in Europe, I at least wanted to let them know I was here. Denis Coenen, their cherubic executive director, was always appreciative of the work I did on their behalf, and not just the risky stuff. He was a brave and dogged investigator, a true crusader. The Russian government actually labeled him a "foreign agent"— he wasn't—and tried him in absentia several years ago, for his work on their assassination campaign of political dissidents abroad. Coenen told me once his last name meant "wise advisor" in Old Dutch. Fitting.

This also gave me an opportunity to reset my body clock. Having gone from the West Coast to the East and back in a day, then Europe two days later, my body had no idea where on earth it was. Denis hosted me at dinner at an upscale yet friendly restaurant in Brussels's Dansaert District. We enjoyed a bottle of Sancerre and a seafood tasting menu I could never have afforded on my own.

"What's new with the Foundation?" I asked, before lifting an oyster shell off a chilled plate.

"I think you know that I've long believed that open source intelligence is the next great wave in information. The intersection with journalism is undeniable and, to a degree, symbiotic. It's getting harder to obfuscate issues now, which is both good and bad." We talked about the challenges of managing the unfathomable amount of information available in the public domain now, and how to make sense of it, and the role artificial intelligence played in all that. I used AI in my own work, probably saved me from having to hire a junior investigator that I couldn't afford to pay.

One could imagine a world where a journalist might set their aggregator algorithm to collect information on a topic—say, compile all reported cases of Havana Syndrome and organize them by symptoms reported. This would be hundreds if not thousands of man hours of research, which an AI could do in potentially minutes. The human journalist might then be able to look at those different groupings and determine that symptoms varied by location. This, in turn, could lead to new branches of investigation. For example, an AI could research if the differences in effects meant there was a different frequency of energy used to cause them. An AI could also model and recognize patterns faster than a human could to answer that question. It would save a journalist potentially hundreds of hours.

"We've got a prototype working now," Denis said. "Even this limited version is paying off. The system showed a link we might not have found between businesses that supply equipment to NATO, through their respective governments. A warehouse fire in Munich, a cyberattack against a French defense contractor, a curious power outage causing allotments of medical supplies to spoil in Turin. All of these things lead us to conclude that an actor—we can guess who—is taking active measures against NATO." Denis lifted an oyster and swallowed it in a gulp.

"This is all real?"

"Absolutely. We think the Russians have been very active in Europe since the war started. With the resources they can spare, of course."

A server brought our next course. "So, how much trouble is Jennifer in?" he asked.

One of the things I loved most about him was that Denis minced no words. He was a cunning cherub with a Van Dyke beard.

"She hates it when you call her that," I said, and Denis waved his wineglass dismissively. "Here's what worries me. A friend in the FBI, someone I trust, urged me to get Jennie to drop this, claiming it was a national security breach. Said there was classified material leaked and that the government is going to charge her with espionage. What I can't figure out is why? Jennie showed me her research. Unless she's held something back, I don't see where she's gotten access to secrets."

"That's strange. Your government has, at least tacitly, supported our work before. Do they think this is a hack or something? Like WikiLeaks?"

"Assange enticed people to actively leak secrets in order to 'expose' the government. He was a political opponent of the Iraq War, not a journalist. This doesn't feel like that. Jennie isn't working out a grudge. Whether or not her source is might be another matter. Do you know about him?"

"A little," he said.

"Someone told me recently that if the government doesn't care about something, they just ignore it and let it die. They only get involved when they really want it to go away. The Justice Department is trying to shut this down, hard. I need to vet this source for Jennie, but I think it's equally important to understand why they want this shut down."

"What do you think?"

"I don't believe Jennie is soliciting people to break the law. That's not her character. As for the other thing, I can't see a reason for a cover-up."

"It seems there are a lot of people with a vested interest in keeping this story quiet," Denis said.

"You're not the first person to tell me that."

"Right, well, we get a lot of threats in this business. This is one of the ones I take quite seriously. Your first job is to keep her safe, everything else is secondary. Promise me this."

I did.

I called it early and went back to my hotel to get some sleep. Before I left, I promised Denis that I'd keep him apprised of the case while I was over here.

The next day, I flew from Brussels to Vilnius.

I hadn't been here in many years. It's a hidden gem of Europe, with its baroque architecture, framed on its eastern side by the gently curving Neris River, rolling hills, and abundant trees. The city's Old Town was beautifully preserved, giving it an old-world, noble quality. I'd been here on assignment several times and fell in love with it. The maze-like streets were a godsend for a spy looking to ditch potential watchers. And they made damned good beer.

Before I left LA, Jennie had given me Auer's email address and phone number. She introduced us virtually, and I said I'd call him when I arrived. The responses I got were terse, at best. It felt "pissy," but maybe that was the jet lag talking. Auer didn't immediately respond when I told him I'd landed, so I went to check into my hotel. He texted back a while later, saying he was tied up at work and couldn't meet me until that afternoon.

I typically travel light and never unpack so I can bug out quickly if I need to. I also always bring a small flyaway kit of gear that includes a compact, basic disguise kit, minor surveillance equipment, scopes and mikes, that sort of thing. The Europeans have some of the strictest privacy laws in the world, so in coming here I was careful about bringing things that might trip alarms. I was also pretty good at making things look like other, less conspicuous things.

With a few hours to kill, I decided to refresh my knowledge of the city. I spent most of the afternoon walking around it like a tourist, though in my mind I was committing its labyrinthine corridors to memory and trying to recall the surveillance detection routes I'd once planned and executed here. I did treat myself to one of their excellent dark beers after walking a circuit of several miles. While I sipped my beer at an outdoor cafe, I started framing the questions I wanted to ask Auer and Fedorov.

Once I'd finished, I walked off my beer, continuing my foot tour of the city.

Around four, Auer texted and said he could meet at six. He gave me a location outside Vingis Park, which was on the western side of town. Auer said he'd be in a black windbreaker and jeans. The location made sense; it was not far from the US embassy, a short bus ride. If memory served, they were on the same street and separated by just a few miles. I decided to make my way there now, using a combination of public transportation and walking. Running a full surveillance detection route still seemed excessive to me. Even if the FBI decided I was worth following all the way to Europe, I found it hard to believe they'd actually do it. Still, I worked some doublebacks into my route to check for tails.

Vingis Park had a few meandering trails and nicely groomed lawns carved out of a primeval forest. Tall European elm, Scots pine, and alder trees formed thick, dark corridors that framed the paved pathways through the park. There was a famous amphitheater in the park's center, a curved, silver structure at the head of a huge lawn. I was to meet Auer on those grounds. That meant a substantial walk from the entrance along a long, straight road. I'd given Auer a basic description of myself and said I was in tan pants, a navy short-sleeve button-down, and a ball cap. My first thought at seeing this long, straight line I was forced to walk: Auer was playing junior spy and wanted to see if I brought anyone with me.

Instead, I showed up an hour early and took a winding path through the park to arrive at the lawn. We were to meet at the opposite side from the amphitheater, in the southeast section of the oval-shaped field. I found a pine to lean against and waited.

It would stay light well past nine this far north, but with the height of these trees, the shadows grew long quickly. I clocked Auer by his clothes from a distance and gave him a slow nod when I saw him looking my way. Even from here, I could see he was on the athletic side of lean, dark-haired and tanned. Auer's posture was tense, edging in on aggressive, with shoulders bent slightly forward.

The details filled in as he neared.

I closed the distance between us, and when I was close enough, I said, "If you're a diplomat, I'm Allen-fucking-Dulles."

"Excuse me?"

"Hi, Connor. It's nice to see you again."

5

"What are *you* doing here?" Connor Bishop asked.

"That is one hundred percent *my* line," I said.

Well, a CIA officer pretending to be a diplomat telling a journalist about a Russian walk-in was probably the best explanation for why the FBI was involved.

A deer in a truck's headlights on a country highway moved more than Connor Bishop did right now.

About ten years ago, as part of the workup to joining Nate McKellar's black ops unit, Nate had most of us cycled through the CIA's National Clandestine Service schoolhouse, what we affectionately refer to as "the Farm." Nate was a firm believer that the best way to hone your craft was to teach, so he had us all worked into the rotation as instructors on top of our own training. I led the blocks on how to establish and maintain cover, and I remembered my students, to include young Connor Bishop.

It took a minute, but the camera-flash of surprise on his face was replaced by something else, which I took to be somewhere between panic and despair.

"When I taught you at the Farm, I was under an alias. We were about to go into an unacknowledged unit, so they gave us covers, even when we were at the schoolhouse." I shouldn't have even told him that much, but it was the simplest explanation.

"Oh shit. You're not…"

"No, I've been out for a few years. I'm a private investigator now. Mostly, I work with the Orpheus Foundation through Jennie Burkhardt. That's why I'm here and not her. Now that that's out of the way, why don't you tell me what's really going on?"

Having one of his Clandestine Service instructors show up in a Lithuanian forest was probably not on Connor Bishop's bingo card for today.

"Well, I guess we should take a walk, then," Bishop said.

Viewed through this new lens, his selection of the park made more sense. Its long approach would give him ample opportunity to observe me, so he could verify I was alone. It would also decrease the likelihood of running into someone from the embassy and give him multiple escape paths if he did.

"Lead the way," I said. Bishop indicated for me to follow, and I took up pace next to him. We moved in silence along the edge of the green, both of us watching the people on the large field. Some at play, others relaxing after a day's work.

We reached the edge of the clearing and Bishop vectored us onto a path leading into the woods.

"Jennie told me you were a State Department whistleblower. That you had information, from an informant, proving a Russian weapon caused the Havana Syndrome. She hired me to vet the informant. Now, I find out that you're CIA. Talk fast, Bishop, because I'm already halfway to the airport."

"Fedorov is real. You understand there is a lot I can't tell you, now that you're not with us anymore. I'll fill in the blanks as best I can."

"Do better than that. The FBI is investigating my friend. If I find out it's because you're sloppy, or you're angling for some get-back because they wouldn't take your walk-in, I'm going to tell them everything I know."

"Don't do that," Bishop said evenly. "Just hear me out, please." He kept his eyes focused on the pathway ahead of us, occasionally looking back over his shoulder. "I met Fedorov here in Vilnius. The Lithuanians have a robust tech sector. They're into nanotechnology, lasers, software. It's one of the fastest growing in Europe, and companies from more expensive markets—Germany, Switzerland, France, and the like—are setting up shop here to take advantage of the lower cost while they can. My portfolio is mostly economic intelligence and technology. I met Fedorov about six months ago. He works for a Swiss-based subsidiary of a German electronics company."

"Infinitechologie," I said.

"That's right. My interest gets piqued when I find out he's actually Russian, and a dual citizen."

My first thought was Fedorov was a sleeper agent, which the Russians termed "illegals." People placed into deep cover who lived as citizens of another country until activated. However, Russian citizens, particularly in their business class and, most infamously, their many oligarchs, increasingly lived abroad from the motherland to take advantage of the capitalist West. Figuring out who was a legitimate member of society and who might be a sleeper agent was one of the preeminent counterintelligence problems in Europe today. "Fedorov was coming here every six weeks or so, as he's setting up the Lithuanian operations for his company. I introduce myself as a State Department officer, and we start meeting for coffee, lunch, cocktails, whatever. Eventually, he expresses a desire to move to the United States. Talks about disaffection with Russia, the current state of affairs, the forever presidency."

"Which you take as your way in," I said.

"Exactly. I tell him that the US has reduced the immigration visas available for Russians, because of the Ukraine war. Then he tells me, 'What if I have some information that your country might find important?' So, he goes on to tell me that he's been covertly buying equipment from Western tech companies on behalf of the Russian government. His Swiss citizenship and position in Infinitechologie gives him a way of sidestepping the multitude of sanctions we and others have dropped on his country. So, I take this to my bosses, and they tell me to cut him loose."

I can already guess the answer, but I ask him anyway. "Why? Seems like a promising recruitment target." Anyone that a case officer proposes to recruit as a potential asset must first be vetted by the Agency's counterintelligence team to determine that they aren't already a spy. The bar for Russian agents is understandably higher.

"They shot it down immediately. They thought Fedorov was a dangle, and ordered me to break off contact. I met with him again to give him the news that I couldn't help him with his visa application."

"And Fedorov doesn't know you're a case officer at this point?" I said.

"Jesus Chris, Gage. What do you take me for?"

I repeated why I was here. "When I thought you were just a State pogue, I was already worried that this was a major security risk. Now, that's basically certain. Do you know what you're doing?"

"Don't lecture me."

"Someone has to, because I don't think you're taking this seriously."

We rounded a corner in the park, and evening sunlight broke through the trees like golden lances. Here, there was a long suspension bridge that spanned the Neris River, both of its ends disappearing into the forest on either side, as though swallowed by the trees. Beyond it, to the north, we could see a lush, green ridge that formed the city's northern barrier. Bishop guided us beneath the bridge.

Connor said, "No. I'm not the only one who is taking this seriously. Fedorov is buying export-controlled electronics for the GRU, I just didn't find out until after they denied recruitment. He told me his handler admitted that it was for a weapon."

"Stop," I said. "You didn't say anything to Jennie about the GRU."

The GRU was Russia's military intelligence organization, though it answered directly to Russia's General Staff of the Armed Forces. Loosely equivalent to our own Defense Intelligence Agency, during the Cold War, the GRU was known as being a particularly brutal, vicious opponent, if unsophisticated. Since the 2000s, they'd pivoted to cyber warfare and were responsible for some of the most devastating cyberattacks against the West. Perhaps most dangerously, they trained criminal outfits in information warfare, equipped them, and then turned them loose. The only mandate was that they not attack Russian targets. It gave the Kremlin a deniable weapon that caused billions of dollars in damages to its enemies without them having to lift a finger or risk their own people.

The CIA and the KGB operated on a kind of "gentlemen's agreement" about the conduct of espionage. They'd harass each other relentlessly but never inflict physical harm. To do so could too easily escalate things out of control globally. The GRU never acknowledged those rules.

This situation was now orders of magnitude more dangerous.

Worse, Jennie had no idea what she was involved in.

The GRU was the Kremlin's preferred tool for "active measures." Which, too often, included actions like assassination.

They would have no reservation whatsoever about murdering an American journalist who threatened to expose their secrets.

I stopped walking and faced Bishop. I needed to be absolutely certain he understood what I was telling him. "Connor, I can't involve Jennie in this. And you should know why this is dangerous. Your leadership had good cause to order you to break off contact. You need to listen to them."

"Fedorov is scared. He wants asylum."

"If you're trying to appeal to my human nature to save a Russian spy, I can spare you the words."

Undeterred, Bishop plowed through. Probably, he'd rehearsed the speech and didn't want it to go to waste. "Russia's president has finally woken up to the fact that the kleptocracy he institutionalized is what's losing him the war in Ukraine. The oligarchs that propped him up bled the country dry, and now he can't fund the army he needs. Problem is, he's figured that out, and the state declared a war on corruption and is purging the criminals. They've already freed up hundreds of millions of rubles that were enriching the oligarchs. They're rearming and reequipping at a terrifying rate. They have a particularly violent method for excising corruption."

"Let me guess, that means purging people like Fedorov?"

"Exactly. This guy's no angel. If he didn't have something worth trading, I'd let him twist."

"And you explained all this to your superiors and they still said no."

"That's right," he said.

"Connor, I appreciate what you're trying to do. But I don't think you appreciate the risk you're asking Jennie to take on by doing this."

"Maybe we should let her choose."

A white-hot streak of fury flashed through me, and I closed the distance between us before he, or I, knew what was happening. Shock splattered on Bishop's face, and he staggered back a few steps. Whatever he'd seen in my eyes scared the shit out of him.

I got myself in check, and Connor used the lull to switch up tactics. "They attacked us, Matt. Fedorov told me it's called Projekt Molniya. The GRU has been working on it for years but could never get the thing small enough to be usable. So, they brought him in to steal the technologies they needed to figure out the rest."

"Molniya" was the Russian word for "lightning."

"Why don't you think they were interested? They give a reason?"

"Not exactly. When I first approached them, I said I had a GRU asset who was stealing Western technology on Russia's behalf. They told me it was a dangle and to drop it. Fedorov didn't know how the recruitment process works, so when I told him we couldn't do a visa, he thought if he gave more information, it'd change our minds. That's when he told me about Molniya."

The process of recruiting an agent can take months, and the case officer doesn't reveal their affiliation with the CIA until they make the offer.

That was another interesting datapoint for me, which raised further questions about the FBI's involvement. Fedorov wouldn't know that "Charlie Auer" was a spy.

I said, "The FBI knows there's a leak."

"That's impossible," he said.

"I *met* with an FBI agent, Connor. Over this. She tried to warn me off, wanted me to talk Jennie out of it."

"How?"

"I don't know how they found out. My friend wouldn't tell me. What I do know is that Jennie is now in the crosshairs of a federal espionage investigation. And that's if she does nothing further. Now I find out that the GRU is involved. And they *will* try to silence this."

Connor didn't react to that news and concealed his surprise well.

"So, on top of the more existential concerns I have for Jennie and her colleagues, my worries about a possible national security leak seem much more real. Are you telling me everything?"

"Yes," he said, and we both knew he was lying. I wished all my relationships were this transparent.

"Before this conversation goes any further, you need to convince me that we aren't breaking our respective oaths."

"Does this mean you're willing to help?"

"It means I'm willing to keep talking to you to better understand the risk that my friend is going to be murdered or thrown in jail. At this point, I'm not inclined to help you. I'm doing damage control for Jennie."

"I understand," he said. There was no bluster in his voice, no challenge to confrontation. Bishop looked at his watch, the universal cue for "I want to be anywhere else." He pulled his phone out, tapped something, and put it back away. "I just sent you an address. If you're still interested, meet me there at nine. It's a bar in Old Town. It'll be packed by then."

"That's not how this works. I just told you the FBI is investigating this leak as potential espionage, and your answer is for me to wait a couple hours to talk to you again?"

"Because you aren't the only person I have to meet with tonight. You trained me, I'll let you fill in the blanks. I also gave you something to think about. If you show up, we'll keep talking. If you don't, I'll know you're out, and I will take my information somewhere else. I believe Fedorov, Matt. I also believe that the Agency telling people this is anything but what it really is constitutes a profound betrayal of trust. I couldn't sit on this and live with myself."

"Do you realize the risk you're taking?"

"I do," he said. I knew in my heart he did not.

The deepening shadows muddled his face and made it harder to read his expression. And because history has a sense of humor, Connor Bishop learned to lie from me.

Prudence, which is decidedly a growth area for me, dictated that I leave Vilnius immediately. As capitals went, it was small, with a population of only six hundred thousand. Though the embassy and its CIA station were small, the officers in my peer group were now getting station chief assignments. My last job was CoS in Managua, Nicaragua, a small post with just a three permanent officers. Chief jobs like that were intended to be stepping stones to the larger commands. The chances that the Vilnius Chief of

Station would know me by sight were high enough that I didn't bother calculating them.

I left the park's looming darkness and spent the next hour winding my way through Vilnius, doubling back and checking for tails, changing my mode of transportation at random. I ate a quick dinner across the street from the hotel, went back up to my room, and changed. I had a message on Signal from Jennie, asking how it was going and telling me she would be in DC meeting sources.

I've always let my conscience guide me. That unflappable dogma has birthed a lot of trouble in my life, and I know that whatever decision I make, I can live with.

This time, I had no idea what "right" was.

I had an obligation to die with the secrets I carried. That's the job. That now included protecting Connor Bishop's identity as an intelligence officer. The fact that it put me in the position that I'd have to lie to Jennie made me sick. It was only the twisted irony that was my life I knew Bishop's true name. Had Jennie any other surrogate here, it would be safe. There were real consequences for me if I shared that knowledge.

Like twenty-five years in federal prison.

And that was just the surface-level secrets. It wasn't even the ones that would get us killed.

The place Bishop chose for us was in Vilnius's famed Old Town.

I showed early and posted at an outdoor cafe down the street.

Fedorov felt like a bait. I knew the Russian playbook, and so far, this felt like I was scanning pages of it.

And I knew Bishop wasn't telling the full truth.

So, basically I had three different groups that weren't telling me the full story or were outright lying.

In other words, a typical case.

And, at the nexus of all of this was why our government worked so hard to convince people a foreign actor wasn't attacking Americans.

Which was what made this case so baffling to me. Two presidencies who diametrically opposed each other actively denied Havana Syndrome's existence. But from the earliest days, speculation of Russia's involvement was in the public domain. If Jennie's theory was correct, it would prove intentional denial and rewriting of objective fact. That's the part I found hardest to believe.

Governments being found to be lying to their people was nothing new. It certainly wasn't uniquely American. Havana Syndrome was different, though. This…they denied it happened and accused the victims of lying about it. Over a thousand of them.

Now, I had a CIA officer claiming to have proof the GRU created a weapon that caused Havana Syndrome, and no one wanted to hear about it.

What did that say?

The cobblestone street, with its four-story structures on either side, extended off into a kind of infinity, eventually vanishing around a corner. There was no one on it that aroused my suspicions. Nine o'clock arrived, and I saw Bishop enter the pub. He walked fast and did a poor job hiding his nerves. I didn't see anyone loitering outside that stood out to me, nor anyone paying too much attention to the bar. And I didn't see any faces on the street that I recognized, so I went inside. The pub's interior was dark, dimly lit by yellowed lamps. Ones that in years past were doubtless ringed with the smoke from cheap Soviet cigarettes. The bar was crowded, serving a mostly younger clientele. It had a good level of ambient noise. I ordered a pint from the bar, a lighter ale since I needed to keep my head about me. Beer in hand, I searched the bar for Bishop, eventually spotting him at a back table. He'd staked out a high-backed booth of thick wood that would mask our conversation. Good choice.

I slid in opposite Bishop. He looked pensive, which wasn't surprising. The earlier meeting, which he expected to control, spiraled completely out of his reach. Not only did he lose the tactical advantage in guiding the conversation, he'd also discovered his liaison to the Orpheus Foundation was an old Agency instructor. I'd been burned in the field myself; it happens to most of us at least once. The moment you realize you're compromised is an instant of shocking, terrible clarity. If you've ever hit a patch of ice on a road, there is that moment when you realize the tires are no longer touching the pavement. It feels like that.

"So, you decided to continue," Bishop said. To his credit, he didn't presume that I was in.

"I was thirsty," I said, and took a long drink. Lithuanian beer is crisp, unfiltered, and unpasteurized. This one was slightly sweet, with a light, biscuit flavor.

"How did Fedorov take it when you told him the Agency wouldn't take him on?"

This was a trick question, and I wanted to see how Bishop responded.

"He doesn't know," Connor said.

"So, he still thinks he's talking with a State Department person?"

"That's right."

Without question, we were toeing the line here.

"Did you tell the chief that Fedorov was a GRU agent?" I asked.

"Yes."

"And you didn't tell them that the Russians were designing an electromagnetic device?"

Connor's eyes darted to the corner and then back. "I'd made one last plea with my station chief. By then, Fedorov admitted that the GRU was building a weapon. I already knew what Washington thought of Havana Syndrome, and the DNI had released their report by then, so I just said it was an energy weapon. I didn't try to link it."

"But Fedorov told you it was?"

"Yes," Connor said.

"Did he ever explain 'why now'? The attacks stopped in 2021. At least, that's the last time any were reported publicly. Fedorov comes forward three years later? Why?"

"Well, like I said when we met earlier, the Kremlin is cleaning house. They're purging corruption." He said that last bit with an unmasked sarcastic cynicism. "Fedorov is worried that means him."

"When we met this afternoon, you said you hadn't told your bosses that the GRU designed a weapon. You said that came later."

"I was being careful with what I told you. I wasn't going to give you information that can bite me in the ass if you didn't show up tonight."

I didn't bother asking if he'd held anything else back.

"Connor, I need you to know the risks you're taking here. Not just with the FBI, potentially. You're violating orders. They *will* punish you." I barked out a grim, humorless laugh. "Ask me how I know."

"I told the chief that I had to back out of this gracefully. That Fedorov was desperate for asylum and we didn't want him showing up at the embassy—here or in Bern."

"That was smart thinking. Do you know if he's going to contact the embassy in Bern?"

"I have to assume so."

"And you told them that Fedorov's job was to basically commit industrial espionage against Western defense contractors, and that didn't move the needle?"

"Yeah. Their attitude was like, 'What's one more?' To listen to Fedorov tell it, the GRU figured the science out but couldn't make it small enough to be practical. Their design wouldn't fit on a flatbed truck. So, using his job as a cover, Fedorov tried to get access to some of the new counterdrone systems the Germans were developing. Make it smaller, more efficient, that sort of thing. He said, after that, what they'd used in Havana would fit inside a van."

I'd never shared my connection to Havana with Connor, and I tried to mask my feelings now.

Instead, I sipped my beer and assembled some disparate thoughts. Tried to get a handle on where this thing was even at. Could I help? There was another fear—and I hadn't fully acknowledged it until now—which was Jennie might do this without me anyway. If I told her Fedorov had nothing to offer, she'd probably back off. But if I told her this was a bad idea because it was dangerous, that'd only spur her on.

People who are ignorant of threats tend not to take them seriously.

And I wouldn't lie to her in order to keep her safe.

Which really left me with one option.

"Okay, so you've told Fedorov that you can't help him with asylum. Does he know that you're talking with a reporter? How does Orpheus come into play?"

"Once my chain of command shut it down, I was thinking about how to get the story out. Eventually, I came across Ms. Burkhardt's reporting. I read her work, and she seemed like she was genuinely interested in exposing the truth. I reached out, using an alias as a State Department employee. I provided her with credentials." Again, Bishop didn't break stride. And he didn't ask for confirmation that I wouldn't betray that to her, relying instead on the unspoken bond between spies. "Once she agreed to interview Fedorov, I asked Ms. Burkhardt if the Foundation could help relocate him. She said they worked with a number of governments and possibly one of them may grant him asylum if the information proved valuable. They would at least put him up in a safe place and help him with a visa."

"Connor, you're putting your career in jeopardy for this guy, someone who probably doesn't deserve it."

"I don't care about *him*. People are on edge, Matt. *No one* believes this is some imagined stress condition, or whatever the bullshit story is now. Especially since they all just up and stopped a couple years ago. Now, people are wondering if it's still going on and Langley just isn't telling us. Once Fedorov came forward, a lot of pieces kind of fell into place for me. And yes, I understand why we have to be super skeptical of any Russian walk-ins. If it's true, they're the last people that would want this getting out."

"You have a point there. Why do you care, though? What is this to you that the chances are worth the consequences?"

"Because it's *still* happening," Bishop said. He set his pint glass down hard enough that the contents sloshed over the side. It was the first time I'd seen him lose his composure.

"What are you talking about? There was this huge spike in 2021, and then it just stopped."

"There was a NATO summit here, in Vilnius, last summer. Three people, all Americans, suffered effects similar to Havana. Intense pressure, mechanical ringing, nausea, vertigo. They came to the embassy, looking for help. We all knew what it meant, even if no one would talk about it." Bishop shook his head. "If this is still going on, we're all at risk, and Langley isn't doing shit about it. You know the Russians as well as I do. They won't stop on their own. And it means the Agency lied to us."

I could not argue with that logic.

We drank in silence, each of us occupied with our own thoughts.

I was closer to believing Bishop than when I'd walked in here, though there was much more he wasn't telling me. I was also no closer to answering the question of how to protect Jennie, though I'd at least talked myself into meeting with Fedorov. If for nothing else, I had to determine whether or not he was a security risk. If Fedorov legitimately believed we were his last resort, he might not react well if we said we couldn't help.

"How did you come to work for Orpheus?" Bishop asked, after a time.

"My exit from CIA wasn't exactly glorious, and it was hard to find work after."

"What happened?"

Telling him wasn't just skirting lines, it was flagrantly ignoring their existence. However, he'd been frank with me, and I had a critical question I still needed to ask. For that to work, Connor needed to believe I was willing to deal. I could talk around the key details and paint him a picture. "I was the Chief of Station in Managua. We knew Russian intelligence was trying to make a play there. The head of ops for Latin America, an oil-slicked weasel named Damon Fox, wanted an aggressive operation to show them we still owned the place. That's a direct quote. I reviewed his op plan—which he had no business writing—told him it was stupidly dangerous and would get my people captured, maybe killed. He told me to do it anyway. So I said *I* would execute it. I wouldn't risk my people over it."

"But if you were the chief…"

"I didn't have any cover. Exactly. It blew up, as I knew it would. Because I thought my people were compromised, I got a Diplomatic Security Service officer I knew to help out. The Russians had flipped one of our agents. Things went…badly. The DSS officer was killed. I got recalled immediately. Fox blamed me for the operational failure, rather than take the heat for his own shittily crafted plan. No one at Langley wanted to hear my side of it. When I got out, I was in a pretty bad spot. Jennie, I've known since college. She's as good as they come. Won a Pulitzer for her work exposing the Panama Papers."

"You know Damon Fox runs all of ops now?"

Ops, short for "operations," or, its official title, the National Clandestine Service, was the collections side of CIA.

"Well," I said, "shit rises faster than hot air. When do I meet Fedorov? No promises, but I'll talk with him and see where this goes."

"That's where things get complicated."

Of course they did.

"Why?"

"Because Fedorov is in Minsk, and he can't leave. I just found out."

6

"Next time you have timely, bombshell information, Connor? Lead with it."

I shook my head, trying to shed the mounting frustration I felt. Connor set a conversational trap for me, and I'd walked right into it.

"What in the hell is he doing in Minsk?"

Connor spread his hands, righteous indignation painted on his face. "I just found this out."

"When, Connor? You don't get to play fuzzy with the facts now."

"Earlier today. He was supposed to be here today, in Vilnius. I was going to introduce you, and that was that. Fedorov messaged me and said he had to go to Minsk now, to meet his handler. Only, his handler didn't show, and now he's being followed."

"I assume he's got his passport. Why can't he just leave?"

"The only way across the border is by car. He can't fly. Belarusian airports only service other Russian client states. If he leaves, they'll catch him. We've got a very narrow window. Maybe a day. I didn't say anything in the park because I didn't know that I could trust you. Once I saw it was you, I first thought it was Langley trying to get me to admit I was coloring outside the lines. Then, when I realized it wasn't, I was trying to decide if I could ask you to get him out. Sorry, I didn't mean to drag it out. I'm sort of making this up as I go."

"Connor, I'm not exfiltrating someone for you."

Unless I wanted answers, in which case, I was absolutely exfiltrating someone for him.

When I got home, I was going to have to have a serious conversation with myself about the choices I was making. What I needed was air, rather than a second round of beers, so we left the bar at staggered times, with me dipping out the service entrance and into an alley.

Connor and I rendezvoused outside a park several blocks away. It was ten, and the last traces of evening were finally gone. Yellow streetlamps lit the cobblestone and washed the white stucco of the surrounding buildings in a dingy glow.

I fixed my best "answers are overdue" glare and waited for Connor to speak.

"Fedorov lives in Zürich, but his company has an office in Vilnius. He travels here at least once a month. His GRU handler called him to Minsk for a 'conference' sponsored by a technical university in the city. All last-minute. Once he got there, he noticed heavy observation."

"What is really going on here? You are already breaking a shit ton of rules, Connor. You do not get to decide which ones to selectively apply."

Connor looked away, sullen, a tight frown drawing down the corners of his mouth. It was clear he was doing the mental math to determine how much he could get away with telling me.

"We know the Kremlin is paranoid about leaks right now. They've launched a massive spy hunting campaign. I can't tell you anything else."

"Is this related to that purging corruption thing?"

"Yes," he said.

"How do you even know any of this? You can't have COVCOM."

COVCOM, short for "covert communications," were the myriad tools case officers used to communicate with their agents in the field. In the old days, it might be a chalk mark on a wall, or a single blind in a window being open when the rest were closed. These days, there were encrypted chat rooms and portable satellite antennae. Not that Bishop could use any of these things, because those tools weren't available until someone agreed to become a spy.

"Relax, I use Signal. He's still got his phone."

"Listen, I came here to vet Fedorov as a source and to assess any potential security risk for the Orpheus Foundation. You're asking me to disappear him from a hostile country, under the nose of Russian intelligence. I can't do that."

"They take him back to Russia, they're going to kill him."

"Those are the consequences for playing for the other side."

"He can provide material knowledge confirming Russia has an electromagnetic weapons program. And he can show they used it against us. Burkhardt can blow this whole thing open. You can't let them keep burying this."

"You have someone in your corner if things go south. You have protection. I don't."

"It's the right thing to do, Matt. "

I didn't care about Grigori Fedorov. He was an anonymous Russian that just found out touching the stove hurt. If I walked away, bad things would probably happen to him—I didn't doubt Connor on that. It was also not my problem.

Jennie, however, was.

She'd invested years into this story. I knew she had other sources, but I doubted any of them could objectively prove what Fedorov supposedly could. Assuming he wasn't lying.

This might also be a way out of Jennie's trouble with the feds.

If we could show that *I* connected her with Fedorov, rather than Connor Bishop—something that would be technically true—that could eliminate the suspicion someone leaked classified information to her.

"You didn't come up with this in the time between our meeting in the park and right now. You've been planning this for some time."

Connor held up his hands. "I have contingency plans. This is just repurposing something I created for a different op and ended up not needing. If it were anywhere else, I'd say just drive across. Problem is, they've shut down all the border crossings but one, so it's an easy phone call from police in Minsk."

"So, how are you planning on getting him out?"

"Cross-border smuggling is a huge problem right now. Thanks to all the sanctions, Belarus has a thriving black market. One of my local assets is an officer with the Lithuanian national police. He arrested some smugglers a few weeks ago and impounded their car. It's a VW Golf with a hollowed-out compartment under the rear seat. Won't be comfortable, but Fedorov could fit. I understand what I'm asking of you, Matt."

"And I can count on you if I get into trouble?"

"Of course. If you get stopped on the Lithuanian side, no problem. My contact will handle it."

"What about if I get stopped on the Belarusian side?"

"My advice would be to not do that. But, if it happens, I will give you a number to call."

"Any issues with me getting across the border?"

"Since the war in Ukraine broke out, the State Department issued a 'Do Not Travel' warning to Americans going there. You'll need a visa, which you can get from the Belarusian embassy here in Vilnius. There's technically nothing barring you from going. They aren't preventing it, but you should expect some level of harassment. The police will harass you if they find out you're an American, and they won't care if you have an international driver's license. You could be arrested just for that."

"Super." I dead-eyed Connor a moment. "Let me ask my question another way. Any issues with me getting across the border using my own passport, or are you going to help me out?"

Connor's mouth formed into the opening syllables of an excuse and closed it.

"You know I can't get you a passport," he said, as if that justified everything and absolved him of consequence. When the look I gave him suggested that wasn't enough, Connor said, "You're going to have to look hard to find a more incompetent and inefficient security service than the Belarusian border police. By the time State Security figures out you're in-country—if they ever do—you'll be long gone."

"You don't think they'll flag my passport?"

"Matt, I'm telling you they don't have the capability to. It's still a manual process. They won't know you're there for days."

Despite Bishop's assurances, this was now an unauthorized espionage operation. We were breaking the law, Belarus's, Lithuania's, and ours. That was a patently bad idea.

So, obviously, I was doing it.

"One last question, before I commit to this," I said. I locked onto Bishop's face, watching for the reaction, the tell. "Is this a CIA operation? Is the Agency trying to lure Orpheus and Jennie out?"

If he'd have exploded into righteous indignation, it would've been to cover his genuine reaction. Connor did not. He only shook his head. "No, Matt. It isn't. It's me, trying to do the right thing against some really shitty odds. But I understand why you asked."

So, I agreed to go to a country where I was unwelcome, where I'd previously operated as an intelligence officer, on a dubious mandate with a hastily created exfiltration plan.

My superpower was seeing a bad idea a mile away.

My supreme weakness was knowing that and doing it anyway.

Minsk wasn't Moscow, though that didn't make it a soft target.

As a nation, Belarus never seemed to get their chance. The resonance of those failures vibrated within the country's very walls, even today. The first instantiation of a Belarusian republic came in the wake of World War I, with territory carved out from Imperial Germany. It barely lasted a year, before succumbing to the external pressures of the surrounding empires, Russia, Germany, and Poland. One of the birthplaces of socialism, Belarus began developing a cultural identity and independent intellectual class, only to have it decimated by Stalin's purges of the 1930s. Belarus gained their relative freedom in 1990 with the collapse of the Soviet Union. Unfortunately, they never truly escaped Russian orbit. In 1994, in the country's only free election, Alexander Lukashenko took power and ruled in the model of the Soviet strongmen he sought to emulate. Lukashenko maintained an iron grip on the country ever since. In 2000, they signed an alliance with Russia, declaring themselves the "Union State," an arrangement not unlike the British Commonwealth. Following Lukashenko's "victory" in his sixth "election" in 2020, the European Union, United Kingdom, Canada, and United States all withheld recognizing him as the country's legitimately elected leader.

Today, the Lithuanian state formally hosted an opposition government in Vilnius.

Though never stationed there, I'd worked in Minsk several times and could attest that state security was dogged, pervasive, and cruel.

Working through ideas that night, I came up with a plausible story that I thought would go over well with the target audience. I'd use a trick that I helped Denis Coenen come up with for foundation employees. Knowing that antagonizing the Kremlin could create serious problems for them in some parts of the world, I'd encouraged Denis to create a fake media company. When the Foundation needed to send reporters into places where press credentials might get them in trouble, they'd instead travel as employees of this entertainment firm, usually researching a documentary or as a concert promoter. Want to get in through some closed doors, tell people you're scouting venues for a Taylor Swift tour.

Posing as a documentary filmmaker, I could pretend to be scouting locations for a new film on Napoleon's disastrous invasion of Russia, which traversed Belarus. Any bureaucrat I spoke with would gleefully support a film depicting the downfall of a famous imperialist leader on the Russian steppes. Denis and I exchanged some messages over Signal the next morning. He loved it and was only too happy to provide documents on company letterhead authorizing my trip. I printed three copies at my hotel.

None of the European telecoms operated in Belarus, so I'd need to buy a cell phone and SIM card there to communicate with Fedorov. I'd bring my smartphone, but only because I had a portable hotspot and needed the VPN to communicate with Connor. He arranged for me to get some Belarusian rubles, the only currency accepted, and advised me not to stay any longer than absolutely necessary. He gave me a Fedorov's phone number and a code phrase, which would be asking him in Russian if I could speak to "Arkady Babkin" when he answered. He would tell me that I had the wrong number, and two hours later, I'd meet him in Minsk's Gorky Park.

"He's staying at the Hotel Minsk," Connor said.

Vilnius is in Lithuania's southeastern corner, not far from the border. If everything went smoothly, it was a two-hour drive from the border crossing to Minsk.

"Matt, I want you to know that I appreciate this. I hope it does some good."

Connor and I met before he left for work in the parking lot of Vilnius's train station. We reviewed the plans for connecting with Fedorov, how we would exfiltrate, and our contingency plans if it fell apart. Connor showed himself to be a shrewd planner and a solid tactician. It was strange being on the other side of this conversation.

Connor handed me the keys.

The car was a black Volkswagen with Lithuanian plates. He showed me how to access the hidden compartment. There was a latch under the seat. It wasn't sophisticated. "There's a forged rental contract in the glove box," he said. I didn't ask where those came from.

"Damon Fox is really the head of ops now?" I said, leaning on the open door.

"Yep," Connor said.

"Well, let's get under that bastard's skin, then."

I had about an hour drive to the Lithuanian border, plenty of time to consider what I'd gotten myself into. I still hadn't written back to Jennie, other than to say I was going to meet the contact. Better that she not know what I was doing.

I was nearing the border now, and traffic began to congeal as each vehicle entered the queue to cross.

In 2022, the Lithuanians completed a fence spanning the entire length of their border with Belarus. It consisted of multiple outer layers of razor wire, and two fences with additional razor wire in the center, just for fun. They'd also closed five of the six border crossings, which limited my options for bringing Fedorov back across.

The border complex was a two-lane road carved out of primeval forest, tall, skinny pines standing like dark sentinels on either side. Gunmetal gray structures covered the road, protecting the border guards from the elements. Lanes for truck inspection branched off to the left. It was early on a weekday morning, and the line into Belarus was understandably short. It was a two-tiered checkpoint. The first, to exit Lithuania, with random inspections to determine if one was smuggling goods into Belarus, followed by one on the other side by the Belarusian border guards.

When it was my turn, the Lithuanian guard signaled me forward.

I didn't speak Lithuanian. While Russian and the Belarusian dialect are common, it's culturally dicey to open with it in Lithuania given the relative recency of Soviet occupation and the lingering animosity toward the Russians. So, I responded with English and hoped that worked. In answering to what I hoped was, "What is the purpose of your trip?" I said, "I'm traveling to Minsk to scout locations for a film. I have a letter here."

The border guard held up a hand, said something into his radio, and, I assume, directed me to wait. I was wrong, he waved me through the checkpoint, and for a moment, I thought I was being admitted, but instead he just vectored me to a side lot to wait further instruction. Then, another pair of guards walked up to me.

"You speak English?" one of the guards asked with a thick accent.

"That's right," I said. I handed him my passport and the letter from Denis.

"Why you go to Belarus?"

"We are making a movie about Napoleon. A documentary. We're looking at locations."

"Belarus is not very safe for Americans. You should turn around," he said.

I gave a short laugh. "I'm sure it's fine. It's just a movie. Everyone likes movies."

"Open your trunk, please. Then step out of the car." I did both things.

Another guard materialized and stood with me some distance from the car, asking questions about where I would be in Belarus, for how long and why. He took my passport and letter. It wasn't long into this conversation that we neared the extent of the answers I'd prepared. While he questioned me, the other two opened the hood and examined the trunk. They walked around the car with a mirror at the end of a pole to examine the underside.

After five minutes with my car, the two inspectors sauntered over to me, full of authority. The one who held my passport handed it to the first guard, who I gathered was the more senior of the three. He paged through it one more time.

"You are free to go, Mr. Gage. However, you should still reconsider."

"Thank you," I said.

I got back in my car. One of the guards removed some cones, and I pulled forward. I drove across the border to the Belarusian checkpoint, and this was an oddly simpler process. I handed him my passport and visa, was halfway into my explanation, in Russian, for why I was entering his country, when he just stamped my passport and handed it back.

There was a duty-free shop at the checkpoint. I purchased a portable phone and a SIM card.

I rejoined the M7 motorway and drove straight to Minsk, reasonably confident that he'd radioed my car and license plate to the highway patrol, internal security, or both.

Probably both.

The Belarusian countryside alternated between dark, impenetrable forest and wide, rolling farmland. I made the trip hugging the speed limit like a one-night stand. A police vehicle appeared behind me about an hour into the trip and stayed with me basically until I got to Minsk. I didn't deviate from my route, pull off to feign needing gas or a snack; I just held steady. The vehicle broke off as I reached Minsk's outer ring, and I breathed a mighty exhale of nervous energy, then deep, calming breaths.

There she was, a dull coyote on the steppes.

Minsk, ugly and brooding, loomed as I neared, neither of us eager to welcome the other back.

I navigated by memories hard earned. It wasn't hard. This was a place you learned quickly to run from.

Connor told me Fedorov was staying at the Hotel Minsk, near city center, on Niezaliežnasci Praspiekt.

Belarus shared Russia's utilitarian and blocky architectural stylings, interspersed with bright yellows and reds. I found a public parking lot a few blocks from the Hotel Minsk and left the car. It was overcast and in the mid-sixties. Connor's assurances that the Belarusians were too incompetent was less reassuring now that I was beneath those cold, gray skies and two hours to my one way out of the country. Before doing anything, I had to make sure I wasn't being watched. I walked several blocks east in a stair-step pattern, over one and down two, and varying it randomly. Periodically, I'd stop to take a picture with my phone, toggling the selfie mode so that I could look back over my shoulder. I'd also rotate the camera around, as though taking a panoramic. I made a loop around the Dinamo Stadium, home to the city's football team, and hopped their light-rail to go back west a mile. Eventually, I'd completed my circle and found a coffee shop about three blocks from the Hotel Minsk.

The coffee shop was a long, narrow room, and perhaps "hallway" was a better name. I ordered a coffee and found a spot in the back where I could make my call to Fedorov. Presumably, Connor told him I'd be calling.

He answered in Russian. I responded in kind, "I'm trying to reach Arkady Babkin." It was rusty, but my Russian was good enough conversationally.

"I'm sorry, there is no one here by that name." *I have received your message.*

"My apologies for the inconvenience." *Two hours, meeting spot alpha.*

I disconnected the call and put the burner in my pocket. Then, I looked down at my watch, marking the time.

Sixty minutes was barely enough time to run a full surveillance detection route to make sure *I* wasn't followed, and that was just to get me in position in time to tail Fedorov. Following an asset to a meet was risky and dangerous. If there was layered surveillance, I could easily find myself in between them. As a case officer, I'd never have done this.

If Fedorov had been an asset, Connor would have trained him on how to spot surveillance and, if necessary, try to evade them. Fedorov told him he was being followed and it wasn't safe to leave. Time to prove that. If I didn't find anyone, I'd just grab him and we'd go across the border and skip the "risking jail in an authoritarian country" part of the plan.

There was a small park next to the hotel consisting of a fountain and small plantings rising up from the pavement. I found a bench that gave me a decent view of the hotel's main entrance. During my SDR, I'd picked up a copy of *Belorusskaya Delovaya Gazetai*, one of the leading Russian-language newspapers in Minsk. I sat down and pretended to read it. Wasn't bad as Russian propaganda papers went.

Connor had given me a photo of Fedorov to memorize and a physical description.

The plaza was mostly empty, and no one seemed to pay any special attention to the hotel. I also kept watch on the bus stop across the street, just in case Fedorov slipped out a side door. In the time I'd sat there, I saw the bus stop fill and empty several times over the course of the hour. No one ever remained.

Time on the clock dissolved, and no one matching his description emerged from the hotel.

7

With fifteen minutes to go, a man meeting Fedorov's description stepped out of the hotel and turned northeast. I stood, dropping the paper in a waste bin. Traffic was light, so I risked crossing the six lanes. It was easier to follow Fedorov from across the street. It also gave me a more objective vantage point to see if anyone else was following him.

As Fedorov crossed the side street marking the end of the hotel's block, a black sedan pulled out of the side street and turned onto the road some distance behind him. I watched the car as it moved about three blocks and turned right onto a side street. Shifting my attention back to Fedorov, I followed him from the opposite side. He wore a dark suit and sunglasses and had thin blond hair that looked like a watercolor that spilled onto a table.

Walking, I kept watch not only for potential tails on Fedorov but also for any excessive interest in me. Intelligence sharing was one of the tenets of the "Union State," and the SVR knew me as a CIA officer after my Nicaragua debacle. A lingering specter of fear followed at my heels like a feral dog.

Halfway to the destination, I spotted that black sedan again. They'd made a right turn off Niezaliežnasci Praspiekt and parked at a garden monument to Soviet revolutionary Felix Dzerzhinsky. The passenger, a bulky man of indeterminate age and wearing casual clothes, stood outside the car and was blatantly following Fedorov's progress with his bull head. With the lack of sophistication on display, I took these two to be Belarusian KGB. The question remained, why were they following him? If Fedorov was a known GRU agent, what concern could he possibly have with the local security service? Why not just tell his handlers?

Or, maybe we weren't clear on which "they" we were talking about.

The stoplights turned red, and Fedorov crossed from his side of the street to mine. He wasn't coming to meet these guys, was he?

No, Fedorov resumed his northeasterly route once he'd crossed, arriving at a bus stop just as one of the city's ubiquitous sea-green trolleybuses pulled up. He queued as the bus disgorged a complement of passengers. I put on some speed, making long strides to cross the Dzerzhinsky Monument without sprinting. Chancing a look back, I saw the presumptive KGB minder scramble to get into his car. Maybe Fedorov was a little better at this than I gave him credit for.

I didn't make the bus.

High walls rose above and across, dark with years of grime and exhaust. These were walls whose buildings had seen terrible things over the decades and, apparently, had learned no lessons. Whatever secrets they kept, stayed with the dead.

The half-block lead that I'd given Fedorov was just enough for him to catch the bus. Forced to walk the remaining distance, I put on some power strides and moved as quickly as I could without drawing attention to myself. The KGB car missed the light and had to wait, which let the bus get farther down the street. I was able to keep it in sight, and it, too, was caught at red at the end of the block. Then the bus disappeared into traffic.

I wasn't worried about losing him, I knew where he was going. And the purpose in tailing him was to determine if anyone else was, which I'd accomplished.

I closed the remaining distance passing, of all things, a McDonald's on one corner with a TGI Fridays opposite it. Way to stick it to the capitalists, folks.

With the bus out of sight, I had to trust that Fedorov knew what he was doing. Keeping an eye out for that black sedan, I cut a diagonal through a large park and resumed my route on an adjacent street. Gorky Park, two blocks away, was on the opposite bank of the Svislach. I cut across the Minsk state circus grounds, blending with its swelling crowds. Swerving through them, I spotted the pedestrian bridge that would take me across the river and into the park.

The bridge, like everything else in this city, was blocky and utilitarian, an edifice to the regime that built it.

Once I was on the other side, I found a path leading me into the woods.

The meeting spot was a small coffee shop in the middle of the park called Puzzle Cafe.

I found him in line and stepped in behind him. Fedorov ordered a coffee and walked over to the condiment stand. Moving next to him at the counter, I said, "I'm a friend of Charlie's. Victory Park Promenade, eight p.m. tonight. You are being followed, and leave your phone in your hotel."

And I left.

All that to deliver twenty-two words.

I booked a room at the Hilton DoubleTree. Being in an American hotel might offer me a little more security, and this one was attached to the Minsk Galleria mall. If I needed a quick egress, this afforded multiple options. The hotel wasn't far from the park where I'd met Fedorov, though I'd had to backtrack to get my car.

Victory Park, where we were to meet, was located on the southern side of Kamsamolskaje Lake. It commemorated a Red Army victory against the Nazis in the Second World War. I'd met a contact there once several years back and remembered the layout well enough. It was a popular tourist destination in the summer, with many enjoying walks in the evening. It was also a reasonable distance from my hotel to cover on foot.

When it was time to leave, I stashed my personal phone in the car's smuggling compartment. Call me paranoid, but I don't trust the sanctity of hotel safes in autocracies. That done, I walked to the Galleria, popping in and out of stores and hopping levels. After a few minutes of this, I navigated to a bookstore, where I purchased a tourist guidebook to Minsk.

Then, I left the mall and picked up a cab outside. I had him take me to a restaurant about half a mile from the park entrance and paid in cash. From there, I maneuvered through a sprawling, Soviet-style apartment complex, avoiding the main roads. I crossed the eight-lane Pieramožcaŭ Praspiekt and entered the park. I had about an hour until my meeting time.

The park's entrance was a monolithic granite edifice with bright yellow Cyrillic lettering depicting the Soviet victory. I ignored this and walked through the unwelcoming arches. Paths snaked through the trees seemingly in every direction. I chose one at random, stopping at intervals to tie my shoes or for some other reason to check behind me. Satisfied I was not followed, I found a bench and waited for Fedorov. It was a cool and partly overcast evening. Fedorov arrived ten minutes early, casually dressed and wearing a light jacket. He approached the metal railing hesitantly and rested his hands on it. I could practically see the waves of apprehension radiating off his body.

I walked up next to him and opened the guidebook, setting it on the railing between us. Anyone looking at us would think I was asking for directions. There was a thick forest behind us and more trees on the opposite side of the lake. The water lapping against the retaining wall provided a good source of white noise.

"Thank you for meeting me. Did Charlie say I was coming?" I said, in Russian.

"Yes," Fedorov said. He was in his mid-fifties, with pale blue eyes and wispy hair the color of straw, both that had the effect of being washed out. His skin was ruddy, suggesting exposure to harsh climates layered with a garden of gin blossoms. His teeth were the product of Soviet dentistry.

"Charlie told me about Projekt Molniya. You're looking to discuss it?" I asked.

Fedorov looked out over the water. "That is correct," he admitted, softly. There was no guilt in his voice, or regret. The volume, I thought, was just so that it didn't get picked up by the wind and carried somewhere he didn't want it to go.

"And Charlie explained the situation to you? That the Americans cannot help you, but perhaps the Orpheus Foundation can? I represent that group. I'll evaluate your information. If it is worthwhile, we continue talking."

"He told me this, yes. Eh, is English better?"

"That's fine," I said, switching to English. Instinctively, my voice lowered a notch. "I'm comfortable with either. I watched you today, and I saw someone tailing you from your hotel. My guess, it was Belarusian KGB. Do you know why they are interested in you?"

Fedorov shook his head. "It isn't KGB. Well, perhaps they are, but if it is, they are acting on behalf of SVR."

The alarms going off in my head were so loud I worried Fedorov would hear them.

Questions screamed into being.

"How do you know this?"

"My...handler, this is the English word, yes? He warned me that the SVR was asking questions about the project. Then, he disappeared. He was not at our meeting place here in Minsk, and I cannot reach him by phone. When I could not, I contacted Mr. Auer to ask him for help."

"Shouldn't that be the FSB's responsibility?"

After the Cold War, the Russian Federation, as part of their "reforms," broke the KGB into two organizations—foreign intelligence, the SVR, and domestic security, the FSB.

"It would be, but the Kremlin doesn't trust them right now. Too many high-profile failures. Corruption, incompetence, and mostly, operational failures in Ukraine."

Even when I was still in the Agency, I'd heard their president wasn't happy with the FSB. Apparently, they'd told him they'd created this network of dissidents, saboteurs, and agents provocateur in Ukraine, and that the president made his final decision to invade based on that. Turns out that network didn't exist, and the Russians discovered a defiant and capable resistance with few assets they could draw on.

Fedorov said, "Charlie told me you had a way to get me out of Belarus?"

"Grigori, so far you haven't told me much that I don't already know. My job here isn't to get you out. I'm here to vet you so that my client knows that the information you have is worth the risk. If you convince me of the latter, I can help you get to safety. Now, can you prove that the GRU is buying Western technology and using that to make electromagnetic weapons?"

Fedorov laughed, and it sounded like polluted water crashing over rocks. "Yes, I can do this. The part about Projekt Molniya that I did not tell Charlie was that I helped design the weapons."

"Weapons? So, you mean there is more than one of them?"

"There are at least three types that I know of. This is why your people suffer slightly different effects. I designed the one used in Havana, and then its smaller versions, which were deployed in Tbilisi and Vienna." Fedorov turned away from me and looked out over the lake. "It wasn't even supposed to be a weapon, you know. We designed it to be surveillance equipment. To read cell phones and computers from great distances. Then, they discovered the waves were harmful to humans and almost undetectable. There is much more I can share, but not until I am safe."

"You know, for fact, that the weapons you designed were used?"

"Yes."

"And you can prove this?"

"Yes."

"Where is this information? Is it on you?"

"It is safe. Nothing more until I am as well."

"That's not good enough. Do you realize what happens to me if I get—" I stopped myself. If Fedorov was a dangle, like I'd feared, he could have a concealed listening device on him. Better not to say anything too incriminating.

Fedorov laughed bitterly. "If I stay here, I am dead. That is a certainty. Moscow is rounding everyone up involved in Projekt Molniya. If I stay here, they will find out I was the one who stole the files. They always find out. I have proof of what I say, but I will not share anything until I am safe. It is the only collateral I have."

So, the only way to really verify that he was telling the truth was to get him out.

Again, this was looking more and more like a trap.

I slid away from the railing and closed the guidebook.

Fedorov reached into his jacket.

My body went rigid, and I flattened my hand, ready for a quick strike.

Fedorov removed a piece of paper and handed it to me. I scanned it. It was a technical schematic, written in German, with proprietary markings from the manufacturer. "This is part of the design specification for one of the Bundeswehr's counterdrone systems." The blueprint showed four small, roughly oval-shaped antennae atop a vehicle. Fedorov continued. "It uses microwaves emitted from here," he pointed at the antennae, "to melt the control systems of enemy drones. Projekt Molniya was based on a similar principle. The GRU's engineers couldn't figure out how to focus the beams properly without melting the antennae. After I acquired these designs, the GRU figured out how to direct a sustained beam without destroying the projector."

Any trap worth the effort would seem authentic enough to convince the mark to take the bait. I chanced a look around us. A dark and gloomy forest closed in on the flanks, water rippled at our feet. I didn't see any movement indicating a potential grab team. Then again, it was now getting too dark to see them.

Still, I wasn't yet convinced.

Fedorov put the paper away.

"What else do you have?"

"Not until I'm safe," he said.

"It doesn't work that way. You don't get to ask people to risk their lives for you without proof."

"I just showed you—"

"A piece of paper," I said. "What else do you have?"

Fedorov exhaled a frustrated mouthful of air. "I have the Projekt Molniya files. Once I am out, and safe, and have asylum somewhere, I will turn them over to Charlie's reporter."

"Okay. Now, before this goes any further," I said. "You said you believed the SVR is here, in Minsk. If you're worried they were going to arrest you, why hasn't that happened yet? Why didn't they just tell you to go to Moscow? And how do you know it's the SVR?"

"I am not sure how much of this was properly conveyed through my texts with Charlie. I was scheduled to attend a conference here, sponsored by the local university. This was pretext for a meeting with my handler. He was worried about the stolen files, not knowing I took them. I knew he wanted to speak to me to see if I knew. The plan was to meet my handler and then depart for Vilnius yesterday."

"That's not what Charlie told me," I said.

"I am sorry. We did not speak on the phone, and there may have been some miscommunication."

Or, someone wasn't giving me the full story.

I said, "We need to leave tonight. I'll meet you at Site Delta at twenty-three hundred. That's three hours from now. Leave your bags, your computer, and your phone, everything, in your room. The only thing you should bring with you is any information you have. If anyone asks, you're just going out for a drink. Ideally, you should leave around twenty-one thirty. Do not take a direct route there. If, for any reason, you are delayed and can't make it, I'll meet you at Site Echo at zero three hundred. Then, Site Foxtrot at zero five hundred."

Connor had three planned meeting locations in Minsk, designated Alpha, Bravo, and Charlie. The three extraction points—meaning the places where I'd rendezvous with Fedorov—were Delta, Echo, and Foxtrot. If one or the other party failed to show at one site, they were to proceed to the next site and time combination. If they failed to show a second time, onto the third. If they failed three times…

Well, you're out.

"I understand. Thank you."

"Don't thank me yet," I said.

With nothing left to say, I disappeared into the forest. I was not stopped.

I took a mostly direct route back to my hotel, though I still had a few miles to occupy my thoughts.

Fedorov's information felt credible enough to buy him the next link in the operational chain. This also gave me a chance to arrive early at the exfiltration point, observe whether security services were in place, and call it off safely.

I returned to my hotel on foot, enjoying the clarity of the cool night air. The last remnants of sunlight were gone from the sky when I neared the hotel. I walked along Pieramožcaŭ Praspiekt, still heavy with traffic, and cut through a now empty parking lot across from my hotel.

The DoubleTree was on the far side of the Galleria, along a gently curving, one-way road. I stepped into the circular carport, which had two taxis positioned for potential fares, a van, and a random collection of other vehicles. There was a man standing at the hotel entrance, leaning against a pillar and smoking while he looked at his phone.

Lights from a parked car flared, painting me in full halogen. A black sedan pulled forward from its parking spot and stopped right in front of me, severing my lifeline to the hotel. The smoker dropped his cigarette and walked forward. Doors opened and closed. I heard another vehicle behind me but did not turn. Instead, I looked to the sides. It would be a hard sprint to the hotel perimeter, but if I made that, I was momentarily out of view. I'd walked the grounds earlier today and knew there was a cluster of buildings on that side, as well as the entrance to the mall. All I needed was to keep my speed and I might be able to lose them in the maze. A long shot, and also the only one.

Probably some local cops looking for a shakedown, tipped off by one of the hotel staff for a cut.

A form materialized in my peripheral. From the sound of shoes scraping around me, I could guess that I was surrounded. The heavy hand dropping on my shoulder confirmed it.

A voice in accented English said, "Mr. Gage, if you would come with us, please. We would like a word."

"I wouldn't," I said. Then, there was movement.

I had no problem arguing with him, just not the gun in his hand.

8

They offered no badges or identification.

"Tell you what," I said, pointing at the hotel. "How about we go and have a nice chat at the bar. I'll buy the first round."

"I don't think so," he said. They knew my name, which meant they were police or KGB. My money was on the latter. Places like this, the hotel staff got a bounty for tipping off the security services when travelers from adversarial countries checked in. Connor told me to expect some harassment.

"Okay, well, if this is an official matter, I'd just like to inform my embassy where I am."

A bleak, ugly chortle passed through the man's lips. "I don't think you understand where you are, Mr. Gage. Now, get in the car, or we will force you to. The latter way, I think you will not like."

One of the men behind me grabbed hold of my arms while another frisked me. They took three of the things I had on me—the burner, my watch, and my wallet. My jacket, a black Harrington-style, was designed with features for people in my line of work. There were concealed carry pockets large enough for a passport or other small valuables—though not a weapon. The exterior padding hid the items from casual inspection, foiling most would-be pickpockets or stick-up guys, as well as the local cops who weren't very thorough. I'd seen it stand up to a frisk, and it did here too. They missed my passport and car keys.

They stuffed me in the back of a black SUV, between two massive forms, neither of whom would win hygiene prizes. The driver moved as soon as the door closed. The hard lessons of calming the mind during times of intense stress came back. I focused on compiling as much detail as possible, anything that would provide clues about who these men were and what they wanted with me. No one spoke. Most appeared to be in their forties, though they could be younger just with hard miles. Fitness level was average. None sported the chiseled features or wiry build of special operators. Squeezed between the two men, I could feel the outlines of their shoulder holsters where they pressed against my arms. Since I could detect two pistols, that meant one of them was a lefty.

We drove roughly south, staying on central streets. There was little traffic in the interior, and the trip did not take long. Local landmarks pointed the way, and we were now just a few blocks from the Hotel Minsk. A cold jolt of terror hit me, and it took all my effort to contain myself. The SUV turned right off the side street and into a sprawling labyrinth of buildings. The main one, I knew immediately. It was a monolith of Stalinist neoclassical architecture, a grotesque simulacrum of many of America's government buildings. The Belarusian Committee for State Security Headquarters, the KGB. The SUV pulled up to a smaller, five-story structure behind it. There was no ornamentation, no styling. It was a simple block of Soviet concrete shaped into a building.

They jerked me out of the car and pushed me inside. Flanked by two of them and another at my back, they frog-marched me through empty hallways. The sound of our footsteps bounced off the walls and reminded me I was very much alone.

Well, at least I could answer the question of whether Fedorov was a dangle.

I took some consolation in knowing that it was me in here, not Jennie.

They "guided" me into an interview room with pale green walls and a Formica table that had been heavily scratched. One of my minders shoved me down in the chair. The room was hot and desperately in need of circulation. The door closed behind me, followed by the unmistakable sound of a lock.

At the Farm, they teach you how to tell time without a watch. An invaluable skill in the field when the light from a watch face or a phone might give you away. It's not perfect, but reasonably accurate for the conditions. I estimated that I was in there for thirty minutes before the door opened again.

The man who'd spoken to me outside the hotel entered and sat opposite me.

"Mr. Gage, what are you doing here in Minsk?"

"Who are you?"

"You may call me Maksim," he said. My practice in the language might've been rusty, but my ear for it was not.

"Your accent is Russian, not Belarusian."

"Very good, Mr. Gage. Though about what I would expect from an ex-CIA officer," Maksim said.

Oh shit.

After Nicaragua, presumably both the SVR and FSB had files on me.

My mind raced to connect the chain of events. I entered the country legally using my own passport. The border guards may have reported me to the KGB. I wasn't known to them, though as I suspected earlier, they may have passed my name to their Russian counterparts as a matter of course. It also may have come from the hotel. Those were the only two places I'd given my name.

I forced a chuckle. "I think your information is a little off, Maksim. I *did* work for the US government, but for the State Department and doing communications. I barely left Washington. Now, I'm making movies."

"Is that so?"

Maksim dressed in a black suit with a blue shirt and no tie. His features were classically European with no hint of Asian influence, suggesting he came from Russia's western regions—Moscow or St. Petersburg. Cobalt-colored eyes were set beneath a straight brow line that gave them an additional focus of intensity. His hair was dark, closely cut and slightly retreating from his forehead. He looked like an ambush predator in an off-the-rack suit. "What kind of movies do you make, Mr. Gage?" I noted that he used my name a lot, as though underscoring the fact that he knew it.

"Currently, we're making a documentary about Napoleon's failed invasion of Russia. I'm here to look at possible shooting locations and try to make some connections with the film bureau."

"And have you?"

"I only arrived today."

"I see. Interesting that a former CIA officer is now...making movies."

"As I said—"

Maksim held up a hand, and I took the hint. "What are you doing in this country, Mr. Gage?"

"I already told you."

"Let's assume that I do not believe you."

"So, what, I'm supposed to change my answer because you didn't believe the first one?"

Maksim said nothing.

I carried on, playing both sides of the conversation. "What are you doing here? Making a movie. I don't believe you. Oh, in that case, I'm a super spy, here to topple your government." I shook my head, feigning frustration.

"What do you think about our special action in Ukraine?"

He changed topics abruptly in an attempt to catch me off guard.

"Well, I'm not involved, so I tend not to have an opinion about it," I said.

"I find that hard to believe. Our president has a saying, 'There are no former KGB men.' I think the same is true for you. Perhaps you would like to hear a theory, Mr. Gage."

This ought to be good. For once in my life, perhaps the only time, I kept my mouth shut.

"I think that your government is afraid to send one of its CIA officers to Ukraine. They know if such a person were captured, it would expose the hypocrisy of your involvement. It would necessitate an immediate escalation of the war. Russia would have no choice but to respond militarily. So, they use people like yourself. A pensioner. A contractor. Someone who gives them deniability. When you get caught, they can just write you off. As they have done with so many."

"I'll bet a lot of extra money writing spy novels. That's pretty rich."

So, they thought I was here as a contract officer to cause trouble for them in Ukraine. This Maksim must be with the Minsk *rezidentura*, the SVR station. That could explain how the loop closed so quickly. I'd known it was possible, that the border guards would report an American coming across to the KGB and that they could eventually kick that over to the SVR. What I hadn't counted on was them doing it so quickly. That was a level of efficiency they didn't seem capable of.

And my cover was wet-napkin weak.

I wasn't in Minsk for the reason they thought I was, though I had nothing to convince them otherwise.

Irony could be a real asshole sometimes.

I also noted that he didn't mention anything about Grigori Fedorov.

"I'm not a spy, Maksim. If I was, I wouldn't have checked into a hotel using my own name, and I sure as hell wouldn't have crossed the border with my own passport."

Maksim shrugged dismissively. "Maybe you're just not that good at it." Then he leaned forward far enough that I could smell the old coffee and cigarettes on his breath. "Mr. Gage, no one knows you're here. Unless you tell me what I want to know, no one will."

Stick to your cover, no matter what. That's what they teach you. *Your cover will save you. Even if it's blown.* One of my instructors at the Farm said that exact phrase to me during my training. It made such an impression, I repeated it to my own trainees. To Connor Bishop.

Maksim hammered me with questions for another hour. Where did I come from? Why was I here? Who was I meeting? Had I been to Ukraine? What was the name of my contact in Minsk?

I deflected, and most of the time, honestly.

"How did you know I was staying at the DoubleTree?" I asked.

"Our partners here in Belarus must vet foreigners as potential subversives," Maksim replied nonchalantly.

"Right. I guess what I want to know is, were you following me all day or just lurking at the hotel. Because if you were following me, you'd have seen a pretty boring pedestrian tour of the city."

Maksim didn't have facial expressions, other than the occasional half-hearted frown. "How do you like Santa Monica, Mr. Gage? It is expensive there, no? For what you pay in rent, you could have an estate in Moscow."

"Yeah, but it'd be in Moscow."

"Pity that a man who has given his life in service to his government can only afford to rent half of a seventy-year-old home. This says something about America, does it not?"

Now I had to listen to a Russian spy's thoughts on real estate prices? Maybe I *should* confess to whatever he thought I did and just ask for the firing squad.

The comment about my house was intended to rattle me, to make me think they'd been watching me for some time. They had my driver's license, and everything else could be picked up online. Still, it was a spider-crawling-on-your-neck feeling to have someone like him say your address out loud, even if it was public record.

"You know, Maksim, I think the one thing we can agree on is that housing prices in Los Angeles are insane. Maybe there's hope for US-Soviet relations yet." I paused, just a second, pretending to catch myself. "Sorry, I meant to say 'Russia.'"

"I would think a man in your position would choose your words with greater care."

"You obviously don't know me very well."

"Curious that your phone is a disposable one. Is this so you cannot be tracked?"

"Nice try. You and I both know every European telecom has boycotted Belarus."

Maksim pushed himself back from the table.

"So, am I free to go now?" I said.

He expunged a bitter gust of air from his mouth, which I took to be a quasi-laugh. "No."

Suddenly, I had images in my head of me sitting in one of those glass boxes where the Russians put the accused when they stood "trial." That box was a one-way ticket to a Siberian labor camp.

Or, more likely, the basement of Lefortovo Prison.

It was the place beneath Moscow where they shot spies.

Maksim left me alone for several hours.

I guessed our little chat session lasted about an hour, so by my calculation, it was close to one in the morning.

I'd already missed the rendezvous at Site Delta, and we were dangerously close to the secondary location/time group. All I could do was hope that Connor had prepared Fedorov well for this. Which was not likely, considering that Fedorov wasn't an asset, at least not one of ours. He wouldn't have had the crash course in tradecraft Connor would otherwise have given him.

Though, I noted that there would be no circumstances for a State Department officer to develop an exfiltration plan. Connor had at least briefed Fedorov on that much. Again, more things that didn't add up to me.

Speaking of the plan, Site Foxtrot was also a problem.

The first two had me picking him up on some dark corner in Minsk. "Foxtrot" meant things had gone to shit and it wasn't safe for us to leave Minsk together.

Fedorov would board a regional commuter train at the city's central rail station and take it ninety minutes north to the city of Smorgon. However, that required me to be on the road at roughly the same time if I was going to meet his train and not leave Fedorov standing conspicuously on a rail platform in a small town where everybody knew their neighbors.

Time crawled by, and Maksim did not reappear.

9

The sound of the deadbolt disengaging in the silent room crashed like metal thunder.

The door opened, and two men pushed through.

"Stand," the first one said.

I didn't recognize either of them.

I stood.

The other one moved around the table, took hold of my arm, and jerked me closer to him. My legs were asleep from being frozen in the same position for so long, and I nearly fell. "Walk," the first one said. I suspected we'd reached the end of his linguistic aptitude, in any language.

They pushed me through the hallway in a circuitous route, through a heavy fire door, and we were outside. It was still night.

The wordsmith shocked me by adding a third item to his repertoire when he growled out, "Car."

He shoved me forward, though his partner hadn't given up his hold on my arm, and I stumbled. Ivan One got in the driver's seat, while Ivan Two pushed me into the back. He slid in next to me. Ivan One fired up the car, and we left the KGB compound. Ivan Two pulled a pistol and held it crossbody.

My hands weren't bound.

I could make a play for the gun.

It'd go off in the struggle, and the driver's chances weren't good. Not that I was particularly worried about him—occupational hazard for being a professional asshole. I was a little bit more worried about the crash that'd follow, but, as they say, one problem at a time.

Not binding my hands was a curious move. If they thought I was a threat, they would have.

We drove north.

It was still dark, but the eastern sky had a soft gray glow to it. It must be later than I'd estimated. The driver angled us to the northwest, as few roads in Minsk followed a typical Western grid layout. No one spoke, though that could just as easily have been lack of ability than nothing to say. We went about ten minutes, then the car stopped abruptly, pulling into a construction site. Even in the darkness, I could see the outline of girders that would become a high-rise in a few months. The dirt landscape was rolling hills of recent excavation and a pit that, from where I sat, was the deepest abyss.

So that was where this would end, a construction site in Minsk at the hands of some SVR thugs.

"Out of car," the driver said.

He'd actually put a full sentence together. Knowing that I'd seen a true miracle on my way out gave me hope there really was an afterlife.

I staggered out of the car, practically tripping over my own feet. They still hadn't recovered from sitting in the same position for most of the night.

Run down the options.

They'd made a tactical error in letting me out first. Because the driver hadn't gotten out to secure me, there was nothing stopping me from bolting. I could easily move to the side, denying the shooter line of sight. Or, I could just step aside, wait for him to get out to finish the job, and make a play for the gun when he did. That was the smarter move.

I got out.

They did not.

The driver opened his door a crack and dropped something on the ground. No sooner had the dust cloud formed, the car jolted forward. Ivan One cranked hard to the right, a dirty ghost billowing up behind the car, lit by a ruddy glow from the taillights. The car fishtailed, because Ivan was a poor driver, and he angled right for me. That was their plan? They wanted this to look like a hit-and-run? Sonsabitches wouldn't even spend a bullet on me.

You're gonna work for it, Ivan, I thought as I dove out of the way. I could almost feel the bumper kiss my shoes.

Flying dirt chased the car like an angry spirit, colored red by the taillights. It bounced once as it drove over something, then sped away.

What...the...actual...fuck?

I was alive.

And alone.

Straining to see in the dark, I searched quickly for what they'd dropped, some clue about what was happening. I found a thick plastic bag, like what you'd use to hold evidence, half covered in kicked-up dirt. I picked it up and shook it off, wiping my hands on my pants. Inside was the burner, my wallet, and my watch. Tearing the bag open, I squinted to make out the dial. It was nearly four. There was exactly fifty minutes until Fedorov was to catch his train.

My plan was to have been there to make sure he got on the train. I assumed they were tracking him by his phone, so there was at least a chance that he could make the train station without the SVR or GRU knowing. I didn't bother powering on the phone. Maksim would've had it on, and if Fedorov had called while I was in custody, the whole thing was off anyway. He'd also delete any calls he made from the record. They'd be tracking the SIM card now, so if it was used, they could geolocate it based on the nearest cell tower. Only reason they'd have given it back.

I dropped it in the dirt.

A quick scan of my wallet showed they'd kept the credit card and taken any cash I had.

Man, these guys really took the concept of "kleptocracy" to a whole new level.

So, I couldn't hail a cab.

Fedorov's train would depart in about an hour. I didn't know where I was, so I didn't know how long it would take to get to my hotel and get my car.

Fedorov was on his own.

I trotted to the edge of the construction site and saw one of Minsk's inner traffic loops. The road system was a series of concentric rings rippling out from city center. This would be the first one, and I could make out the train tracks on the far side of it. At least I had a notional idea of where I was now. Morning traffic was still sparse, so I easily dashed across the four lanes. No trains in sight, so I stepped over the tracks as well. I picked up a street on the far side.

I checked my watch to reconfirm how little time I had, and then I ran.

I'd never brought my things inside the hotel, other than my personal phone and portable network. Both of which I had stashed in the car's hidden compartment beneath the seat. There was no reason to go back inside. Good luck charging me for the room. That card was getting canceled the second I got across the border. That'll show 'em.

Jogging a couple miles in pants, a long-sleeved shirt, and a jacket wasn't my favorite activity. I wanted a shower, but I wasn't going to risk going inside. I assumed that someone in the hotel had sold me out once; I wasn't risking it again. Also, it was a reasonable guess that Maksim had his boys bug my room.

Releasing me made no sense. I couldn't understand how they'd go from accusing me of being a contract operative to leaving me in the dirt at a construction site, with a conspicuous lack of bullet holes.

Had they just believed I was a target of opportunity for a shakedown?

Or did Fedorov evade them and they let me go to see where *he* went? There was no reason for them to assume we were connected. Other than the fact that they knew I was ex-CIA and in town at the exact same time as him.

Wow, seems bad when you say it out loud.

Open question on whether my passport was flagged with the border guards. If I made it across without getting arrested, it was probably only owing to the incredibly inefficiency of this government.

This entire episode was a great reminder that I was a private investigator now and no longer a spy. As Dirty Harry once wisely stated, "A man has got to know his limitations."

A final glance at my watch showed I had thirty minutes until Fedorov's train departed.

I burned precious but necessary time driving a circuitous route of double backs, random turns, and leapfrogs through parking lots as I left town. There hadn't been time to check the car for surveillance devices.

The original route was to take the P108 highway, even though it would stack an extra thirty minutes onto the travel time. It was a rural route, and there was less chance of running into police. Because I'd lost so much time, the only chance I had to make Fedorov's arrival was to take the M7 motorway, and even then, I'd have to risk exceeding the speed limit.

Smorgon is a small town near the Lithuanian border and has the distinction of once being part of the Grand Duchy of Lithuania, Imperial Russia, and the Second Polish Republic, before its absorption by the Belarusian SSR. It was here that Napoleon disbanded his Grande Armée following his failed invasion of Russia and returned to Paris. All facts that would've come in handy had anyone believed my story that I was here to make a movie on it.

Now it's a low, quiet town of square apartments and small houses on a vast plain with intermittent trees.

I'd beaten the train by ten minutes. The adrenaline had long since faded, and what I needed was a cup of coffee and food. Of course, I couldn't get either because some Russian spooks emptied my wallet out of spite. I parked on the street and walked up to the train station, which was a long, single-story building of white stucco with a maroon roof. Everything was closed. There was a ribbon of light on the eastern horizon, and the sky was a burgeoning gray, with low overcast.

Three cars were parked in front of the station, none of them occupied. Nor had I spotted any lurking on the road, though admittedly I hadn't done a true sweep.

The blue-and-silver train slowed with an arriving horn blast and coasted into the station as I reached the platform. No one waited for the train. I approached the station and rounded its north side, near the front quarter of the train. There were large streetlamps lighting up the front of the building and the platform, but the sides were dark, so that was where I stayed.

Doors opened and nothing happened.

A sleepy family emerged from the station and boarded. I also spotted a railway employee that was notionally supervising things.

I'd memorized the departure schedule the day before, so I knew that we had exactly two minutes.

There was no sign of Fedorov.

With fifteen seconds to spare, I watched a man in a dark suit descend the train car's steps carrying a briefcase. The railway attendant called out the departure.

The man on the platform turned to face me, and I saw that it was Fedorov.

A second form materialized in the doorway and quickly descended to the platform.

I recognized him immediately. His eyes were on Fedorov, then they went to me, and we locked.

Maksim said, "Mr. Gage, how surprising to find you here."

10

At the sound of Maksim's voice behind him, the color drained out of Fedorov's face.

Train doors closed, and the horn called out its departure. The huge machine crawled forward but quickly gained momentum.

I took a few steps forward, not acknowledging Fedorov.

"I told you I was making a movie about Napoleon. This is where he packed it up," I said. I'd committed these facts to memory for this cover, and I was damned well going to use them.

Maksim held up a finger and wagged it in the dim light. "It's not a very good lie, but I admire your conviction." He turned his head slightly. "Grigori Fedorov, stop." Fedorov did. Maksim opened the wing of his coat and drew a pistol from a shoulder holster. "Once we saw Mr. Fedorov leave his hotel, we assumed *someone* was here to meet him. We made the mistake of relying on local support to watch him."

"You did all this by yourself?" I said.

"I had men on other trains and covering the exits at the station, in case Mr. Fedorov tried to double back. But I don't need a team to shoot a traitor."

Even for an SVR officer, holding two men at gunpoint on a train platform was brash. Though, admittedly, it was now empty, and Maksim had little to fear.

"What's your interest in...Fedorov, is it?" I asked.

"I told you, he's a traitor. In a way, this is your doing. So, you should take some comfort in that. Until you arrived, we only had orders to observe him. We believed the Americans would send someone to collect him, it was just a matter of finding out who."

"Pretty thin grounds to assassinate a tourist," I said.

Maksim laughed. "A tourist? I think not. A tourist wouldn't run flat-out for two miles to get back to his hotel, only to not go to his room. A tourist wouldn't have thought to lose an observation vehicle. Or known how." Maksim's expression now was one of smug superiority, and I wanted nothing more than to wipe it off his face.

Maksim raised the gun.

Pushing off my back leg, I closed the distance between us. I thrust my left hand out and grabbed the gun; all I cared about was pushing the barrel of its aim. Using that same explosive momentum, I punched Maksim in the throat.

A gunshot cracked out.

Maksim staggered back, and I grabbed the top of the pistol. If I'd have gotten any more force behind that punch, I'd have smashed his trachea. Still, Maksim desperately clawed for air, and his eyes were wide with shock. Keeping my hand on top of the pistol's slide was dangerous; if he fired again I might lose part of my hand in the action. Letting go of the pistol, I tried to grab his forearm. Maksim knuckle punched me in the temple, and an explosion of yellow-white dots flooded my vision.

He couldn't overpower my grip, since I could exert more force pushing than he could at that angle. Maksim twisted his wrist, and I hadn't anticipated the move. It gave him just enough space to maneuver his hand. He switched the pistol's angle and brought it dangerously close to my midsection.

Maksim fired a second time.

The bullet drilled into the concrete and pocked a section right next to my foot. The barrel was about three inches from my leg.

I stepped in, slamming my right shoulder into his body. With as much force as I could muster, I pushed with both legs and forced Maksim backward. He backpedaled several steps, and I saw he was inches from the edge of the platform. It wasn't a steep drop, but if I could knock him off, it might give us enough time to get away. Maksim wouldn't have a car here.

I lunged forward.

Maksim fired.

My first punch landed on his jaw, and the wild, unfocused look in his eyes told me I'd landed a good one. My second was a body blow to the stomach. He brought the gun up, and I caught it just in time to block it with my right hand. We struggled to control it. Jesus, this guy had a grip. I couldn't wrench it out with both hands.

With both of Maksim's hands on the pistol, I jerked my right arm back and punched him in the throat again. He staggered back and brought one of his hands up instinctively to block. I grabbed his wrist and brought it crashing down on my knee with all the force I had. The gun fell from limp fingers, and I kicked it away. It clattered across the platform.

I side-kicked him in the stomach.

He backpedaled several steps, already recovered.

"You're going to—"

A succession of gunshots cut his words off and shattered the morning's silence.

Maksim's body jerked with each impact, and his eyes went wide. Four dark circles appeared on his shirt. A breath later, they'd spread out, covering his chest. His face was a mix of incomprehension and pain. He stumbled back once and collapsed.

The light faded from his eyes as blood leaked out onto the bricks.

Fedorov stood in shocked silence with a zephyr trail of gun smoke climbing out of the barrel.

Even if I thought he'd be worth the effort, I knew Maksim was too far gone to save. The only thing we'd get for the trouble was actual blood on our hands and burned time we couldn't afford to lose.

The operator part of my brain snapped the world into violent focus. We needed to move.

Closing the distance between us, I grabbed Fedorov's arm. "We have to go."

Fedorov just stared at the body, either still processing what he'd done or unable to do even that.

"Goddamn it, get rid of that thing," I barked.

"Right. Yes," he said. He dropped the gun on the platform. The briefcase he'd had was at his feet.

Swearing to myself, I kicked the gun onto the tracks.

Maksim forced the confrontation, he'd pulled the gun. None of this was my fault, and none of that would matter. A Russian intelligence officer was dead, and we were in a client state. There would be no accounting for actual circumstance here.

Fedorov grabbed his briefcase, climbed into the passenger seat, and we were gone. I'd take a succession of rural highways until we reconnected with the M7 motorway in Ashmyany, and from there, the checkpoint.

We drove in silence.

When the adrenaline wore off, the realization of what he'd done sank in.

Almost anything in this world can be undone.

Except taking a life.

Now, our only chance of escape was making the border before the local police guessed that was where we were heading.

I pushed the car hard over those back roads, driving as fast as I dared. Knowing we'd hit more populated areas as we got closer to the M7, I pulled off the road and stopped. "Get out," I said. I did the same and checked both directions for oncoming traffic. Fedorov, confused or scared, maybe both, stayed put. "We don't have a lot of time," I said. I opened the back door, leaned in, and popped the rear seat up. Fedorov got out of the vehicle.

"You expect me to get into that?" he said, over the top of the car.

"How do you think this works? You're on a watchlist. The first thing they're going to do is call the airport and the one border crossing that's still open. And now we've got a dead body to worry about."

"What if we're caught?"

"One crisis at a time," I said, and pointed at the hole.

Fedorov stared at the space for a few seconds, as though trying to calculate the geometry of it. He was shorter than me, but anyone over age ten would be cramped in that space. I made another sweep off the road, spotting a vehicle in the distance, from the direction we'd come. I didn't see lights on top of it, but certainly by now Maksim's body had been discovered. The station agent had probably hid under his desk when he heard the first shot and called the authorities from there. "Goddamn it, get in. We do not have time for this."

Fedorov looked at me for a hard second and knelt into the compartment. I pushed the seat down before he was even in place, closed the door, and took off before that other vehicle got anywhere near us.

I tuned in to local radio to see if I could pick up any news, but I didn't find anything.

There was a decent flow of traffic on the M7, which calmed my nerves a little.

Until I hit the wall of trucks waiting for clearance. The line stretched about a mile. The Lithuanians thoroughly inspected every vehicle coming through because of the smuggling problem.

Good thing this plan relied on my being able to successfully hide a guy in a trunk.

The line dragged on for about two hours. I was now on about hour thirty without sleep, and over twelve since I'd eaten last. About the same since I'd used the bathroom too. At this point, pressure on the bladder was about the only thing keeping me awake.

Traffic crawled forward, and eventually the lane split, with trucks routed one way and personal vehicles to the other.

A border guard signaled me to pull into the inspections station. I rolled the car forward and handed him my passport. He snatched it out of my hand, scanned it, and took several steps back from the car. Then he mumbled something into his radio.

The border guard walked back to the car and leaned down, appraising me with dull, cold eyes.

"Please step out of the car," he said.

"Is there a problem?"

The guard repeated his command.

Fedorov, who'd been in that compartment for about three hours, would have no idea what was happening. I didn't know the man's nerves, and he could be on the verge of panic.

"Okay, I'll get out now," I said in Russian and a voice above conversational level. The guard looked at me quizzically. "This is a routine inspection?"

He did not respond to that either. I stepped out. A pair of guards materialized out of the background, and they were all over the car. Before I knew it, all of the doors and the trunk were open. They removed everything that wasn't attached to something and a few things that were. Meanwhile, the guard in front of me hammered questions about what I was doing in Belarus. The rapid-fire cadence was enough that I couldn't keep up with that and pay attention to the two guards poking around the car. The full day without sleep was catching up to me, and being jet-lagged on top of it. Concentrating on the border guard speaking in a language that I was several years out of practice with and knowing when to be evasive took every ounce of mental strength that I had.

After our third round of "what is your purpose in Belarus," the guard turned, having been signaled from one of the others at the car. I turned around.

Then he handed me my passport and waved me forward with a disinterested gesture.

They left the car with every door and compartment opened, *except* the back seat. As quickly as I could, I closed everything and got back inside.

Sparing no seconds, I left Belarus.

One down.

There was a long line of semi-trucks waiting on inspection, but the personal traffic was much lighter, and I was called forward quickly.

The Lithuanian guard took my passport and asked me to step out of my vehicle. He proceeded to ask me a series of questions about my trip, while another guard walked around the car with a mirror at the end of a stick. Once he'd completed his route, he said something to the one asking me questions, who then directed me to open the trunk. I did so, and the second guard proceeded to take the trunk apart. Again.

This time, it was much faster than on the Belarusian side. The guard handed me my passport and said that I was free to go. I closed everything up and left. There was a gas station just over the border, and I pulled in and parked. I turned and pretended to reach for my bag in the back; instead I lifted the seat cover up an inch. "We're through, Grigori. There are too many people around to get out. Do you have any money? The SVR sort of stole my wallet. It's a long story."

Fedorov swore, and there was jostling. He pushed a twenty-euro note through the gap.

"I'll be right back," I said. Leaving my charge in the dug-out hole of a Volkswagen, I went into the gas station for a poorly regulated Eastern European energy drink and a protein bar.

Vilnius was safer than Minsk, but not by much.

The Russians had assets here, and by now, they would be looking.

I wanted to put fast miles between me and that dead SVR officer's body.

Borders didn't make you safe. Not against these guys.

We could get out that night on the Polish flag carrier, Lot, and connecting through Warsaw, get into Brussels a little after midnight. I called Denis and told him we were coming and to secure us a couple hotel rooms.

With Fedorov cooling his heels in my hotel room, I stepped out to call Connor on Signal and let him know we were safely out of Belarus. "We need to talk in person, now."

Ten minutes later, Connor and I were mutually smoldering outside the hotel, a pair of volcanoes looking to duel in lava and ejected rocks.

"Why am I hearing reports of a dead SVR officer in Smorgon? What the hell happened, Gage?"

"They were watching Fedorov. I spent all night in a KGB interrogation room. They only let me out to see where I'd go. Missed our first two windows. When I met Fedorov in Smorgon, an SVR officer had followed him there. I assume they didn't grab him on the train so they could see who picked him up. The guy pulled a gun on me. I tried to get it away from him. Fedorov picked it up and shot him." I paused to let that sink in. "Choose your next words carefully, Connor. Here's what's going to happen. I'm getting Fedorov out of here so that he can do what was promised. You are going to do whatever you have to do to make this go away. Vanished, Connor. If this ever gets back to me, I've only got one name."

"All right, all right. I'll see what I can do."

"No. You will not 'see.' You will defy the laws of physics, *Connor*. I don't want this buried, I want it disintegrated."

Connor fumed but said nothing. Reading expressions can be difficult and often misleading. Watching him, though, I saw the breaking dawn of a grim, new understanding behind his eyes. Connor was learning, in real time, that the things he set in motion were now spinning far beyond his control.

"Connor, you wrote a good op plan," I said, softening my tone and checking my own anger. "I mean that. Especially for the short time you had. Your backups worked and worked well."

"Thank you for saying that."

"I'm serious. We got him out. But you now need to be exceedingly careful. The Russians know something happened, and they'll obviously suspect you guys. I mean, Vilnius Station. You've got to think through how you manage that. You also need to remember how thoroughly CIA and NSA have penetrated the Russian state. The issue isn't just when the local *rezidentura* starts nosing around, because maybe you can control that. This thing really gets off the rails when it gets reported up through channels and we're listening in. Or an agent tells their Agency handler about an exfiltration from Minsk and an American was involved. That will get attention at headquarters."

Connor nodded, and I could see his mind already working the problem. That was a good sign. He wasn't panicking, wasn't looking for me to solve it for him. I debated telling him that all Fedorov showed me was a paper of dubious origin as his proof of passage. Ultimately, I decided it was something I'd want to know.

"I suppose this is something I should've pressed harder on in the park," I said. Maybe accepting some responsibility would ease him into it. "What kind of proof did Fedorov give you? How'd he convince you that he could back up his claims?"

"Before I pitched him to my chief, I had him show me some docs. Mostly tech specs. Why?"

"He showed me a piece of paper in Minsk. Under any other circumstances, it wouldn't have been enough for me. He said the material in his possession was the only currency he had to buy passage with, wouldn't show anything else until he was safe."

"I saw enough to convince me he was on the level, plus he could speak in detail about Molniya."

"Okay," I said.

Connor nodded softly. "All we do is collect pennies for the ferryman."

Jesus, that was grim. Even for me.

Connor left, saying he needed to check in with some assets in Minsk to assess the fallout of our little op.

I gathered my things from the hotel, checked out, and went to the airport with Fedorov. Before I left the hotel, I wiped down the Volkswagen and left it in a public parking lot in town at a spot Connor and I agreed on earlier.

Well, at least I knew that I could still execute an improperly planned, hasty exfiltration out of a hostile country.

Still got it.

Fedorov, for the time being, was safe. The question of his value to Jennie's investigation remained open.

There was also the matter that he'd killed a man during our escape. And, to my eyes, it seemed pretty easy for him.

Fedorov and I didn't speak much.

Once I collapsed into my seat, all I could think about was the light going out of Maksim's eyes and the sight of his blood slowly expanding from his body.

My back pressed into the seat as the airplane climbed into the darkening sky. There was a thought I hadn't been able to banish. Something that just didn't add up for me. Maksim said they believed the Americans would send someone to collect Fedorov, and Maksim followed him to prove he was a spy, believing he was fleeing to meet his handler. That was something an American law enforcement officer might do, someone whose job relied on verifiable proof. None of that applied to a Russian intelligence officer. And as I focused my mind on those last minutes on the platform, something else struck me. The surprise on Maksim's face when he saw me. It wasn't just that he didn't expect to see me *there*, he didn't expect to see me able to *be* there. Like, why was I out of jail?

Unable to sleep, I drank.

Denis met us at the airport.

He had a couple coffees in his hand, which couldn't be a good sign.

He pushed one of them into my hand as soon as I saw him.

"It's Jennie. She's been arrested."

11

Once we got to the hotel Denis arranged, we called Thomas Coogan, the civil rights attorney that worked with the Foundation on occasion. Coogan represented me when the FBI had gotten a little aggressive and before Danzig and I sorted it out. Coogan was a good man and a good attorney, and I was grateful he was handling her case.

It was evening in Los Angeles and late as all hell in Brussels.

"They're charging her with contempt of court," Coogan said in his gravel-laden baritone.

"How is that possible? She hasn't even been to court," I said.

"I'm not sure you've got the full picture, Matt. The Justice Department accused her of receiving leaked classified information and demanded that she turn over her files and sources three months ago. She was given two weeks to comply at the time. When she didn't, they started fining her. Eight hundred and fifty-four dollars per day."

"We paid the fees on her behalf," Denis added.

"Jennie didn't tell me any of this when I agreed to meet Fedorov," I said. "Just that the FBI was harassing her and she was worried about surveillance." As I replayed that first meeting with Jennie back in my head, I thought she was being paranoid at the time. As soon as possible, I needed to warn Connor. The Agency's counterintelligence apparatus must have gotten engaged somehow, perhaps notified the FBI.

Something about that still didn't click. Fedorov was a rejected recruitment target who didn't know he was talking to a CIA officer. Could any of that technically constitute secrets? Of course, I was forty plus hours without sleep, and three of those were pounding airplane whiskey. So, perhaps I wasn't connecting all of the dots I should've been.

"Gentlemen, this is all of the information I have right now. Rest assured, I'm on it, and I will be filing a motion for release first thing tomorrow. It won't go anywhere, mind you, just an opening shot. Meanwhile, we need to prove that Jennie hasn't received classified information."

"I can help with that," I said. Denis and I traded a look. "I'll be on the next flight to LA."

Turned out the next flight wasn't for another day, so I got much needed sleep. And food.

I spent the day debriefing Fedorov with Denis and a few members of his team.

"The GRU recruited me in 2012. I'd been living intermittently between Switzerland and St. Petersburg since attending graduate school in Geneva in the 1990s," Fedorov said. "I am Russian by birth, but my mother's family was Swiss, and I maintained Swiss citizenship and identification under my mother's maiden name, Künzler. I think this is what appealed me to the GRU."

"Who recruited you?" I asked. Denis asked me to coach Fedorov through the opening stages so they could focus on making notes and framing the investigation.

"A GRU officer, Major Antonin Zolin. He asked me to help with an 'engineering project.' 'Unlawful and predatory sanctions by the West,' Major Zolin explained, had crippled the Russian economy. They needed patriotic citizens, such as myself, to help the motherland modernize its industry to better compete on the global stage. I believed Major Zolin, at the time. I didn't have a favorable view of the Americans at the time and believed him that the West was unfairly targeting the Russian government and its people. So, I agreed. Zolin would tell me which technologies they desired, and I used my position in a German-owned technology company with military contracts to acquire the things on Zolin's list. Initially, I thought I was helping them acquire components to build a new synthetic aperture radar. By 2014, I believed it was some type of electromagnetic defense system, a communication scrambler, or perhaps a counterdrone system. The Russians had just invaded the Crimean Peninsula, and electronic warfare was a significant part of that campaign."

"But you always knew that Zolin was GRU?" I asked.

"Not at first, actually. It was several months in before he acknowledged it. Once it was quite clear what I was doing and after I'd broken some laws on their behalf. By then, however, I suspected they were not having me steal defense technology for the sake of it."

"What do you mean?"

"By mid-2014, Major Zolin tasked me with acquiring the specifications for an acoustic anti-riot weapon the Swiss were developing for their defense forces. I failed in getting anything useful, and Zolin was quite angry. I looked back through what I had been seeking for him and had enough disparate pieces of information to conclude the GRU was building a weapon. I informed Zolin that I could more effectively target what they needed if I knew what they were trying to build. Perhaps I could even help improve the design, reminding the major that he was an electrical engineer by trade. I was summoned to Moscow and thought I'd gone too far. It was there, at GRU headquarters, that Major Zolin introduced me to Colonel Aleksandr Orlov, who read me into Projekt Molniya.

"I was greatly relieved when he shared electronic copies of a score of documents he'd hoarded over the years. Those included documents he'd acquired from technology and electronics companies in Germany, France, Lithuania, Italy, and the UK. He even said that he'd been to the United States on multiple occasions."

Denis asked how Fedorov contributed to the design if he lived in Zürich. Fedorov said that he traveled to Moscow several times a year and that he'd review concepts. He'd provide his input, using what he'd learned interacting with the various Western companies to inform his suggestions.

Fedorov repeated what he'd told me at Victory Park, that there were at least three versions of the weapon. The one used in Havana was the first and largest, taking up most of a van. The version deployed to Vienna in 2021 could be worn as a backpack and was aimed like a rifle. Though, Fedorov added, it was unstable and still prone to overheating and melting down. They continued working on the design, and he believed the one used at the NATO summit in Vilnius was much improved. This variation in weapon designs, and other factors, Fedorov explained, was what accounted for the variety of symptoms across geographic locations.

During a break, I stepped out to make a phone call to an old friend in the Belgian State Security Service. I wanted to let him know that Fedorov was here and likely now a GRU assassination target. Luc first chastised me for not being in town long enough to buy him a pint, but said he would pass the word on to his counterparts in the federal police.

There was little else I could offer to the Foundation's effort with Fedorov. I'd gotten him here and given my assessment to Denis that he seemed credible enough to consider. Fedorov thanked me for getting him out.

Did I owe Fedorov my life?

Maybe. I'd beaten Maksim in the fight. Though in killing him, Fedorov likely guaranteed our escape.

"Thank you, Matt. I know you risked a lot for this," Denis said. I'd told him over dinner what I'd done to get Fedorov out. There were lingering concerns about this being a Russian snare, and I wanted his objective read.

"You need to keep Fedorov's association with you a secret, as much for his security as your own," I said. "If the SVR put this stuff together, it could lead them here. I've got a friend in Belgian intelligence that I'm going to try to connect you with."

"Thank you, Matt."

I also asked that he not tell Jennie any of this, for those reasons. He said that he wouldn't.

The next morning, I flew home.

I hit Los Angeles at four the following afternoon.

Though the FBI has holding facilities at its field office in Westwood, they booked her at LA County women's facility at Lynwood. Coogan met me at LAX, and we drove to the jail. Visiting hours ended at four. Coogan made special accommodations with the sheriff's department to get us in after hours, saying that I was a consultant for her case and that we needed to see her tonight. We processed through security, and they led us to a now empty visitation room. I thought I was prepared for seeing one of my oldest friends, someone that I'd been involved with, in a blue jumpsuit. I was not. It hit me harder than I thought possible.

It wasn't just the image of seeing someone I loved in a jail suit, it was the knowledge of how she got here.

A guard escorted her to the table, admonished us again that there was no physical contact and we could not hand her anything.

"Are you okay, Jen?" I asked when she sat.

"No one is messing with me yet," she said. "They've got me in gen pop. Mostly, they leave you alone. When they found out I was a reporter, a few ladies wanted me to write stories on them. Tell their side. You're never going to believe this...turns out, everyone in here is completely innocent. The word is getting around that I'm in here because I told the government to go fuck themselves, and that bought me a little credit. When did you get home?"

"Like an hour ago. We came straight here. I met with Charlie Auer," I said, sticking with Bishop's alias. "And I met Fedorov." Images came back—the interrogation room, the train platform, four blossoming holes in Maksim's chest.

"Matt?"

"Sorry. Fedorov...he's been stealing...or illegally purchasing...Western defense technology for a Russian military intelligence unit. However you want to phrase it. We think he's been doing both. He's been at it about twelve years. A very long story short and definitely not to be repeated here, but I got him to Brussels. He's with Denis, being debriefed now. Fedorov is a tricky character. He's not providing the best information, the real concrete proof, until he's got asylum somewhere. But he says he's got all of the project files. No way to believe him until we see it, or don't."

"Even what you've seen so far, that's proof, right? I mean, that's it. That clearly shows the Russians did this."

"Well, it means they had the capability." I turned to face Coogan. "What we're still missing is proof that the Russians used those capabilities on American citizens."

"Knowing the Russians developed a weapon doesn't really help Jennie's story," Coogan said.

"I agree. Too much room for official denial," I said.

"Thomas, what are you doing to get me the hell out of here?"

Coogan cleared his throat. He was tall, with a crane-like gait and the afterimage of a once-athletic frame. His shock-white hair and clean-hewn face reminded me of James Coburn. His voice was equally resonant with an almost jovial cynicism.

"I've filed a motion with the court to have you released and have advised the federal prosecutor that this constitutes a First Amendment violation. I've also reached out to contacts in the media. Journalists across the country are up in arms over it. We can expect significant, national coverage."

Jennie, as usual, cut right to it. "How the hell long do I need to be in here? Why am I not out right now?"

Coogan refrained from rolling his eyes and instead patiently explained the government's rationale. "They're alleging that a government employee broke the law and knowingly provided you with classified information. Furthermore, they state that there is no constitutional protection for sources."

"That's some articulate bullshit," Jennie deadpanned. "I'm almost impressed."

"The government's attorney told me, 'You need to advise your client that the First Amendment only goes as far as her right to publish story, but she can't violate the law to do it.'" Coogan held his hands up, as if to compel Jennie's invective back by force. He failed, and we waited for the tide of profanity to wash back out to sea. "I only wanted you to know what we're up against."

When we'd met at that bar in DC in what felt like a year ago, Danzig warned me this would happen. I didn't take her seriously.

"Thomas, a reporter going to jail to protect her sources is almost a cliché by now. They've made their point, now we need to make ours." Jennie held up an open palm and closed a finger with each point. "I want the ACLU involved. I want you to contact every news network, media organization, paper, and basement blogger you can find. I want them lighting fires. I want them committing ideological arson all over the goddamn internet by morning. And. I. Want. To. Be. Out. Of. Jail."

Coogan spoke softly. "I understand."

Jennie smoldered for a bit, keeping her own counsel. Coogan looked at me, and I only shrugged. I didn't know what to say any more than he did.

After some long moments of this, Jennie shifted her gaze to me. Her eyes bright and hot, resolute. I felt like she was assessing me anew. "You have to do this, Matt. Until I get out."

"Do what?"

"My investigation. Their plan is to wait me out. Keep me here until I eventually give up my sources. The government can wait forever, they know I can't. They also assume that as long as I'm in here, nothing is happening out there." Jennie shot a hand toward a window, drawing a stern rebuke from a guard to "watch it." "What they aren't counting on is you."

Well, *someone* was, since Danzig knew I was involved from the drop. Instead, I said, "Of course, I'll help however I can. Do you need me to talk to someone?"

"No. Thomas has my research. Because I voluntarily turned myself in, they didn't need to bash down my door with an arrest warrant. I took everything I had from my office at home and signed it over to him."

"We've got it all at the firm, locked in a safe," Coogan said. "After she was processed, the FBI executed a search warrant of her home. We assume looking for the source's identity. Now that the evidence is in my possession, they can't access it because of attorney-client privilege. Certainly, they'll argue that over national security grounds. I'm confident we can beat that."

"Okay. That doesn't answer my question, though. Thomas has all your raw material, but what do you want me to do with it?"

"Fedorov is one part. He proves that the Russians made a weapon and used it against us. The second part is that two presidential administrations knew about it and covered it up."

"And the third part is why," I said. This was a thought I'd had for some time as well.

"Yes," Jennie said, pointing at me for effect. "Most of my reporting so far has been on the Russian side of this, which ultimately led me to Fedorov. I've interviewed about fifty people for this story, most of them in our government or somehow connected to Havana Syndrome. Their names, contact information, and what we talked about are all in the files I have to Thomas. I think some of them know more than they're revealing."

"If they wouldn't tell you, what makes you think they'll open up to me?"

"Because you have a way of getting information out of people that I don't," Jennie said.

Her words bore an implication that I was immediately uncomfortable with.

I turned, again, to Coogan. "Thomas, can you give us a minute? I'll meet you outside."

"Why can't I just—"

"Because I'm going to say some things that probably shouldn't be said in front of a lawyer."

A dour, knowing smile crawled onto Coogan's mouth. He asked Jennie if she needed anything, and when she said no, he stood to leave.

"I'll be outside, Matt. Talk soon, Jen," Coogan said, and he left.

"Jen, we need to be absolutely clear on what I can and cannot do for you."

"Matt, you're reading between the lines and coming up with the wrong thing."

"Am I?"

"You're a damn good investigator, that's what I meant. You know when someone is lying to you."

Not at the moment.

Jennie continued. "Now, there's a handful of names that I thought were worth focusing on. People I was about to go see when Thomas convinced me to surrender. They're all marked with a note to follow up on my spreadsheet. Audrey Farre is the chief of staff for the Senate Intel Committee. Start with her."

"Why didn't you tell me about your court order when you hired me?" I asked.

By way of answering, Jennie only looked to the side.

"What would you have done with that information? I have a lawyer, and he's on it."

For starters, because it got me jammed up with the FBI again, but I let that slide for now. "Far as I can tell, Auer covered his tracks in talking to you. He didn't reveal anything classified and just facilitated an introduction with a source."

"So?"

"So, I'm having a hard time believing that he's the reason the FBI is up your ass. There aren't dots to connect there. And it's not clear how the Bureau could possibly have found out about it in the time we've had."

"What are you getting at?"

"I met with Katrina Danzig before I went to Europe. She pressed me on this case, told me to talk you into giving up. She knew about this thing right away."

"So, I was right about them spying on me."

"It's a reasonable guess. The point is, they believe there is a security breach, and it's not Charlie Auer."

"Or they're trying to convince you there is," Jennie countered quickly.

"Auer told me everything that happened. I don't see how anything official tripped there that would've gotten the FBI involved. Now, Auer is in trouble for some other stuff related to Fedorov, but that's not your problem. I don't see how the FBI decides there is a leak from just your reporting. It doesn't add up. That tells me Auer isn't the person the Bureau is looking for. Who is that, Jen?"

"No," she said, with the unwavering authority of gravity.

"Does that mean you have someone else you're talking to?"

Jennie didn't answer.

"Is that person's information in the documents Coogan has, or do you have it stashed somewhere else? Like, maybe a safe deposit box or an encrypted drive somewhere?"

"Now I understand why you didn't want Coogan here. Everything you need is in his office. Talk to Audrey Farre," Jennie said.

Danzig's words sounded in my mind like she was right here the room. *Burkhardt is going to be accused of cultivating assets within the United States government for the purpose of accessing classified information. Where do you think they'll say she learned how to do that?*

Those same words hovered right behind my teeth.

And stayed right where I put them.

Jennie didn't need the extra burden of my guilt, so maybe that was why I didn't say anything.

I left the jail complex and found Coogan waiting outside. Jennie had another source, I now believed. The one who likely set all of this in motion. I understood why she didn't want to tell me. As long as I didn't know, she reasoned, the FBI couldn't compel me to disclose it. But in not telling me, she limited the number of sources I could draw on with material knowledge of the case.

Jennie released stories on Havana Syndrome about every six months. Recently, she'd also been doing podcast tours, which I'd listened to on my various flights. Her latest piece was a critical look of the Intelligence Community's study and how it contradicted the volumes of previous medical and technical analysis—both from independent and government-commissioned sources. Jennie quoted an "anonymous source with material knowledge" who confirmed several senior officials believed a hostile government was responsible for Havana Syndrome.

It hit me, that could be the line that got her in trouble.

Jennie's strategy, I believed, was to use Fedorov's information to prove that the weapon existed. The government would deny it, but the public would assume they'd do that anyway. That could shift the focus away from her official source and put the government back on the defensive. I'd agreed with Coogan when he said Fedorov's information didn't help Jennie's story much, or her case. Now I was rethinking that. This would undoubtedly fuel some uncomfortable conversations in Congress, and with the public.

The problem was that, so far, all Fedorov could do was provide tenuous evidence that the Russians were developing such a thing. All we had to go on was his word that they'd really done it.

And the chain of events linking Fedorov with Connor Bishop wouldn't stay quiet forever.

I walked down the concrete path to where Coogan waited outside, skimming his phone, furiously triaging the messages he'd gotten while inside. As if reading the thoughts cascading through my head, he said, "What was that Jennie said about intent and cover-up? How is this any different than, say, Watergate?"

"Because most of the time when the government tries to make something go away, it's because they broke the law and don't want anyone to find out. Jennie's argument is this is a deception operation. They want people to believe it's something other than what it is. We figure *that* out, and we've got something to trade for her freedom."

"You're not suggesting that we give them evidence in exchange for her release? Kill the story? That's exactly what they want us to do. She'll never go for that."

"I'm not. It's more of a shell game. We give them something that they want, which they think answers the question of a leak. Meanwhile, the Foundation does a full court press with Grigori Fedorov and his ties to the GRU."

Coogan chuckled next to me.

"What's so funny?" I said.

He looked back at the jail complex behind us. "You and I first met in a place like this," he said. "Now I understand why the FBI put you there."

12

We agreed to meet at his office downtown first thing in the morning.

I went home and, using a commercial signal detector, swept my home for listening devices. Finding none, I poured a double of Lagavulin, put Soundgarden on my stereo, and framed my plan for the next day.

Sleep was ugly and troubled.

Still on European time, I was up before the sun, so I decided to use the gifted hours. I loaded my open water kayak into my Land Rover and got some reps on the water. When I'd first started hanging out at Ray's, I'd done it with the intention of picking up surfing. Ray told me the ocean could sense my energy and said I was too angry to surf. I mostly capitulated and opted for the kayak. I felt a little guilty doing something as trivial as exercise while Jennie sat in a jail cell. I wasn't worried about her safety, necessarily, though it was still county jail. It was more that this case was evolving quickly, and it didn't matter how much information I was able to gather if she wasn't around to write the story. True to form, Jennie was actually working from jail—to the extent that circumstances allowed. She'd use her phone allowance to leave me messages about things to follow up on, questions to ask, or whatever thought she wanted me to capture. It was surreal, even for me, which was saying something.

The sun lit the water as I paddled out into the surf, making sure to stay clear of the Dawn Patrol veterans for whom these waves truly belonged. After an hour of hard paddling, I beached my kayak and trudged up to Cosmic Ray's. They opened for the Dawn Patrollers, selling to-go coffee and breakfast burritos.

"'Sup, Matt," Vin, the guy at the window, said. "Where you been?"

"Case," I said. He nodded, as though we both knew the secrets of the world.

I posted at a weathered picnic table in the sand and ate and drank in silence. Once I'd finished my breakfast, I loaded the kayak onto my Defender and drove home to clean up and join the slow moving knife fight that was LA's morning commute.

Coogan's law firm, Case Ritter and Company, was a global practice that specialized in international conflict resolution. Coogan ran a carveout within the firm handling civil rights. While this had him, on occasion, directly opposing four successive presidential administrations over the detainment of enemy combatants and suspected terrorists without due process, Coogan had just as often mediated on behalf of the United States when Americans were unlawfully detained in other countries. And there were sometimes conflicts when an official representative of the government would not be welcome, and Coogan would act as a proxy. The Orpheus Foundation retained Case Ritter because of how often they'd come into the crosshairs of powerful organizations.

Case Ritter's offices were located in the US Bank Building in LA's downtown core.

I arrived shortly after nine. Coogan had a junior attorney waiting to meet me and who promptly showed me into a spare office they'd set aside.

"Here you go, Mr. Gage," the kid said. It was an interior office with a desk, computer, and phone. I signed about a dozen nondisclosure agreements, none of which I'd actually read. Then he gave me a guest login and password so I could access the materials stored on their secure server. Copies of the physical documents were placed on the desktop or in boxes stacked on the floor.

Staring at the mounds of research Jennie compiled, I couldn't help but wonder if Sisyphus hadn't had an easier go.

Jennie maintained a detailed spreadsheet of whom she'd spoken with, organized by date and subject matter. It also included relevant background details, such as occupation and their physical location. From this, I compiled a smaller list of the people I wanted to interview. Based on her tone earlier, I assumed that the person who was the source of her troubles with the Bureau was not on this list.

I'd also gotten several updates from Denis on their progress with Fedorov. They were flying in a consulting physicist from Cambridge to help piece together the actual mechanics of the system he described.

Last night at the jail, Jennie said there was a Senate Intel Committee staffer that I should talk to. I'd found a phrase connected with her name, "CINDER SPIRE." It sounded like the kind of nonsensical phrase that the IC used as a cryptonym. She'd also made sure to write it in app caps, which was how we used them. A cryptonym could be the code for an intelligence source, a new tool, or an operation. It was just a way of obfuscating something's real meaning so it could be discussed openly.

The problem would be in the meaning.

Coogan appeared at the door, and I looked up, bleary-eyed, to realize that I'd been at this for hours.

"I've had lunch brought in. Care to take a break?"

Grateful for the distraction, I followed him to a small conference room. I assembled a plate, grabbed a coffee and a water, and joined him at the table.

"How goes it?"

"Jennie is thorough, I'll give her that." A smile formed as I stabbed some food with my fork. "I used to copy her notes all the time in school."

"What have you found so far? Any ideas on next steps?"

"She mentioned a handful of sources she thought might be holding out. I'll start there. Probably, that means flying to DC and talking to them in person." I took a sip of coffee and considered my next words carefully, mindful of whom I was speaking to. "Tom, I didn't want to say this in front of Jennie, because right now what she needs is hope, but I think she's in real trouble. I mentioned that I'd met with an FBI friend. She was convinced Jen had received classified, and she wouldn't bullshit me. I think it's possible a source revealed secrets, possibly without telling her." The words CINDER SPIRE sparked in my mind, and I couldn't unsee it. If Jennie had gotten access to code word material and used that in her reporting, there was nothing I could do. No amount of truth stacked up on the other side would matter.

"My opinion, and granted I'm an outsider to all this, is that I think the government tends to over-classify. They want to control the flow of information to the public, so they declare everything a secret."

"I don't think you're wrong, necessarily. But you'll also have a hard time proving in court that disclosure won't result in grievous damage to the United States, or whatever the official phrase is. Still, unless I see what that is, I can't assess how much trouble she might be in. She won't tell me what the thing is that the Bureau is keyed in on."

"Maybe she's protecting you," Coogan offered.

"That helps precisely no one."

"And your Bureau friends aren't a help there?"

"They're not going to tell me. Though, there's always the possibility they're bluffing too."

"What do you think about Fedorov? Seems like if his information is true, that undermines whatever argument the government has," Coogan said.

"Fedorov is guilty of espionage in about five countries that I know about, including ours. He's going to someone's jail over this if he can't find someone willing to trade."

I didn't bring this up because it wasn't relevant to my conversation with Coogan, but it was to the case. Fedorov wasn't thinking broadly, yet, because he was worried about his life. Now that he was out of immediate danger, he was going to. That guy was a sure flight risk, for one. He was also a mercenary. Whoever was going to keep him safe and out of jail was where he was going to land.

"On the one hand, we've got the very real possibility that Jennie did break the law. On the other, one of her significant sources *did* without question."

"I don't see a legal way out of this." I didn't even tell him about the cryptonym I'd found in Jennie's notes. That, I got nervous even looking at.

"That's usually my department, but I understand your point," Coogan said softly.

"Do I think that the Justice Department went too far in trying to keep this quiet? Yes. Do I believe the Intelligence Community is pushing a story to deflect from the actual cause? Also yes. But I worry that I can't deliver the truth without breaking the law. Or, at the very least, exposing the kinds of national secrets I swore to protect. That has consequences for me, and not just moral ones."

"I agree with you, that's a lot to consider. Let me offer this." Coogan pushed the remnants of his own meal aside and sipped water. He took a moment of quiet reflection before continuing. "About fourteen years ago, I represented Khaled Alzahrani. He was a senior al-Qaeda commander that some of your coworkers captured in Afghanistan, December 2001. They got him at a small training camp where he was prepping a specialized unit for another strike on America. They captured him with troves of intelligence, his signoff on operations plans, everything. I know, because I saw it as evidence. Heavily redacted, of course, but nonetheless. Unquestionably guilty and absolutely unrepentant. The reason I represented him was that his interrogators waterboarded him, among other things. He was tortured repeatedly for several years. The government can't put him in court because it will force them to acknowledge to the public that they authorized torture. Everyone knows it happened, but no president has ever actually admitted it. It's just like an open secret they hope dies with time. So, I'm representing this man that I know is a terrorist, a true believer, and if he was released tomorrow, the first thing he would do is kill Americans. The reason I took his case is because during his confinement, we listened to our greater devils instead of our better angels. In trying to defend this beautiful and flawed country, we fell short of the thing we were trying to protect. If brave people don't speak up when that happens, who will?"

"What happened to Alzahrani? He never saw trial, right?"

"No," Coogan said, shaking his head. "No, he didn't. He took his own life in 2014. The Department of Defense wouldn't even acknowledge the twenty-five or so suspected suicide attempts at Guantanamo. Called it 'manipulative self-injurious behaviors.'" Coogan pushed himself back from the table and stood. "Matt, you're the only one who can decide what's right, for you. I won't presume that you came here asking my advice. Follow your conscience. I'll support you one way or the other. The reason I brought up the Alzahrani case was that my job was to defend someone unrepentantly guilty, because that's our system and I had to hold the government accountable for their actions. I'm not comparing him to Jennie by any means, it's more about the point of sometimes we listen to our devils. Just be cautious about listening to yours."

I flew to DC the next day.

There were conversations that I needed to have, and those were best done in person.

My first target was Audrey Farre, Jennie's contact on the Senate Intel Committee. From Jennie's backgrounding, I'd learned Farre had been an Air Force intelligence officer before applying to the CIA. She served another ten years as an analyst and eventual member of the Presidential Briefing Team. After leaving the Agency, she joined Senator Deacon Howell's staff. Senator Howell, a long-serving legislator from New Hampshire, was appointed to the Senate Select Committee on Intelligence in 2018. SSCI memberships are term limited, and when Senator Howell moved on, Farre was hired as the deputy director of staff overseeing all SSCI staff activities.

I'd taken a red-eye from LA so that I didn't burn an entire day traveling, checked into my hotel room near Reagan National, and called Farre in the morning. The call went straight to voicemail, so I followed up with a text identifying myself and that I was representing Jennie. Farre called me an hour later.

"I only have a few minutes," she said.

"Would it be possible to meet in person? I wanted to ask you a few questions about Jennie's reporting." I kept it generic, knowing they'd only spoken on this subject and not wanting to put her in a difficult position since she was likely taking the call from her office in the Hart Building.

"I don't think so. Look, I told Jennie what I knew, we had a nice chat, and that's about as far as it went. Sorry, I don't think I've got anything else to add."

"Ms. Farre, Jennie is in jail. The FBI fabricated a charge and locked her up to shut the story down. They wouldn't do that unless something about this scared them."

"If the FBI is involved, then I definitely don't want to be."

"What do you know about CINDER SPIRE?"

Farre hung up.

I placed a dozen other calls throughout the course of the day. None of them were returned. All I'd said was that I was a colleague of Jennie's and was following up on their conversation.

The FBI wouldn't have access to Jennie's research, so they shouldn't know who her potential sources were. Not for the first time I wondered if Jennie's surveillance paranoia was well grounded.

While I was being serially hung up on, I continued feeding Jennie's notes, research, and even finished articles into a tool I had called Echo-Trace. It was an investigative platform that aggregated open source intelligence and used artificial intelligence to pattern match, conduct link analysis, and summarize massive arrays of raw data. It was a powerful research tool and only available to members of law enforcement or licensed private investigators. I'd hoped this could give me a few new leads or parse the data in a way I hadn't.

That afternoon, I took a break from cold calls and research to stretch my legs in the sweltering DC summer heat. I regretted this decision immediately. The region was pinned beneath a historic heatwave with mercury pushing a hundred.

Ten minutes into my ill-conceived stroll, Denis called me on Signal.

"How is Jen?"

His question reminded me that I hadn't updated him since getting back to the States.

"Oh, man, I'm sorry I hadn't gotten back to you. She's holding up okay. All of her files are at Case Ritter's office, so that information is secure for now. The Justice Department has no problem bullying a journalist, but they're going to be a little circumspect about picking a fight with a company full of lawyers."

Denis laughed at that. "Listen, I wanted to talk to you about Fedorov," he said, once I'd finished updating him on what I was doing.

"Why? What's going on?"

"Remember that physicist I said I was bringing in?"

"Yeah, guy from Cambridge, right?"

"Yes, exactly. Among other things, he consults with the UK Ministry of Defence. Spectrum warfare, he calls it."

"Okay," I said, drawing the word out like it was old gum.

"He said Fedorov is lying."

"Lying? About what?" My dialogue with Fedorov by the lake in Victory Park played back through my mind as Denis continued with his consultant's assessment. As much as I'd focused on what Fedorov said at the time, I'd evaluated how he said it. The human body, in conversation, offers a roadmap of insight into the speaker, if you know how to read it. If I hadn't believed he was credible, I wouldn't have snuck him out of Belarus.

"Simon can't attest to the quality of the intelligence Fedorov claims to have. I'll defer to you on that. What he can say, quite authoritatively, is that there is no possible way that Fedorov designed a microwave weapon."

It wasn't until Denis said my name several times that I'd realized I'd gone silent.

13

Denis wasn't sure what to do about Fedorov, but he was certainly concerned. He worried now, as I had initially, that Fedorov might be a dangle by Russian intelligence. Intelligences services used tactics like this all the time—often just to see if they could get someone to bite. Given Lithuania's NATO membership and proximity to Ukraine, it seemed an obvious target for them. The Russians would have no way of knowing at the outset that Fedorov would end up interviewed by the Orpheus Foundation. However, it would be a delicious target of opportunity for them once the Americans declined to speak with him. Plausible, yes, though I didn't want to believe it. Denis said he wasn't going to press Fedorov because he didn't want to scare him off, and his Cambridge physicist friend only shared those conclusions with him.

Another possibility was that Fedorov was simply a liar who'd overplayed his hand. Worried that he'd be swept up in the Kremlin's anticorruption fever, Fedorov took what he knew to the highest bidder. Not a problem, necessarily, if what he knew was tangible and valuable.

Denis's consultant suggested otherwise.

I asked Denis to keep humoring Fedorov for now, and I'd get back with him as soon as I could.

So now, on top of the fact that how Fedorov acquired the information was questionable, the data itself was too.

EchoTrace returned an interesting hit.

I'd asked the program to analyze all of Jennie's data and any public domain information and to correlate any instances that used keywords associated with deception. The idea was to see what else might be reported or discussed about "cover-ups." I scanned the summaries EchoTrace returned, and one name surfaced several times—Harold Floss. Floss was an electrical engineer and physicist who'd spent most of his career with the Naval Research Laboratory here in DC. About three years ago, he'd left abruptly and now worked with a small defense contractor in the area. What made Floss interesting to me was that his name kept popping up in online forums and a few fringe chat groups, mostly about government conspiracies.

Floss didn't cover his tracks as well as he thought he had, and EchoTrace connected his handle on some of those forums with another website, eventually linking it back to him.

Floss was fifty-four, unmarried, and lived in Springfield, Virginia, one of the metro area's outlying suburbs.

He could easily be discounted as another crackpot yelling on the internet, except that when he believed he was anonymously posting on a Havana Syndrome thread, he cited his expertise as an electromagnetic weapons expert. I backed this up with research papers he'd published in some technical journals while at NRL. Floss was also fairly open about his résumé on various professional networking sites.

Floss's argument was that the Russians didn't have the technical know-how to pull this off, but the US did. Someone asked him if he thought we'd seriously attack our own people, and he said, "No, not intentionally." Floss repeated the refrain multiple times and in several different forums that this wasn't the Russians but the work of the US. That he'd designed what he'd called, "something similar for the Navy."

I'd known from my conversations with Colonel Rick Hicks that the US had been working on sonic weapons going back to the Cold War, but something about Floss's continued drumbeat struck me.

So, I called him.

"Mr. Floss, my name is Matt Gage. I am a private investigator."

"How did you get this number?" he asked immediately.

I paused. This was going to be a long conversation.

"Mr. Floss, I'm investigating Havana Syndrome, and I've come across some of your work on the issue. I was wondering if we could meet."

"You're not a cop, are you? Because you have to tell me if you are."

I loved it when someone's attempt at verbal judo was basically rehashed lines from *Law and Order*.

"I am not a cop, and I'm not working with any. In fact, they're trying to shut me up."

Floss chewed on that. My plan for this conversation was to draw him in, show that I was one of the ones "they" wanted to silence.

"Sorry," he said. "I don't know anything about Havana Syndrome."

I named the aliases he posted under and on what website. "I can show you screen grabs of your posts, if you like. Or we can just skip to the part where you admit all that and tell me what you know."

"You're a private detective, who are you working for?"

"I'm working for a reporter."

"Who?"

"No. You've haven't earned that information. You said on a forum that Havana Syndrome wasn't caused by the Russians. That they didn't have the capability, only we did. What did you mean by that?"

"I'm not talking over the phone," he said.

"You know where the Jones Point Lighthouse is in Old Town?"

"Yes," he said.

"Okay. I'll be there at four."

I hung up and kept working until it was time to leave. Jones Point was a public park on the southern tip of Alexandria beneath the Woodrow Wilson Bridge that connected Virginia with Maryland suburbs across the muddy flow of the Potomac. I'd chosen the location because of the dense trees on two sides, and the bridge overhead would make eavesdropping difficult. Not that anyone would be, but Floss was the type who assumed someone was always listening in.

Honestly, I was expecting an archetype and might have missed him because of it. What I was looking for was an overweight man with furtive eyes, a closeted loudmouth that just needed you to challenge him with a few facts to get him going. What I found was an unassuming, middle-aged man of average height and build, mustache, and round glasses. He dressed in jeans and a Virginia Tech polo.

"Mr. Gage?"

"Mr. Floss," I said, offering my hand. He shook it.

"You think the Russians aren't responsible for this? Your posts are pretty specific," I said. I didn't know enough about his business to know whether he'd crossed a line or not, but Floss seemed to be straying dangerously close to the edge of "shit you shouldn't post on conspiracy forums."

"Navy's been worried for years about drones. Destroyer goes into a port in a foreign country and some local tries to fly over. Happens all the time, they just don't talk about it. They're worried about sabotage or surveillance. That kind of thing. Like, what if someone drops a listening device onto a ship? One of the projects I worked on—"

I held up both hands.

"Hold up. I don't want to know what you did," I said.

Floss's expression soured. "Relax. It's over. Anyway, we use spectrum analyzers to detect outbound transmission. It's one of the ways to search for surveillance devices. My project was to couple that with a microwave beam that once we detected it, we should shoot it. Called it the 'bug zapper.'" He laughed. "Anyway, we had some interest from some folks up the road." Floss put a heavy emphasis on the latter, as though I'd know what he meant. Of course, NRL was at the southern end of the DC metro area, so "up the road" could mean half a dozen intelligence agencies within ten miles.

"You mean CIA?" I said, just to name one.

"Yes," he hissed, like I'd shouted it. Then he looked around, as though black helicopters and men wearing CIA jackets would materialize from the trees. I'd need sandbags on my eyelids to keep them from rolling.

"They were interested because they wanted to use it to counter enemy surveillance?"

"That's right. They were worried about people eavesdropping at our embassies. You know that there's so many bugs in the Moscow embassy, it's like a goddamn roach motel."

"What'd they do with it?"

Floss shrugged. "Never told me. We sent a concept over and never heard from them again."

"You posted that 'we did this to ourselves.' What did you mean by that?"

"Exactly that. They took the design we made, built it themselves, and then used it more or less the way we'd intended," Floss said.

"Which was?"

"To scan for bugs and then zap them."

"What would happen if a person were struck with such a device?"

"All the stuff you hear those Havana Syndrome victims talk about. We brought in some human physiology and neuroscience experts to talk about it during the design phase. We were worried someone on a ship or on shore might be hit. Asked all those 'what would happen' kind of questions. Just like you say. They said you'd have vertigo, fatigue, trouble concentrating, ringing in your ears like really bad tinnitus, but it'd never go away."

"And once you saw the reports in the media about Havana Syndrome happening at our embassies, you thought the Agency, or someone, possibly applied your design?"

"That's right," he said. I noted a grave pride in the way he said it.

"How do you explain the instances where it happened in someone's home? Or out in the local area?"

Or a Havana hotel?

Floss's eyes narrowed, and he hung a condescending look, as if to say, *Come on, man*. "Who do you think has all those addresses? Or the plates of the cars? I read the stories. I know. The Agency took the design, but they didn't do any of the homework, so they didn't know the effect it'd have on people. They just used it and didn't consider the consequences."

"I find it hard to believe that once people started reporting symptoms, they'd keep it up."

"They had their reports, man. Surely you've seen them. All those experts said nothing was wrong. Then they have a bogus story that it was broken air conditioning or something."

This was going nowhere.

Harold Floss was exactly what I'd suspected, a lonely person who found validation proving things to strangers online. I untangled myself from the situation as gracefully as I could, mindful of offending or denigrating him, and told Floss he'd been very informative.

When I got back to my computer, I set up EchoTrace to flag any further posting from his various aliases just to make sure he didn't start talking about me or the case.

I grabbed dinner in Old Town to let traffic die off.

While I nursed a beer, I thought through what I'd learned so far. Floss was, in technical parlance, off his rocker, but there was a nugget of useful information in the otherwise incoherent conspiracy blather. And it was supported, in a way, by that one bit of data I had from Jennie's notes. The code word. We'd never test a weapon on our own people. We might use a device for the purposes that Floss suggested and remain ignorant of the human cost. Until we weren't.

Something Thomas said about the nature of classification came to the fore and how the government tended to call everything a secret so they could control the flow of information. The same could also be true of their mistakes.

There might be something to that. The kind of thing you hid with a code word.

My phone started blowing up with texts from friends, old colleagues, and more than a couple former college classmates. Jennie's incarceration for not revealing her sources just made national news, and people were pinging me about it. As Thomas Coogan expected, journalists across the country picked that flag up and charged the hill with it. Even our College of Journalism issued a statement of standing in solidarity with her as she made a tremendous personal sacrifice to uphold the First Amendment and sacred duty of the profession to protect the people who risk their lives and livelihoods to turn the lights on.

Audrey Farre called as I was paying my check.

"I just read about Jennie Burkhardt," she said. "I know you told me it happened, it just seemed more real when I saw it in print."

"This is as real as it gets."

"If I spoke with you, what would you do with that?"

"My first goal is to get Jennie out of jail so she can continue her work. But Jennie's hypothesis is that the Intelligence Community knew the Russians attacked us and covered it up. I intend to prove whether or not that's true."

"You understand the position that puts me in? I'm ex-CIA."

The words *so what, so am I?* burned a spot on my tongue, but I held them in.

"Audrey, I'm a private detective, not a reporter. My client is. I'm just carrying on her investigation while she's being unlawfully detained. Whatever agreement on confidentiality that you and Jennie had applies here. All I'm interested in is the truth. If Jennie's hypothesis is correct, then I want accountability. One has to follow the other. This isn't some WikiLeaks bullshit. We're not kicking over rocks to see what's buried there."

"Okay, okay. I got it. There's a Barnes and Noble in Clarendon. Can you be there in an hour?"

I pulled up the map on my phone to examine just how dark the red lines were.

"I'll figure out a way."

"Second floor, science section in the upper left corner. I'll wait ten minutes, and then I'm gone."

Luckily for me, I'd taken every combat driving course the US government offers and one they won't admit exists. I made it with five minutes to spare.

The bookstore is in Arlington's Clarendon neighborhood, one of DC's innermost suburbs. The large, two-story bookstore was in a U-shaped outdoor shopping plaza, wrapped around a fountain and small playground. Once inside, I took an escalator up to the second floor and navigated to the science section.

It wouldn't be obvious to anyone else in the store, but I could pick out Audrey Farre immediately based on her positioning and body language. She hadn't forgotten her training, and that was nice to see. She sat in a large chair with her back to the rear corner, giving her full visibility of the second floor. There was a book open in her hands, which she pretended to skim, but I could see her staring over it, looking for me. The only acknowledgment I got was Farre holding my gaze for just a second before returning to her book. When I was four steps from the bookshelf, she stood and replaced the volume, pretending to scan for another one.

Farre was in her late thirties, blond, and dressed in work attire that had seen a full day at the office. I walked up to the bookcase and selected one off an adjacent row.

"We never met at HQS," she said, using the Agency shorthand for Headquarters Station, or Langley. "I had to brief about you in the PDB once. We redacted your name from the briefing, of course, but I had the source material. We had to tell POTUS about Managua." Audrey spoke in low tones and without looking at me. "Damon Fox is a festering asshole of a human, for whatever that may be worth."

Maybe Audrey was my kind of people after all.

"Can you tell me about CINDER SPIRE?" All I knew about the reference was that the phrase appeared in Jennie's notes next to Audrey's name. It didn't say what the association was, so I didn't know if it was something Jennie learned from her or something she wanted to ask Audrey about.

"I'm not talking about that. And you should stop asking."

"Understood."

"On the phone, you used the phrase 'kicking over rocks.' I'm going to give you one to kick over. You do with it what you will. I will not put it in context, and I won't answer follow-up questions."

"Fair enough."

"In June of 2021, POTUS and Putin met in a summit in Geneva. I think you would be very interested in that discussion. Particularly, the five-minute private exchange that wasn't recorded or scripted."

Audrey replaced the book she'd pretended to examine.

"Good luck," she said, and left.

I waited until she was gone, and then I departed as well. I went back to the car, grabbed my backpack, and then returned to the bookstore. I bought a coffee from the Starbucks inside and set up at a table. There's no such thing as a "secure hotspot," though at least I was accessing the internet through a VPN.

The 2021 Geneva Summit was intended to reset relations between the Russian Federation and new US administration. The official topics listed were arms control, cybersecurity, and the fate of the anti-corruption activist Alexei Navalny.

I knew the last reported cases were in 2021, several months before the summit. There was no mention of Havana Syndrome in any of the articles I skimmed. I used EchoTrace to return anything on Havana Syndrome and the summit. It could run down my query on the client side, even when my laptop was powered down.

Then I set up another search on the national security staffers listed as participants at the summit.

A meeting between the US and Russian heads of state was a big deal. It required months of coordination, both public and clandestine across multiple government agencies and the National Security Council staff. The details of that coordination would live on in the collective institutional memory, if I could find someone willing to talk.

I closed my computer and made fast steps for my car. Hopefully, by the time I got back to my hotel, EchoTrace will have produced a list of any publicly reported connection between Havana Syndrome and the summit and the analysis on where those NSS staffers were now.

No sooner was I in the car than my phone rang. The caller ID flashed a giant "UNKNOWN."

Knowing many of the people I'd been trying to reach were privacy inclined, I answered.

Before I even said hello, the other party said, "Why are you in my town, Matt, asking questions you shouldn't be asking?"

I knew that voice, and it was the last person on earth I wanted to hear from.

Damon Fox.

14

Damon Fox didn't cross my path for most of my Agency career, but I'd known him by reputation and steered clear. He wasn't dangerous because he'd been a subpar case officer, bumbling ever up the ladder. Fox was dangerous because he'd been an exceptional one. Now he plied those field-honed skills at Langley and Washington with the precision of a true maestro of the dark arts. Fox wormed his way into a role as a White House liaison, and that put him in a position to build relationships in the broader national security universe and earn favors on the Hill with House and Senate Intel Committee members.

By the time I'd finally met Fox, I was emerging from a black ops cocoon to assume my first station chief position in Nicaragua. Our formal introduction was Fox informing me I wouldn't be taking the job. He wanted one of his coterie in the role. He'd already stocked much of the Latin America pond with his own sycophants. Even though I had little traction at Langley, my mentor, Nate McKellar, had plenty, and he intervened on my behalf. The assignment stuck. Until it didn't.

I can still see those words, the epitaph of my Agency career, burned into my memory like the afterimage of staring at the sun.

. . .

FROM: DIR LATAM OPS
 TO: C/S MANAGUA
 SUBJ: C/S IMMEDIATE RETURN TO HQS
1. By order of Director, Latin America Ops, Chief of Station relieved of duty immediately and directed to return to HQS.
2. Cease any and all operational activity immediately. Direct staff to await further instruction from LATAM OPS.

"Surprised it took you this long to call, Damon. I've been in town for eight whole hours. I'd assumed you were watching my phone."

I *may* have threatened him with physical violence at one point.

"There's that signature Matt Gage wit that I've missed." A poorly manufactured laugh fell out the phone. "Matt, I'm going to send you an address. And I'll expect to meet you within the hour. Do yourself a favor and be there."

The Agency maintains some private residences in the DC metro area. These serve a variety of purposes, from transitory housing for relocated spies to clandestine meeting sites that CIA security personnel can fully control. There were no vehicles in the driveway when I arrived, though the lights were on. I'd never been in one of these places before, only known they existed. One of the missions we did in Nate's unit was smuggling a Chinese businessman out of Guangzhou after we learned the Ministry of State Security found out he was spying for us. Once his family was safe, they stayed in a place like this for a few weeks as they acclimated to the United States.

I parked on the street and walked in like I owned the place. It took the security officer hanging out in the living room absolutely by surprise. The house was a mid-century two-story with box store furniture.

"Relax, ace. I'm not armed."

"It's fine, Don."

There he was.

Damon Fox was five nine and now in his mid-fifties. He was built like a runner who skipped meals. Fox had brown hair, styled by committee and sporting a shock of gray at the temples. Polite observers would call it "dignified"; I'd argue it was the result of unrepented guilt.

Fox wasn't on the take, but he dressed like he was.

It takes a special breed of asshole to wear a custom-tailored, three-piece suit during a DC summer.

He traded a look with the security detail, and the latter faded out of sight. Fox walked over and extended a hand. "It's nice to see you, Matt." His face cracked in a smile. I shook his hand, because that's what you do.

"LATAM Ops to running the NCS in, what, four years? That's got to be a record," I said.

Something, a look I couldn't read, moved across Fox's face like fast-moving clouds. He ignored the question.

"Please, have a seat." Fox gestured magnanimously to the generic-looking living room. Sure. I walked over to a couch in his Potemkin front room and sat. Fox strode to a bar in the open space between the living and dining rooms. He grabbed a tumbler and set it next to a glass that already had two fingers in it. "Memory serves, you're a Lagavulin man, right?"

"That's right," I said.

Fox pulled a bottle of Johnnie Red out of the bar, poured a slug into the empty glass, and walked it over to me. He held the one already poured in his other hand, and once it hit the light, I could tell we were not drinking the same thing.

Fox sat across from me. I sniffed my glass and took a sip, not wanting to give him the satisfaction. I hated blended whiskey, and I really hated Johnnie Walker. It was probably in my file.

"So," Fox said after a languid sip of his own glass, before setting it down. "You're in town, asking questions you shouldn't be asking. I get it." He held up both hands in a plaintive gesture. "Your girlfriend is in jail, and you want to help out. Be a hero."

"She's not my girlfriend, she's my client."

"Right. I keep forgetting. As I understand it, so do you. At any rate. Ms. Burkhardt found herself in trouble. You're going to protest that, and frankly,

I'm not interested. You'll forgive me if I decide to take the Justice Department's interpretation of the law."

I couldn't wait until I could use *that* line against him.

"I'm having a hard time understanding why I'm having this conversation with *you*, Damon. I'd need a computer to quantify the number of things I would rather do than spend five minutes with you and your cheap scotch. If the Agency is scared that I'm asking questions, that probably means they have a reason to be. What did *anyone* hope to gain by sending you here? Or did you think that you, the great spymaster, could somehow talk me onto your side?"

"I've never liked you, Matt. There's no secret of that. You're reckless and arrogant, and you don't know when to keep your mouth shut. I knew you weren't ready for a station chief job, not coming off of McKellar's unaccountable goon squad. You needed time to get back on the reservation. We were going to offer you a pick of top assistant chief jobs. Athens, Rome, Tokyo. Get back into the flow. Then you'd have gotten your own station. Instead, Nate pushed, and they forced you on me. We saw what happened. I also knew you'd be hostile to me here, and you didn't disappoint." Fox leaned forward, picked up his drink, and made a show of the sip.

"This has been a fascinating trip down revisionist history lane. But please get to the point. You're not going to help me, and you're not going to convince me to back off. So why are you wasting my time?"

Fox sighed and set his tumbler down on the coffee table, then leaned back into the couch.

"Ms. Burkhardt solicited classified information from a government employee and is now in jail for that. They will charge her with espionage, and they will con—"

Temper overrode self-control and better judgment. The words were out before I knew I was speaking them. "I *heard* all that from the FBI already." A smug hint of a smile blossomed on his lips before he put it away, and not before I saw it. Which he also knew. I hated him knowing he scored a point.

"Right. Well, you are allowing your feelings about a woman to cloud your operational judgment. We've been here before. Truly, I hope it ends better for Ms. Burkhardt than it did for Angel Kelly."

Holding my tongue probably meant controlling my fists, so I opted for the lesser of the evils. "Her death is on you as much as it is me. You had no business planning an operation you weren't running, in a theater you didn't know, over a situation you knew nothing about."

"History seems to have judged this differently than you do. Nevertheless. I didn't have high hopes that you'd see things my way. I did hope that you still loved the Agency you served as much as I do, and together, we could find some common ground. I invited you here as a last chance to not only prevent a serious breach of national security but also to save our organization from unnecessary and inaccurate allegations."

"You really thought I'd give up her source?"

Fox shrugged. "I am in a position to help you, Matt. A second chance. I can get you work. You know how much we pay our contractors? Enough that you wouldn't have an office in a tiki bar. I can even expunge your record." Fox let the implications of that speak for themselves.

Former spooks often find the transition to civilian life challenging, and it can be difficult to find meaningful work without a network to vouch for you. I was blackballed with a generation of senior officers, many of whom now had lucrative gigs in the private sector. Even as a PI, there was plenty of work I couldn't get because my detective résumé wasn't that deep and I had few people that would speak on my behalf. All because of Damon Fox.

Fox running the CIA's operations directorate made him the nation's chief spymaster and one of the most powerful and influential men in the Intelligence Community. If not the dark machinery that turned cogs in the world.

And he had it out for me.

Now he was offering to wipe all that out and put me on the right side of my own history.

"What do you want from me?"

"Give me Ms. Burkhardt's information and her contacts. I'll see to it that she's released no later than tomorrow."

"What, exactly, would you do with that information?"

"We're deeply concerned about where it came from. The first thing I do is give it to our CI people and have them run the traps. After that, we quietly work to repair the leaks. I know Ms. Burkhardt has done a lot of work on this story, and I imagine with that amount of time invested, it's very important to her. I can offer her some exclusives, as well as be an off-the-record source for future work. *The Washington Post* has had the lock on intelligence reporting for thirty years for good reason. That doesn't always need to be the case."

"What about the *story* itself?"

"I don't follow."

"The GRU attacked our people, Damon. You can't seriously believe this report the National Intelligence Council released."

"There is so much more happening below the surface. If I could trust you, even a little, I might clue you in. If you actually understood what was going on, what the stakes were, I think you'd be a little more cooperative. Maybe even supportive."

"You didn't answer my question."

"Yes, I did. You just didn't like the answer, so you pretended not to hear it. I see some things haven't changed. Burkhardt's story isn't going anywhere, for a lot of good reasons. I'm offering you one last chance to cooperate with us. And to get your life on track. It is far more grace that you deserve to be extended, Gage, but I'm willing to be magnanimous in the interest of national security. Her facts are wrong, the person who leaked them has an agenda, and it's going to cause the country a lot of unnecessary problems at a time when we can't afford to have them."

Fox took a final, small sip of his drink, which I suspected was mostly for show. He set the glass down on the table.

"You know what I'm worried about right now, Gage? Active measures from three different countries in a presidential campaign. That has *global consequences*. I'm worried about the CHICOMMs deciding that given the instability we have at home, we're too preoccupied to help defend Taiwan. And I'm also worried that since we seem to have been kicked out of half a dozen African states—thanks to Russian influence ops—now we've lost eyes on the kinds of Islamic terrorists that might actually pull something awful off here. And instead of focusing on *those* problems, I have to deal with Matt Gage and his girlfriend who want to write a newspaper article."

"The GRU attacked our people," I repeated. "Even for someone like you, that has to count. I have a source who will confirm it. Now you're asking me to give you all of her research so you can put it in a burn bag?"

"A source, you say? That's interesting. I've gotten some...curious reports out of the European Division about a suspected American who may have been involved in the unlawful exfiltration of a Russian citizen from Belarus. A person on a watchlist as a known foreign agent. This suspected American is also implicated in the murder of a Russian intelligence officer." Fox leaned forward in his seat, and when he spoke, his voice was a low growl. "We will harass the other side relentlessly, Matthew. But the thing that sets us apart from the animals we face off against is that we *do not harm them*. That is the inviolate rule of our profession."

"You're complicit, Damon."

Fox leaned back in his seat and then stood, smoothing out his suit. "I see that you've learned nothing in your time on the outside. I did what I could. You are now on your own. You're in the cold, Gage, and that will have consequences. The FBI is going to talk to you. I can't stop that now. You probably won't like what they have to say."

I rose and stared down America's top spook.

Then I left without another word.

Back in my car, I navigated out of the neighborhood to Westmoreland, a four-lane divided street that connected McLean and Arlington. They flashed me with the lights about two miles south of the safe house. I pulled off Westmoreland onto a residential street, and two cars followed. One stopped behind me, the other in front. Four men in suits belched out of the cars and surrounded mine. "Turn the engine off and step out of the car," one said when he approached my door. I did as I was ordered.

"Matt Gage, you're under arrest for espionage."

The next stop on my tour was a windowless room in a nondescript government building outside DC. One of the FBI agents took my keys and followed with the rental car, which meant they now had my phone and my laptop. What safeguards I had on my phone wouldn't stand up to the Bureau's white hat hackers. I hadn't stored any of Jennie's background research on my local drives, which were also partitioned and encrypted. My browser activity was anonymized and wiped after each session, so they shouldn't be able to find the secure containers I had stashed all over the internet for hiding case details.

I bring all this up because once I was in that small cell, with a slab anchored to the wall for me to sit on and a urinal and sink, I had nothing to do but contemplate how exposed I might be. If and when they got into my phone, they'd have my contacts and they'd have the record of calls I made outside of Signal. So, Audrey Farre and Colonel Rick Hicks, for starters. I wasn't sure, but there might be a way to connect me to Connor Bishop's alias, Charlie Auer.

Lights out came about an hour after I was processed, so I had a lot of time alone and in the dark.

Great metaphor, that.

At some point, I must have drifted off because the explosion of light in the room jarred me into a confused and disoriented, groggy wakefulness. I washed up using the toiletry kit they'd issued me and spent a half hour doing calisthenics in the cell—a circuit of pushups, bodyweight squats, dips, lunges, and ice skaters. Acting like you're in captivity is the worst way to manage being in it. Sometime later, a guard pushed a government-issued jail breakfast through the slot in the cell door. Cue the Dostoevsky quote about judging a society by the quality of their prisons.

I asked through the slot for my phone call. The guards did not respond.

After "breakfast" came more waiting. I estimated this to be about two hours. Then a guard opened the cell door and told me to follow him. He had another uniformed officer with him. They led me to an interview room and handcuffed me to the table. A few minutes later, an FBI agent entered. He was a Black man about my age, close-cropped hair and a mustache, gray suit.

He sat opposite me.

I wondered who was watching through the one-way glass.

It was an interesting play having Damon Fox try to get something out of me first. I almost wondered if that was the point. They'd know he was the last person on earth I'd talk to. So why him? Fox was hubristic enough to believe he could coax something out of me, though that didn't seem like the play. A night stewing in an FBI cell didn't give me any fresh perspective.

So much didn't make sense.

"Mr. Gage, my name is Special Agent Cedric Rawlings. It is ten oh three." Rawlings then specified the day and date.

"Are we being recorded for quality and training purposes?"

To his credit, he maintained his composure. Must've been here before.

"Mr. Gage, this morning we'll be discussing your role in a concerted effort by an organization to solicit classified information from the United States government. I understand you served in the Central Intelligence Agency for about nineteen years. I also understand that the Agency terminated your employment for cause."

Again, I turned toward the one-way glass. "I would like the record to reflect that I have asked for my phone call and have thus far been denied."

Undeterred, Rawlings continued. "As I stated, we will be discussing your role in an effort to solicit classified information from the US government."

"Does your file include the FBI's legal attaché, Brad Keane, that I exposed for sleeping around enough that it caused a diplomatic incident? And, in so doing, put himself in an actionable position by foreign intelligence operatives? That I advised him of this and, to save his career, he made up some allegations about me?" I feigned a confused, frowning expression. "That's in there too, right?"

Rawlings's eyes flitted over to the one-way mirror, hung there long enough for them to read him, and then returned.

"Agent Rawlings, I can save us a lot of time. First of all, I quit. The Agency HR people listed me as 'terminated' to spite me on the way out. That was Damon Fox's doing. Second, I took the fall for something I protested heavily and is documented in cable traffic. Unless Fox wiped those too. I've never unlawfully received classified information. There is no leak that I'm aware of. The Orpheus Foundation is not WikiLeaks. I would never disclose national security information. I do, however, think you can appreciate that if the government is lying to the American people, someone has responsibility to expose that, right? Of anyone, you all should be able to appreciate that. After all, the Watergate leaker was an FBI agent."

Rawlings's eyes simmered for a long stretch in the room's cold silence.

"Are you done?"

The comment about my termination was intended to knock me off my feet, get me rattled. They wanted righteous indignation and fury, frothing at the mouth so I wasn't thinking about being evasive when they hit me with the real questions.

"You're aware that security officials in Belarus are reporting that a Russian diplomat was murdered in a small town north of Minsk? I understand you recently traveled to Europe. Care to tell us what you were doing in Vilnius?"

"I flew to Europe to meet with the Orpheus Foundation's executive director. I then traveled to Vilnius to meet with a prospective source on behalf of my client. She wanted me to vet them. I'd also like to state for the record that source was not a representative of the US government."

"What did you discuss?"

"I'm sorry, I'm not at liberty to say."

"Mr. Gage, you're suspected of espionage. The penalty for this could be twenty-five years in prison. I suggest you cooperate."

Now, that was interesting because espionage is incredibly hard to prove in court. Law enforcement officials basically had to catch someone with secrets in hand. They didn't have that, and we both knew it.

"What were you doing in Minsk?"

"I already told you."

"Do you know the name Fyodor Vasiliev?"

"No," I said. I'd never seen Fedorov's identification and had taken it for granted that he was lying about who he was, so the fact Rawlings was coming at me with his actual name wasn't surprising. I kept my reaction in check.

Rawlings came at me from several different directions, and I more or less stuck to the truth. I told them I was there to meet a source, who was a foreign national, and I didn't confirm his nationality. Nor did I acknowledge that I knew how Maksim died. Rawlings was good and he tried to back me into an admission. Still, the conversation wasn't fundamentally different than the argument I'd had with Fox last night. Overall, I'd say I gave nothing up and held my own.

"Mr. Gage, unless you cooperate and tell us who is leaking classified information to your client, Jennifer Burkhardt, you will be charged with the murder of Fyodor Vasiliev."

Wait, what?

That meant "Fedorov" wasn't an alias for Vasiliev…that must have been Maksim's real name.

Rawlings checkmated me with expert skill. Even with all of my counter-interrogation training, I hadn't seen this move coming.

They were going to use the threat of charging me with a murder I didn't commit as leverage to admit who my source was and give up everything Jennie gave me.

This seemed like the time when I needed to get a lawyer.

15

There was no clock in my cell and they confiscated my watch, so I marked time by the "meals" they served.

Eventually, they gave me my phone call. I told Coogan what had happened. He had the foresight not to say that he told me so.

It was the first time since that first conversation with Jennie that I had the enforced quiet and solitude needed to objectively consider what'd happened to date. The brain has a way of processing information in the background and not offering up its conclusions to the conscious mind until periods of relative calm. It's why you can sometimes wake up in the morning with a flash of intuition after going to sleep with a problem.

Fedorov remained indiscernible. During those long hours, I vacillated between absolute credibility and none at all, with stops at every increment along that spectrum. The datapoints lingered that I couldn't reconcile. He seemed to be correct about it being a weapon, just lying that he had anything to do with it. Why?

This thinking led me to the other thing I couldn't reconcile: the timing. Why now? What did Fedorov gain by risking his life to smuggle this information to the West *now*? The Intelligence Community already concluded it was "highly unlikely" that Havana Syndrome was the work of a foreign power. The US government was not pursuing any punitive action against any suspected antagonist. As far as I could tell from my conversation with Fox, the Agency wasn't dedicating resources to this either. So, if the Russians were off the hook, why press the issue? Was that the point? Fedorov was smart enough to know that once our country accepted the official conclusion, his information had measurably less value.

Which led me down a darker path.

Was this just an elaborate deception operation? Get the CIA to question itself? Introduce doubt into the IC, the administration, and the public sphere? That was an intrinsically Russian move.

The second morning, two guards marched me into an interview room for a second round of questioning. Interrogators want their suspects to know they control every aspect of their life. You have to have a long walk, under guard, just to have a one-sided conversation that might be the slightest chance to prove your innocence.

Rawlings asked his questions in an impassive, professional manner. They were all some flavor of the previous evening's round.

At the end of it, the guards took me back to my cell.

"Gentlemen, hold up a minute." Rawlings's slightly Southern drawl echoed in the hallway behind us. I'd already moved into my holding cell and turned to see the guards staring back at the agent. He exchanged quiet words with them and then filled my doorway. "Matt, there are people in the Bureau who are trying to paint you as a vindictive opportunist."

"Is that what you came all the way back here for? You guys tried that once already."

"I don't think you're working for the other side. I've spoken with Damon Fox. I know about your history. For what it's worth, he doesn't think you're a traitor."

"I'll sleep better knowing that."

"You really don't like making it easier on yourself, do you?" Rawlings said, seemingly more for his benefit than mine. "I think you're trying to do your job, and maybe you're letting personal feelings for your client get in the way of it. It wouldn't be the first time that's happened, would it? One of our agents spoke with Elizabeth Zhou."

"You assholes leave her out of this," I said through gritted teeth.

"I'm not your enemy, Matt. I have a job to do, same as you. I don't want to believe you murdered a Russian intelligence officer in cold blood, but as a cop, my training teaches me to follow the evidence."

"I didn't shoot that man," I said.

"If you didn't, you're protecting the person who did. Either way, it's now an international incident with a hostile country. I don't need to explain to you how much of a problem that is. And there's still the question of how Grigori Fedorov got out of Minsk."

"What would you do if I could prove Russian intelligence was responsible for this? Where would that go?"

Rawlings's face softened and then dipped into a slight frown.

"I wouldn't do anything with it, Matt. That's not my job. I'm here to find out who is giving national secrets to a reporter."

"Then I guess we don't have anything more to talk about. Look, I appreciate you coming down here for an off-the-record chat. I know what I saw, what I was told. I don't know who Jennie's source is inside the government, or if she even has one. And I didn't kill Fyodor Vasiliev. We can spare the taxpayers the cost of you asking me those questions a third time."

"You seem like a good person, Matt, if a little misguided. I hate to see what's coming to you."

"Now I understand why we're having this conversation where the tapes aren't rolling. You didn't want it on the record that you know this is bullshit."

His eyes flashed, and I knew I went too far.

"There was some doubt. You're doing a goddamn good job of eliminating it."

Agent Rawlings left.

We did not meet again in the interview room.

Another day's worth of jail food passed before I saw the guards again. I'd been here about three days at this point.

I'd gone from an offer of absolving my sins with the CIA and a new future of steady, high-paying work to the option of turning Fedorov over to the government and a chance to walk.

Both of which I'd pissed on.

Good work, me.

Though, in my defense, the latter would've had them handing Fedorov over to the Russians in order to quiet Moscow down. He'd never be seen again.

The door opened, and they instructed me to follow. I didn't have anything else to do at the moment, so I went.

Instead of being led to the interview room again, as I expected, they processed me out of the detention center and gave me my personal effects.

Special Agent Rawlings was waiting for me when I stepped out of the changing area where I put on the clothes I was arrested in.

"Your lawyer is here," he said. Then he handed me a card. "You can do the right thing, Gage, and help us. There's more going on than I think you appreciate. If you change your mind, call me."

I accepted the card and said nothing.

"This offer expires faster than the milk in your fridge. Keep that in mind."

I was escorted out of the federal building with my things, where I met Thomas Coogan outside. Someone brought my rental car out.

"You must be getting really close to something, because these guys sure are pissed off at you," he said. "Or you're just being you."

"Probably a bit of both."

I wasted no time once I was out of jail. First, I needed to replace my phone and laptop. I wouldn't even turn these on until I had replacements. The FBI had my gear for three days. I'd never trust that hardware again. Replacing and reconfiguring would burn a few hours. I thanked Coogan for flying across the country to meet me. He said he needed to ensure the Bureau actually complied with my release. They hadn't formally charged me with anything, so they couldn't hold me longer than seventy-two hours. Coogan planned to raise hell about it anyway and would be meeting with the ACLU and other watchdog groups while he was in DC. He didn't expect anything to come of it, but wanted the FBI to get some bad press out of harassing me.

"They can't prove you were involved in anything Jennie may allegedly have done, so they couldn't hold you," Coogan said. Then he added, "Yet."

We agreed to meet up over dinner for a more detailed debrief and plan the next steps.

Once I had a clean phone and laptop, I posted to my hotel and caught up on what I'd missed.

I sifted through the missed calls and texts. The most relevant was Rick Hicks telling me the FBI pressed him on our association. He wished me luck with my case, but asked that I not contact him again. I noted that was on my regular voicemail and not on Signal, so it was available to any ears that might have been listening.

Because I could run queries on EchoTrace's servers, the app was able to keep working even when my computer was shut down. It completed the link analysis of the senior National Security Council members involved in that 2021 summit with Russia.

Anthony Carter was a counterproliferation official on the NSC until 2022, when he returned to a security-focused think tank.

Raj Patel was the summit's chief cybersecurity policy coordinator. He was still with the NSC.

Amara Johnson coordinated the counter-terrorism agenda; she was also still with the NSC.

Victoria Townsend led the NSC's Russia policy. Interestingly, her deputy was a Colonel Taylor Mercer, United States Marine Corps. I looked up Colonel Mercer's bio. He was a military intelligence officer with a strong background in Russia. He'd written some papers for service schools that were posted online. I downloaded them and had EchoTrace summarize them for me.

I opened Signal and saw that Audrey Farre's contact information automatically populated, meaning she had an account. I called her through the app. "Audrey—it's Matt Gage, please don't hang up. I'm following up on what you told me. Do you know a Colonel Mercer? He's a Marine officer assigned to the National Security Council."

"Gage, I cannot have this conversation with you."

"Can you connect me with him?"

She hung up.

Shit.

A few seconds later, Signal pinged.

Farre sent Colonel Mercer's cell phone number.

I called him.

"Mercer," he said.

"Colonel, my name is Matt Gage. I'm a private detective. I've just texted you a copy of my California PI license to this number so you may verify my identity. I'm supporting an investigation into Havana Syndrome, and I was given your name as someone who might speak with me about the 2021 US-Russia summit."

Click.

Dead air.

Coogan and I met for drinks and a quick bite in the District.

"Let's start with the good news," Coogan said. "As it currently stands, the US Attorney is not charging you with espionage. I think you're aware that's incredibly hard to prove in court without surveillance or being caught trying to sell secrets to an undercover officer. However, that's not stopping them from charging you with obstruction of justice. I also don't need to tell you that has a much lower bar to prove."

"So why aren't they?" I asked.

"I convinced the US Attorney that stunt they pulled with Mr. Fox constituted entrapment and I'd play hell with it in the press if they did."

"Glad that's out of the way."

"This isn't a clean slate, Matt," Coogan said gravely. "I've bought you a little time, but not much. I think we can beat this espionage thing in court, should it ever come to that. The thing I worry about is this murder charge."

"That's complete bullshit. And they can't prove it."

"They tell me they can."

"And that's how we know they're lying. Fedorov shot that man. This is just a power play to get me to hand over Fedorov so they can silence him. Call their bluff. Demand to see their proof."

"I've already done that," Coogan said. "They won't, but it's a move to force the government to show their cards. They can't go to trial without discovery. I believe they're posturing to force you to cooperate, but part of me wonders if they've actually got something."

"They don't," I said.

"Moving on. Jennie is not going to reveal her source, under any circumstances. She also attests that source has not revealed classified information and that this entire thing is the government using its power to silence a whistleblower." It felt like he was reading off a cue card. "She still believes that her best chance at getting the government to drop the charges is to prove what she's alleging."

"Then what the hell is the point of this? What'd I spend three days in jail for?" I snapped.

Coogan blinked a few times. "I suspect that has as much to do with your relationship to Mr. Fox as it does your case with Jennie."

"Sorry, Tom. I didn't mean to bark at you."

He waved my apology away.

I continued. "I think my question is valid, though. Jennie won't tell me who her source is because she doesn't want to compromise their identity. That person is the key to this, which is why she won't reveal it. So, I'm supposed to run around and dig up shit, talk to people that she has identified, for what?"

"She doesn't believe this person is the whole story. A large part, yes, but not the whole thing. She thinks Fedorov's portion is equally important. Two sides of a coin, is how she put it. What's your take on him? Is he credible?"

"Yes and no."

"That's clarifying," Coogan quipped.

I looked around the restaurant, mostly out of habit, to see if anyone was paying attention. I lowered my voice anyway. "He provided solid intel. Based on what I saw, I believe Moscow has built an energy weapon. Possibly more than one. And I think they've also been waging an industrial espionage campaign against Western tech companies to make up for their own limitations. However, Denis thinks he's lying about some of this. He brought in an independent expert who poked a bunch of holes in Fedorov's story."

"So, he's lying about some of it, just not all of it?" Coogan asked.

"That's about where I land," I said.

"Does Jennie have a story without him?"

"Without knowing what her source knows, I can't answer that. Though, if Jennie was all that ironclad on this person, I doubt she'd have me doing all this. I think what Fedorov knows, and claims to have in his possession, is vital."

"Has he shared any of it yet?"

"A little. Denis said he's waiting for asylum before he shares it. He told me the same thing. I don't suppose there's anything you could do on that score."

"Not if he's potentially guilty of espionage," Coogan said.

We drank in silence. Coogan had given me a lot to consider. Eventually, I said, "So, my take is the government genuinely has something they're trying to keep out of sight. They've thrown too much at trying to get me to be quiet. Before the FBI tried to scare me off, I could've been convinced that maybe Jennie was wrong. Not now."

"What's your next move?" Coogan asked.

"I spoke with someone on the Senate Intelligence Committee, one of Jen's contacts. She told me to look into this summit between the US and Russian presidents in 2021. Coincidentally, the attacks also stopped that year."

"Think the summit had something to do with that? If so, what does that prove?" Coogan knew the answer, and I could tell he was coaching me on how to navigate the question.

"If the attacks stopped following a summit between POTUS and the Kremlin, we can conclude the president knew the Russians were attacking our embassies and told them to stop. Of course, there's no official record of this conversation that I've been able to find. We still need someone who was there to confirm it. I have two leads of people that might talk to me." And one of them had already hung up on me.

My phone started vibrating. I looked down at the number.

"Would you excuse me a minute?"

"Of course."

I picked up. It was my landlord. "Jim, hi. What can I do for you?"

"Matt, hi, I guess you're out of town? The police called me because no one could get ahold of you. The house has been broken into."

16

My landlord didn't have any other information and gave me the number for the Santa Monica police detective that handled the burglary. I called him, told him I was away on business but that I could try to be back tomorrow. They needed me to inventory my valuables and see if anything was stolen.

Honestly, I was more concerned with something being left behind than taken out.

If the FBI entered my house to search it, they'd have left a copy of the warrant. If they were planting surveillance devices, they would've had to have filed a warrant with a federal magistrate. I didn't know if that was something Thomas could get a judge to admit, but I'd bring it up.

This also wasn't a casual burglary. When I'd moved in, I'd convinced Jim to upgrade the locks and told him the make and model to get. If those were picked, they'd have been pros. That narrowed the list of suspects considerably.

I'd learned in Minsk the Russians knew my name and address from looking at my driver's license. Looked like that knowledge hadn't died with Fyodor Vasiliev.

There was a flight leaving Dulles at ten o'clock, which I could just make. I changed my ticket on my phone, told Thomas what happened and that I needed to leave. Thankfully, I hadn't been here long enough to unpack, so I grabbed my bag and headed to Dulles.

I genuinely didn't remember the last night of decent sleep I got, but I'd be willing to bet it was before Jennie called me with this case.

The police were done with my home by the time I got back to Santa Monica. It'd been dusted for prints, and they hadn't found anything; I'd learned that from the detective on the phone. I called his cell, left a message to say I was back in LA and that I'd inventory my valuables as he'd asked.

The house was a mid-century two-story that Jim split into two apartments. I had the bottom floor and the garage. The upstairs neighbors were a young couple. They were nice, I'd invited them over for a drink when they moved in. The woman was an ER nurse, and the husband worked for one of the aerospace companies in Santa Monica, so they rented this place to be what we call "California close." Meaning, they were about five miles away from work and it could still take forty-five minutes to get there. Apparently, the nurse had been returning from a late-night shift when she saw the perpetrators exiting the property. Because I traveled so much for cases and sometimes internationally, I let them know when I was going to be gone. She saw the burglars leaving and called the police. They, too, thought it was a professional job because they didn't see signs of forced entry. In fact, the police asked if I used a maid service (I didn't) and had also grilled Jim on his alibi for that time.

The first thing I checked were the two concealed safes I'd had installed when I moved in.

The first was my gun safe. That was in the bedroom closet and not that well hidden. It was locked with a biometric keypad. A dedicated safe-cracker from an intelligence service could get through that, though all they'd get would be my Glock 34. The other safe was concealed in the floorboards, also secured with a biometric lock and some additional security. You'd need to move the bed and some plastic boxes first to even see it. I kept my valuables there, hard drives that needed protecting, cash in several currencies, and a clean passport with an alias that maybe I neglected to turn back into Langley and claimed was destroyed.

Anyway.

Whoever was in my house didn't find either safe, or, at least, they didn't open them. I had a sensor connected to each of the doors, which logs opening and closing times. The only way to check it was to open them, so that was the first thing I did. My Glock was in the first, and passport, money, and hard drives were in the second. The timestamp was the last time I'd been home.

Jim, the landlord, knew I was a private detective, so he was aware that I had a pistol in the house. I did not tell him what I did prior to my PI work, just that I worked in "security." He asked me if I thought this had anything to do with one of my cases. I told him I didn't think so.

The detective met me midmorning, and we walked through the house. I told him about the gun safe and showed him, also showed him my permit. Since it hadn't been touched, I did not mention the other safe.

I told the detective that I had accounted for what few valuables I had, and that maybe my neighbor coming home scared the burglars off.

"Any enemies you can think of? Someone that might want to harm you? Maybe someone from one of your cases?" the detective asked.

Buddy, we don't have that kind of time.

"I don't think so," I said, even though I knew that was a lie.

If I'd have known at the time the damage that deflection would cause later, I might have been more honest.

In the moment, though, I didn't think a small-town beach cop could offer much help if I told him who I thought was really in my house. "I mostly do investigations for a group of reporters."

"Gotcha. Well, if you think of anything, let me know."

I thanked him for his time, took his card, and saw him out.

There's a fine line between being a paranoid nutcase who thinks "they're all out to get me" and definitively knowing that to be true.

Which was why I kept electronic-sensing equipment in the house.

After a thorough search, I did not detect anything inside. However, I did find a portable GPS tracker stuck to my Land Rover.

I called Special Agent Rawlings.

"Decided to come to your senses?" he said.

"Someone broke into my house. I know you guys would leave a copy of the search warrant, so I'm certain you're not the ones who illegally entered my home." I said that in a tone that begged for challenge, but Rawlings did not rise to it. "Now, I'm fifty-fifty on who put the bug on my car."

Rawlings was dead quiet for a long time.

"That wasn't us, Gage."

"Well, maybe we can be on the same team, then."

"The ticket price to that show hasn't changed."

"Are you kidding me?"

"Russians think you killed their man. Whether you did or you didn't probably doesn't matter in their eyes."

"And you're going to let them get away with this, just because I won't give up my client?"

Sometimes, you can hear a shrug.

Especially when a company man does it.

"What's it going to be, Gage?"

I noted that when he was first trying to get me on his side, Rawlings used my first name. Now, it was just "Gage."

"You know that I cannot betray my client's trust. Jesus Christ, Rawlings, that's what this whole thing is about. I don't know who Jennie's source is, or even if they work for the government. I do know that she has a First Amendment right to protect that individual, and you cannot ignore that just because," I waved an arm, even though he couldn't see it, "national security."

"I told you when we last spoke that I thought your intentions were good, just misguided. There's an opportunity to change that now, and you seem unwilling to take it. If it was the Russians who broke into your house, and you keep this up, whatever happens next is on you. I'm sorry, I truly am. Now, are you willing to help us?"

"Cedric, I'm practically begging to work with you, I'm just not betraying my client to do it."

"Unless and until, Gage," he said, and hung up.

First, I let Denis know about the break-in and my suspicions. Then I gave a similar heads-up to my friend in the Belgian security service. I thought about calling Katrina Danzig but decided against it. What would be the point? She made her position clear when we last spoke, and I knew her well enough to know she wouldn't side with me over the Bureau.

I wanted to go see Jennie, reassure her I was on top of this. Also, to share what I'd learned in DC. Did she know what CINDER SPIRE was, or about the summit? I'd burned half the day with the police and inspecting my place, and if I drove to Lynwood, that would be the day. Momentum was building—in good ways and in bad—and I didn't want to take my foot off the accelerator just yet. I called Coogan's assistant to let him know I'd be coming by to review the files again.

I wasn't really aware of the time until Coogan's assistant poked his head into the cube they let me use.

"I'm heading out for the night, Matt," he said. "I've told security that you're going to be here, and there are a few folks still burning oil."

"Thank you," I said.

"I don't know if Thomas had a chance to brief you or not, but we think we've got a compelling argument for getting Jennie transferred to home confinement. There's precedent."

"That's great," I said, half listening. "Anything I can do to help?"

"Yes. I'd like to debrief you on your trip to Washington and, specifically, the circumstances around your detention. Thomas wanted a fuller accounting of it."

"You got it," I said.

He said he'd reach out for a convenient time and left. I looked down at my watch, it was about seven.

Jennie didn't have notes on CINDER SPIRE beyond the name. She also didn't have anything on the US-Russia summit, so I was taking that to be new news. I'd made another attempt at Colonel Mercer's phone earlier that day. Straight to voicemail.

There wasn't much in the public domain regarding the summit. Billed as a chance for a new president to "reset" Russian relations, the subtext was the goal was to back them down from invading Ukraine.

A series of questions emerged that I'd never previously considered.

What if it wasn't only the Russians?

We had good reason to believe they'd outsourced the first round to the Cuban DGI. Maybe they weren't the only interlocutors involved.

Given the known limitations of Russian engineering, I wondered if they'd actually gotten these weapons from their allies in the People's Republic of China. Perhaps at this summit, Putin admitted where they'd acquired the technology from in exchange for a pass on US reprisal and global condemnation.

Perhaps it was never the Russians.

Perhaps I'd allowed my career-long animosity toward the Russian Federation, its diabolical, reptilian president, and their vindictive, abhorrent intelligence apparatus to cloud my thinking. If anyone had the capability to use electromagnetic weapons in such a way, it was the Chinese. We knew they were expanding into the Western Hemisphere, with a significant emphasis on Latin America, using the argument that it was a region America had simply forgotten. Frankly, both things could be true. The People's Liberation Army could've designed the devices and given them to the Russians to field test. It might explain the differences in symptoms between locations. It was also impossible to discount the fact that there were dozens of cases in Guangzhou. That gave Beijing a lot of deniability.

Putting all of that in the context of an undocumented sidebar at a summit, I could see Moscow saying the Chinese were to blame. That was exactly the kind of power move Russia's president would play against a new opposite number in Washington. Considering that Russia would invade Ukraine just seven months later, it played back as wise deception and a daring chess move. Would a US president risk starting a war with China over this? Doubtful. Not when weighing the consequences of it becoming a global conflict almost immediately.

This cast the Intelligence Community's report in new light and explained why the government was trying so hard to keep this buried.

These thoughts flowed through my mind as I watched the sun disappear over the horizon. While the sky above darkened, lights below winked on in sporadic pops and waves, tracing illuminated outlines of Los Angeles.

A potential China angle changed this story dramatically. It didn't explain Grigori Fedorov or his information, though it certainly called into question his credibility.

I wondered if *that* was the secret Jennie was protecting.

Was that the live grenade her source had given her?

Tomorrow, I'd go see her and ask her in person. For now, I needed some sleep.

I exited the elevator into the cavernous garage beneath the building.

It occurred to me that I needed check in with Dylan soon, let him know how we were progressing on this case.

I reached my Defender, squeezing in between the van that had parked too close.

A door slid open, and unseen hands grabbed me from behind.

The dark mass of an arm snaked around my upper torso. I felt a sharp stab in my neck. Pain spread like a wildfire from it. Already, the light washed out and the darkness at the edges of my field of vision closed in.

The last thing I saw was the open maw of the van.

Then it was dark.

17

Consciousness broke against the rocks in my brain in intermittent waves, as if the body were trying to wake and the brain arguing against it. I'd partially wake, realize I didn't want to be there, and then pitch backward into the abyss.

Eventually, someone got tired of that and punched me in the stomach.

That ended the cycle.

Air exploded out of my lungs and I forcibly tried to sit up, but restraints held me in place.

I couldn't move. Eventually, enough faculty returned and I could orient myself. I was lying down, maybe at a slight downward angle. Everything hurt. Whoever did this kicked the shit out of me first. Probably not the cops, then. Dim pinpricks of light penetrated the sack over my head, a constellation of dirty stars.

Suddenly, what felt like a bucket full of water slapped me in the face. I couldn't see it coming to flinch.

There was a whispered command, but I couldn't make out what was said.

Water poured over my face, and I was drowning.

It went into my nose, my mouth, into my eyes. I coughed and gagged and more water poured in, choking me. Jesus, I *was* drowning!

Then it stopped.

My chest heaved, trying to force air back into my body. I was still trying to catch my breath when they did it again.

Water crashed onto my face.

"Stop!" I cried.

It did not.

I couldn't breathe. Water just flooded into my mouth, up my nose. I was drowning, and I was going to die on this plank.

The terrible knowledge of what this was crept into some part of my brain, and maybe that made it worse.

Water stopped.

"You will breathe now," a voice said. It wasn't straight English, but I was too addled to place an accent.

I gulped air. On the fifth or sixth breath, they hit me with the water again.

It stopped, and someone ripped the soaked shroud from my head. All I saw was light, impossibly bright and shining in my face. Dark and disembodied forms hovered at the edges of the lamp, like reverse halos.

I was breathing hard, like I'd just sprinted up a hill. My heart throttled so hard in my chest, I worried it was going to crack a rib.

"Where is Grigori Fedorov?"

Thankfully, I'd been trained for this and knew how to respond appropriately.

"Fuck you."

Apparently, that was not the answer they were looking for.

Someone violently forced the hood back over my head, and they hit me with the water again. Longer this time. Though, time is subjectively elastic when you're drowning.

As the water poured onto my face, I tried to count the seconds, give my brain something else to concentrate on. My best guess was that I was at twelve when they stopped. If you'd have asked me, I'd have said three minutes, because my body was trying very hard to convince my brain that it was dying.

"Where is Grigori Fedorov?"

I'd gone through this in training, and there was one thing I knew for certain.

Everyone breaks eventually.

The unknown speaker asked again where Fedorov was. I answered in Russian, "Up my ass."

That got a laugh.

Then another five rounds of waterboarding. They'd stop long enough for me to breathe and to make sure I wasn't going to stroke out on the table, then hit me for more.

It's an especially invasive and cruel technique that tricks the subject into believing they are downing. It taps into the mind's most primal fears and the body's reflex to survive lethal danger. Most people can tolerate it for about ten seconds.

They stopped and asked the question again.

My heart rate was in serious redline territory, pulse hammering in my head.

The hood got yanked off, and a disembodied voice asked again, "Where is Grigori Fedorov?"

"He's in New York, I think," I said, coughing.

"Where in New York?"

"I don't know. My job was to get him here. After that, it's not my problem."

"There is no record in the Customs and Border Protection system of Grigori Fedorov entering this country."

"We gave him a new passport to travel under," I said, extending the lie.

"So the American government assisted Fedorov's escape from the Republic of Belarus?"

"Yeah," I said.

It's your problem now, Fox. Fuck you.

As soon as I thought that, his words rang out in my memory. *You are now on your own. You're in the cold, Gage, and that will have consequences.*

What had he done?

"Where am I?"

"Somewhere no one will miss you," a shapeless voice said. "Why did you murder Fyodor Vasiliev?"

"I didn't."

I assumed my interrogator was Russian, but I still didn't know.

This time they didn't bother with the hood, they just held the scratchy cloth over my face and hit it with water. My body rebelled immediately, going into paroxysms of jolting panic. I fought against myself, *knowing* that I wasn't drowning yet unable to convince my body that I wasn't.

The water stopped. I heard the heavy Velcro ripping, and restraints came off. Hard hands grabbed me, pulled me up and over the side of the board, and I was on all fours.

"Breathe," someone commanded. I did, and then vomited water.

I was given a merciful few seconds to breathe.

"Why did you murder Fyodor Vasiliev?"

Sputtering words leaked out of my mouth. "I didn't."

They yanked me back onto the table with all the gentleness you'd expect from a group of sadists, tightened the straps, and I was too weak to resist.

"Why did you murder Fyodor Vasiliev?"

I stuck to my answer because it was the goddamn truth, if he'd just listen.

We entered a cycle of question—truth—water—question—truth—water. This went on for too long.

Eventually, I collapsed. I just wanted it to stop.

If it stopped, I could breathe and think and figure out how to get myself out of this.

"Did you shoot Fyodor Vasiliev?"

"Yes," I said.

The crushing weight of my failure would've pushed me through the floor if I weren't strapped to the table. Knowing that everyone breaks is cold comfort when it's you.

I didn't want to believe Damon Fox would go this low, not just break the law but piss all over it. Then again, I didn't know what in the hell he was trying to hide.

Breath came hard now, my heart was thundering so hard in my chest, it was difficult to catch it. I was drenched and shivering uncontrollably, as much from shattered nerves as the temperature.

I felt the hot breath of someone on the side of my face, and a man whispered in my ear, "You will die in this room."

No one said anything for a long time. Despite the cloth draped over my face, I closed my eyes, because I didn't want to see the blurry, wet light anymore. I concentrated on my breathing and tried to calm myself, get my heart rate down.

"Where is Grigori Fedorov?"

"I...told...you..." The words came between heaving gulps. "I left...him...in New York."

They hit me with more water, pouring it over my face, down my throat. I fought against my restraints, but they were inexorable. I couldn't move. I couldn't escape. And the water just kept coming.

I didn't know how long this went on, only that my body had given out and my mind felt like it was torn apart and pushed back together.

Then it stopped.

"Are you lying?"

"Yes," I said.

The other thing we learned over the span of dark years doing this to terrorists was that when you convince someone that they are drowning, they will do or say anything to make it stop.

No one spoke. I couldn't hear anything over the sound of my own breath through the wet cloth. This time, they left it draped over my face. My head was immobilized by a thick strap that they'd ratcheted practically to the gray matter, and it had no give. My body shook with shivers.

Still, no one spoke.

I heard the inconsistent patter of water dripping off the table and onto the concrete beneath.

You know when you're truly alone.

I stayed that way for a very long time. Wet and shuddering in the dark, strapped to a table, with that wet sackcloth over my face and bleary light pinpointing through.

It was impossible to calm down. Maybe my heart slowed a touch, but it still felt dangerously fast. I knew from training that was the adrenaline.

Nothing happened for a long time.

Then, a door slammed hard in the darkness, and it startled me enough that I jumped. Heavy footfalls approached.

"We will try this again," the voice said. "Where is Grigori Fedorov?"

Even though I knew what was coming, I said, "New York."

Water crashed into my face, down my throat, up my nose, and it didn't stop. Breathing was impossible. My body jerked on the table, raged against the restraints, but it did nothing. I was literally drowning. The water kept coming.

Then it stopped. Wet, heavy Velcro tore and rough hands dragged me over the side. This time, they didn't help me down. White lights exploded in my eyes as I hit the concrete, unable to brace myself because I couldn't see it coming. Someone yanked the hood off. An explosive coughing fit followed, and then I was puking up water and whatever was left in my stomach.

"Breathe now," a different voice commanded. Then they were hauling me back onto the table and strapping me down.

The room was dark, cold, and smelled of damp concrete. A halo of halogen light splashed an oblong aura on the ground. Dark formless shapes moved outside the light. My eyes hadn't adjusted to the new inputs yet, so they remained inky blobs.

There were sounds I couldn't make out in the distance, but it was distinctly mechanical. Then, a metallic, whipsaw of a motor starting, rising in pitch and then settling back to its dull chug. I could smell the gasoline and exhaust.

There was the sound of metal on metal, and I heard the electric *crack* of contact made, heard the sparks leaping off the leads and smelled the ozone.

My heart rate spiked again.

God, not this.

"One last time, Mr. Gage. Where is Grigori Fedorov?"

"New" wasn't even out of my mouth before one of them shoved the blunt ends of the alligator clips into either side of my rib cage. My body thrashed hard against the restraints as electricity jolted through it. I screamed. It was a raw, primal expression of visceral pain.

Well, at least I knew this wasn't Fox.

"Where is Fedorov?"

The motor chugged away, already filling the room with exhaust fumes, and I could smell the ozone from the electrical leads.

I said, "New York," anyway.

My body flinched in anticipation, but nothing happened.

"Where in New York?"

"Safe house...swear to...God...I don't know." I gulped air, prayed for time. "They didn't tell me."

They hit me with the alligator clips, and my body rocked with shocks. I screamed.

"Are you lying?"

"No!"

"Why did you murder Fyodor Vasiliev?"

My mind hurriedly tried to re-create the last few horrifying moments. I *hadn't* admitted to that.

Right?

Christ, he was switching lines of questioning to throw me off, catch me in the lies. Had I admitted to killing Vasiliev? Maybe I had. I honestly didn't remember.

If it kept them thinking I was honest about Fedorov being in New York, I'd have to commit to it.

"Vasiliev...wouldn't let us leave."

"You *were* breaking the law," he said. The interrogator stepped into light around me, and I could finally put a face to the disembodied voice. He was tall, with inky-black hair and an angular face. Black eyes, vacant and soulless wells, stared back at me.

"So, the Central Intelligence Agency used you to help Grigori Fedorov escape illegally from Belarus. You will have an interesting trial in Moscow, I think, Mr. Gage."

I didn't reply. A chuckle. It sounded like bones rattling in a can.

"We know everything about you. We shall expose your numerous crimes in Nicaragua. We shall expose your country's imperialist designs on the free peoples of that and other countries in the region..." Nicaragua? He kept droning on about crimes, but I'd stopped listening, frozen dead in place. "Oh, there will be a full accounting of your actions. Perhaps...what was her name, Agent Angel Kelly? Yes, I believe that was it, perhaps Agent

Kelly's family will finally hear the truth and receive the closure they deserve."

If I could choke the life out of him for even putting her name in that sewer of a mouth, I would.

"You are alone, Matthew. Your government has denied you, they have disavowed you. They disowned you. They call you a criminal. They will not negotiate for you. We will make sure you hear them admit it, it will be played for you at your trial. Then, you will go to gulag, where you will have ample time to think on your crimes against the Russian Federation, if not the world. That is what this is about, Mr. Gage, exposing America's legacy of imperialism, of lies, throughout the world."

This was an exquisite tapestry of bullshit, even for a professional liar like him.

"I am not an unreasonable man, Matthew. You and I, we are similar. We are spies. We understand the great game, yes? Unfortunately, there are those above me who do not see it the same way. The bureaucrats. They want revenge, they want justice. If you tell me where Mr. Fedorov is, I can make things easier on you."

"I'll bet," I said, and my words came out in a wheeze.

My interrogator sighed heavily, as if to tell me, *I tried*.

If they wanted Fedorov this badly, the information he had must be legitimate.

"The Orpheus Foundation," the interrogator said with an oily drone. "This is a CIA front, yes?"

"No."

"Forgive me, Mr. Gage, if I don't find you convincing. But, a...*former* CIA officer now working for a group of reporters who target the Russian Federation with misinformation and lies? I think your ouster from the Agency is nothing more than an elaborate cover. Something to throw the dogs off the scent, no?"

Oh, that's not good.

That conclusion couldn't be further from the truth, though from a Russian's perspective, I could see how he got there. The Foundation's relentless campaign against Moscow only buttressed this argument. That this was the only conclusion he could reach was so deeply paranoid that it was intrinsically Russian.

And from this, a new danger birthed.

Denis and the Foundation were now at risk.

Jennie, at least, was relatively "safe" because she was in jail. The others were in imminent danger.

A renewed panic crashed into me that I fought to control.

I didn't know where I was, and neither did anyone else. There would be no help for me.

This was an exceedingly aggressive play for the Russians. It was hard to believe they had an operation this size in LA.

Nice work on your counterintelligence, FBI.

My interrogator spread his hands to show me what happened next was out of his control. He pretended to look sincere.

"You will now be taken to Moscow for trial. Considering the charges against you, Mr. Gage, your guilt is assured. You can help yourself, of course. This is your last chance. Tell me where Fedorov is."

"And what, you'll let me go?"

He actually laughed at that, and I believed it was genuine.

"Of course not. You've committed crimes against the Russian Federation and our many allies throughout the world. You will stand trial. However, cooperation on your part, now, may mean the difference between five years in gulag and twenty." He paused for effect. "Or death."

"Pass," I said, with as much spite as I could muster.

"You don't do yourself many favors," he said.

"You'd be surprised how often I hear that."

The interrogator extended an index finger, and I saw a looming shadow come closer. There was a blunt, hard stabbing in my side, and my entire body exploded with pain. Electricity shot through me. Violent seizures rocked me like earthquakes. I screamed. He pulled the source of it away just long enough for me to catch a breath and realize it was over, then he hit me again. My body jolted uncontrollably. I was a marionette watching the world's most twisted puppet show from the inside. He started and stopped several times, I lost count. The intervals were the only thing that changed.

Sometimes the space between was long enough for the terror to build, other times it wasn't enough to catch my breath.

Eventually, it stopped.

I smelled smoke, and I knew it came from me.

I had never in my life known pain like this. Randomly, a muscle would jerk as if current were still being applied.

Body and mind were equally beyond their limits.

I stared back at my torturer, and in that moment, I resigned to kill him. Somehow, some way, that man would die by my hands.

The Russian stepped back into the circle of light and looked at his watch. "We've been at this for two hours. I'm impressed at your stamina. All of this can stop, Matthew," he said, in a shockingly civil tone. "Please, let's end this. If your government was interested in Grigori Fedorov, they would have accepted his offer as a walk-in. If you don't tell me where he is, I will have to assume the Orpheus Foundation is hiding him. In which case, we will look for him there. How many more must pay for your sins, Matthew?"

All the circular logic, the backtracking on questions was all intended to trip me up, expose my lying.

The Russian stepped out of the light. I knew what was coming.

"This is your final chance," he said from a distance.

A jolt of electricity blasted me, my body shook. So much pain. They pulled the contacts away just before I'd have gone into cardiac arrest, waited a few seconds, and hit me again just for spite.

I screamed.

"Fedorov is in Zürich," I said. The words erupted from my mouth so fast, they came out practically as one.

"So, not New York, then? Why is he in Zürich?"

Between heaving gasps for air, I said, "Because he thought he'd be safe there." A pause, to collect my thoughts. Had to sell this. He already thought the CIA was involved. "Plan was to bring him...to New York. But it was too risky." I stopped again to breathe.

"Where in Zürich is he?"

"Park Hyatt, but he's gone by now. I told him to change hotels every two, three days. Stay in American-owned properties as much as possible." He'd know if I gave him an exact location, I was lying.

The Russian officer feigned a look of grim concern. "Honestly, I'm disappointed in you, Matthew. I hadn't expected you to give Fedorov up. People really are disposable to you, aren't they?"

What. A. Bastard.

The Russians were desperate for this information to stay hidden and were going to some extraordinary lengths to keep it that way.

Which only made my failure so much worse.

Hopefully, I'd bought Denis and Luc, my pal in Belgium's security service, some time.

There would be no trial in Moscow, that much was certain.

I also doubted there would be something as sublime as a Siberian work camp.

There would only be an unnamed cell beneath the Lubyanka, the infamous former KGB headquarters where the FSB invented crimes against the state and tortured and murdered people pronounced guilty of them.

"I look forward to seeing you in Moscow, Mr. Gage. Since your country has restricted flights to my country, you will be traveling by boat. Assuming you make it. I understand the seas can be...unpredictable...this time of year."

The interrogator jutted his chin in a kind of nod to someone unseen, and they ripped me out of my restraints. Bolstered by a man on either side, they zip-tied my hands and dragged me out of the room. They followed that up with a forced march through a twisting maze of hallways. The one sign I saw was in Cyrillic. We exited the hallway into a dank and cold garage. We stopped next to a white panel van that had no windows. One of the goons opened the van's door and shoved me inside. Two men, both armed, followed me in. Two more got in front.

There wasn't much of a Russian ex-pat population in Los Angeles, and their government didn't have an official presence. Then it hit me.

We were in the Russian consulate in San Francisco.

18

I worked it out as we left the compound.

After knocking me unconscious in Los Angeles, the Russians drugged me and kept me sedated for the five-hour drive up here. It made sense. Consulates and embassies were considered sovereign territory under international law, so the Russians would have no fear of US law enforcement breaking down their doors while they tortured and interrogated me.

Now, they'd put me on a boat, probably one of the innumerable "fishing trawlers" they used that just happened to be decked out with electronic surveillance gear. I'd enjoy a leisurely cruise across the Pacific or, as my interrogator intimated, they'd just shoot me and dump me over the side of the boat in the middle of the ocean.

That threat made less sense, though, once I'd figured out I was in the consulate. It was too easy to disappear a dead body from one of those places. If they wanted me dead, that would be the place to do it.

They turned north and drove toward the bay.

It was night.

They hadn't bothered putting the hood back on. Either sloppy tradecraft or they didn't expect me to be able to tell anyone what I saw.

They were Russian, so probably a bit of both.

I'd never spent much time in San Francisco, though a case brought me up here recently, and I was generally familiar with the geography. Old habits kicked in, and I tried to zero our location. I counted fifteen blocks, heading north before a left turn that put the bay on the van's right side. The inky image of a large hill rose to the left, and the Golden Gate Bridge glowed in the distant foreground. The van pulled onto a road empty of cars. Headlights illuminated a steep, tree-covered slope to the left. If there were streetlights, they were unlit.

The van's headlights tracked past a sign reading, "Torpedo Wharf."

They parked next to a building, a white two-story that looked like it used to be an old military structure. Like the street we took here, the lights were also out all around the grounds, which didn't seem right.

Doors opened, and they yanked me out onto the pavement.

With a guard at each elbow, they frog-marched me to the low pier. There was a cut chain lying on the ground. Wind whipped in from the bay, I was already soaked and cold. Uncontrollable shivers racked my body again.

"I don't think we're supposed to be out here, guys," I said, fighting to control my chattering teeth.

If they spoke English, they didn't show it.

With a pistol at the small of my back, they guided me down a long pier. It was too dark to see how far it pushed into the bay, but we walked for a while. It was cold and the air thick with the pungent smell of the ocean. The Golden Gate lorded overhead, bright against the murky night.

One of the Russians pulled a cell phone out, made a call. A few seconds later, I heard an outboard motor approaching.

One of them stayed in the van and another at the wharf's entrance. With the two at my sides, we walked into the night. I wasn't sure how much farther we went, though I judged us to be close to a hundred yards offshore. Partly cloudy skies above, the moon a fingernail sliver of white light. We'd be invisible from the shore.

Not that anyone was looking.

I spotted the boat by its running lights as it pulled up along the pier.

Here, we had a bit of a logistical problem.

My hands were tied behind my back, and it was about a ten-foot drop from the pier to the boat.

"Stop," one of my minders said.

The other trotted off. I assumed he was going to help secure the boat to the pier.

We stood in the cold silence. Every muscle hurt, and each time I moved I seemed to discover some new spot they'd violently introduced themselves to while I was in their care.

The one who'd gone to guide the boat commanded his partner to bring me over.

"I can't climb with my hands tied behind my back, comrade," I said, in Russian.

He told me to shut up. I mean, those weren't the exact words he used, and it included a characterization of my mother best left unrepeated.

He pushed me close to the edge. One of them had a tactical flashlight with a red lens. I could see the rope ladder descending into what looked like a private fishing boat. Not something that'd make the trip to Russia, though it could probably get us to the trawler or, God help me, submarine they had parked off the coast.

All I knew was that if I got on that boat, I was a dead man.

And so were a lot of other people I cared about.

I felt movement behind me.

I hadn't eaten in over twenty-four hours. I was still woozy from whatever they'd drugged me with, and physically exhausted from the torture. My reserves were gone.

What I'd summoned up there was just hate.

These men kidnapped me, beat me, tortured me, and they'd threatened a woman I cared deeply about. Perhaps it wasn't until that moment I realized how much. All I knew standing, frozen, on that pier was that someone would pay. Here, now.

The only thing I had on me was surprise.

"Climb, or I kill you," the Russian said. Die here or die there, nice options.

I heard the metal "snick" of a blade opening, and he cut the plastic ties around my wrists. He pushed me forward.

I snapped my head back, slamming it into his face. I heard a wet crunch and knew I broke his nose. He staggered back. I stepped forward and kicked the kneeling man in the face. The force of it knocked him over the side. There was a dull thud and cry of pain as he crashed to the boat below. Alarm was up now. The ones on the boat would be scrambling up the ladder, gorillas full of spite.

I whipped around. The Russian I'd headbutted staggered, holding his nose and gushing blood. Closing the distance, I grabbed him by the throat and put all my force behind it. I ran, driving him backward. With a surprised cry, we went over the side. There was an instant of dark descent, and we crashed into the water. Momentum carried us into the murk, driving down into the cold blackness.

Better in the water than outnumbered two to one on the pier.

The Russian, completely disoriented, panicked. I could feel his arms flailing, his legs kicked mine as he scrambled to find "up" and reach it. He must have let go of the knife when we hit the water. My hand was already at his throat, so I wrapped my arm around him in a choke hold. I squeezed, and wrapped my entire body around his so he couldn't escape.

The man thrashed and flailed, kicked and screamed a muffled roar.

Use that oxygen, pal.

He pawed for a gun. I locked my legs around his, securing him, and used my other arm to push his head down, increasing the pressure against my arm around his throat. His body spasmed once, and I felt him go slack, unconscious.

I pushed away from the body and floated off, leaving it to sink into the deep. Kicking once, I tried not to crash the surface so I didn't give my position away. The wharf's barnacle-covered wooden supports loomed over me like creatures rising from the depths. Russian voices shouted at each other in the distance.

I pulled myself along the wharf in the opposite direction. The sound of the water covered my movements.

Then the boat's motor kicked up, and I saw its running lights through the gaps between the pillars. It was coming around.

A large flashlight, its cyclopean beam diffuse in the murk, tracked across the surface. They scanned where we'd hit the water for several seconds while I furiously pulled myself along the wharf, now adding my legs to kick off from the stanchions.

The light beam tracked over to the wharf itself now.

I took a lungful of air and slipped beneath the surface.

Kicking, I drove myself downward and then straight. There was no light in that bleak abyss and navigation was impossible, so I instead opted for speed. I swam as far as my lungs would take me, breaking the surface eventually to breathe and get my bearings. I'd cleared the wharf and squinted to discern the shadowy outline of shore in the darkness.

The boat closed the distance, its occupants tracing across the surface with what I now realized was an actual searchlight.

As it tracked back in my direction, I dove beneath the surface just in time and held the plane at my unknown depth as best I could. From the murk, I watched the light's jittery path above. It moved away, but I held my position, despite the burning in my lungs and muscles. My prudence was rewarded when the light retraced its arc, passing back over me.

Then, everything was dark again.

Slowly, I rose to the surface, breaking through and taking in air as quietly as possible. It took all my willpower not to inhale, and I bet I was louder than I thought.

The boat was still there, moving now back over to the dock. Shouting voices added to the sound, and I could make out the form of one of them bolting down the wharf for the boat. I guessed they were going to add to the search since none of them wanted to return to their boss to explain how I'd gotten away.

I flipped onto my back and kicked, fanning with my arms and letting the tide do most of the work. It was all I could muster. I swam until my legs dragged on the rocks beneath and then turned to walk the rest of the way, staying low in the water. This area was completely dark, though I could make out the gloomy shapes of buildings in front of me. The Russians must have cut power here. I crawled up the wet boulders and hauled myself onto the concrete path, collapsing onto my back.

My chest heaved and my extremities felt too light, like they weren't getting enough blood. Unless I tried to move them, and then I got waves of remembered pain.

The immense and glowing form of the Golden Gate Bridge was all I could see in the night.

Russian voices carried out over the water, and I knew that I couldn't linger. Their friend would float to the surface eventually. Maybe they'd find him, maybe they wouldn't, but if they did the pessimistic math, they might reason only one of us swam away and it wasn't him since he wasn't calling out. That would train them on the beach.

I had no chance in a fight.

My body had nothing left to give.

Willing myself to stand, I rolled over onto my stomach and pushed up to all fours. Searing pain blazed out from my ribs where they'd hit me with the clips. Now that my eyes fully adjusted to the night, I could make out the shadowy shape of a man stalking back and forth at the end of the wharf. They'd killed the boat's motor and it was now drifting, but the searchlight still tracked across the water.

If there was only one of them on the wharf now, that meant the last one would still be in the van and I'd have to get past him to escape. While I was on a road now, this was a two-lane drive that ended at an observation point beneath the Golden Gate Bridge. The cliff above it was unscalable, and I didn't have the strength left to swim.

The only way out meant sneaking between a couple buildings and past the van. I moved around one, putting the single-story structure between myself and the water.

I could see the van from here, and the man in it. Beyond this cluster of buildings, a road slowly crawled up the tree-covered hill. The hill looked steeper than I could climb, but I might be able to make it up the road before they figured out which way I went. Also working in my favor, there were two roads out of here. This gave me an even shot at escape. Further, this second street went through heavy tree coverage with ample hiding places. But to go where? I wouldn't make it very far in this condition. Also, they had all of my personal effects.

Modern society rotated on two fundamental axes, smartphones and credit cards, and I had neither.

There weren't even payphones anymore, so I couldn't even make a collect call for help.

If I was going to get out of here, I needed to steal their van.

There was just the minor problem of a Russian operative between me and it. He was also armed, and I had no chance to overpower him.

The van faced me, pulled next to a row of stanchions to prevent vehicles driving between the buildings. The Russian now stood in front of it, his face partially outlined in a spectral glow from his phone.

He was about fifty feet away, too far to make out his side of the conversation.

I didn't get a great mental map of the layout on my way in. There were two long, low buildings parallel to the water. The van was parked in an open space between those buildings and the ones I now hid behind.

The question was, how to get the driver away from the van.

I disappeared back behind the building and crept around to the other side. In the distance, I could see the boat's red and green running lights and the dark form of someone moving on the pier, searching.

I crept to the edge of the building.

Hopefully, the patron saint of bad ideas had a soft spot for me.

Leaning back around to face the van, I said in Russian, "Come down here and help us, damn it." I adjusted the pitch of my voice to sound like I was calling out from a distance.

Quickly, I moved back around the other side of the building and to where I'd started. I could see the fool standing there next to the van. He took a few tentative steps forward. Hugging the wall, I crept along the side, minimizing my profile.

The Russian took a few halting steps toward the water. I was at the edge of the building, we were maybe twenty feet apart. He had the phone to his ear, and the glow from it was wrecking his night vision. Otherwise, he'd have seen me.

Crouching low, I crept a few feet away from the building. Moving with aching slowness, I rolled my shoes over the pavement to quietly propel myself forward. My muscles screamed in agony over the pace and the position.

The Russian walked past me with some angry strides but stopped to peer through the darkness at the wharf. He pulled his phone out again and made another call.

A bitter realization washed over me—the keys wouldn't be in the van, they'd be on his person. I hadn't seen a physical key/ignition combo in ten years.

Damn it.

To get out of here, I'd need to win a fight I was in no condition to have.

With the Russian's back now to me, I stood, bringing some much needed relief to my leg muscles. He was fifteen feet away, perhaps? There was only one way out of this, and it required fast, decisive action. I closed the distance between us in four long strides, reached out, and wrapped an arm around his neck, yanking him backward. Taking the Russian completely by surprise, I pulled him off his center of gravity but didn't have the strength to hold him up.

I lost my balance and we both fell backward, with the Russian landing on top of me. His phone clattered to the ground. By some miracle, I'd kept my choke hold intact, but it wasn't working. My opponent wasn't losing consciousness, and my strength was fading quickly. Hoping this guy hadn't ever wrestled, I used my weight advantage to corkscrew him over and plant his face in the pavement. He grunted in pain. I bashed his face in the ground.

The Russian jabbed his elbow backward, striking my ribs in the wounded spot. A reflex shock of pain blasted through my body, and I flinched and loosened my hold on him. The Russian started to struggle out. He was up on one knee now and driving to his feet. Maintaining the grip around his shoulder and neck with my right arm, I knuckle punched him in the side of the head several times. Each hit landed with waning force, but I knew that bastard saw stars.

I thrust my left hand into his jacket pocket and felt for the keys.

Got them.

The Russian kipped up to his feet, and I fell backward to the ground. He turned.

He growled out a guttural curse in Russian. It wasn't particularly clever.

I kicked one leg out and wrapped it around his, then scissored the other like I had his buddy in the water. I pressed my legs tightly together and wrenched over, knocking him off-balance again. The Russian pitched over. I released my legs as soon as he hit the ground, pushed myself off the pavement, and sprinted for the van. It was the last trace of strength I had left. The sound of shoes scraping on pavement followed me.

He gained ground fast and would be on top of me in another few feet.

Still gripping the stolen van keys, I felt for a metal key on the ring. I flipped it in my hand, pushing the key through my knuckles.

I stopped, pivoted, and punched.

The Russian barreled right into the path of my fist as I did, the key scraping across his face. He screamed, grabbed his eyes, and fell to the ground. He rolled back and forth, crying out in agony, clutching his face. He roared unintelligibly.

I kicked him once for my trouble, turned, and staggered to the van before I collapsed. When the dome light came on, I saw my things in a heavy plastic bag on the floor. I put that on the seat next to me and drove like hell.

I called 911 with a report of suspicious activity at Torpedo Wharf while I drove. I might have added a couple details to encourage the police to get off their ass. The Russians got a problem with it, they can sue me.

I navigated to the 101 and drove south. It was nearly one in the morning. I found a convenience store that was still open, bought a thirty-two-ounce Gatorade and a protein bar, and sat in the parking lot until my hands stopped shaking.

Then I opened my phone and dialed Nate McKellar.

19

Nate had been my mentor for most of my time in the Agency. When I'd started out as a private detective, Nate hired me to investigate the death of a friend. Turned out, his "friend" had once been an asset Nate recruited in Beijing and then, breaking a few rules, helped emigrate to the US after they feared he'd been burned. The Chinese Ministry of State Security found Johnnie Zhou and blackmailed him into their employ. Nate had hired me because he knew I'd keep it quiet. Later, he admitted that he also hired me to find out if he'd been compromised. He figured if *I* couldn't link Johnnie and him in Beijing, the Agency couldn't do it either. That all blew up when the case exposed a Chinese espionage ring here in the Bay Area.

Because of his long and distinguished service, the Agency allowed Nate to quietly retire. That was also a good way of keeping the lid on the clandestine operation he led under the guise of running a tech firm.

Nate made his choices and said he didn't blame me for what happened. That didn't alleviate the guilt I felt over being the catalyst for ending his career. We hadn't spoken much since.

Now that he was no longer accepting middle-of-the-night calls, Nate set his phone to mute notifications at night, and it took a few tries to get him.

"Matt? What?"

"I went fishing, but nothing is biting," I said.

He was awake instantly.

"Where are you?"

"At a gas station just outside SFO."

"I'm on my way."

I texted him the address.

The line about fishing was a code phrase we'd used when I'd worked for him. In that context, it meant your cover was blown, the opposition was in pursuit, and you needed help immediately.

Nate met me thirty minutes later. By then, I'd wiped my phone and dropped it in the trash. The Russians had it long enough that I couldn't ever trust it again. First the feds and now them. I was beginning to worry about the expenses I was racking up. There would come a point when my nonprofit client would decide they couldn't afford to cover the trouble I was getting into.

Nate pulled up in a Rivian SUV. It was a perfect cover for living in Silicon Valley.

"What happened to the Tesla?" I asked.

"Didn't want to keep funding the laser that guy is eventually going to build to blow up the moon."

"Fair," I said.

"What in the hell did you do, Matt?"

So, I told him.

By any reasonable measure, I should've been under the care of a doctor.

Or most of a hospital.

Instead, I asked Nate to drive us to his house so we could debrief.

Nate lived in a mid-century rambler in Los Altos, a community on the southern end of Silicon Valley.

While I talked, he stitched me up. Nate hadn't forgotten how to field dress wounds and took care of the burns on my rib cage and the multitude of cuts I'd acquired. Since he didn't have anything stronger, I opted for ibuprofen and scotch to manage the pain.

We finished our conversation in his office, surrounded by the artifacts that defined a life in covert intelligence. I'd been present for some of them and noted with pride the one on the wall that I'd given him. Nate handed me a glass of scotch and I drank it, which helped me discover all the cuts I had in my mouth.

I told him absolutely everything, even the part about Connor Bishop. I'd left his name out but kept the other details intact. I debriefed as I had so many times before, with Nate following along and interjecting only the occasional clarifying question. We both knew the ritual. The time for critiquing my moves was after the facts were on the table.

His eyes burned with cold fury at what the Russians had done to me. Never in his long career had he seen such a blatant violation of the unspoken norms guiding the trade of spies.

"They're scared, it would seem," he finally said. "You need sleep. Take the guest room, and we'll continue in the morning."

Within five minutes, I fell into a black pit that had no bottom.

I awoke to the smell of fresh coffee and the gradual realization that I'd slept past lunch.

Sitting up took an act of will that I hadn't known I could meet.

My clothes had been washed and folded and were sitting on a chair next to the bed. There was a bottle of ibuprofen and water that had long ago warmed to room temperature. I availed myself of both, dressed, and walked out to the kitchen, where I saw Nate at work at the stove.

"Here," he said, and handed me a mug.

Nate fixed me a breakfast burrito with bacon, avocado, and a nuclear-grade hot sauce that had to have been smuggled into the country through an elaborate underground. He set a glass of orange juice next to me. "It's California, drink it anyway."

Being a Floridian, I had specific opinions about oranges and beaches. I found both lacking in California, but I took it anyway and was grateful.

"I made some calls while you were out," Nate said. "Kept your name out of it."

"Thanks. You find out anything?"

Nate nodded. "Let's start with what we think we know. I spoke with some old friends in the counterintelligence division. We think the leader was an SVR officer named Anton Malyshkin. Don't know for certain it's him, but we know he's been operating out of the San Francisco consulate, and your description fits. He runs the same kind of black ops squad we did. CI doesn't know what he's doing here, or if they do, they aren't saying on a nonsecure line. You said he started off asking about the SVR officer this Fedorov fellow shot outside Minsk."

"That's right," I said.

"Okay, that tracks. It makes sense they think you killed him and that Fedorov's extraction was some kind of black bag job, since the SVR knows you. It also tracks that they'd try to kidnap you and exfiltrate you to Moscow."

"But they asked a lot of questions about Fedorov, and they made threats against the Orpheus Foundation."

Nate nodded, agreeing. "We won't know for certain for a while, I suspect. Prevailing theory is the Kremlin is worried that whatever information this Fedorov has will get into the public domain."

"You think the SVR is running cleanup?"

Nate shrugged. "It's possible. Could be they're just coming after you because their guy got killed. Still, they had Fedorov under surveillance in Minsk. That's the part that doesn't make sense for me. Why is one agency spying on the asset of another?"

"Well, if the SVR believed Fedorov was talking to the other side..." I stopped myself. "But that'd be state security, not foreign intelligence," I said.

"Yep. Again, it doesn't make a lot of sense. So, look, I suspect you're going to hear from the Feebs on this," he added, using the Agency's nickname for the FBI. "Do yourself a favor and don't do what you normally do in these situations."

Saying nothing, I focused on my breakfast.

"Thank you for picking me up, Nate. I owe you."

"No, you don't. You pulled punches on the Zhou case and let the FBI run you ragged rather than give me up. Anyway, the Russians crossed the line, and they're going to get hit back hard." Nate refilled his own coffee cup and then leaned against the counter. A grim smile flashed across his mouth. "You didn't hear this from me, but there is going to be a fire alarm at the Russian consulate soon. Some of our folks, some of the FBI's folks are going to be mixed in with the first responders. Need to open every room to clear it, you know? They're paying particular attention to the basement. Russkies are going to have a hard time in this town for a while to come. I suspect they are also going to drive themselves crazy looking for bugs. Now, this is just some get-back to tell them we know what they did and they aren't going to get away with it."

"What about the people who grabbed me? FBI got people at the airports?"

"Sure do."

I pushed the plate, scraped clean, aside and lifted my mug in both hands. "What did you make of the Havana Syndrome cases?" I asked.

I hoped Nate understood I was asking his honest opinion as a member of the Senior Intelligence Service.

Nate walked over and joined me at the table, as though the act of closing the distance formed a kind of pact. "On the long list of shit I wasn't supposed to say to you today, yes, I always believed the cases were real. I've read Burkhardt's reporting on it. Generally speaking, I think she's spot-on. Couple areas, she's off base, but that's to be expected. Before we go any further, you need to promise me that none of what I tell you leaves this table. Ever."

"It won't," I said.

"You said Fedorov is a GRU asset. Unit 29155 is the one you're looking for. For years, they were the service's technical development group. Recently, they pivoted to carrying out assassinations"

"Why is the Agency denying that it even happened?"

Nate shook his head slowly. "I don't know, and that's the honest truth. In the early days, leadership assumed someone was using an ultrasonic or other electromagnetic device. Most assumed the Russians gave Cuba's DGI something to test out. A few thought it was the Chinese, but it would've been too provocative for them at the time. Personally, I think the CHICOMMs have the means to do it but lack the tradecraft and the will to pull it off."

"Think the Russians got the weapons from them?"

"Possibly, though it wouldn't matter if they did. I wasn't at headquarters when this happened, mind you, but you hear things. I think—and I want to be clear that this is speculation—that initial opinions were divided on whether or not it was really a weapon. After Vienna, there wasn't much doubt. Too many incidents and too many locations."

"Then why didn't it get any traction? And why the bullshit report?"

"As to the former, a lot of the old guard thought people were playing up symptoms. Said they should just tough it out. There wasn't a lot of sympathy. I remember hearing 'intelligence is hard, get back in the game.' Hard to classify wounds you can't see. I don't agree with it, I'm just saying how it is. As to your second question, and again, this is speculation. Let's say the Agency is divided on whether or not this is real. Let's say, then, information comes out that says it was a weapon. Imagine what that does to the diplomatic corps? To us? Who is going to want to serve in an overseas post if they know we can't protect them? Can't protect them at work, can't protect them at home? Hell, even on the way to or from. And this is a potentially life-changing injury."

"That's the exact reason not to say it was nothing. My contact says the Russians did it again at the NATO summit last year in Vilnius."

Again, I didn't want to put Nate on the defensive here. He deeply loved the Agency, for all its many flaws. This conversation wasn't supposed to make him choose between that and a righteous answer.

"I wasn't on the Seventh Floor when those conversations were happening, so I can't give you any direct insight. All I have are my guesses. Look, Matt, I know what's going through your head right now, and I would urge caution. If you're right, if Burkhardt is right, put the evidence out there— that's what she does. Let the chips fall. People will demand accountability, or they won't. But you'll have done your job. Now, I know *you* and I know how you can be when you're backed against a wall. I don't know that there's ever a *good* time to carry on a one-man, covert war against a Russian intelligence service. But I do know this isn't it."

I smiled. "Roger that, boss." Then I said, "Damon Fox is really the head of the NCS now? That was…quick."

"Bad news travels fast."

"How'd he do it? I mean, I assumed it involved a goat sacrifice or something, but still."

Nate chuckled. "Did a favor for someone. You know he was dialed in with the White House. Not too hard to figure out."

I debated contacting the San Francisco police but ultimately decided against it. The anonymous 911 hardly counted. Nate had engaged the CIA's counterintelligence function, and they'd notified the FBI of the incident and the perpetrators. He didn't tell me exactly what he said, just that he'd kept my name out of it. Bringing the police in might just bring extra attention on the Agency that I didn't need right now. Though part of me really wanted to rub this in Fox's and Rawlings's faces.

I got myself on an afternoon flight from San Jose to LAX. Nate drove me to an Apple store to replace my phone. Again. The kid who checked me out suggested I invest in their replacement plan. I suggested some things he probably wasn't flexible enough to attempt.

Once I had my newest phone, I messaged Denis. It was middle of the night in Belgium, but he needed to know what was coming. I told him I'd be there as soon as I could.

My next call went to Coogan.

"Good news, we're making progress on getting Jennie house arrest."

"Thomas, you've got to pump the brakes on that."

"I'm going to pretend I didn't hear that."

"Russians grabbed me from the garage underneath your office two nights ago. They drugged me and brought me up to the consulate in San Francisco. I was interrogated for a long time. For the time being, man, she's safer in jail. You don't know these people like I do."

"Matt, I can appreciate what you're going through."

"No, Thomas, you absolutely cannot. On any conceivable level."

I let him stew in the silence for a bit.

"Right. Well, Jennie is my client, and I have an obligation to *get her out of jail*. Where she is *unlawfully* imprisoned. I can hire private security, or better yet, federal marshals."

I didn't see how that was better. Arguing was worthless.

Nate insisted on driving me to the airport.

"Matt, you have to be careful. They know you got away, and they know where to find you. Stay moving, and I'd call that FBI friend of yours."

"Yeah, that's a good idea."

Assuming she'd take my call.

I flew home, collected my Defender from the garage, and drove home.

Danzig hadn't returned my call in the time it took me to fly to LA.

Back at my place, I poured three fingers of scotch and watched the sky darken over the ocean from my porch.

Nate shared two incredibly valuable pieces of information with me. First, I had a tangible reason for why the Agency might try to cover Havana Syndrome up. It didn't track that it would be the only reason, but it was a start. Second, I had the unit name of who CIA thought was behind this.

In telling me that designation, Nate was telling me the Agency—on some level—admitted the GRU had an EM weapons program.

Now, it was up to me to take it from there.

That, and make sure that line never traced back to Nate.

There was no question the Russians were taking extreme measures to hide their involvement in this. The question now was how to convince everyone else.

20

I woke up to a strange update from Denis.

There had been a series of arsons, break-ins, and cyberattacks across Europe in the last few weeks. Two days ago, there was a fire at an industrial plant in Hamburg. Here's the kicker. Each of the companies attacked were on the list Fedorov gave us.

I called Connor Bishop through Signal. It was evening in Lithuania, and I'd thankfully caught him before he started work that night.

"Gage, what's going on?"

"We have problems, and they aren't small ones. An SVR grab squad nabbed me at a garage in Los Angeles." I told him what they did and didn't spare the details. "They knew all about Minsk and about Fedorov. Wanted to make sure you knew, but I also want you to run the traps on potential leaks. I know this was a tight operation on your end, still, it's worth running down."

"Okay. Will do. I'm sorry you had to go through that. Did they hurt you?"

"Not permanently," I said, with some effort.

"Is Fedorov still in Brussels?"

"Yes. I have an old friend with Belgian intelligence who's keeping an eye out. Orpheus hired security. Fedorov is probably safer in Western Europe than he is in the US, frankly. They put the questions a little rough, and I had to give them something. I told them Fedorov was hiding out in Switzerland. Think it was convincing, but you should be looking at counterintelligence reports anyway."

"Okay. Matt, I'm sorry for getting you into this. I had no idea."

"Don't, Connor. It was the right thing to do."

We agreed to stay in touch.

I drove to the jail to visit Jennie.

She listened, stone-faced and staring at the table while I recalled everything that happened while I was a guest of the SVR.

After it was done, all she could say was a breathless, "Oh, Matt." Tears welled up behind the words.

"The good news is, this proves we're on target, the Russians know it and are scared. Denis says Fedorov has more information, but he won't give it up unless someone grants him asylum. Which the government won't do."

"Do you think this changes their mind at all?"

"Doubtful. I've got a couple tricks left, though. It'd be a lot easier if I could see what he had."

"You believe him, though?" Jennie asked in a way that was looking for reassurance rather than confirmation.

I didn't tell her about Denis's consultant poking holes in some of Fedorov's claims.

"I sure believe the Russians," I said. "Look, if Fedorov is telling the truth, it means he's stolen trade secrets from defense contractors in five countries. I don't blame him for holding out for a guarantee of protection. Still, it's weird to me, given all that, our side won't listen to what he has to say. I don't have a good answer for that yet."

"Charlie Auer, he's not really State Department, is he?"

"Not really," I said.

"That explains why they don't do anything."

"Yeah," I said, but decided against adding anything else. "I'm going to have to go back to Brussels and see Fedorov. I need to convince him that no one is going to help if he doesn't share everything he's got."

"What if that is all there is?" Jennie asked.

"I've learned enough in the last couple days to suggest it isn't. Coming after me here is a panic move. I'm willing to bet Fedorov has more. If the Agency won't act, maybe the FBI will."

Jennie looked down at the table, silent for a long time. Then, she lifted her eyes to me.

"Matt, I love you."

"Yeah, I know." She'd been casually saying that since college. It was kind of her offhanded way of saying "we're complicated friends."

"No, I mean, I *love* you. I can't believe what you've done. I mean, I know you, I *can* believe it. It's just, no one else would do that."

Oh. That's different.

"It's the right thing to do. Sometimes that still happens." I slid my hands across the table and touched hers. Was this really happening? "I love you too, Jen."

"No contact," a guard shouted from across the room. Everyone in there stopped to look at us.

After twenty-five years of dancing around it, we finally expressed our feelings for each other. But she was in jail and I was being hunted by Russian intelligence.

It's enough to make one question their choices.

We shared a moment of knowing silence.

In time, I said, "What do you know about CINDER SPIRE?"

Jennie shook her head. "Nothing."

"How'd you hear about it?"

"Audrey Farre gave it to me as a lead, as long as I promised not to disclose where it came from. She would only tell me that was a hook. She said I had to figure out what it is. I wanted to ask you if you could ask any old Agency buddies."

Well, if the Bureau knew Jennie had that code word, it might explain why they thought she received classified.

"Something tells me that's a big part of the answer. So far, I'm striking out. No one wants to talk about it. Farre wouldn't say what it was, just that I should focus my efforts on the 2021 US-Russia summit in Geneva."

"Oh, that's new. She didn't tell me anything about that."

"Yeah. And it was in the context of CINDER SPIRE, so I have to believe they are related. The meeting was supposed to reset relations with Russia after the new administration took over. I keep bouncing off that code word. I've worked my way up to this Marine colonel, Taylor Mercer, on the National Security Staff, but he hung up on me. I've got little else. We know that the attacks stopped after 2021, at least until '23. There was an incident at the NATO summit in Vilnius that year."

"That at least explains Auer's involvement."

"Yeah, he more or less saw it happen. Russian military intelligence is leading this, which you already knew. Don't know what happened at the summit, but if it's true that they reached some kind of agreement, the Vilnius attack is a dangerous escalation."

"Why would Moscow risk it?" Jennie asked.

"Because they aren't afraid of a reprisal," I said. "I think that's true, but it feels too simple. Or at least incomplete."

"Please keep at it, Matt." She smiled softly. "I'd squeeze your hand, but I think they'd hit me with the firehose."

"I should get moving. I need to find a hotel for the night."

"Why?"

"Someone broke into my place. Didn't steal anything. After what just happened, I've got a pretty good idea who it was. I don't really want to be in there."

Jennie set both hands on the table in front of me, close to touching but not quite. "Matt, please be careful."

"Careful doesn't get questions answered."

"I'd rather have you than the story." She looked away. "All I have is time to think in this place."

I should tell her, "That's just the jail talking." That once she was out of isolation, she'd think differently.

It would be so much safer for her if she did.

Instead, I said, "I'll be safe. Well, safer than I usually am."

Had I known what was to come, I wouldn't make promises I couldn't keep.

Driving away from the jail, I'd known I should've pressed her on her source. Did the Justice Department's claim have any merit? Was I the moving target for everyone to chase while Denis ran down the story? If it had been anyone but her, I'd have assumed that's what was happening from the drop. I didn't want to believe she'd do that, though in my darker moments, I admit that I wondered.

Why didn't I ask?

Because when a woman says she loves you for the first time, there's gravity to it. You don't think about anything else.

And maybe a county jail wasn't the place for that.

There'd been too many red-eyes for me to do another, so I decided not to return to Washington until the morning. My body was in no condition to try sleeping on a plane. Every movement reminded me that I was too old for this shit. I didn't have a regular doctor and couldn't afford medical insurance anyway, but even if I had those things, all the doc would do would be to order bed rest. Which I would promptly ignore.

So, my way was more efficient.

I needed familiar faces after the events of the last few days, so I packed up my laptop and went to my office. The late afternoon crowd at Cosmic Ray's was mostly regulars who'd been surfing all day and had finally called it.

"Hey, Magnum PI!" I turned to see Ray behind the bar in a tie-dyed shirt, his hair salt-streaked and washed out hanging on either side of his weathered face. I walked over and chatted him up for a few minutes. He asked me if I wanted the usual, but I demurred, opting for a beer. "Case?"

I nodded, picked up my beer bottle, and slowly walked over to a booth. Moving hurt.

My phone rang. It was a number that I didn't recognize, but a 202 area code—Washington.

I answered.

"Good afternoon, Mr. Gage. I hope I'm not disturbing you."

"That depends on who you are."

"For now, I prefer to keep that to myself. Let's just say that I'm a friend with a common interest."

It hurt too much to frown, so I left my expression blank. "You're going to have to do better than that."

"You're on the right track asking about the 2021 Geneva Summit, but you aren't asking the right questions."

Questions about CINDER SPIRE bubbled to the surface, but I caught myself before I asked about it on an open line. "Care to enlighten me? What questions should I be asking?"

"Not over the phone. Where are you now?"

"Where are you?"

"I'm in Washington," he said.

"Well, I'm not. But I could be, if it's worth it." Fedorov had been with Denis for about a week now. In leaving him there, I'd inadvertently put a target on the Foundation's back. Especially now.

"I assure you it will be. When can you be here?"

"Tomorrow, best I can do."

"Then it will have to do. I look forward to speaking to you then."

He hung up.

I drank in silence and wondered if I'd done the right thing. The most important thing was to get Fedorov to safety and convince him to share all of his intel with me. However, it was also true that the attacks stopped after the Geneva Summit and I needed to understand why. If I could prove that, it would also prove the government acknowledged it was real. That might pull the carpet out from under their case against Jennie.

Coogan called shortly after.

"Hi, Thomas. I'm—"

"Our office has been burglarized."

"What did they get?" Sometimes you ask questions you already know the answer to as a way of daring the universe to prove you wrong.

"Everything from Jennie's case." After a long moment, Coogan said, "Matt, that's not everything. The police want to talk to you. They want to know where you were."

21

According to Coogan, it happened two nights ago, when the Russians kidnapped me. Police said it was a pro job, someone who knew how to defeat industrial security and top-of-the-line safes. They figured the perpetrator stole a building's access card and reprogrammed it to give them access to any floor. The security company's monitoring software was hacked into, and the cameras showed an archival feed from a previous day. They also deactivated the motion sensors on the floor so the lights wouldn't activate and indicate occupation. They opened the safes with portable drills.

If I hadn't known better, I'd have asked if his company hired a red team to test their security.

But I knew better.

This was a pro job.

And that was why the police wanted to speak to me.

I'd never shared this with Coogan, but I had that training. With the right support, I could've gotten into his office and taken those files. The SVR would know that.

The LAPD interviewed all of the firm's staff and knew I'd been issued a badge and access card. Said I needed to come in and account for my movements that night. Which of course I couldn't do. No one could.

The SVR would know that too.

Too much of this still didn't fit.

Nate validated Fedorov's claims about the GRU's involvement. But it was a different service, and a fierce rival at that, who'd kidnapped and interrogated me. Presumably, the SVR were the ones who broke into Case Ritter too. And, I assumed, my house.

Had the Kremlin dispatched the SVR to clean up after the GRU's screw-up?

That could explain why they tried bringing Fedorov in from Minsk.

The Kremlin pitted all of their intelligence services against each other to keep any one of them from getting to be too powerful.

Coogan said I was a "person of interest" for now. I told him that was complete bullshit. He agreed, but the partners were freaking out. He suggested I turn myself in to the police and clear it up quickly.

The next part, though, was icier than coldcocking a blind man.

"Matt, the partners have said I may continue to represent Jennie in the matter of her incarceration but that we have to wrap it up quickly. They will not allow me to represent you, in any matter. I have a list of firms that I can recommend—"

I set the phone on the table and just let Coogan continue talking. Eventually, I hit the disconnect button. I left Ray's.

Everything was now at risk.

The SVR had the names of everyone Jennie spoke to. Every lead. They had CINDER SPIRE, whatever the hell that was. They had the "Charlie Auer" alias, his email, and the email record of his contact with Jennie.

I didn't have the time to waste trying to convince the LAPD that I was in San Francisco being interrogated by Russian intelligence officers instead of breaking into a law office. No one could confirm that for certain, not even Nate. I thought about calling Nate and having him tell the police I was with him, but they'd ask questions about what we were doing. And that would inevitably bring us back to my captors.

To be clear, I agreed that giving the police a full accounting was the right thing to do, I just couldn't afford to do it now.

Their theory was bullshit anyway. What reason could I possibly have for breaking into a law office and stealing my client's files?

I quickly packed and headed for the airport, changing tomorrow's flight to an overnight. Again, a four-digit first-class ticket.

From the airport lounge, I sent out a flurry of messages on Signal, informing Jennie's contacts that their information had been compromised and by whom. For those who didn't have Signal accounts, I risked phone calls or texts, knowing it'd be late in the evening for them.

Most importantly, I called Connor. It was morning where he was.

"Connor, listen, I don't have a lot of time."

"Jesus, what now?" he said, exasperation evident. Though I knew it was at the situation rather than me.

"Before she was arrested, Jennie turned all of her research—notes, contacts, transcripts, recordings, all of it—over to her attorney so the government couldn't take it as evidence. He secured it in a safe at the firm. The night the Russians grabbed me, someone broke into the law office, dismantled the safe, and took everything."

"Oh shit."

"That's exactly right. Jennie never identified you by name, but the 'Charlie Auer' alias is in there, along with whatever contact information you gave her. I'd delete everything you have, scrub all of your devices of the Auer legend and any contact you'd had with Jennie."

"Jesus Christ. Okay. Shit." The outgassing of profanity was a natural part of the processing. I knew how he felt.

Connor was in trouble now, and serious. Because of his connection, however tenuous, to a Russian intelligence operation, he had an obligation to notify the Agency's counterintelligence unit. However, doing so would expose his participation in an unauthorized exfiltration and everything that followed.

I didn't have time to get into that with him, and his career was not my problem. Connor was responsible for his own choices, I could only hope he made the right ones.

"Does this mean Fedorov is exposed?"

"We have to assume he's in imminent danger. Now, under questioning, I lied and said I'd stashed him in Zürich. Hopefully, that buys us a little time. At least enough for me to get to Brussels. I'm flying there, after a quick stop in Washington."

"What do you need from me?"

I froze, unable to answer the question. I was in a place so far removed from reality, I didn't even know how to ask for help. Instead, I stalled. "Just keep your phone near and watch your back. Stay on top of regional security and counterintelligence reports. Let me know if you get any hits. I don't want you any more exposed than you already are."

It was early in DC when I landed, and I got downtown before traffic turned into cooling tar. I got a hotel downtown, changed the bandages on my wounds, and then called Denis. Since he was already briefed on my abduction and interrogation, I could just focus on Case Ritter and how I'd been cut off from my lifeline here in the States. Denis reassured me the Foundation would continue to cover my expenses, and they'd see about other representation. In his defense, he hadn't seen an expense report yet. I told him I was in Washington for one day and would be in Brussels tomorrow. He promised to notify Belgian authorities and hire security guards for the office.

For all the good that would do.

I told Denis I'd see him in Brussels.

Assuming I wasn't a fugitive.

The anonymous tip would've been a perfect frame-up if I hadn't escaped. The breadth of it didn't hit me until I'd had time to process. Fired ex-spy breaks into law office and steals document to keep his reporter girlfriend's national security violation out of the public eye. It was just stupid enough to be believable.

Since I was here, I decided to call Danzig.

This was risky. I didn't *think* there was enough to arrest me on; I also didn't want to test that theory too far.

"Hi—"

"You need to turn around and get the goddamn hell back to Los Angeles, Matt," Special Agent Katrina Danzig of the Federal Bureau of Investigation calmly advised. And by "calmly," I mean "practically screamed into the phone."

"Will you hold on a minute?"

"No, I will not. You are a person of interest in a police investigation. The LAPD brought the Bureau in to consult. Your name was flagged, for obvious reasons in our systems, and because I have sinned, they called me." I could hear the genuine weariness in her voice.

"Stop yelling and let me explain. Where can I meet you?"

"No, Matt. If you were in any deeper shit, you'd need a snorkel. Look, I know you didn't do it. But you need to turn yourself in and give them an airtight alibi for where you were."

"Why in the goddamned hell would I break into my client's law office and steal her files? It makes zero sense." I regretted the outburst as soon as the words were out of my mouth. Danzig was my friend, had stood tall for me many times, and deserved better. The realization sparked that she didn't know. About San Francisco, or Anton Malyshkin, any of it.

"Rawlings is making waves about this, which means it's probably coming from Damon Fox. They're saying you're trying to disappear evidence before Justice can get it in discovery."

"That's farfetched, even for them," I said.

"They're going to yank your license, Matt."

"I'm sorry for snapping at you. There's an explanation for all of this, but we probably shouldn't do it over the phone. Where are you now? Can we meet?"

"I'm already at the office. There's a sculpture garden on Constitution, across from the National Archives."

"Okay. I can be there in ten minutes," I said.

I was fried, mentally and physically. I'd needed another few nights of good sleep to fully recover from my ordeal with the Russians. Nate also suggested some sessions with a trauma counselor, as if I had time for that. My dreams were...not good. Mostly light-flicker images and feeling like I was drowning.

And I'd killed someone.

Not wanting to fight for parking this time of day, I took a rideshare to the sculpture garden.

Moving like a poorly constructed marionette, I limped across the grounds and sought shelter beneath a tree. Not that it did any good against the heat. While I waited, I watched people across the street queuing to enter the National Archives for a chance to glimpse some of the most consequential documents in history.

"This better be earth-shatteringly good."

Turning at the torso, I saw Danzig fast-walking up to me. Her jacket mostly covered the service pistol clipped to her waistband, and I attributed her attitude as more to do with being forced to wear a jacket in this heat and less with me.

"Jesus Christ, Matt," she said, just shy of breathless when she saw me.

"You want to know why I couldn't have broken into *my* lawyer's office? Because at that exact moment, I was being transported up to San Francisco. An SVR hit squad knocked me out and kidnapped me out of Case Ritter's garage. I woke up about a day later, turns out, in the basement of the Russian consulate. We had a few rounds of Q and A." I lifted up my shirt to show the welts, bruises, and bandages. "I don't even know where most of these came from. These," I pointed to my ribs with my other hand, "are from a generator and alligator clips." I let go of my shirt, and it fell back into place. "They were going to put me on a boat and take me to Moscow for a 'trial.'" I was in a bad enough mood that I included air quotes. "I escaped before they put me on the boat. Nate McKellar will verify this. I called him after I escaped and spent the night at his house. The Russians know I've put most of this together and are trying to take me out. Pretty sure they called in the 'anonymous tip' the LAPD is working off of." I gave her the chain of events, both in LA and SF, and what I assumed the Russians' strategy was.

And I told her what Denis relayed to me about the sabotage.

Danzig exhaled, put her hands on her hips, and tried to will the tension from her voice. It half worked. "I should've guessed that was you." Danzig's last posting had been in San Francisco and only left for DC a few weeks ago. Doubtless, she'd have heard about this right away.

"That is also why you need to get your ass back to Los Angeles before they hang an arrest warrant on you. You should be able to clear it up in a few days."

"We don't have that kind of time," I said, not masking the urgency. "They have all of Jennie's leads. Her research. Her contacts and where to find them. This is the national security risk that you people should be worried about, not whether or not someone told her a secret. Look, Fedorov is the key to this thing. He can prove the GRU built an energy weapon—microwaves, ultrasonic sound, something like that—and that they used it on us. I was fifty-fifty on him until San Francisco. Now I know how far they'll go to silence this thing."

"My colleagues in SF say it was the SVR. Is that what you heard?"

"Yeah. The SVR was watching Fedorov in Minsk, too. I think they're the ones trying to clean up the mess."

"Where is Fedorov now?"

"He's safe," I said. Danzig blanched, but I shook my head. "I'm not telling you unless we can work out some kind of deal. He says he's got hard proof but won't share it unless there is a guarantee of asylum."

"I understand he asked for that and was denied," she said. We both knew what she meant. Danzig was well informed for someone who wasn't assigned to this, but Rawlings was probably back-channeling to her in hopes that she'd feed him something.

"I came here because I need help." I waved a hand over my body. "You saw what they did to me. They're going to kill Fedorov as soon as they find him and burn whatever he's got."

"Are you willing to sit back down with Rawlings and tell him everything you know?"

"If you can promise me we'll take care of Fedorov."

Danzig took her sunglasses off and pinched the bridge of her nose.

"If you agree to meet with Rawlings, I'll get Fedorov an interview with us and State. If his intel is good, they might be persuaded to grant him asylum. We can also look at covert resettlement. Again, if he's legit. If the Russians are targeting American companies, or our allies, that's something we'd want to know."

"And what if his information goes against the government's narrative about Havana?"

"You know damned well I can't influence that. I'm a cop, I don't make policy."

"I'm not asking you to. I just need to know that I'm not going to risk my life to bring him back here only to have Rawlings pull a vanishing act."

"Jesus Christ, Matt, will you listen to yourself? Everything isn't a conspiracy, and the government isn't some massive machine designed to grind you up in its gears."

Could've fooled me.

"Damon Fox tried to get me to give him everything Jennie had, sell her out. In exchange, he was going to wipe my slate. Offered to bring me on as a contractor, and a highly paid one. I told him to go to hell. Not ten minutes later, Cedric Rawlings rolls up on me, lights and sirens, and I spend three days in the hole. Threatens me with espionage charges. Seems to me, someone in government is really nervous about Jennie's story getting out. And maybe, just maybe, there's a good reason for that. So, if my source can prove the GRU created a weapon and used it against us and caused thousands of casualties among embassy personnel over the last decade, it sort of goes against the narrative that the Intelligence Community and the administration have been trumpeting as fact, doesn't it. You'll forgive me if I'm just a little skeptical about making a trade."

I watched the storm clouds build on Danzig's face, her skin flush with the leading edges of fury and then quickly dissipate.

"Matt, you are my friend, and I care what happens to you. I am worried about you. I'm worried that your personal feelings about Burkhardt are undermining your objectivity." She held up a hand to ward off a protest. "For once, please don't argue. I also worry that your experience at the Agency is clouding your judgment. I'm not saying that those feelings aren't justified, just that I think you're truly not thinking clearly here." She paused and made sure that she controlled my absolute attention. "Now, you need to listen to this carefully. Rawlings has video footage from that train platform in Belarus. I don't know how he got it."

"I can give you a couple guesses," I said. That's normally the surprise evidence they throw on you in an interrogation to knock you off-balance so much you've got no choice but to cooperate. If Danzig was telling me, that could only mean Rawlings told her and they were still interested in some kind of deal. The "what" and "why" remained unclear.

Danzig grimaced and continued. "You are very quickly running out of options. Rawlings can put you in Belarus now. I haven't seen the footage, but I know it shows you and Fyodor Vasiliev fighting. It also shows him getting shot, but you're out of frame, so that doesn't help your case. We don't know yet if that part is doctored. Now that you've got this thing in Los Angeles—which I agree is bullshit, but you must recognize that it is a thing until it isn't—Rawlings has enough that he can move on you. He can arrest you. You say Fedorov shot him, turning him in is going to be the only way you clear your name."

"But what happens when I do?"

"Well, he's got to account for where his information came from. You've already admitted the GRU used him to steal trade secrets from the US and our allies. That will have to be reconciled. We don't particularly care if he shot an SVR officer, but someone does. We also care that you are complicit in his escape. At a minimum, you're guilty of smuggling him into Lithuania."

Irony was an asshole sometimes. Fedorov had his passport on him, we just couldn't use it.

"Kat, I appreciate your telling me this. And I'm sorry that I got you involved."

"Bring Fedorov in and turn him over to us. We'll debrief him on the Havana stuff, but I can't make promises there."

"I understand."

"Matt, this is your best shot at staying out of jail. Maybe your only one."

22

I spent the rest of the day making phone calls, warning Jennie's contacts about what was coming, following up on the messages I'd sent out while in flight. Colonel Mercer still wouldn't answer the phone. Neither would Rick Hicks, and he'd asked me not to call him, but I needed to warn him anyway. Reactions from Jennie's sources were generally what you'd expect for a situation like this.

Audrey Farre summarized the broad sentiment.

"I fucking *knew* I shouldn't have talked to her. God. This is what I get for trying to do the right thing."

"I'm sorry, Audrey," was all I could say. She had a right to be scared. Her life was forever changed. The bad guys knew her name and where to find her, worse, they knew she had information they wanted to keep quiet.

She hung up on me.

There was little left to do here. The leads had run out. All I could do was fly to Brussels and pray I got to Fedorov before the Russians did. We had to assume they were coming for him.

I didn't hear from my mysterious contact until late in the afternoon. I only had today to meet with this guy. My flight to Brussels was in the morning.

"Gage," I said.

"Are you ready to meet?"

"Yeah, and I'm running short on time. It needs to be today."

"I can agree to that. However, I have two conditions," he said. Because of course he had conditions. I'd finally noticed a tinny, almost mechanical quality to his voice. Like he was speaking through a bad connection or a very cheap phone.

Before I could even agree to it, he said, "First, I will never agree to be interviewed. I'll talk only to you. Second, you cannot use anything I give you on background."

"No dice."

"What?"

"Is the connection bad? I said no. If I talk to you, and Jennie Burkhardt can't use that in her reporting, what is the point?"

"I thought you were interested in the truth."

"If I can't share it, it's just trivia. Fun facts. The point to all this is to hold people accountable. You offering to tell me something I can't do anything with is a waste of my time."

"My name cannot be associated with this…situation."

Jesus, I hated this town. No one could give you a straight answer, and everyone was too important for the unvarnished truth.

"I have a vested interest in the facts getting out, Mr. Gage, but my involvement must remain a secret. A reporter being in jail to protect her sources is a noble thing, but I don't want her resolve to be my last line of defense."

"Look, you've contacted me twice claiming to have information useful to my case, but you're also putting conditions on that saying I can't give what I learn to Ms. Burkhardt. So, why is this worth my time?"

"Because I can prove the White House knew the Russians attacked our embassies, and I can prove the weapon they used to do it is responsible for Havana Syndrome. I promise it will be worth your time. I'll text you an address at eight p.m. You'll have fifteen minutes. Be in Northwest DC."

"All right. I'll be wearing a—"

"That won't be necessary."

He clicked off.

Okay, then. Not at all weird or ominous.

The text came at the expected time.

Vote was still out on whether this was a bad sting.

An address, as well as instructions to park several blocks away and approach from the alley behind the house. The address was on R Street, which is the affluent part of Georgetown, if that tells you anything.

I left my rental car on 32nd Street, beneath the canopy of hundred-year-old maple trees and yellow streetlights. The houses on this string of blocks were three-story city mansions and suggested connections to power that couldn't be measured with such pedestrian concepts as "money." Cutting up the middle of Reservoir, I found the alley indicated in the message. Well, an "alley" only relative to the houses that fronted it. This was fancy boulevard anywhere else in the country.

I found the house at the top of the alley, hidden behind ten-foot concrete walls with iron bars on top and enough trees to start a forest. There was a detached garage facing the street. A form emerged from the darkness when I got close enough to be a threat. Man, late twenties, military haircut and build, navy polo and khakis. He had an earpiece and a visible sidearm.

"What's your name?"

"Matt Gage," I said.

"ID?"

"I am now reaching for my wallet," I said, and did. I removed my PI license and handed it to him. The man surveyed it in the half light and handed it back.

"You can go through, sir." He motioned with a knife-hand for the property. "You can access the residence through the patio. One of my associates will see you up."

He opened the wrought iron gate, and I slid through. I stayed on the walkway so as not to trigger any of the half dozen alarms I assumed would be on the lawn. It was clear that no one over twenty pounds had walked on it in some time. A long pool stretched nearly from the back fence to the patio. Water burbled softly in the darkness.

I walked briskly to the house, noting that the exterior lights on the ground floor were off. There was a wide concrete patio, with stairs up to the main floor. The entire area was shrouded in darkness. I ascended the steps, staying close to the right side, which was shielded by one of the wings. A door at the top of the steps opened, revealing a dim wedge of light. "This way, Mr. Gage."

What the hell was this?

The house was mostly dark, except for the parts that I needed to move through, but I could see it was decorated with generational wealth.

The guard who let me in wore a jacket and announced my entry to the next link in the chain through a lapel mic. He led me through an opulent maze to a door with a band of light shining through the gap beneath it. The low thunder of hard bop jazz resonated through the door. It seemed off. I'd have expected Wagner.

The guard opened the door, exchanged a look and a nod with someone inside who I couldn't see, and then motioned for me to enter. The room's single occupant stood to greet me, and I understood the security.

Former National Security Advisor and Ambassador, Joshua McDonough.

McDonough headed the prior administration's national security team, though he'd been a fixture in Washington power circles since the eighties. An avowed interventionist, he'd once offhandedly quipped on a Sunday talk show that he'd "organized a coup d'etat." The revelation, for anyone else, would've been scandalous. For McDonough, it simply validated his reputation, if not raison d'être.

The door closed behind me.

"Have a seat, Mr. Gage. Can I get you a drink?" McDonough spoke with a voice that was raspy with age and authoritative from experience.

I noted the tumbler of whiskey next to his massive leather chair. It'd be rude to refuse.

"Sure," I said. I walked into the room. It was a quaint study, in the ways that rooms in a castle could be understated and sublime. The decor played to type, vaulted ceiling and dark bookcases on most of the walls, with paintings of ships and busts of Greek philosophers in between. Seemed a little cliché to me, until I realized that the owner probably was the reason that cliché existed.

McDonough poured me a glass from a crystal decanter and handed it to me. He was a hard man to miss in a crowd, and I didn't fault him for the subterfuge. McDonough cut a tall, looming presence, with a high mound of gray hair and a bushy, drooping mustache. The man was immediately recognizable for his numerous and highly visible roles over the last two decades and frequent appearances on the Sunday talk circuit.

I accepted the glass, sniffed it, and took a sip. This was exceptional scotch, and I'd wager it was bottled during the Cold War. So, here's to symbolism.

McDonough sat, and then I took the chair opposite him.

"Of all the people I expected to see on the other side of that door, Mr. McDonough, I have to admit, you were not on that list. You've got an impressive home."

"Oh, this isn't mine. This is a friend who agreed to let me borrow his library for the evening while he's out of the country."

Yeah, I could guess the type. The kind of people who use "summer" as a verb.

"You've still got a security detail?" I asked.

"No, I need to pay for that myself, unfortunately. Hopefully, it's not permanent. The IRGC has a standing kill order on me. Apparently, we did one too many drone strikes." He chuckled in a way that conveyed no humor and at something that wasn't a joke. The Islamic Revolutionary Guard Corps were the Iranian paramilitary fanatics that bolstered the Ayatollahs, keeping the theocracy in place, and had a notoriously poor sense of humor. McDonough was believed to have recommended, if not directed, the assassination of an infamous Iranian general several years ago.

"I know something about your history," he said.

Not surprising that he maintained contacts in the Agency. Since the Agency's shift in focus post-9/11 from pure intelligence gathering to aggressive counterterrorism, there was a strong cadre of officers, many of whom were now in senior leadership, that believed in the same kind of interventionism as McDonough.

It was fair to assume that he knew most of the Agency brass, from his time as National Security Advisor. The comment was intended to remind me of that, and of the power dynamic extant in this room.

"And I know a little of yours. Which is why I'm curious that we're speaking."

"It's no secret that I have little in common with the current president." He said "current" as a way of underscoring the transitory nature of the thing. It wasn't hard to guess what he implied. "These attacks began during my tenure. We quickly determined the Russians were behind it, a conclusion supported by your former organization." McDonough sipped his whiskey and set the tumbler on a stand, next to a volume of Churchill's writings. I doubted that was a coincidence. "In '19, we were attending a series of meetings in London with the British government. Three members of my personal staff were attacked on that trip. Two of them are suffering considerably to this day, one cannot work. Unfortunately, my tenure with that administration ended shortly thereafter, so I was not in a position to do anything about it."

Ahh, that's right. He'd had a rather public disagreement with his notably volatile boss and resigned. McDonough, I suspected, was the type of person for whom personal loyalty was a gravitational force. He expected it, demanded it even, of his subordinates, but returned it in kind. As a policymaker and power broker, McDonough would never have been in a position to avenge his personnel. People who wouldn't have been in that position but for their loyalty to him. Now, he was compelled to do something about it.

"I understand your boss didn't want to antagonize the Kremlin," I said.

"That is correct. My disagreement with him was mostly about that, though I made it about other things when discussing publicly. I didn't want Moscow knowing the truth of it."

"You contacted me because you think I can help you, is that it?" I asked. "People loyal to you were hurt, and you think I might be in a position to help you. That's what this is about."

"Thus, my question about what are your interests here. I hope this is about more than just getting your girlfriend out of jail."

"Your intel is about twenty-five years out of date, but sure. I think the FBI arrested her because the government is scared that Jennie's reporting proves Russian culpability. Further, it shows that this Intelligence Community finding is bullshit. If not entirely manufactured. That's not why I took this case. And I've seen first-hand these conditions weren't caused by broken AC units, or crickets, or whatever bullshit they've come up with."

I cut myself off there. McDonough hadn't earned the right to anything else.

McDonough studied me. His craggy face was expressionless, except for the slight bobbing of his mustache, which I imagined was a sizable workout for his upper lip.

"Then it appears, Mr. Gage, that we're temporarily aligned." McDonough leaned back in his chair and picked his scotch back up. He drew a distinction on "temporary."

I understood, then, the depth of potential trouble I was navigating.

Joshua McDonough was a powerful man. He tended to get what he wanted and, I could imagine, could be quite vindictive when he did not.

As evidenced by his coup d'etat comment. Not that he did it, but that he was brazen enough to discuss it on a talk show.

"The national security community is a small one. Many of the staffs, those who are below the level of political appointment, tend to stay in their roles irrespective of who the current political officials are. This is essential for continuity on issues that transcend political boundaries. Such as this one."

There's only so much pontificating I can take when I'm not being paid for the trouble, and I'd already passed my limit.

Time to cut to it.

"What is CINDER SPIRE?"

He chuckled slightly. "Straight to the point, I like that. You're well informed. Or, Ms. Burkhardt is. There's about ten people on earth who know that name." He paused to study my face, assess my resolve. I could back out of this now. Cryptonyms only held secrets, and this was one I wasn't meant to know. Learning about it could have consequences, severe ones. McDonough was testing me; he was also giving me an out. I could keep that specific genie bottled, if I chose. I said nothing, but my expression said to get on with it. He took a drink and set his glass down. "Very well. It's the code word for a covert operation we devised during my tenure in the White House, working in collaboration with your old organization. We defined the outcome we wanted, and spooks came up with a plan. The intent was for it to be reciprocity for Havana. We were going to hit them where it hurt, reallocate billions they had stashed in foreign banks and then destabilize their operations in Africa. Cutting them off from the precious metals and rare earths they've been extracting would lose them billions more and put us in a position to recapture the initiative there. We had a presidential finding authorizing us to present options, and we advised the Senate Intelligence Committee of potential covert action, which I suspect is how you found out about it."

Now I understood why he'd shared this with me.

This was staggeringly secret. I could go to jail just knowing this existed. If I told anyone, I'd get locked into one of those cells they don't make keys for.

In telling me, McDonough sealed us in a pact that I could never betray.

I'd give him this, he was a diabolical son of a bitch. Good to keep in mind when the offer came.

"I left the White House before we could enact it, but the plan remained on the books." By "the books," he likely meant in a file that the National Security Council's Russia desk would have. That explained why Colonel Mercer wouldn't take my calls. I wondered if he'd told McDonough I was asking.

"What does CINDER SPIRE have to do with the 2021 Geneva Summit? I learned about one in context of the other. I know POTUS had an off-the-record chat with his opposite number there. He threaten the Russians with it?"

McDonough chuckled again. "When it came time to have the summit, the plan found some new life. Unfortunately, now they wanted it to be something of a stick, an 'or else.'" McDonough leaned forward in the chair, the leather creaked. "In the months leading up to the summit, Havana Syndrome cases had reached their highest-ever levels. And it'd now spanned two different administrations, so we knew that it wasn't retribution for a particular president's actions. At this point, everyone in the know knows Moscow is responsible. It was the worst-kept secret in town, in a town where leaking is a varsity sport."

"But you're outside the walls at this point," I said. "And not a friend of the administration, I could tell that much from the Sunday TV hits."

"As I said, there is continuity between successive administrations in national security. Strategic issues like arms control and terrorism don't fundamentally change just because a president does. Or at least they shouldn't. Some like-minded colleagues remained on the National Security Council staff, and we kept in touch. As the White House prepared for the summit, they knew they needed some options to come to the table with, in case the Kremlin refused to back down. CINDER SPIRE found new life. The plan was attractive to them since it'd already been vetted by the requisite congressional authorities. And since the plan had technically been developed by the previous administration, they had a level of deniability should it have been leaked. It showed a level of sophistication I didn't think that team was capable of." The wings of his mustache took flight in what must've been his version of a smile.

"So, POTUS has this off-the-record chat with Putin and tells him to knock the attacks off, or CINDER SPIRE?"

"You're getting warmer, but I still wouldn't serve the dish." McDonough reached for his drink. "I've been at this game a long time, Mr. Gage. *Every president in the last twenty-five years believed they could 'manage' Russia*, could negotiate with them, could curtail them. They were all of them failures. What they refuse to understand is that the Kremlin only views the world in terms of chess. *Everything* is a game, moves and countermoves."

This would be a fascinating lecture in a grad school class on great power politics, but it wasn't answering my question. He confirmed what I suspected, though not in a way we could use. And it still wasn't clear what McDonough wanted from this.

At least the scotch was good.

"So far, you haven't told me anything I didn't already know, except for filling in some of the details on CINDER SPIRE. Which doesn't really help the story." I slid forward in my chair, a subtle signal that I was getting ready to rise.

"CINDER was the stick, Matt, but you never asked about the carrot."

People talk about "oh shit" moments a lot, but unless you've experienced one, I don't think you can appreciate that instant of perfect, terrible clarity. It's a lot like that last breath before a traffic accident when you realize everything is about to come to an absolute and abrupt stop.

"Because the Intelligence Community report was the carrot," I said, slowly. The corners of McDonough's mouth drew up into a smile at a rate eerily paced to the cadence of my words.

"Everybody walks away," he said, spreading his hands in a flourish. "If you know this president, then you know that he's more the carrot type. He's not doing anything that's going to risk a war with a nuclear power."

"The nerve," I deadpanned.

"The report was a way for the White House to back down from the potential of conflict with Russia."

"That doesn't make any sense. The Russians attacked us, repeatedly, and you expect me to believe that the president went into that summit to give them a way out?"

"Of course I do." Anyone else would've said, *Believe what you want.* "Think about it, Gage. What is the world like in 2021? We know the Russians are about to invade Ukraine. The entire world is in the midst of a pandemic. The Chinese are credibly threatening Taiwan. And those are just the biggest pieces, they are by no means all. This is not the time to go picking fights with a nuclear power."

"Sounds like you agree with him," I said.

"Not quite, but suffice it to say that I understand the statecraft at play. And the stakes."

"Well, they traded an awful lot, and it didn't work."

One of McDonough's caterpillar eyebrows lifted a few notches. "What do you mean?"

"I don't think Vlad is living up to his end of the bargain. There was an attack in Vilnius last year at the NATO summit."

McDonough lifted his glass from the side table. "Yes, well, I would not be surprised to learn that the Kremlin had no knowledge of that beforehand."

"Seriously," I said, incredulous. "You really think there's something going on here that Putin didn't personally authorize?"

A throaty, rattling sound poured out of his mouth that I discovered was intended to be a laugh. "You, of all people, should know how much they outsource. Think of their cyberattacks. The GRU is responsible for many, but not all. Often, they give exploits, 'hacks' in the common parlance, to criminal organizations and have them carry it out. Most of the cybercrime against the global banking system is done by transnational criminal outfits using tools created by Russian intelligence. Putin encourages it. The only standing rule is they can't target any Russian interests."

It hardly seemed possible, that the GRU would give a weapon like this to a contractor or, God forbid, an organized crime outfit. Or that the Kremlin would allow something like that out of their control, especially after a deal was made that let them escape without any accountability.

But the idea that Moscow would risk the relative stability by going back on the 2021 arrangement, especially now that they were overcommitted fighting in Ukraine, didn't track either.

There was more to this question, and the answer was critically important to the case.

"What do you get out of this, McDonough? Why come forward, and to me?" I asked.

"Oh, I want the same thing that you do, though for somewhat different reasons. The Kremlin must be held in check. We reduced our military presence in Europe, and Russia invaded Ukraine. They attack us constantly in cyberspace and farm those capabilities out to criminal organizations to do their bidding. They've practically kicked us out of sub-Saharan Africa. They must learn that will not be tolerated. I also think that this report is, pardon my language, a crock of shit."

"No argument there. How do you see an investigative journalist helping with that?"

"It's no secret I'm not a big fan of the press. Oh, it can be a useful tool on occasion, but broadly speaking, I think the best secrets are kept."

"You don't want this getting out, do you?" I asked. "You just want the *threat* that it might."

McDonough spread his hands. "As much as I would like for the president to get egg on his face for even proposing something as stupid as this, let alone actually *doing* it, we need to be mindful of the broader consequences."

"You mean consequences for the administration should the story get out that the report is fabricated? Call me naive, I thought that was the point."

"It is naive, yes. Mr. Gage, we have a president not running for reelection. What, exactly, do you think happens to him? Precisely nothing, is what. Oh, there will be demands from the public, and Congress might even act on them. The Agency, and others, will get dragged into hearings and, in all likelihood, we'll have another Church Committee. You know as well as I do that crippled clandestine operations for a generation."

He wasn't entirely wrong there. But he wasn't entirely right, either.

The Church Committee, a Senate select committee in 1975 led by Senator Frank Church, was an investigation into allegations of the CIA and FBI spying on American citizens. The subsequent reporting revealed not only that but also a campaign of assassinations, regime changes, and other active measures throughout the world. This opinion wasn't exactly popular in the Agency, but a lot of bad things were exposed, and I thought it was justified. Though, in an effort to "reform," they gutted the Directorate of Operations and seriously undermined the Agency's human intelligence collection. That action had dangerous aftershocks for almost twenty years.

"Maybe the president skates, but there are people beneath him that won't. And this should absolutely be exposed. My client isn't going to spike her story so that some future generation of spies can get quiet payback against the Russians. For the record, that doesn't work for me either."

"Maybe not. Then again, maybe it does."

His words hung in the air between us.

He waited for me to ask him why. He needed me to do it to reinforce the power dynamic. I didn't want to give him the satisfaction. So, I leaned forward in my chair and squinted my eyes to match his, just a few degrees short of late '60s Eastwood. We stayed there, unblinking and unflinching, long after it was ridiculous, because I hated the stupid gamesmanship that was coin of the realm here and I wasn't going to let him win.

McDonough stood, strode over to the bar, and refilled his tumbler from the decanter.

"Washington runs on three things," he said as he poured. "Money, bullshit, and favors." He replaced the decanter on the runner and returned to his seat. "As it happens, I have quite a bank of the latter. I have a vested interest in seeing the Russians punished for this. While I don't expect the president to publicly overrule his National Intelligence Council, it would be entirely possible for 'new evidence' to emerge. They even acknowledge this in that report of theirs. This change in direction would give certain actors... freedom of movement. This is unlikely to occur if the president is humiliated in the press for his rather dubious negotiations, however justified that may be." McDonough paused to let his words seep into my consciousness. He knew how to sell an idea, I'd give him that.

"Mr. McDonough, that's a great line about what Washington runs on. Let me tell you what *I* run on. Straight answers. You got fired in the last administration and are no friend to this one. Why am I talking to you about anything? Do you seriously believe you can attack the president on the Sunday talk show circuit and then convince them to quietly overturn the Havana Syndrome report?"

McDonough stared at me, as if I was somehow stupid for having to vocalize it.

"There are enough news outlets looking at this story that the White House, and the broader Intelligence Community, is worried it's going to get out. I am offering a way for them to correct the narrative without losing too much face. The fact that the Russians have already reneged on the deal just gives them more of an incentive to do so. However, I restate my framing argument, that they will not go for this if a reporter exposes that report for what it was."

"What about the victims?" I asked.

"Well, once the Intelligence Community is forced to formally reconcile their position, they'll be much more inclined to support those claims. People will get help. If the IC is made to look foolish, I doubt those same leaders will be willing to change course. Remember what I said about Washington running on favors."

Then, he dropped his bomb. "In exchange for your assistance, I can have the charges against Ms. Burkhardt withdrawn."

"How?" I said quickly. In truth, I was knocked flat, but I wasn't going to show my belly to Joshua McDonough.

"You will just have to trust that I can handle things on my end," he returned with an equal deadpan.

And there's that *second* thing he said this town is run on.

I leaned back in my chair, took up the tumbler, and had a solid pull.

"You're asking a lot and giving nothing in return but your word. No offense to you, Mr. McDonough, but we run in different circles. Your word isn't worth to me what you think it is."

To my great surprise, he laughed at that.

"No, I suppose it wouldn't be." Then, just as quickly as it flared, the playful light in his eyes died and his face was again a grim and craggy visage. "All you need to know is my government career began in the Justice Department, and I forged deep and lasting relationships. I wouldn't have proposed this if I didn't know I could deliver on it."

"You'll appreciate that this isn't entirely my decision to make," I said.

"I do." There was more than a hint of tired annoyance in that response. It irritated him that I wouldn't just decide to do the thing he wanted me to do in the moment.

"How long do I have before you need an answer?"

"Not long. Is there something more important?"

"Yes."

"And that would be?"

"I'm trying to prevent a murder, and we'll leave it at that."

On the surface, this was certainly what *I* wanted. Dylan West and the others would get the recognition and treatment they'd deserved. The Agency would, at some point, carry out retribution against the perpetrators. I'd have Damon Fox end up owing me a favor. I harbored no illusions that he'd ever pay it back, but he'd live the rest of his life knowing that I had the truth of it. And that I could expose him whenever I wanted. Most importantly, Jennie would be released from confinement and all charges dropped.

All it meant was convincing Jennie to spike the thing she'd gone to jail to protect.

23

On the flight to Brussels, I was reminded that I was only a couple days outside of insufficient recovery from violent torture.

I hoped my justifying the International first class ticket as "medically necessary" would cut it. Judging by how I still looked in the mirror, I suspected it would.

I landed in the late afternoon and was glad to learn everyone here was still alive.

Brussels is a quirky town, unlike any other in Europe. Cartoons and animation aren't just art forms here, they're cultural icons. The juxtaposition of the thoughts racing through my mind—how to protect myself and my colleagues from a Russian hit squad—while looking at statues of the Smurfs, the Snorks, and Asterix throughout the city was cognitively divergent enough to be hilarious.

The Orpheus Foundation office was in a historic building in Brussels's city center. One of Denis's staff met me outside to give me a badge for the elevator and walk me through their security procedures, introduce me to the hired guards they had. From there, it was to the war room where Denis, Fedorov, and a few others camped out.

The room was on the third floor, overlooking the street. The shades were down, and I saw they had small ultrasonic generators beneath the glass. These created visually imperceptible vibrations across the surface and frustrated any attempt to use laser microphones to eavesdrop. The conference room table had stacks of papers, with Post-it notes and colored tags sticking out at odd angles. The whiteboard had markings scrawled in English, Belgian-Fench, and Russian, and in half a dozen colors. It was stuffy and felt lived in.

Denis, wearing his usual black hoodie and jeans, rose when I entered the room. I could tell immediately that he was exhausted, and the eyes behind those glasses looked haunted. Fedorov stood too. He wore chinos and a button-down that didn't suit him. We exchanged a look, but no words.

We sat, and Denis asked for his other employees to leave the room.

I said, "This is where we are. The SVR knows about Grigori's escape and that I helped. They assume the US government facilitated it, and I wasn't in a position to convince them otherwise. They interrogated and tortured me, intended to take me back to Moscow. I was lucky to escape. They have everything that Jennie Burkhardt collected for this story. Thousands of pages of research, names of sources, and their contact information. We should assume both of you are at risk. Though, I think I threw them off the scent and they don't know you're here."

"How did you do that?" Fedorov asked.

"I'd rather not say," I said. I still saw Malyshkin's leering, shadowy face every time I closed my eyes. "I spoke with a friend in the FBI. She said that she could arrange for you to meet with someone to debrief and assess what you have to offer. There's no guarantee of resettlement or protection, just a chance that they will hear you out."

Fedorov shrugged. "It's better than what I have right now."

"Maybe, maybe not. There is the question of how you acquired this information. They may decide to arrest you, or extradite you to Germany or France. I made as good of a case as I could. If what you have to offer is good, they may not charge you." I spread my hands. "You deserved to know what you were walking into."

"I appreciate that, and for you telling me the truth."

"I hate to sound callous, but does that affect our ability to tell the story? And what about Jennie?" Denis asked.

"Probably that you can't use anything Grigori gives them in a deposition. This is a part of the law I'm unclear on, but given the lengths my government has gone through to control this narrative, assume she can't use anything from his testimony until it's public record."

"I see," Denis said.

I didn't tell them about my meeting with Joshua McDonough or the offer he made.

"The other option is we tell the FBI no thanks. Jennie's lawyer is working on getting her released to home confinement. If he's successful, she writes the story based on Grigori's information. With this option, the idea is to create enough momentum in the public that the government's case is undermined by the weight of fact. Or that the revelations in Fedorov's materials are so explosive, what they have doesn't matter. We do need to clear something up first."

"The weapons discrepancy," Denis said.

I turned to Fedorov. "Grigori, I know you didn't design the weapon, but I don't doubt that your handler had you secretly buying components. After getting burned by the US embassy in Vilnius, you felt like you needed to amplify your position a little. So, you made up the part about designing them."

Fedorov flashed red with embarrassment, and his eyes fell to the table.

"For whatever it's worth, I don't fault you. I don't think there was any malice intended. You just want to live to see the end of this." I looked at Denis. "We cool?" He grimaced, annoyed, but nodded a grudging acceptance. "Good. Here's the part I needed to be clear on. It was an SVR black ops team that grabbed me in Los Angeles." I saw a question forming on Denis's lips, a journalistic instinct he couldn't turn off. "Just trust me that I know and I'm not going to tell you how." There was more I could say, but I had enough lingering suspicion about Fedorov that I just wasn't disclosing information that'd come from Nate.

I shifted my gaze to Fedorov. "The SVR assumed I shot their man in Belarus, but that wasn't the only reason they interrogated me. They wanted me to give you up. That same night, they broke into the law firm and stole everything related to the story, which I told you about earlier. This has to be part of a larger operation. What I want to know is, why is the SVR trying to make Projekt Molniya go away. It wasn't theirs. And how is it related to Vilnius, because that's when everything seemed to have kicked off. Tell me what you know."

"The group within the GRU is called Unit 29155. They are commanded by a man named Colonel Aleksandr Orlov. Initially, he was charged with developing this weapon, but he was also permitted to test it."

One point for Nate.

"In Havana?" I asked.

"Yes. And with the data gained, Orlov made improvements to the weapon. This is where I came in. My job was to identify Western companies that produced corollary technologies of interest to Russian objectives. Orlov knew Russian industry would not be able to make the necessary improvements in the time that the Kremlin required."

"Did the DGI use the weapon in Cuba, or was that GRU?"

"They gave it to a DGI team, but my understanding was there was a GRU minder present. As well as a scientist to document the findings," Fedorov said. So far, he'd validated not just what Nate told me in his kitchen but what I'd suspected for years. "Once Orlov believed he had a workable solution, the Kremlin changed the unit's mandate to direct action. However, they still wanted to make the weapon more efficient, smaller, so I continued securing the required technologies from defense companies in Europe and a few in the United States."

"The GRU rapidly escalated their attacks in late 2020, early 2021, and then stopped abruptly. Why?"

"All I know from Orlov was that the General Staff ordered him to shut down Projekt Molniya. However, you probably know that my government, and the GRU in particular, has a habit of contracting some operations." Point to Joshua McDonough for being incredibly well informed.

"You're saying Orlov contracted the attacks?" Denis asked.

"Not initially. Just in Vilnius, as far as I know."

This revelation changed everything. And complicated them. Without question, I should give Fedorov over to Danzig. Unaccountable mercenaries running around with an energy weapon certainly met the "clear and present danger" threshold. This was information the FBI and CIA needed to have, and needed now.

The problem was, there was no reason to believe the CIA wouldn't just bury this again.

McDonough's offer rose up again like the unquiet dead of my subconscious. *They'll use it as an excuse to 'find new information.'*

Of course, in neither of these scenarios was Jennie permitted to write the story.

"So, what do we do?" Fedorov asked.

Million dollar question, that.

What I needed was time to figure out how to thread this needle. How to keep Fedorov alive without betraying my client.

"You will be safest in the US. But I need to remind you that the FBI will almost certainly arrest you. Unless you can give them indisputable information."

"I understand. And yes, I agree that America would be safer. I should go back to my hotel and pack," Fedorov said.

"How far is it from here?"

"A few blocks," Denis said. "We can get a driver if we need."

I didn't love the idea of him going off on his own, but I suspected Fedorov needed some time alone. I also needed a few private words with Denis. "I'll meet you there in an hour. We'll get some dinner and talk about getting you out of here. We won't be able to get out tonight anyway," I said.

Fedorov nodded, stood, and left.

"Could we do both?" I asked.

"I don't follow," Denis said.

"What if you have the same information that your government does? You've been interviewing him for a week. But the real goods are the stuff he was hiding in exchange for asylum. Assuming he'd give us copies, could you use them?"

"We could, but there's the question of provenance. Well, this is all hypothetical since I haven't seen them. But, let's say it's legitimate. We need Fedorov to stipulate where he got them from to prove we didn't make them up."

"So, we need Fedorov no matter what. Hold on," I said, grabbing for my phone.

I messaged McDonough in Signal. **Confirmed GRU outsourced Havana weapon. Code-named Projekt Molniya. What kind of protection can u offer my source?**

J. McDonough: **Something like WITSEC**

Even if I didn't take his deal, there was strategic value in telling him about the GRU giving this technology to mercenaries. Like he said, secrets were part of the currency that turned that town's gears. That information would make it to certain ears now.

"I think Jennie is in a lot of trouble," I said, honestly.

"So, where do we go from here?"

"There's a second offer, one I didn't mention to Fedorov. I'm bringing it up here because it'll have complications for you. A former government official wants to prevent the story from getting out. Says that there's a quid pro quo to be had, where the government quietly 'finds new information' disputing the Intelligence Community report. That then triggers equally quiet acknowledgment and support for the victims and somewhat less quiet retaliation to the perpetrators. Says he can get Jennie's charges dropped." I paused to make sure I had his complete attention. "Denis, this is help she may need."

"And you trust this contact? Don't suppose you'll tell me who it is."

"I trust him as far as his intentions. This path lets the government save face. I think he can deliver on what he's promising."

"How does Grigori come out in all this?"

"Probably settlement somewhere, new identity," I said.

"You've turned the corner on him, then?"

Being evasive with Denis left me with a sour feeling in my gut. I've taken a lot of risks on his behalf over the years, and he's repaid that with rewarding work. Probably kept me in my house. Anything I'd learned from Nate, though, couldn't be shared with a reporter, no matter how much I trusted him. "Oh, he's not who he says he is. I'm almost convinced he's a GRU officer, but my instinct is that his information is probably on the money. For the record, Denis, I don't know what the right answer is. If I accept this offer, Jennie will never speak to me again. She'll never take it on her own. If I don't, there is a real possibility she goes to prison."

"She won't care," he said.

"That's coming from someone that's never seen the inside of a cell. Federal prison is different."

"These are just scare tactics, though. Even if they prosecuted her, it'd just be a fine. Certainly a substantial one. She wouldn't actually go to prison." While his voice had conviction, the lie was evident in his eyes.

"She could be looking at ten years."

The reason Jennie and my relationship serially failed was because we're wired exactly the same way. When you're young, looking into a mirror like that can be terrifying, instead of cautionary or instructive. Jennie would absolutely make a stand over what she believed and would ride that all the way to federal prison. Just to show them she would.

"Maybe you're right, I don't know. We can't strategize with her incarcerated," Denis said.

"The other thing is if she gets into home confinement. The Russians got me in the garage underneath Coogan's law firm in downtown LA. What do we think they're going to do when she's on the street?"

"If she's on house arrest, there'll be an ankle monitor or something, right?"

"That's not a panic button, Denis. And these guys broke industrial-grade security. The government is not going to put a federal marshal at her doorstep. I'm worried this makes her exposed. And if I'm running around *for* her, I can't be standing watch *with* her."

"Have you considered that maybe it's time to step aside?"

"What do you mean?"

"Jennie hired you to vet Fedorov, which you've done. When she was arrested, she asked you to finish the investigation. You've proved, to my satisfaction, that the Kremlin are the perpetrators."

"But we still don't know why they covered it up?"

"Maybe that's our fight, not yours. If you're genuinely worried for Jennie's safety, she'd rather you were nearby. As would I."

"What aren't you saying?"

"Matt, you know how grateful I am that you've risked your life for our work, more than once. But we're a nonprofit. I can't keep covering this stuff. The insurance people already wanted me to cut you loose."

I'd already lost my legal coverage and now my financial backing too?

"You can't seriously be asking me to quit."

"Not asking, necessarily. However, I want to know how much more of this is in your interest, and the story's? Maybe it's time to step aside, focus on keeping Jennie safe. I think we've got the facts we need. There is also your health to consider. You didn't give me any details, but I can already tell you should've gone to hospital, not come here. Where does this end for you?"

"What about Fedorov?"

Denis's shoulders lifted. "He made his bed, Matt." Denis grimaced, paused, and took in a breath. He laid both hands on the table. "That's harsh and unnecessary. I don't want any harm to come to him, and that's what I wrestle with. I think he needs more protection than my limited private security can manage. Still, he isn't your client, Jennie is. You can't make a deal that affects her story without consulting her. It isn't right. It doesn't matter what your intentions are."

Left unsaid was the fact that Jennie and the Orpheus Foundation had been chasing this story for years. They were close, now, to conclusively unravelling a dedicated deception by two governments. They weren't going to give that up easily. And not because I asked.

Before I left, I asked Denis, "When did you come around on Fedorov?"

"What do you mean?"

"You said you had serious questions about his credibility. But you'd kept him here a week and thoroughly debriefed him. Kept security up, at considerable risk to you and your people. What changed your mind?"

"A warehouse fire in Hamburg. He's not a dangle. The Russians wouldn't use him to give us a list of companies and then burn them down. Fedorov is more than he says he is, but his information is right."

They'd booked Fedorov in a hotel walking distance from the office. One of Denis's people snagged me a room in the same building. I grabbed my bag and headed out. A dreary rain blew in from the North Atlantic, painting the city in greasy streaks. Thankfully, I didn't have to walk far. Unlike a typical American hotel, the ones in European cities tended to be converted from whatever the building had previously been. The lobby was small, with a single desk, brightly lit and with a single large window facing the street.

I knew Fedorov traveled under his Swiss passport, so I asked the manager if Gregory Künzler was in.

"I'm sorry, Mr. Künzler checked out. He left about an hour ago."

24

The hotel manager didn't have any information on where Mr. Künzler had gone. I stepped away from the desk while she was checking me in and called Fedorov.

Straight to voicemail.

I called Denis to see if Fedorov had circled back to the office.

They hadn't seen him since he left.

Fedorov was in the wind. I had no way to track him.

The manager gave me my key, and I handed her my bag, asking for it to be sent up to the room. I called Connor while navigating for an Uber on my phone.

"Fedorov is gone."

"What do you mean, he's gone?"

"He checked out of his hotel and disappeared."

"Are we sure he disappeared?" Connor asked. It was a fair question.

"I'm not sure of anything right now."

The app told me I'd have a ride in three minutes. I asked Connor to hold on while I texted Denis and asked him to send people to the train stations. If Fedorov was what I thought he was, he'd know to hide his tracks. My car arrived.

I ran back over to the front desk, grabbed my duffel from the now confused hotel clerk, and stepped out into the squall.

"I'm headed to the airport now," I told Connor. "Do you have any idea where he might go?"

"I'm thinking," he said. After a couple seconds of churning, Connor said, "He used to talk about this cafe in Cyprus."

"Cyprus?" Actually, that made a lot of sense. Cyprus had earned the nickname "Moscow on the Med" because of the number of Russian expats living there. It also offered easy access to Istanbul and Athens, two international cities where it would be easy for someone like Fedorov to disappear. There were rumors, too, that it was a popular tax haven for Russians to stash money outside the Federation. "It's a big bet to make on a coffee shop."

"Oh, it's not just that. He's got property there, and he didn't exactly cop to this, but I think he's got money and potentially a clean passport. Why would he leave, though?" Connor asked. It was a good question. I had to be careful with my answer since I was in a car.

"Sorry if I break up, I'm in an Uber," I said. Connor would be smart enough to pick up on the code I was about to improvise. "We'd talked about the deal and how the new investors were looking for a hostile takeover. He knew their meeting with me was pretty confrontational. I guess he got cold feet and decided to pull out. I'd really like to find him, though. Make sure feathers aren't too ruffled."

"Okay, I'm tracking," Connor said. "Far as I know, the US isn't explicitly barring entry from Russian citizens, so he could enter on a tourist visa. That's the other possibility. Assuming he's flying. I gave you my guess, do you have any idea where he might be going?"

"None."

Connor finished my unspoken thought. "If he took a train or car, he could be anywhere in Europe without having to flash a passport. That limits my ability to track his movements."

"What kind of flexibility do you have in your schedule?" I asked. "Say I could get a meeting between the three of us."

"You're asking me to get involved? You know I can't do that."

"This venture was your idea."

"Let me know where. I'll figure it out."

We disconnected the call. I pulled up a flight tracker app that showed the departures from Brussels International Airport. There were no flights to Cyprus. Most likely, you'd fly to Istanbul or Athens and connect. There were multiple flights to London and Frankfurt, both major international airports that could have him in America, Asia, or Africa within hours.

The driver let me out at the departures terminal, and I stood under the overhang with rain crashing down behind me, frozen. No clue what to do next. There was nothing to suggest Fedorov took a flight out of here, other than the cold logic of it. If it were me, I'd have taken the train. Almost any form of modern travel leaves a digital footprint now. Assuming one isn't using a forged ID and ghost credit card, a rental car leaves a long trail in some easily hacked systems. Planes compound that problem, because you're adding extra digital touch points and the travel systems are typically dated and, therefore, easily hacked. The only advantage to traveling by air is getting to the destination faster and hopefully to a place where you can lose the hypothetical watchers. But a train can be a great way to disappear. Especially in Europe. And if you really want to vanish, get a regional commuter ticket, as those don't require ID.

If Fedorov had any tradecraft, he wouldn't be on a plane. At least, not at this stage.

I opened my phone.

I called him again. And, again, he didn't answer.

It was certainly possible that the opposition grabbed him off the street. Waiting until Fedorov checked out would be a smart move, throw us off.

If he ran, the question of why he'd do it would have to wait until I found him.

Denis's security people hadn't observed anyone watching the building or their staff. Of course, I didn't know how good any of them were. If they were little more than bouncers with an hourly rate, they wouldn't pick up a foreign intelligence service.

I was tailspinning, and that was counterproductive. The mind has a way of thinking the worst when it's fatigued. Assume Fedorov ran until we had evidence to the contrary.

The next question would be where would he go? That was an immediate problem because in European Union airports, the terminals were separated into the ones that serviced Schengen Area countries and the ones that did not. The Schengen Treaty established open borders within the European Union. Once a traveler went through security, they either went to the Schengen Area or non-Schengen Area. So, if I guessed his destination wrong, I would be in a different terminal and unable to cross over.

Where might he go?

The US was a possibility, but he wasn't getting there directly tonight. I could buy a ticket for Switzerland and still post at the Heathrow or Frankfurt gates to see if he showed up there. The trick was if Fedorov was going to Cyprus as Connor suggested. Cyprus was not within the Schengen Area. There were too many possibilities, and I had no concrete evidence he was taking a plane.

Most people, when they're scared, they run for what they know. Seek psychological safety.

Fedorov kept talking about the information he had, the files he'd stolen from Moscow. Where would those be safest?

His home or a Swiss bank. Fedorov would be going home.

I bought a ticket for the eight p.m. flight to Zürich.

Brussels International is not a large airport. It's U-shaped, with one arm for the Schengen Area flights and the other for those that aren't. There was no sign of Fedorov in the security screening area. I orbited the departure hall, scanning the strip of small cafes and the seating area. No sign. Next, I scanned the departure board for what I guessed were Fedorov's most likely destinations and went to those gates. Again, no sign. That feeling of iced clarity when you realize you were dead wrong seeped into me.

My phone rang, Connor calling on Signal.

"Matt, I've got him."

"Where? How?"

"I'm tracking his phone now."

"You didn't do that before?"

Connor dropped his voice to a violent hiss. "He's a foreign national, not an intelligence target. I can't just follow whoever the hell I want. I'm using a national asset for this, and there's going to be a record of it."

I understood. Connor was putting himself in some deep shit.

"I can triangulate his location, and it appears he's on a train. I'm not risking anything else by doing a passport search. Too early to guess where, but he's currently moving southeast."

That didn't exactly narrow it down. The only thing that wasn't southeast from Belgium was Denmark. Still, Connor was taking a serious risk on my behalf, and I was grateful for it.

"I bought a ticket for Zürich. I was betting on him taking a plane, guess that was off. My flight gets in around nine."

"You can't know," he said, though his tone was snide. Connor was helping me and angry about it. He'd handed Fedorov over to me and expected that to be the end of it, to cover his involvement. Now he was finding himself in deeper than he'd wanted to be and having to go to greater lengths to mask it.

"Doesn't look like my flight has Wi-Fi on board, so I'll be dark for three hours or so."

"I'll do what I can," Connor said. Then, "Shit."

"What?"

"His phone just dropped off the net."

Looked like I wasn't the only one going dark.

Or the SVR was on the train.

Whichever it was, we likely wouldn't know for hours.

My plane touched down in Zürich, and I powered my phone back on to a flood of texts.

Connor reacquired Fedorov by picking up his portable hotspot on the train and then tagging his laptop's IP address. I didn't ask Connor how he had this to begin with. The train was now in France and continuing southeast. Germany and Switzerland were the two best guesses, with Austria and Spain as a distant third and fourth. It would be several more hours before we knew what his destination was.

I also had a message from Coogan. He'd gotten Jennie released to home confinement. As a condition, the court prohibited her from working on the story, and she was not allowed to use her internet or phone for research or interviews. His message didn't indicate whether the government was providing additional security. A wave of panic hit me, now that Jennie was out in the open. This distraction wasn't helping. It'd be hard to concentrate on finding and securing Fedorov when I was worrying about Jennie at the same time.

I found a room at a hotel a few blocks from the Hauptbahnhof, where Fedorov would roll into sometime tomorrow if God was smiling on me and I'd guessed right. The hotel was a small, squat building in Zürich's Old Town. It was just two short blocks from the water, and I could see the city's yellow lights smudged on the lake. Once I was in my room, I called Coogan. I didn't tell him where I was, I couldn't trust him with that information anymore now that I was no longer a client. Of course, that was the first thing he asked and said his attorney friend was trying to get in touch with me to sort this situation out with the LAPD. I suggested he direct them to the Russian consulate in San Francisco.

"Hire a security detail and put them on Jen's building. If anything happens to her, it's on you. I told you she was at risk, and you didn't listen."

I hung up.

Tired of everyone.

I called Jennie. She'd just gotten home and showered the jail off her.

"Matt, are you still in DC?"

"No," I said.

"Can you come here? I'd feel better if you were around."

It felt like someone with an especially cold hand reached into my chest and squeezed my heart.

"I'm...I'm in motion right now. Better that you not know where."

"Is it about Fedorov?"

"Jen, I need you to listen to me very carefully. The Kremlin does not want whatever Fedorov knows to get out into the open. Enough so that they're going to risk aggressive operations in the US. You have got to be careful. Don't trust anyone. If someone says they're a cop, a fed, whoever, make them provide proof first. Any time someone visits you, call their office to confirm before you let them in the building. Better yet, have the building's security do it. I asked Coogan to get you a security detail. Not sure he's going to follow through with it or not. Even if he does, I don't know how long it'll take to get them in place. I'll be home as soon as I can."

Connor messaged me around midnight to say that Fedorov's train was in Strasbourg. That meant any destination in France, Germany, Switzerland, or Spain was still in play. I really wished I understood what Fedorov's game was.

He knew the Russians made a play for me.

I told him I'd get him safely to the States.

And then he vanished.

None of this made sense.

According to online schedules, the Strasbourg train would arrive in Basel at five in the morning. That line would continue on to Bern. If Fedorov was coming to Zürich, where he lived, he'd take a regional commuter train. That ticket wouldn't require an identity, and he could pay cash for it. Anyone following him would lose him in Basel as long as his phone remained off.

I grabbed a handful of hours' sleep before the alarm jerked me awake at five. I showered and drank all of the in-room coffee. I'd only gotten the room for one night, so I dropped my bag with the desk clerk and said I'd be back in a few hours. Then I stepped out into the brisk and gray morning. The Swiss architecture immediately snapped me back to Vilnius and the start of this thing.

A full night's rest helped. My injuries had faded to dull aches, but I was still reminded of them as I moved. I'd put fresh bandages on the electrical burns, which were healing as well.

A growling vacancy in my stomach reminded me that I hadn't eaten since sometime early yesterday. I had almost ninety minutes before I could expect Fedorov's train, and the station's many cafes would be yawning into business shortly. Zürich's Hauptbahnhof was one of the largest and busiest in Europe. If he was smart, Fedorov wouldn't tarry long. He'd pick up what he came for and go to ground somewhere. Connor's Cyprus supposition might well prove correct. Fedorov could conduct his business and then disappear into the European rail network by lunchtime.

I entered the train station complex. First, I headed to the multilevel mall, which they referred to as "ShopVille," so I could grab breakfast and a coffee. Then I checked the arrivals board for the inbound train from Basel. Track eleven, ten minutes.

The station's surface tracks sat beneath an arched ceiling of gray metal and glass, accessed by a below-ground terminal. The platform itself was a single concrete isthmus reaching out from the main building like stony fingers.

I'd had no further contact from Connor. He was an hour ahead and should be up and running now.

I waited on the platform at track eleven until I saw the train arriving and then walked back to the outer row of shops, where I could safely watch. By now, there were enough morning commuters in the main hall that I could fade into a crowd.

And then he appeared.

Fedorov descended from a train car wearing a rumpled suit and manhandling his luggage with tired gesticulations. The throng of passengers descended with him, though few were as bleary-eyed. Fedorov looked like a business traveler, with a rolling suitcase and his laptop bag threaded on the handle. I faded into the background and watched him pass into the main hall.

I fought the urge to run over and brace him, ask him what in the hell he was doing.

Because he came here for a reason and, whatever it was, didn't want me to know. Spooking him would just make him turtle. And I needed to see if he was playing for the other side.

I fired off a quick update to Connor. Then, I clocked Fedorov's fellow passengers as they dispersed into the main hall, scanning to see if anyone was watching him. About half carried luggage, likely on the train from Strasbourg to Basel. A blond couple stood in the central hall, the woman reading the arrivals and departures board while her male companion surveyed the massive room. I saw another man, dressed as a business traveler, who lurked in the fringes of the swelling morning crowd. He was also surveying the entry hall, and I noted that his attention seemed to land on Fedorov.

Fedorov maneuvered to the far side of the hall, where he accessed a bank of luggage lockers set inside an alcove. In my earlier sweep, I'd scoped out the locker area, figuring he might use them. They were divided into two groups—silver for credit card and blue for cash. Fedorov stepped into the blue locker alcove, paid, stashed, and was moving.

So, he wasn't planning on staying long.

Of course, a train station dead drop was a trick so old it predated all of the tradecraft textbooks.

All he needed to do now was slip someone the locker number, if that was the game.

Following him with my eyes, I watched as he pushed through the southern exit. He crossed the street to the Bahnhofplatz, mixing with the crowd there waiting on the train. I followed at a distance, crossing to the covered platform just as the Strassenbahn arrived. The Commuter, the man who'd ridden Fedorov's train in with him, followed as well. I stayed about ten steps behind him so I could watch his hands while keeping Fedorov in frame.

The Strassenbahn platform was crowded, providing good cover in a small space. I stayed near the outer edges of it, still able to keep Fedorov in sight. Zürich's Strassenbahn, or light-rail, was a blue-and-silver tram connected to an overhead wire network.

The air smelled faintly of mechanical grease and ozone.

The doors opened, and people flowed into and out of the train in a tightly choreographed dance.

I spotted that blond couple from Fedorov's train, along with a few other faces I recognized from my spot check.

There was a bit of jostling, and I lost Fedorov. I quickly realized that I didn't have a ticket for the light-rail and that it was an app-based payment system, which I wouldn't have time to download. Well, I'd just have to sneak my way onto the train and play the dumb tourist card.

The Commuter was shouldering his way through the crowd, moving up near Fedorov.

It was impossible to tell if this was a tail making his play or just an asshole who didn't like waiting in line. Orbiting around the group, I slid in alongside the train's rear car. The line was thinner here, and I could slip on. Following someone on a train was a risky play, especially if they could immediately identify you.

I had to make a decision about whether I was getting on or not.

Staring down the platform, I saw Fedorov was still queuing to get on. The Commuter was right behind him. Damn it, I was too far. The GRU's typical move was to inject someone with a concealed poison-tipped device—an umbrella or a ballpoint pen—and then fade back into the crowd. The marks rarely saw it coming.

Fedorov patted himself, as if looking for something, and stepped out of line.

The Commuter bumped him and stepped onto the train.

Fedorov jostled further out of the way.

The doors closed and the train departed, with Fedorov on the platform.

He gingerly stepped across the tracks as the Strassenbahn cleared the platform and headed south into Old Town.

Only, Fedorov wasn't alone.

That couple I spotted in the central hall followed.

25

Old Town Zürich held the traditional architecture of Western European cities, tightly packed four- or five-story white buildings with burnt-orange tile roofs. The structures wrapped around an entire block, with a courtyard or parking in the center. The streets were narrower than elsewhere in Zürich. Sometimes there was a fingernail's width of alley between buildings that you could duck into, but usually not.

It had a "walls closing in" feeling that I didn't necessarily need right now.

Fedorov's little maneuver on the platform wasn't bad.

But the couple hadn't fallen for it, and I was convinced now they were watching him. He'd crossed over from the train platform, dodging the slow-moving traffic alongside the Bahnhof, and the couple followed him. I lurked about a quarter of a block behind them. I didn't see any obvious signs of distress, so perhaps that bump on the train platform was just that —an impatient traveler bulldozing his way onto a train.

The next block had a small park, lined by trees and with a statue in the center. People occupied benches with cups of coffee and pastries wrapped in paper. Fedorov angled across the park, heading toward a cafe on the far side. The couple kept pace with him, staying at a distance. Once in the park, the couple separated, with the woman following Fedorov into the cafe and the man staying outside. He was clearly orbiting, and now that his mark was inside, he wasn't trying to blend in.

My guess was they were a sleeper team activated once the SVR learned Fedorov was in Brussels. The man was on his phone now.

I traversed the park quickly and then entered the cafe. The woman wasn't in line. Rather, she stood in the background, pretending to wait on an order. Fedorov was in line for a coffee.

There was no choice but to break cover. I couldn't risk these two being a covert kill squad.

I slid in behind Fedorov, pulling my phone out and busying myself with the screen. I lifted the phone to my ear, vamping a call. Leaning forward slightly, I said, aware of the parallels to our first meeting, "Grigori, you're being followed. Man and a woman. The woman is inside. I'm here to help you. Meet me at the university, on Tannenstrasse. Can you remember that?"

"Yes," he said softly.

"Will you go?"

He paused.

"Yes," he said.

"Okay. Take a cab. Once you have your order, leave the cafe through the side. I'll try to distract them." From behind, it would just look like I had no respect for personal space.

He said, "Okay," again and ordered a coffee to go. He paid and accepted with nervous hands.

The barista handed me a coffee, I said, "Danke," and then sub rosa to Fedorov, "Now."

He pushed his way through the crowded room, and I maneuvered my way over to where the woman stood. She was now watching him. I walked over to her, interposed myself into her line of sight with Fedorov, and said, "*Entschuldigen Sie, könnten Sie mir mit einigen Anweisungen helfen?*"

The woman looked at me with a confused, annoyed expression that quickly turned to something else.

She tried looking around my shoulder, so I moved that way, dominating the frame.

"*Ich spreche kein Deutsch*," she said dismissively, and pushed past me, trying to get to the hallway Fedorov disappeared down.

Turning, I left the cafe and crossed back into the park, aiming for the woman's companion. He was still on his phone.

I walked up to him and said excitedly, "Sorry, excuse me. I think your wife is ill. She just collapsed in the cafe." I pointed anxiously at the building. The man looked at me, then to the cafe. He left his position, dashing across the street.

Walking around the corner, I saw Fedorov hustling back up the street in the direction of the Bahnhof, where he could find a taxi. Neither of the couple emerged from the cafe yet, so I decided to make myself scarce as well. I disappeared down a different street, heading back to the Strassenbahn.

Eidgenössische Technische Hochschule Zürich, the Federal Institute of Technology, was a sprawling university campus in the city's center. It was just over a mile from where I'd met Fedorov and would be filled with people and easy to blend in. Because he'd taken a cab, Fedorov arrived before me and had the good sense to wait at the Strassenbahn pavilion amid a small crowd of students and faculty. We made eye contact, and he started walking around the corner. I caught up with him on the sidewalk.

"What the hell are you trying to pull?" I asked. I vectored us across the street, taking us deeper into the city.

"What can I do? My government wants me dead, and yours wants to put me in jail."

"Why didn't you say anything?"

"I don't owe you an explanation."

"Don't you think you owe Denis one? He risked his organization just listening to your story. Don't forget who got you out of Minsk. If it weren't for me, you'd be in a cell underneath Lubyanka right now. And if I hadn't shown up *here*, those two would've gotten you for sure. Speaking of, that man who bumped you waiting to get into the train."

"What about him?"

"Did you check to see if he stuck you with anything?"

"I didn't feel anything," Fedorov said. Now concern washed over his face, quickly draining to fear. He slid a hand into his shirt to feel down the left side of his torso. "Seems okay," he said. "Matthew, I am not going to be a pawn. Nor will I be the meat that bickering parts of your government fight over."

"I have someone for you to talk to," I said.

"You also said you don't trust the people she answers to."

"That's right. But I'm asking you to trust *me*. I have an idea."

He laughed bitterly. "Oh, I should like to hear this." There were times the Russian in him was unmistakable.

"We need to get off the street," I said. We walked a few blocks until we found another cafe, just off campus. It was filled with students. We ordered coffee and food to blend in and maneuvered our way to a table at the back that couldn't be seen from the street. "Now, can you please tell me what you're doing here?"

"I told Denis all along that I wasn't sharing my best information until I received a guarantee of security from someone. He tried to convince me to strike a bargain with the Belgians, but so far they have not been receptive. We agreed that I would be interviewed for what I'd promised to share with Ms. Burkhardt, but unless I could assure my safety, I wouldn't reveal anything else. I have always been clear on this."

"So, what is that?"

Fedorov lifted his oversized coffee mug, took a sip, and held the mug up so he could speak behind it. He didn't want anyone to be able to lip-read him. "I have all of the Projekt Molniya files," Fedorov said without intonation. "Colonel Orlov disagreed with the Kremlin shutting his project down. He believed it was too valuable to just let go of. If the president didn't want it, he'd find a third party that did and would pay handsomely for it. As GRU, Orlov had connections in Syria, Eastern Europe, and other places. He gave me all of the project files and ordered me to hide them while he found a suitable buyer."

"Only, he didn't find one?"

"You spoke of cells beneath Lubyanka like one who knows. I suspect the colonel has been introduced to them. When Orlov did not show in Minsk, I knew his plan had failed and he'd been discovered."

"What do you have?"

"I have the schematics for the weapons. Test results. I have internal correspondence, official memoranda, and mission reports. Perhaps the one you are most interested in is the mission report from the Vienna operation. The others, I could not get, but this should be sufficient to prove Russia's guilt. I even have a copy of the citation Colonel Orlov received when the General Staff officially closed Projekt Molniya."

"Why did they order him to stop?"

"You already know about the summit in 2021. The General Staff directed him to cease operations, but he was permitted to continue developing new prototypes in case Projekt Molniya was reactivated. However, those resources were quickly redirected to the war in Ukraine so they could use the devices to attack drones. The project was to stop entirely then."

"The attack during the Vilnius Summit last year, was that Orlov looking for a buyer?"

"No. As I said, he was…eh, unhappy, with his orders. Orlov believed that because the Americans were not acknowledging the weapon, they would not disclose any such uses. As such, he believed he could use it again and no one would know. Or that they would call it 'stress.' He wanted to use that as a selling point to potential buyers. There were mercenary operatives he'd used before for other missions. Orlov hired them to test the latest iteration at the summit."

I paused a moment to consider the implications. Nate's speculation was correct that they'd outsourced it, though I didn't believe he'd considered the possibility of a GRU colonel going off the reservation.

"He wasn't worried that he'd be discovered?"

A grim smile cracked Fedorov's lips. "You don't know Orlov. He is like a cat. Crafty, perhaps too much so for his own good."

"Well, the Kremlin knows something is up."

"It would seem so," Fedorov said contemplatively.

"I wish you'd told us this yesterday. The fact that you knew Orlov went out on his own, against Moscow's orders, dramatically increases your bargaining power. I think my government has to sit up and take notice now."

Fedorov shrugged, an almost disinterested gesture.

"And you've got all this electronically?" I asked.

"I do. I also have additional companies that the GRU targeted. These are based in the United States. I made multiple trips to technology companies in Connecticut, Texas, and California."

"Some of the businesses you stole from here on the continent have had acts of sabotage. Fires, cyberattacks, things like that. That can't all be coincidental."

"I have no more information than you do. But it wouldn't surprise me if the GRU was trying to hide their involvement. Orlov's deputy was not sophisticated."

"Seems like sabotage would do the opposite, wouldn't it? Eventually, someone does pattern matching and figures out the common denominator in all of these is that they're defense contractors and microelectronics manufacturers, right? I mean, Denis did that. Now, he had the benefit of your list, but you can see how someone puts this together."

Fedorov shrugged. "I didn't say it was a sophisticated plan, Matthew. Just that it was my guess. However, it's not exactly a secret that the president does not fear the West. He believes he can act with impunity and moves accordingly." Fedorov looked for answers in the cooling coffee mug in front of him, tendrils of steam climbing slowly into the air. "I am sorry that I ran. I believe you have always been honest with me, Matthew. And you also helped me escape from Minsk. For that, I am forever in your debt. I ran because I am scared and I don't know where to go."

"Grigori, I need to know the truth, because it will have implications on what we do next."

He said nothing, his watery eyes downcast.

"Are you a GRU officer?"

"No," he said brusquely. "I was always an agent. My father was a senior member of the politburo, but he crossed a powerful party member, and it became unsafe for us. We fled. However, we were not welcome in the West. We struggled for a long time to find a home, and they were very poor. It was hard for him, as he once had power and now had none. Mother was just happy to not have to queue to purchase bread and old cabbage. I was disillusioned with the West, because of how they treated us. Eventually, I returned to Russia and settled in St. Petersburg. I attended university and was recruited there. Not to join, but to spy for them, which I did for twenty years. My mother is Russian, not Swiss. The service forged the documents I needed to establish Swiss citizenship and used an asset in the government for the rest. My recruitment officer, Major Zolin, said that he would absolve my father of his 'disloyalty' if I joined."

"What happened to your parents?"

"They died very poor."

Now was the time for hard choices.

McDonough could get Jennie out of jail and free, could get Fedorov secretly settled in the US somewhere. And he said he could negotiate care for the Havana victims. All that required was that I trust him.

Danzig, however, would not make any assurances about Jennie's case. The Bureau needed to debrief Fedorov. CIA also needed to know. Whatever feelings I had for that place, this transcended it. I believed this information was worth a trade, certainly enough to keep Fedorov out of prison for espionage.

And I needed him to admit he shot Fyodor Vasiliev.

Both of those options would require Jennie to drop the story. And Jennie would never agree to any condition that prohibited her from reporting on this. Not after she'd spent time in jail. The Foundation could publish whatever they wanted, they weren't a US institution, they just wouldn't have access to Fedorov or his information.

This was now bigger than a story.

I was responsible for a man's life.

I wished I could see a way out of this that didn't have me betraying my client.

"You are very quiet," Fedorov said.

"This isn't *un*-complicated," I said, forcing a laugh. Fedorov had, finally, shared what I believed was the full truth. He'd need to back that up with the files he possessed, but I had no reason to doubt him here. That didn't mean I trusted him enough with the plan.

Not telling him gave me more time to figure out what in the hell I was actually doing.

"You know, I really like Switzerland, and I shall be sad to leave it. Moscow is terrible. The weather is abysmal and the food is worse, and those are the two most charming things. I grew up in Soviet Russia; in many ways, now it is worse. I'm not an ideological man, Matthew. They tell you we are at war with the West, that we always have been. Maybe, for a time, I believed it. Do you know why the weapon was named this? Putin called it *Vtoraya Molniya*."

"Second Lightning," I said. That told me much about its primacy with the Kremlin. "First Lightning" was the Soviet's code name for their first nuclear bomb.

"Hence, Projekt Molniya. Then I read about all of the people who were hurt. One of them was a child. This is not right. I did not want this to be my legacy." Fedorov traced a finger absently on the table, lost in his thoughts. He exhaled heavily, exorcising some personal demon. "Those documents I told you about are in a safe deposit box with the bank LTL-Suisse. My hope is to put them in the hands of someone who can do something good with them."

My phone buzzed. I ignored it.

"We still need you, though. Whatever documents you have in your possession aren't worth much if you aren't also there to say where they came from. It'd be too easy to say they were faked."

Fedorov smiled thinly. "I was counting on that, too."

"You did a brave thing. I wish we'd gotten to this place sooner, but I understand your reluctance. It's easy to convince yourself you see spies in the shadows."

I glanced down at my phone. There was a notification on Signal. I opened it, saw it was from Connor. He'd just arrived in Zürich.

Well, that explained why I hadn't heard from him.

The better question was what in the hell was he doing here?

My hotel was in Old Town, and I didn't want to go back there with Fedorov, just in case our two tagalongs were still in the area. But we needed a staging area. I booked a room at the Europa Hotel, about two miles south of where we were now and in a high-traffic area. I sent Connor the address. I called the place I'd stayed in the night before and for a reasonably usurious fee, they agreed to have my bags sent over.

"We should be moving," I said.

26

"This is officially bat-shit crazy," Connor said when I'd given him the full debriefing in our hotel room.

We were still working under the fiction that Connor's name was Charlie Auer; we'd never disclose a case officer's true name to an asset. By now, it was obvious to Fedorov that his old friend Charlie did not work for the State Department.

"We passed 'bat-shit crazy' about ten exits ago," I said. "So, here are the risks as I see them. One, the SVR has a robust operation inside the United States. They broke into the law firm representing Jennie Burkhardt and stole all of her research on this story. Information going back years. She'd given it to Case Ritter because she didn't want the Justice Department to seize it. Assume the SVR knows what we know and knows who we know. Also, Jennie's legal team convinced a judge to transfer her to house arrest, so also assume she is under threat. I've spoken with my FBI contact, and they will not offer any protective services for Jennie, because she's been accused of a federal crime. Now, my friend wants to interview Grigori and claims he'll get a fair shake if they believe what he has to offer."

"Do you trust her?" Connor asked.

"Her? Absolutely, just not the people she works for. The Bureau, somehow, claims to have surveillance camera footage of the train platform in Smorgon."

"Shit," Connor said.

"Yeah. Allegedly, they see me and Vasiliev fighting and then Vasiliev shot, and I'm not in frame when it happens."

"So, they're claiming you did it until they hear otherwise," Connor said, eyes flicking to Fedorov.

I nodded my agreement. "That's my problem. It doesn't necessarily have bearing on what we do."

"Of course it does," Fedorov said, indignant.

"Not entirely. The Intelligence Community still wants this thing buried, for reasons I have not been able to figure out yet. *That* is the critical piece. *That* is the story. We need to understand why the coverup. I think the material in Grigori's possession forces that conversation."

"Surely, with what I will turn over to you, this will change, no? It is indisputable truth."

I considered those words for a long time. "My friend, I have been in this game long enough to know that the 'truth' can always be disputed. There's an additional wrinkle, which is that in 2021, the US and Russian presidents met in a summit, here in Switzerland. There was an off-the-record conversation between the two leaders. What was said was never documented, but I spoke with someone who had knowledge of it. They told me POTUS offered the Kremlin an out if they stopped attacking us."

"The ODNI report," Connor said.

"That's right."

"And that agreement held until last year," Connor said.

"Until last year," I agreed. "Grigori tells me that the GRU gave at least one of the weapons to a third party. Probably an ex–special forces team, now contract killers, and that they did this without the Kremlin's approval. The Projekt Molniya director thought he could get away with it, use this to find an outside buyer."

Fedorov rose and emptied the contents of his pocket, setting them on the nightstand. It was a wallet, keys, and a cigarette lighter. Then, he excused himself to the bathroom. Seeing the lighter struck me as a strange thing to carry around, since I hadn't ever seen him smoke.

When the fan came on, Connor asked, "So, your plan is to escort Fedorov back to the States and turn him over to a contact in the FBI?"

I held up a finger to my lips, and Connor nodded. I walked over to Fedorov's things and quickly inspected them. Starting with the lighter, a cheap gold number, I opened the cap and kept it up just long enough to see the flame. Then I went to the phone. Tapping the front just got me his lock screen. Satisfied there were no more shadows I could jump at, I continued.

"After we make a stop by his bank so he can access his safe deposit box. Since I know the opposition is here, I'd like to be on the move tonight. I'll feel better if we can at least get to London."

"What about all this stuff with the Orpheus Foundation?"

I held my hands out. "That's something I have to negotiate with the Bureau."

Connor paced. "I don't like it, and I don't trust the Feebs. There's also no guarantee they don't arrest him."

Connor was worried about his own exposure, for sure. With good reason. I wanted to help him, but I wasn't sure if I could. I had too damned little leverage as it was.

I dropped my voice so Fedorov couldn't hear through the door. "There's another offer on the table, which I haven't shared with him. Joshua McDonough approached me. He's the one who told me about the summit and the deal. He wants what Fedorov has, and he wants it not to be reported. In exchange, he can get the IC to say they found 'new information' to overrule the report. Havana Syndrome is quietly recognized and people get treated."

"And maybe we finally punch these assholes in the mouth for what they did."

"That too. McDonough says he can get Fedorov asylum, relocation, and says he's got the traction in the Justice Department to get Jennie's charges dropped."

"Now I understand why you didn't bring it up," Connor said dryly.

"There are no good options." Looking around the room, I somehow landed on Fedorov's phone sitting on the nightstand. "Dam—" I caught myself before I said, "Damon Fox." Probably jumping at shadows, but I didn't complete the sentence. "I got arrested, then threatened with worse.

So, it's not like we can run this up *your* chain of command. It's this or nothing."

"Why not just let Jennie write her story? Let the chips fall. Wasn't that the original plan?"

"Well, she's pretty limited in what she can do until she's off house arrest. And she's not allowed to work as a journalist as a condition of her release. I'm also genuinely questioning, now, whether the government has a valid case. Regardless of the story, there's her safety to consider."

Every minute I spent away from Los Angeles was one more minute that Jennie was unguarded. Malyshkin's people had grabbed me in a downtown garage. They could easily get to Jennie in her condo.

Fedorov flushed the toilet and then ran the faucet.

"What are you going to do?" Connor asked.

"Get him to the US. After that, I am not sure what to do. Getting him to the FBI feels like the right thing, but there's no guarantee he doesn't get arrested. McDonough is a little deep state for my tastes, but if he holds up his end, that gets us what we want." And my client wouldn't speak to me again and I was probably on the hook for my five-figure expense tab. "Neither of those things are what my client hired me to do."

Connor said, "We need a car. You can't fly out of here, you have to assume Ivan is watching the airport. We get whatever Grigori has in that box, and then we head south. We're only a couple hours from Milan. You guys take a train south to Rome and fly to the US from there. I'll stay here and run interference." Connor walked over to the window, pushed one of the curtains aside, and stared down at the street below. "When you get him back, do what you have to do. But you need to promise me that you're going to get his information to Burkhardt. Don't let them bury this. Don't let them bury him."

Fedorov emerged from the bathroom, walked over, and resumed his place on the bed.

Connor disappeared for an hour to secure a car.

I wanted to scope out the street out front but decided against it. Fedorov had earned a set of constant eyes.

Connor texted me when he was out front in an Audi Q4.

"Let's go," I said.

The hotel was a sliver, occupying maybe a third of the space in this building. We pushed through the door, finding the street in its full, early afternoon rush. Connor sat in the small black SUV, idling just off the corner and steps from the door. I motioned for Fedorov to get in the back. I walked around and got in the passenger side. The car was moving before my door closed.

LTL-Suisse was a privately held, independent bank owned by a prominent Swiss industrialist family with ties to the old nobility. Their headquarters was north of us, in the city's modern core, but they maintained an office south of Old Town that still served as home to the traditional Swiss banking industry. They were near the Swiss legislature and state bank and within view of the emerald waters of the Zürichsee.

Connor had to loop around the block, bringing us south along the river that fed into the Zürichsee, then he continued south, instead of passing over the Quaibrücke. When the route correction bubbled up out of Fedorov's mouth, I looked up into the rearview mirror and said, "Just checking for tails."

Connor drove south with the Zürichsee on our right. It was a beautiful summer day with a soft breeze and intermittent clouds. I saw countless boats on the water. Connor stayed on the road as it turned into an expressway and then followed that further south into a residential district. We wended our way through the neighborhood, stair-stepping through the blocks—over two and up one, following the irregular contours of the medieval streets. When possible, Connor looped back around, and we both kept an eye on cars behind us. He found a sports complex, where we parked for a few minutes to see if anyone followed.

"How much of this job is driving around in circles," Fedorov asked.

"Most of it," I said.

On every level.

Eventually, we worked our way back to the Quaibrücke. Traffic slowed as we neared a convention center that fronted the Zürichsee and a yacht club that was doing brisk business today. "LTL-Suisse is on the next street," Fedorov said. Connor nodded and drove past it, turning right on the very next street. He went up three blocks, over, and then turned back south. Connor slowed at the crosswalk, we got out, and he drove off down the street. Fedorov led me into the building.

This building, once LTL-Suisse's headquarters, was a nine-story building of blue-green glass and steel, erected in the 1990s on the site of the previous one. Viewed from the front, one saw a single side at a rounded angle. When viewed from above, it looked like a cresting wave. Fedorov approached a teller, produced his Swiss identification, and in perfect Swiss-German, asked to access his box. The young banker asked him to follow. I was politely informed that I was not permitted back there.

About five minutes later, Fedorov emerged from a heavy wooden door with the jovial young banker in tow. Fedorov held a zippered pouch in the bank's blue, green, and white livery. Fedorov's anxiety was palpable. I could practically see him vibrating from across the room.

I messaged Connor that we were coming out.

Fedorov walked up to me. With a lifted eyebrow, I asked, "What's up?"

"It's not every day you walk out carrying a bomb." He smiled, but it faded quickly. "Maybe I shouldn't make that joke."

"Do you have physical documents in that?"

"Everything is electronic. They are on a solid state drive."

"Here, hand it to me."

"Why?"

"Because I've got some concealed pockets."

Reluctantly, Fedorov opened the bank pouch and handed me a small, black plastic drive, about the size of two fingers. I slid that into the concealed carry pocket in my jacket and closed it. Then, I put an arm around him and guided him from the building, leaving the bank pouch on a counter near the door. Connor was nowhere to be found.

We stood on a corner at an intersection, and I gave a look up and down in each direction. No sign.

I dialed.

"Where are you?"

"Traffic accident two blocks over. Just happened. Hold on, let me see if I can turn around."

I hung up. "He'll be here in a minute. Traffic accident," I told Fedorov, who just nodded. I saw a Mercedes Sprinter, with their comically tall roofs, idling next to Stadtbank Zürich on the next street. It had a courier service emblem painted on the angled hood. There was a man behind the wheel and another standing outside next to the van, looking at a tablet. I only clocked them because I was already on edge and in the practice of noticing everything.

Fedorov and I nervously ticked off the minutes in silence, standing outside the bank.

A black shape whipped around the corner, and Fedorov jumped.

The Audi.

Connor pulled up next to us, and we got in. Then we were off, heading back east in the direction of our hotel.

The plan was to grab our things, check out, and make it to Milan by dinner. Connor zigzagged a few blocks north to make a right onto Dreikönigstrasse. We followed that out of the banking district, making our way deeper into Old Town. We turned right on Bahnhofstrasse, now a few blocks up from the lake.

"Did you see a courier van outside the bank?" Connor asked, the wary tone of hard-earned street time rising in his voice.

"I did," I said.

"They've made every one of our turns."

"Let's move."

Connor accelerated and pulled around the car in front of us. Watching in the rearview, I saw the van leap forward. We sped toward the lake, with the green trees of a city park flashing by on the left. Before us, I saw a chaotic scene of two traffic lanes in either direction with a light-rail in the center, pedestrians everywhere. Traffic fed the massive intersection in four different directions, all bookended by the lake on the far side.

"Hold onto something. This turn is going to be tight," Connor said, whipping around another car and accelerating toward the intersection.

The car pulled hard left. Horns erupted around us.

Fedorov screamed in pain.
And then I knew why.
A crushing pain filled my head, pushing out all thought.

27

The sound of a thousand pissed-off cicadas fighting over a bandsaw filled my ears.

My head felt like it was in an industrial press, inexorable exploding pressure ambivalent to my pain. I couldn't see, everything was fuzzy, as though looking through a half-filled dirty glass.

And then it ended, just as abruptly.

Connor got us off the X.

He weaved around a car to the right, putting the Audi half up on the sidewalk, then jerked it back onto the road. We had to get out of here, now, and it was the only thing that mattered.

I looked over at Connor, and he seemed okay, was still in control of the car. I couldn't tell if he'd been hit too.

Connor blasted into the intersection, and a wave of horns followed. He braked hard and cranked the wheel, power-sliding through a gap in the cars. Screaming through two lanes of traffic, he jerked the wheel again and into a hard left turn that nearly put us on two wheels. Connor forced the Audi into a lane already brimming with cars, seemingly in defiance of physics. They made space, repelled by inherent survival instinct, and Connor drove that thing like a rental with a force field.

We rocketed down the street with the lake on the right and the concrete island holding a light-rail stop on the left. In another fifty yards or so, we'd be on the Quaibrücke. That far side meant safety.

Connor screamed, a feral, guttural sound, something dredged up from his most primal ancestry. Then I felt it too, a hard punch in the face, a hot wave of force, and that maddening, metallic buzzing followed. I heard Fedorov behind me choke off a scream, something that just died in his throat.

Connor fell forward, his head slumping against the steering column.

When his body hit, the wheel jerked to the side and the car skidded off the street, narrowly missing the glass booth on the train platform.

Instinct took over. I unbuckled my seat belt, slid left, and straddled the center console. Leaning over, I pushed Connor's unconscious form back into his seat and grabbed the wheel. Then I kicked his foot off the gas pedal. This move, I'd only ever done in training.

I wrestled control of the car back, jerking the wheel to the right to swerve off the light-rail tracks and back onto the road. People, screaming, dove for cover, and I got us off the concrete island just before we crashed into a bench. Cars were blasting by, and there was nowhere to merge without slamming into another vehicle at full speed.

The light-rail tracks and oncoming traffic were on the right. Beyond that, a wide paved boardwalk facing the lake's northern shore. We were in the inner left lane. The safest thing to do was just to stop the car, but that left us exposed to our attackers.

I'd rather face them on open ground than risk innocent lives.

But first, I had to stop the car. In order to reach the brake, I practically had to move into Connor's lap. The tires screamed in response, and the steering wheel locked. I snapped forward, slamming face-first into the dashboard as we got rammed from behind. Airbags exploded, catching me right in the middle, and I was forced backward violently. With my face pressed between two of the deployed cushions, I felt, rather than saw, the car's front end rip violently to the side as we skidded to a stop.

Horns blasted from every angle with panicked shouting in between. My whole body was a single, exposed nerve, furiously throbbing with fiery pain. Connor moaned; at least I knew he was alive. I collapsed back into my seat. My eyes refused to focus, making everything an intermittent blur. One of the rear doors opened.

I knew I had to move. Our attackers would be here to finish the job. I tried grabbing the door handle, but my arm just fell in a limp slap against the side. I felt like I was on a violently rocking ship about to capsize in high seas. A wave of nausea crashed over me, and it seemed like I'd been pitched upside down, even though I knew I was leaning upright against the door.

I heard horns, a crash, and then screams.

Then, nothing.

I awoke to a rhythmic, electronic beeping.

Dim light hit me as my eyes fluttered open, but that was all I could make out. My vision was cloudy and smeared. Gradually, focus returned, like playing with the zoom lens on a camera, first the outer rings became clear and then the inner.

I was in a hospital bed and, I noted, I was not handcuffed to it. So, that was something.

How'd I get here?

And *why* was I here?

A female voice spoke at the fringes of my perception, but none of the words made sense. Individually, they were familiar to me, but when strung together in a sentence, I couldn't comprehend it. I tried to sit up, and that got her attention. The woman, who I deduced to be a nurse, placed a gentle hand on my shoulder and guided me back down. She said a few more things I didn't understand, and I blacked out.

When I came awake the next time, I felt slightly more aware of my surroundings.

The nurse was back with a soft, gentle voice, but I still couldn't understand a word.

"I'm sorry," I said, my own voice sounding like it'd been dragged through gravel. "I don't understand."

"You don't speak German?" she said after a moment, in accented English.

I paused to consider the question. "I thought I did," I said.

The nurse found that funny.

"Luckily for you, I speak English."

She handed me a large plastic cup with a straw climbing out of it and asked me to have a sip.

The nurse adjusted the bed so that I could sit up.

"It would not surprise me that you can't remember. You took quite a hit to the head."

Pieces started to come back to me.

A terrifying blast through an intersection. A chaotic chase through traffic. Horns, screams, and the agonizing sound of metal twisting beyond its proportions.

I didn't remember a crash.

"Where is Connor," I rasped.

"Connor?"

"One of my...one of the guys with me in the car. The driver. Sorry, I meant Charlie, not Connor." I cursed myself for the slip and hoped the nurse just chalked it up to the head trauma.

"Herr Auer? He was driving, I believe. He is resting comfortably now. He was hurt very badly."

"Oh, right," I said. The nurse didn't give any indication that she noticed my calling Charlie by a different name. "What about our other friend?"

A look passed over her face. "Oh, I'm afraid I don't have any information about anyone else." She flipped through a chart. "Do you feel up for a visitor? The doctor would like to speak with you."

"Sure," I said.

A doctor entered and conducted some pro forma examination. Asked me questions, did I remember anything? He was particularly interested that I claimed to have once been fluent in German but could not remember a word. He explained that I'd sustained a traumatic head injury in the crash, and they were evaluating me for additional complications. The doc used a few terms that I didn't understand. They sounded serious and technical. I described what I could remember, the pressure, like a heat wave but with force, and the sounds. Pain and buzzing, a swarm of furious insects in my ears. It was starting to come back now, in fragments of detail with blurred edges. He said they'd do a battery of scans, CT and MRI, to get a better picture. It seemed like I'd sustained the least grievous injury.

"A gentleman from the police would like to speak with you about the accident, if you feel able. If you don't think you can, I can send him away."

As much as I didn't want to talk to a cop right now, sending him off didn't seem wise.

"It's fine," I said.

"Okay, good. We will talk more later. I'm particularly interested in this question about language."

You and me both, doc.

A man walked in a short time later. He was professionally dressed, but instead of a suit coat he wore a stylish, lightweight field jacket.

"Good evening, Mr. Gage," he said in English, and produced a badge and credentials. "I am told you don't speak German. My name is Gunter Schiller, and I am with the Swiss Federal Police. I am very interested in understanding, from your point of view, what happened? We know Mr. Auer was driving the vehicle, though he has not yet regained consciousness. We'd like to understand why he was speeding through a crowded intersection and driving like he was being chased."

I was too tired to lie, so I gave Schiller the truth. Or at least the closest approximation that I could.

"It's because we were," I said, and gave the cop a few seconds to absorb the information. "I'm a private detective. My client is a journalist. She hired me to vet a source, who is a Swiss citizen." Damn it, what was Fedorov's Swiss name? I couldn't think of it.

"You're having some trouble remembering," Schiller said, a statement, not a question. He picked up my chart and started thumbing through it.

"He's a dual citizen. I knew him as Grigori Fedorov."

"A Russian?"

"Yes."

"Was his name Gregory Künzler, perhaps?"

"Yeah, I think that was it." I reached for the water and took a cooling sip. "Fedorov…Künzler was offering information on a Russian intelligence operation to my client. The Russians were trying to prevent that. We went to…" I paused. Something about this scene felt off to me, but I couldn't tell what. Maybe this wasn't the time to share that Fedorov had stolen Russian intel hidden in his bank box.

"You went to…" the cop prompted.

"Sorry, I'm a little fuzzy. We were on the way to Künzler's hotel to get his things, then the airport. I was to escort him back to the US."

Why were the federal police questioning me on what—to them—should be a reckless driving case? As far as I knew, there were no civilian casualties, and they didn't know Connor's true identity. Of course, I'd just told them about the Russians.

"You were saying?"

"I'd like to see the men I was with."

"That will not be possible for some time. Mr. Auer is unconscious and heavily sedated."

"What about Fedorov? I mean, Künzler?"

"I am afraid I have some bad news. Herr Künzler is dead."

I collapsed back into the bed, feeling like something dark and heavy had just been dropped on me.

"Truly, I am sorry," the Swiss cop continued. "It was a hit-and-run. Herr Künzler was disoriented from the crash and stumbled out of the car, unfortunately into traffic. A car that was fleeing the chaos struck him."

A fragment of information snapped into focus.

"Was it a delivery van?"

The cop cocked his head slightly. "Why, yes. Did you see it before you lost consciousness?"

"Call it a hunch," I said. "We made a stop for Künzler to settle some business in town, and we saw the van. When we were driving, Auer made a few turns to avoid a traffic accident and said the van was following us. He accelerated, and it matched speed. I was already wary of pursuit because we'd had some run-ins with Russian operatives on this case. Then we felt it."

"What is 'it,' exactly?"

"It was like a weight pressing against my skull, the air felt hot, almost electrically charged. I heard this intense ringing or buzzing sound, followed by nausea and disorientation. Künzler screamed. I think he got the worst of it. Auer, too. That's what this case was about. The Russians developed an electromagnetic weapon, they've been using it against Americans for years. I think that's what it was. I bet...if you canvass some of the people who were in that intersection today, you'll come up with a dozen reports of similar symptoms."

Telling Schiller was a calculated risk. Partially, it was to add another datapoint to the story. I wanted there to be some documentation that the Russians weren't abiding by this agreement they'd struck with us in Geneva. Schiller also had a right to know those assholes were playing in his front yard. Still, this could backfire in some spectacular ways.

"What stop did you make?"

Like that.

"I'm sorry. I'm having a hard time putting details together. The timeline is pretty fuzzy. I'll probably be able to answer your questions better in the morning."

Schiller considered this, and I felt like he was sizing me up. Then he nodded and said, "Yes, I suspect you need some rest. I am sorry about Herr Künzler."

"Thank you," I said.

After Schiller left, I hit the nurse's call button.

"How are you feeling, Herr Gage?" she said in English.

"About as well as you'd expect. I was wondering if you could bring me my things. I wanted to check my messages and let some people know that I am safe."

"Yes, of course. They're actually right here." She walked over to a small cabinet in the room and opened it, pulling out a clear plastic bag. It had green lettering, but it was all in German and I couldn't read it. Which was strange because I knew that I *knew* German. She set the bag next to me on the bed. "Is there anything else I can get you?"

"No, thank you."

She left.

I tore into the bag and rummaged around through my clothes. Thankfully, they hadn't had to cut me out of anything. More importantly, the police hadn't confiscated it as evidence. Because it was just my clothes. I pulled my jacket out, felt for the hidden pocket and separated the folds, then unzipped the nearly silent zipper.

Fedorov's flash drive was there.

My phone was dead, and I didn't have a charger, so that was out.

Holding the drive in my hands, I said, "I'm sorry, Grigori."

He'd fled because I'd downplayed the FBI's willingness to help. I'd let my experiences, my distrust of the feds to color my judgment, and Fedorov paid the price for it.

I had long hours in the dark to consider my options. Without Fedorov, I wasn't sure what else I had. The GRU report should've been the decisive article. The problem was, Jennie needed Fedorov to verify its provenance. If she couldn't prove it was true, anyone refuting the story could argue that she'd manufactured it.

And there was the simple fact that I'd promised to protect him and I failed.

Fedorov played a part in hurting Americans, people like Dylan. Not a pivotal one, though, and the GRU would have done this without him. He'd also tried to make it right. Not making excuses for the man, and he still came forward anyway knowing the risk he took.

Without Fedorov, there was no deal with the FBI. That put me in a tenuous position.

Jennie didn't have a story anymore. Connor couldn't go on the record, and even if he did, he was a secondhand source. Maybe Denis's people got enough from Fedorov in their interviews that they could get something for Jennie to use. Fedorov couldn't validate the intel I had in my possession.

It was like holding a lottery check made out to a different name.

The case had never been about Russia. We'd known it was them. The case was about our government, that they'd known the truth and covered it up. We'd just needed the Russians' evidence to prove it.

I knew there was more to this, but I couldn't connect the disparate pieces of information flitting about in my head. One of the major conditions associated with Havana Syndrome was an inability to concentrate. Victims reported intense brain fog. I'd known from Dylan that he'd spend hours composing a simple cable only to have someone read it and it be nearly incomprehensible.

The nurse said earlier Connor was still unconscious. I hit the call button, and a tired voice asked me a question in German, which I still didn't get. I asked, in English, if one of them had an iPhone charger that I could borrow so I could let people know where I was. Eventually, a nurse came in, and it took another ten minutes to find the right kind of adapter. After the inexorable stretch of time for my phone to boot up, it exploded into life with unread messages.

I looked down at the logon screen. Something wasn't right. The phone showed the wrong date. Had it been damaged in the crash? My body must have shielded it from the worst of the microwave, because it still worked. I turned on the TV and found a news channel.

The phone was right. I'd been out for a full day.

The Russian hit squad had a full twenty-four hours with no one watching them. They could be anywhere.

28

Once my phone had enough charge, I called Jennie on Signal. She'd sent me a string of messages earlier letting me know that she'd been released to home confinement, and that an ankle monitor was undeniably humiliating. Then she said if she had to wear "this goddamn thing" there was a list of people she wanted to murder so she at least looked like it belonged on her. Another message said a condition of her release was that she was not allowed to access the internet or work on this story until her court date. Then she answered that with, "Yeah fuck that."

"Matt, where the hell have you been?"

"Unconscious," I said.

"This is not the time," she snapped.

"I'm not joking. I just woke up. I'm in a hospital in Zürich."

"You're what?" She ripped into a rapid-fire, belt-fed string of questions. None of which were intelligible in my current state.

"Jennie, listen to me," I said, breaking in. "Did Coogan get you the security I asked him to?"

"What? No."

"No? There's no one there but you? No one in the lobby?"

"No, why?"

"Son of a bitch." I pinched my eyes shut. The strain creeping into my head was manifesting as a rip current migraine. It'd crash onto the shore, grab me, drag me under and out to a sea of pain. "I don't know how much of this I'd told you, but I guess I can't trust Coogan to do it, so forgive me if I'm repeating myself. Russian agents kidnapped me out of Coogan's garage. They interrogated me and beat me up pretty bad. I escaped before they could exfiltrate me to Moscow."

"You told me all that."

"Right," I said, trying to remember. "Those same people broke into the firm and stole everything from your case. They have all of your research and all of your sources, their contact information. I told Coogan that if you were going to get released, they *had* to protect you."

"Matt—the police think you did it."

"I know. I'd hoped this would blow over by now, but it didn't." I took the phone off my ear so I could scan through messages. There were several missed calls, voicemails, and a text from an LAPD detective. "The Russians framed me, obviously. It was such a half-assed job, I hadn't put much effort into refuting it. That appears to have been a mistake. I'll…call…" But my voice trailed off. Who *would* I call? The Bureau wouldn't help. Coogan probably believed me. I assumed this was coming from his bosses. Not that it mattered, at this point. Maybe I could talk this cop into helping, though I had nothing to offer him. "It gets worse," I said. "They attacked us here, in Zürich. I'm pretty sure they used the microwave weapon."

"'Us' who?"

"Me, Charlie Auer, and Fedorov. Fedorov had all of the GRU's files on Projekt Molniya."

"Do you have it?"

"I think so."

"You *think* so?"

"Jennie…ease up. They were following us, probably hacked Fedorov's phone. They hit us with the microwave while we were driving. The files are electronic, and I don't know if they were damaged. Auer got it the worst, but I got hit too." My ears rang.

"Oh my God, Matty," she said, just shy of breathless.

"I managed to stop the car. But Fedorov…Jennie…Fedorov is dead."

The other end of the line was pin-drop silent.

"The Swiss police just told me. Hit-and-run. I'm certain it was the Russians." My mind was a jumble of thoughts, and it was hard to put them all in order. There were things I knew I needed to tell her, but I couldn't remember what they were. "I have to get out of here," I said.

"It sounds like you need to stay in the hospital."

"I'm not safe here." That much I knew without help. The men who'd killed Fedorov could still be in Zürich, and they might know Connor and I survived.

Thoughts swirled in my mind, dead leaves kicked by the wind.

There was something about Fedorov that I needed to tell her.

Something about his files. Then, it snapped into focus. God, but it was hard to concentrate.

"We have a problem. Another one, I mean."

"I was worried the other shoe would drop at some *really* inconvenient time."

"It's about the files. Without Grigori, we can't prove where they came from."

"But I know it came from him."

"No, you don't. You know that he handed me a hard drive, which I still haven't looked at. Neither of us can prove where it came from." Puzzle pieces slowly congealed into a picture. "The government is trying to kill this, they will just say you made up everything. Or, worse, they use this to hang you. They are trying to prove you illegally have classified information. You write a story with raw intelligence and your answer is, 'Well, your honor, my source died trying to get this to me.' There's nothing to back you up."

"Except you," she said.

I couldn't go on record about any of this now without exposing Connor's involvement. Maybe there wasn't a way to hide that now, I didn't know. It was so hard to think about two things at once.

"So, what do you expect me to do with this?" Jennie poured a lot of anger, bitterness, and cynicism into that short question, and I really wanted to believe it wasn't directed at me. In that moment, I couldn't be sure.

I didn't have an answer.

Wait, maybe I did. Perhaps I was reaching for anything, but I remembered McDonough's proposal.

"When I was in DC last, a former official contacted me." I pinched my eyes shut, trying to remember the details. "I met with him. He...confirmed the intel community's report was a smoke screen. That it was the White House's idea."

"What? Matt, that's everything. That's what we've been after. Who was it?"

Revealing the name was dangerous. I could trust Jennie to keep it quiet, though I also knew what she thought of him personally and that she'd rather light herself on fire than accept help from Joshua McDonough. I didn't want her personal feelings to cloud her judgment on the offer.

"For right now, this has to stay a 'condition of anonymity' kind of thing. I have his permission to make an offer, but he wants his name out of it. Just know that he was a high-ranking national security official."

"Will he ever go on record?"

I actually laughed at that, and it didn't help my position at all.

"Oh, he'll confirm that POTUS told the Kremlin to stop attacking our embassies. The Intelligence Community report was designed to give Moscow and Washington an excuse to step back."

"Then why is he telling you this, but he won't go on record with it?"

"He thinks he can make a deal with the Agency. Support for the victims. He said the administration will use it to say they found new information that reverses their position on Havana Syndrome. Saves face. And he says he can make a deal with the Justice Department, get them to drop the charges."

"But the price tag is that I don't write the story, isn't it? That's why you're sugarcoating it."

"He said the administration won't play along if we expose what they did."

"And you agree with this?"

Fatigue fell on me like a wall without mortar, a few loose bricks and then the whole damned thing. It all caught up to me in that moment. The human body, let alone the mind, can only be in fight or flight for so long before it has to crash. I figured I'd passed that point a few days ago and was just too stubborn to admit it. "Jen, my head got microwaved, and I crashed a car. Then the guy I was here to protect got killed. The only thing I agree with right now is codeine."

I expected a little empathy from her and learned the hard way it was not on offer.

"You didn't answer my question," she said, words cold and smooth like new ice.

"You did hear the part where I almost got killed, right?"

"Sometimes it's hard to know when you're being serious and when you're being sarcastic to make a point. But you need to answer me. I can't believe you'd even consider this. You're protecting the same people that kicked you out."

"I'm not protecting *them*, Jen. I'm looking out for the operators, the rank-and-file people like me that are just trying to do a hard job that doesn't need to be made harder. People like Charlie Auer. And I'm trying to protect you. If you try to run with Fedorov's information without him to back it up, the federal prosecutor could claim you got that from your source. You will have to reveal who it is so *they* can testify that it didn't come from them. If you don't, they'll nail you to a wall. This isn't worth it."

"No," she said, hard and flat. "What isn't worth it is for me to have just spent two weeks in jail and enduring months of harassment for defending my constitutional rights. I'm not making a deal, Matt. If I do that, if I give up a source, I'm done as a journalist. Is that what you want? Sources are based on trust, and you're asking me to burn my credibility to the ground, for what? Some deep state bullshit? I expected better from you."

"Jen, this is everything you wanted. It's proof, it's accountability, and it's support for the victims."

"And it's all in the dark!"

Anger flash fired. "Is it the truth that's important, or that you get credit for it?"

"What did you say?"

The words just boiled up and over, were out before I could contain them, before I even knew what I was saying. "You have no concept of what I've gone through for this. I appreciate you spent some time in jail. I have broken laws for you, been tortured and nearly killed. More than once. Now

I've got someone that can get you off the hook with the feds and get victims support they deserve, but you don't want it because it means you have to give up your story. So, I'm asking what's really important here?"

Jennie's pause felt like the passing of an age. When she spoke, her voice was ice-cold and hard. "I hired you to vet Fedorov, and when they tried to shut me down, I trusted you to carry on the fight. I thought you believed in the same things I did. I'm sorry you were hurt, I truly am. What I don't want is your backroom Washington power-broker bullshit." Jennie's voice trailed off like distant thunder. I said nothing to fill the void. "Just get me the information I asked you to collect, and I'll pay you what you're owed."

There's something deeply unsatisfying about being hung up on in an app.

At least a dial tone gives you closure.

29

I'd replayed that conversation with Jennie a hundred times in my head. Where had that rage come from? I never lost my cool and certainly not with her.

And I'd left out so many details that mattered.

I hadn't explained the risks Connor and I took. And I hadn't said anything about Colonel Orlov, or mercenaries, or Vilnius. I didn't say anything about the FBI thinking I shot Vasiliev. In the moment, none of those things came to mind. My thoughts were just this mass of fog and gauze. Even now, it was hard to concentrate. I tried calling her back once, to explain it all. I left a voicemail, and when I played it back, it didn't make any sense. She didn't return my call.

All I knew now was that I had to get out of here, had to keep moving. Our attackers were still out there. I would have to assume they knew Connor and I were still alive. There were few hospitals in Zürich, so it wouldn't be hard to find us.

I wasn't safe here.

Though I didn't want to leave Connor and I didn't know what condition he was in, I had information that I needed to get back to the States.

Jennie's life was absolutely in danger, and I had to do something. I'd bring her the files, like she'd asked. That's what she was paying me for. And

I needed to clear up whatever this situation with the LAPD was. Hopefully, in doing that, I could convince them to keep watch over Jennie. I'd have to take my chances with the feds. And so would she.

Sleep found me in time, but it was fitful, the dreams vivid and horrifying.

The next morning, after I'd finished the food-like things that passed for hospital breakfast and was drinking a watery coffee, one of the nurses appeared in the doorway and asked if I felt up for a visitor. I didn't feel great, but the injuries I'd sustained in San Francisco were healing now that I'd finally gotten real attention on them. Of course, I now had a fresh stack of new hurts on top of them, but at least there was industrial-grade pain medication for that. The ringing in my ears subsided, and I found it easier to concentrate. One of the nurses found me an English-language newspaper and encouraged me to try to read a little. Not so much that I strained myself, but they wanted to make sure that I could, since I'd said I'd been fluent in German before the accident and now couldn't speak a lick.

I told the nurse I'd see the visitor, assuming it was that Swiss Federal Police officer.

"Matt Gage." It was familiar, like a song you'd heard before but couldn't remember the title of.

She stepped into view at the foot my bed, dressed for lies.

The day before, that Swiss Federal Police officer told me the State Department was sending a consular officer over to interview me. I should've known that it wouldn't have been.

Natalie Harper and I came up together in the Agency and had been cordial, if not friendly. We hadn't known each other well and didn't play in a lot of the same sandboxes, but I'd known she was a good case officer and a decent human. Still, after the FBI cleared my record, I'd heard from some old colleagues offering support and saying my getting run out of the Agency had been bullshit. Natalie Harper was not one of them.

Harper was about five foot eight, mid-forties with shoulder-length hair that threaded a tight needle between blond and brown. Whatever color her eyes were, they were the angry shade of it.

"What are you doing here?" I said. Sometimes I like asking the obvious question.

"I think the better question is, what in the actual hell are *you* doing here?"

"Not sure that's any of your business," I said.

"It is when you involve one of our officers."

"Sure you don't have that backward?" I asked.

"I don't know what you thought you were trying to accomplish, but you got a man killed. And damned near one of our people too."

I was in a terrible position here, and my mind was still fuzzy enough that I knew I couldn't talk my way out of it. I could *maybe* convince Harper that I didn't know Connor was CIA. Of course, that would require a full chorus of bullshit singing in harmony to pull off.

Instead, I'd try to flip it back on her, buy myself some time to think.

"How is Connor?"

"He's still recovering. They've got him sedated. I wasn't allowed to see him, because I'm not family, and the doctor would only tell me so much. Same as with you." She recited those statuses clinically, and without empathy.

Natalie was my peer, which meant she'd likely be a station chief or a deputy at a larger posting. My guess was that she was not the chief at Bern Station, because that was a declared position—the one role in an embassy the CIA explicitly acknowledged they filled. But she'd told the hospital she was a State Department consular officer doing a wellness check, so I assumed she was here undercover.

Connor was traveling under the Charlie Auer alias. I didn't think hospitals notified embassy staff when Americans were admitted, though maybe a combination of the circumstances and Connor's injuries changed that. Because Harper was here now, I had to assume that was what happened. There was no way to know if Harper was, as she said, trying to keep an off-the-books operation quiet, on behalf of Connor's boss at Vilnius, or if Damon Fox somehow knew that I was here and was trying to put blocks in my path.

Until I knew better, I figured Natalie Harper was not on my side. I would not tell her about the files I had.

"Natalie, why are you talking to me? If you say you're here to look after one of your people, I believe you. I'm not one of them. What do you want with me?"

"I'm here to clean this three-ring shit circus up," she said.

My first thought was, *You're going to need a bigger broom.*

"I clocked a pair of watchers on Grigori Fedorov when he got off the train. Then a different group chased us through town. It was a Russian hit squad."

"And you can prove this?"

"I know the SVR nabbed me off the street and interrogated me in California." On the off chance Harper would report this directly to Fox, this was the kind of thing I wanted in that cable.

"I think that's an overactive imagination and someone too used to jumping at shadows. The *facts* are that you drove recklessly through a crowded street and crashed a car. Then one of your passengers, dazed from the crash, wandered into traffic and got hit by a car."

"You cannot seriously believe that's all it is," I said, though I knew she already believed it.

"Consider this a warning, because it sure as shit isn't professional courtesy. We have too much going on in this region right now to have it get blown up by you. There are things you need to answer for, Gage. The Russians claim one of *us* exfiltrated a Russian national out of Belarus two weeks ago. And during that...operation, an SVR officer was murdered."

"Yeah, I've heard all this."

"Well, the FBI has it now. I suspect they'll have questions for you." Harper looked at her watch. "In fact, you could probably be expecting the LEGAT and the Regional Security Officer over from the embassy by the afternoon. If they aren't here already."

The LEGAT, or legal attaché, was an FBI agent who was the senior Justice Department representative in a country. About the last person I wanted to talk to right now. Because, unlike Natalie, the LEGAT could arrest me.

Harper narrowed her eyes but said nothing else.

Seemed like a strange threat, unless she was here just to twist the knife. Maybe a veiled threat not to invoke the Agency when the Bureau guys pressed me on Fedorov's escape. Wouldn't put it past her.

Add that to my running list of problems.

I didn't care that a random Russian intel officer thought I shot one of his pals at a Belarus train station. I did care that the FBI thought that, especially since my alibi was riding a slab.

"Is that all?" I said.

Harper shook her head, put a hand on the door, and made to leave.

"Natalie, wait."

She turned.

"Connor reached out to me, but he used an alias to do it. The only reason I knew he was with the company was because I'd taught him at the schoolhouse." I didn't know if admitting that would do Connor any good.

Natalie Harper regarded me in silence for a moment and said, "Gage, you're not one of us anymore. For your own sake, I hope you take that to heart." Then she left the room.

Now, I had to think about getting out of here.

Checking the time, I figured that the nurses weren't due to look in on me for another thirty minutes.

The hospital had given me a set of pajamas and a robe. I changed into my street clothes, which were decidedly worse for wear, and then put the hospital clothes over them. I had my jacket folded up and tucked beneath the robe, making sure Fedorov's drive was still secured in the hidden pocket.

I popped my head out into the hallway to check the nurse's station, and I understood. Harper stood by the elevators talking with the Swiss Federal Police officer who'd interviewed me yesterday. He had a couple of friends with him. So, I was under guard after all. Obviously, the elevators were out. However, there was a stairwell at the other end of this hallway.

Harper had something in her hand that I couldn't see, but it might have been a tablet, which she'd set on the counter at the nurse's station. She and the Swiss cops were now huddled around that.

Harper's admonition, *you're not one of us anymore*, echoed in my mind.

We'll see.

Harper and the Swiss cops were looking at her tablet and not at me, so I slid out of my room, closed the door, and made fast steps for the stairwell.

Once I was down the stairs, I balled my hospital clothes up and tossed them in a waste bin. I found a side exit on the ground floor and disappeared into the cloudy morning.

They'd taken me to the Zürich University Hospital, which was not even a mile from that hotel I'd stayed in. Hopefully, they still had my bag. My clothes were pretty ripe, and the shirt had blood on it. Walking through the cool morning helped clear my head, and immediately I started thinking about how easy that was to get out of the hospital.

First, there was Natalie Harper telling me the FBI was on their way. At the time, it felt like a threat, but now it seemed more like a warning. Then there was her occupying the Swiss police's attention at the other end of the hallway. That distraction gave me enough time to slip away. Had she really helped me escape? Me being in the wind reduced the number of questions CIA needed to answer to the Swiss by a lot.

It took the focus off "Charlie Auer," though at the expense of putting it squarely on me. Harper could spin whatever story she wanted. Gifts come in strange packages, and I wasn't in a position to turn one down. If the Agency's pathological bent toward damage control helped me out, so be it.

The hotel manager, thankfully, still had my gear. I told them I'd been in an accident and thanked them for keeping it for me. After changing clothes in a bathroom, I walked to the Bahnhof.

First thing, I needed to get the hell out of Zürich and plan my next move.

I needed time to look through Fedorov's documents and confirm they hadn't been wiped out. Make sense of them, see what use they could be. If any.

Three and a half hours would have me in Munich. I bought a ticket and navigated my way to the appropriate platform. Once I got there and found a hotel, I could adjust my return trip to LAX to leave from Munich. Hopefully, I'd be home late tomorrow.

Jennie would have the documents. And I could get medical attention in a language I understood.

The consequences of my hasty exit from the hospital were now manifesting in the form of a dull, throbbing forced march of pain in my skull. The last round of narcotics were wearing off. The click-clack of the train and mechanical swaying as we rolled over tracks didn't do anything to help.

I shut my eyes, as though that would ward off the pain. I dozed a bit, and thankfully, I didn't miss my connection.

I got a room at the Hilton Munich Airport and chased a handful of aspirin with a glass of Glen Whatever-the-Hell-Was-Behind-the-Bar.

My phone buzzed in my pocket.

McDonough.

As if I needed the universe to remind me of my narrowing options. And my head was already hurting enough. I'd want narcotics to talk with this guy even if I hadn't been in a car accident.

"What is it, McDonough? This isn't the best time."

"I suspect it isn't," he said. The jovial lilt in his voice made me sick to my stomach. "I'll be fast because I'm sure you have a great deal on your mind. I'd hoped that you hadn't forgotten about our agreement."

We didn't have an "agreement." He gave me a Faustian offer, and I told him I'd consider it. Though, I suppose that's how people like him thought. The word "offer" was just a polite way of saying, "This is what I expect to happen."

"As I understand it, Matt, you've found yourself in even deeper shit than the last time we talked. I am your only friend in this town, believe me. From what I hear, the sand was already running out of your hourglass before you started tapping it with a hammer. I can make your problems, and Ms. Burkhardt's problems with the Justice Department, go away. But I can't help you once you're in their custody."

"Duly noted," I said. "Is there any world where you'll consider letting Burkhardt write her story? Even if she constrains it to the facts she currently has, which is proof of Projekt Molniya?"

"There is not."

"That's what I thought. You'll hear from me soon. I promise." I disconnected the call.

Exhaustion came like a squall. It came on so fast, I paid my check and staggered back to my room, surely seeming a stumbling drunk to anyone peeking in the hallway. I'd pushed myself too far and should by all rights still be in the hospital.

I felt like I was looking at the world through a series of broken mirrors with everything at odd angles to reality. Somehow, I managed to get my door open and stumbled to a bed. I saw a couple of them, so I aimed for the one in the middle.

30

The phone rang, and I answered without thinking.

History will rightly judge this a mistake.

"Gage, this is Cedric Rawlings."

I was completely disoriented. How did Rawlings get the phone number to my hospital room?

"Agent Rawlings," I said drowsily.

"First of all, why aren't you in the hospital?"

Wait, I wasn't in the hospital?

Munich. I'd gone to Munich.

Memories fell into place like a glass breaking in reverse.

The drumbeat in my skull returned.

I sat up and tried to force myself awake. All I knew was that I was in no condition to go toe-to-toe with him.

"I've got some new information. There's some things you need to hear."

"Like hell I do. The legal attaché from Bern was supposed to interview you, today, about what happened there. And you disappeared."

Interview? That's rich.

Wait, he said *there*. That meant he might still think I was in Zürich.

"Someone tried to kill me...us. And it's not the first time since I started this case either. Since I haven't been getting any help from your side, I decided not to stick around."

"There are three dead Russians in Zürich, and you're missing," Rawlings said flatly.

"What?"

I turned on the light on the nightstand and looked for the remote.

Rawlings was still talking. "Here's what I know, Gage. You say someone tried to kill you. I've met you, so I believe that. Now, three men are dead. Just like in Belarus. And there's an unclaimed body on a slab in San Francisco that looks a lot like someone we've got on a watchlist as a suspected Russian intelligence office. Or, he would if he weren't waterlogged."

"Well, if I was in San Francisco killing a spy, I couldn't have been in Los Angeles breaking into a law office. So, at least there's an alibi for that," I said.

"You think this is a goddamn game? Everywhere you go, Russian spooks are ending up dead. Way this looks to me is they took a swing at you, and you're getting some payback. Or maybe you're just settling some old scores." Rawlings wouldn't say more on a nonsecure line, but the implication was enough. I could assume from that little bit that Fox had talked to him.

"I didn't shoot that man outside Minsk. That was Fedorov, not that you could ask him about it now. They got him yesterday."

"Convenient, that."

"I've had it with your half-assed accusations, Rawlings. A federal credential doesn't give you the right to just make shit up and call it evidence. The Russians murdered Fedorov to keep him quiet. I didn't know anything about the three new ones until you told me about it just now."

The words were out of my mouth and zipping across the ether before I'd realized that I'd walked right into the trap he'd set. If I'd had half my faculties, I'd have seen that coming.

"Seems like motive to me," he said, with conviction. "Gage, you've got twenty-four hours to turn yourself into the LEGAT at the US embassy in Bern. After that, an INTERPOL Red Notice goes out on you, and every police agency in Europe is going to have your picture. Not even you can hide from that."

"I've got proof, Rawlings."

"Then turn yourself in and we'll talk it out."

"Damn it, why won't you listen to me? Fedorov gave me all of the Projekt Molniya files. I can prove everything."

"Turn yourself in. Twenty-four hours," Rawlings repeated, and hung up.

I turned the room's TV on, searching for some news on the accident. There was nothing on the local stations, not that I could understand the coverage anyway. The only English-language network I could find was CNN International, and they were reporting on the war in Gaza.

I fired up my laptop, connected the hotspot and VPN, and surfed.

Three Russian men with ties to organized crime were found dead in Zürich this morning.

I stared at the screen until my eyes hurt.

The three men, each with suspected ties to an Eastern European crime syndicate, were found dead in Zürich, in an execution-style killing with a single bullet to the head. Not that it was proof, but when the KGB would kill a traitor or suspected spy, they'd shoot them in the face to deny the victim's family an open casket. The news site showed their pictures, which were mug shots from three different law enforcement agencies. The one in the middle—I recognized him immediately. I didn't know him until I saw it, but it was the wide, bald head and dead eyes staring at me from across the street as we left the bank.

They were the ones in the courier van who chased us through Zürich, the ones who hit us with the microwave gun, or whatever the hell it was.

And someone had shot each of them in the head, and the Federal Bureau of Investigation thought it was me.

Just once, it'd be nice if there was a body that the feds didn't think was my fault.

Obviously, I wasn't getting back to sleep.

I wasn't getting back to Los Angeles, either.

DC was an unavoidable next stop. Even if I went home, the Bureau would just jerk the chain and make me come back there.

It was four in the morning, so I got after the room's coffee machine and tried to assemble the facts in my mind. It felt like looking at a puzzle with ninety percent of the pieces in place, yet still unable to identify the picture. It was hard to concentrate, hard to think straight.

Okay—start with what I know.

The GRU built the weapon, so it stood to reason our attackers were connected to Projekt Molniya.

Fedorov told me the GRU used contractors for the Vilnius attack. My bet, those three dead bodies in Zürich were contractors too. But who'd killed them?

It was possible the GRU decided to silence their contractors. That seemed a little canny for them. In my experience, the GRU would call the asteroid that killed the dinosaurs a precision weapon.

Malyshkin.

I told Jennie they found us because they were tracking Fedorov's phone, and maybe that was true. But I'd told them where to look. When Malyshkin tortured me, I had to give him something, so I'd said Fedorov was going to Zürich. In the moment, it was a lie that I could sell. He lived there, it was a reasonable guess. I didn't want them looking in Brussels. I'd done it to throw the SVR off our trail; instead, I'd led them right to us.

I wanted to scream, for all the good it would do.

And I could only ask forgiveness of Fedorov's ghost so many times.

Natalie Harper was another thing that didn't add up. I know a delaying tactic when I see one, and she clearly ran interference. She said the LEGAT was on their way to debrief me and gave me a time frame. Why would she help me?

Getting me out of the hospital made it easier for Harper to shape the narrative around Connor Bishop. From that angle, I could see it.

But letting me loose with Fedorov's intel meant CIA couldn't control the story.

And it seemed like more grace than the Agency had afforded me of late.

I'd powered up my laptop and scanned Fedorov's drive to make sure it hadn't been damaged.

Everything was there.

At first glance, it looked like what he'd described to me. Weapons designs, multiple versions, and I could trace the evolution of the system through the years. I saw the mission report detailing the GRU's attack against the American embassy in Vienna. There were also the technical designs stolen from Western defense companies and, in some cases, lists of components Fedorov purchased under the guise of working for a Swiss military tech firm. At a minimum, I could warn them about potential sabotage.

I didn't want to believe all of this had been for nothing.

I could connect a Russian-made weapon to attacks on American embassies. And I could confirm the United States government, including two presidents, knew about it. I could also confirm that the Intelligence Community authored a report at the White House's direction that refuted all of the above.

The part I couldn't answer was *why now*?

If everything McDonough told me was true, why would the Russians risk the deal they'd struck with the White House? It was basically a get-out-of-jail-free card.

McDonough also downplayed CINDER SPIRE, that covert counterattack he'd helped design. But when Jennie learned about that from Audrey Farre, she'd been told to start there.

There was something about CINDER SPIRE, the Geneva Summit, and that conversation that was still missing, and that was the link I was looking for.

I knew someone who could answer that question, too.

I reached for my phone and dialed.

...Which went straight to voicemail.

"Colonel Mercer, this is Matt Gage. I'm the private detective that tried to reach you regarding an investigation into Havana Syndrome. It's very important that I speak to you. Please call me back as soon as you get this."

I grabbed the room's complimentary notepad and pen and wrote down the questions I wanted to ask Colonel Mercer, if I ever got to speak to him. Focusing still took effort, and I didn't want to stumble through that conversation, should it actually happen. God only knew how long this would last.

I was physically and mentally exhausted, knew that I needed rest, and understood with equal certainty that I couldn't afford to take it. Every second felt like stolen time.

With just a few hours until my flight to DC, I messaged an old colleague to see if he was awake.

Mickey, a.k.a. Mikhail Iliescu, was a Romanian hacker and *mostly* reformed criminal. He'd learned his trade working for some Eastern European syndicates before we'd shown him it was much safer and more profitable to play for our team. We'd used him as a contractor when I was in the Agency, and I'd used him as a consultant throughout my time as a PI. If I needed something done in cyberspace, Mickey was my guy. Mickey also maintained a conduit into some of Europe's darker information tunnels and was a valuable source of intel. I'd broken a slew of rules connecting with him once I was out and telling him my real name. I was also in a place where I didn't care about them.

Mickey called me back a few minutes later. "Matthew, how are you, my friend? You know this is early for me, yes?"

"Sorry. And yes, I know. I'm in Germany, so at least it's early for me too. I was wondering if you could track some names down for me."

"Sure thing. How soon do you need it?"

"ASAP." I cut and pasted a link to an article showing the mug shots and names of the three Russians executed in Zürich. "I think these guys are all contract hitters for the GRU. Probably former Spetsnaz."

"Okay, this shouldn't be too hard."

"One more name. There is an SVR officer named Anton Malyshkin. I don't have much to go on, other than a name."

"That might be more problematic, but I'll see what I can do."

"Thanks, Mick. I owe you."

"That is correct," he said matter-of-factly, and hung up.

It hit me that I'd never told Denis about what happened with Fedorov. While a hit-and-run following a traffic accident wouldn't exactly be international news, three hit men being murdered would be. Surely he was following local coverage in Zürich. I messaged Denis to let him know I was safe. He'd called earlier when he'd heard about the accident. I confirmed that it was us, and that Fedorov was dead. I told him I had all of Fedorov's documents, as well as my fears about proving their authenticity without

Fedorov. Denis shared those concerns but said we'd work something out. He pressed me for my next steps, and I told him I'd let him know. He asked me to consider bringing the drive to Brussels and returning to the States from there. I said I'd think about it.

When it was time, I grabbed my things and went down to the hotel's restaurant for a quick breakfast. While I was eating, I got a text from Jennie.

Jennie: **Hey—where are you?**

I stared at my phone for a good long while, thinking about what to say to her. Since I can only read women I'm trying to recruit, I couldn't tell if this meant she was still mad at me, she needed something, or it was a peace offering.

Me: **Does this mean we're speaking again?**

Admittedly, I was in a dark place and was just looking for some kind of reassurance that at least we were back on some kind of footing.

Jennie: **I'm sorry. It was my fault. Where are you?**
Me: **Munich**
Jennie: **When are you coming back to LA?**
Me: **IDK. Have something I need to do first.**
Jennie: **What is it?**
Me: **You hired me to get info for you. Who knew what when. Answers are in DC. Heading there now.**

I stopped typing, as it finally registered this was over SMS and not in Signal. Jennie and I both had iPhones, and their messaging app was fairly secure. The danger with an SMS system was the carrier retained copies of the data transmitted over their networks. They couldn't read it, necessarily, but could turn it over to a court. Not only was Signal encrypted, the company didn't retain copies of the messages, and users could set their messages to auto-delete after reading.

I didn't want to tell her that I was out of both options and time. I had to turn myself into Rawlings, at least to clear up this thing with the three dead operators in Zürich. After that? McDonough's offer was looking like my, and Jennie's, only real way out.

Jennie: **R u still there?**
Me: **Yeah. Why are you using SMS?**

I watched the rolling ellipsis as Jennie typed a response, stopped, and then finished her thought.

Jennie: **New phone. FBI took my other one. Still getting it set up. Do you have anything from Fedorov?**

Me: **I have everything.**

Jennie: **Have a safe flt. B careful!!!**

She didn't sign off the way I'd hoped, and anyone in my position would understand exactly what I meant. Despite everything going on around me right now, despite what I was in the middle *of*, what I wanted in that moment was some reassurance that I had something to come back *to*.

The hours until my flight burned quietly away.

Nine hours to come up with a plan.

31

My flight landed at Dulles at four thirty, and I was reasonably certain it was a Friday.

Vertigo started on final approach, and I'd barely made the lavatory when we landed to heave my guts up. The nausea faded to a headache I couldn't penetrate with the bottle of aspirin I'd brought from Germany.

It wasn't until I'd cleared Customs that it hit me I wasn't arrested. The way Rawlings made it sound, I should have expected FBI agents fast-roping from black helicopters the second I stepped off the plane. Could be that he was bluffing and didn't have enough to detain me on.

I rented a car, secured my things in the trunk, and entered the gladiatorial arena that was DC-metro traffic in evening rush.

Late summer heat pressed down on me with a particular fury. A row of thunderheads had been building off to the west and were making their inexorable march toward DC. Special Agent Rawlings did not try to reach me again, even after the twenty-four-hour clock expired, triggering my alleged international fugitive status. I'd booked a room in Crystal City, which might as well have been on the other side of the earth, but it was close to Reagan National and had easy access to the District. To my cosmic amazement, it only took me ninety minutes to get there from Dulles. My body was stretched to the breaking point by the elasticity of international travel as my day clawed into its twenty-fourth hour.

I dropped my bags at the hotel and was heading out to grab food and coffee when my phone buzzed.

I flicked an eye down at the screen. It was Colonel Mercer.

Mercer was my last, real lead. He was the one who could confirm that the White House ordered the Intelligence Community to fabricate some justification that they could offer Moscow at that summit.

"This is Gage," I said.

"Mr. Gage, I'm only going to tell you this once. I'm not interested in speaking with you. I wanted to tell you personally so there was no equivocation. Is that clear?"

I'd had enough of people hoarding answers while those without suffered, or died.

I could almost hear me snapping in my mind.

"No, it isn't. Let me tell you what is. I have specs for a Russian-made microwave weapon, Colonel. A defector smuggled them out. I have files from the GRU headquarters confirming they used it against our embassy in Vienna. Something tells me you know about that even without that document. I absolutely should not be telling you this over a nonsecure phone, but I don't have any options left. I'm tired of everyone in a position to do something doing nothing. Acting like if they pretend hard enough, it'll just go away. Hundreds of our people—dips, spooks, staffers...*families*—have been injured, many permanently. And add me to that list too, now. Some have taken their lives because the government they served told them it never even happened. Now, I think you might have information that we need to end this thing. You can talk to me, and I'll hear your side. Or I just give everything I have to my reporter client, she writes her story, and the fucking lot of you can sort this out in front of Congress. How is that for *clear*, Colonel?"

The air was filled with a hot and dangerous quiet.

"What do you want from me, Gage?" The aggression was gone from his voice, but not the wariness.

"Answers that only you can give. If there is something you genuinely can't, I'll respect that. Someone in power knows the truth. They are covering it up, and I want to know why. I will light a lot of things on fire until I find that out."

"Where are you right now?"

"Crystal City," I said.

"There's a parking lot outside the Courthouse Metro. That's not too far from where you're at. I'm just leaving the White House now. I should be there in less than thirty minutes."

"Thank you, Colonel."

Arlington's Courthouse neighborhood sat atop a bluff at the Potomac's dogleg bend, with Georgetown on the other side. The scene was a mix of local government, contractors, and tech companies. It was nearing seven, and streetlights were coming on. The air was thick and hot, charged with violent unspent energy. Thunder growled in the distance.

Colonel Mercer cut an unmissable figure as he sauntered into the parking lot, even though he wore civilian clothes. He was in a navy polo and chinos, his uniform likely tucked into the issued ruck slung on his shoulders. He was six feet even, wiry, with corded muscle and a precisely engineered high-and-tight haircut. He had a hawk's eyes.

Mercer slowed when he saw me, approaching warily.

"Thanks for coming," I said.

"Did they really hit you with it?"

"They did, in Zürich. It was two days ago."

"Christ, why aren't you in a hospital?"

"That's a great question." My eyes tracked across the parking lot and the surrounding buildings. The sky was an ugly gray-green color, and it was nearly nighttime dark. The streets were full of the usual Friday evening crowds, though people seemed to move with a nervous urgency atypical of a late DC summer.

"Ask your questions. You must appreciate that there are some things I will be unable to answer, either because I am not privy to that knowledge or because you aren't cleared to know them."

I nodded my understanding.

"I can prove the GRU designed and fielded an energy weapon at the Kremlin's direction. I can prove they gave it to the Cuban DGI to field test in Havana. Attacks continued for approximately five years, with a major surge in 2021. Up until the Geneva Summit that year. Another source confirmed a five-minute, off-the-record conversation between POTUS and the Russian president. The attacks stopped immediately after that summit. Shortly after, the Intelligence Community published the results of a study concluding that Havana Syndrome is a 'mass psychological event.'" I paused, taking in his reaction. To his credit, Mercer wasn't giving me anything. You could've carved his expression from a block of granite. "Colonel, I'd like you to confirm a theory. The president wanted a way out. He was looking for a way to back down from this and not go to war over it. He asks the IC to produce a report that would let him do that. And if the Russians refused his offer, he had a pretty ugly get-back plan to unload on them."

A scoffing smirk painted across Mercer's face.

"I know about CINDER SPIRE."

The look drained away. "There's about ten people who know that whose job title isn't 'POTUS.' Now we're talking breach."

"Did the White House direct the Intelligence Community to justify a medical explanation?"

"Tell me how you heard about SPIRE."

"Will you answer my question?"

"Yes," he said.

"Joshua McDonough," I said.

After a long, cold moment, Mercer said, "That makes sense." He shook his head slowly and exhaled, as if exorcising something. "I'm a little different in that my tour on the National Security Staff bridged two administrations. I was supposed to rotate back to Marine Headquarters about two years ago, but the current advisor asked if I could stay on until the end of the term. Anyway, I came in at the tail end of McDonough's time as advisor. He approached me after they'd shut down the embassy in Havana and asked me to coordinate with CIA to come up with a CONOPS, that's—"

"I know what a CONOPS is," I said dryly.

"Right, well, he wanted one that outlined some broad clandestine operations we could conduct against the Russians. I outlined the effects, and the Agency's ops people would come up with the actual plan. Before you ask, I will not go into the details of either in a parking lot."

"Did you coordinate this with the Senate Intel Committee?"

"The Agency handled that and just notified me when it was done," he said.

Which would be how Audrey Farre learned about it. In order for a president to authorize a covert operation, one that is intended to be publicly deniable, the Agency has to advise Congress that they're doing it. It's the times they don't that the Agency really finds themselves in the shit.

"How did you come to be in contact with Joshua McDonough?" Mercer asked.

I told him. I described the anonymous Signal messages, the irritatingly cloak-and-dagger meeting, and the information he gave at that meeting in Georgetown.

"What does McDonough get out of this?"

"He was hoping that I'd give him the GRU intel," I said. "He's planning something. He told me that he's got some op cooking with some senior Agency people that are pissed we're not hitting back. Personally, I think there's more to it than that. There's a fifty-fifty shot his party takes the White House in November. If they do, he's got a major intel coups to hand over in exchange for something like being named Secretary of State. He told me that you two were buddies, by the way. He said the reason he came forward was because you weren't comfortable doing it."

I'd landed that shot perfectly.

Mercer clearly took notes being in the West Wing as long as he had. He concealed his reaction deftly, but I saw the hint of it anyway, and I knew McDonough had lied. In our meeting, he'd told me Colonel Mercer had been his ally in the administration. I could tell from the colonel's reaction, however well he masked it, that nothing was further from the truth. It was the simple gut reaction of pure, venomous loathing.

"Your expression tells me that isn't entirely accurate," I said. "I don't know that McDonough broke any laws. I also don't know that his name is going to come out of this very clean. If you're not colluding with him, now is a great time to get on the right side of it."

Mercer looked away, at some point behind me and to the side. "Just because I understand the game doesn't mean I like or approve of the rules. Joshua McDonough can go to hell. He wants power for the sake of power, not for the good it might do. No, I'm not working with him. And there's no way I would. I cannot stand him, or those like him." Mercer paused to collect his thoughts, and perhaps offer a silent prayer to whatever god of bureaucratic vengeance might shine upon him. "I think he was manipulating you. Certainly he had his way with the facts. Is he the one who told you the White House directed the CIA to come up with that report?"

I nodded.

"Most of your information is right, but you're off on one key detail." Mercer paused for the span of several breaths, to make sure he had my absolute attention. "That report was CIA's idea."

"It was?"

"My point person at Langley was a special assistant to the Director. We'd revived CINDER SPIRE leading up to the Geneva Summit. The idea was, this was the stick POTUS was going into the meeting with. Stop the attacks, or else."

"So, they believed Russia *was* attacking us?"

"Opinions were mixed, and that's the truth. I don't actually know what POTUS believed. Most of the staff thought *something* was going on. Just before the summit, the Director's staff reached out and said they'd been studying this. What if POTUS suggested to the Kremlin that this could all go away? Everyone back down, walk away."

"And they just took it?" Anger roiled, and I fought to keep my temper in check.

"People in the administration didn't know what to make of Havana, because it started with their predecessor. Some think it's plausible the Russians had a weapon, others don't think they'd would ever be that reckless. All that mattered at the time was it was one more crisis we could take off the board. So, POTUS did. For what it's worth, the CIA Director believed the report, and the president trusts him implicitly. That's how this guy works. If the Director said gravity was failing, POTUS would grab a hand rail."

"So, the Agency offers a way out to present to Moscow. Moscow agrees, the attacks stop, and then the report comes out."

"Yes. I mean, the CIA Director and the Director of National Intelligence both testified before Congress on this. That pretty much shut down any questions." It would, because if it proved otherwise, they'd both be guilty of perjury.

"And when I told you that I had proof the Russians did it?"

"That's why I'm here, Gage."

I got my phone out and navigated to some photos I'd taken of Fedorov's documents. For the chances he was taking, Mercer deserved more than just my word. I handed him the phone and let him swipe, narrating as he went. He landed on the GRU's post-mission report from Vienna. With a grave expression, Mercer handed me back my phone.

The Agency, rather than the presidency, buried this.

"What was the name of your person at Langley?" I asked. Before he even said the name, I knew.

"Damon Fox."

Fox crafted this plan, gave the White House the way out they were looking for—even if they wouldn't admit it—and allowed everyone the plausible deniability they needed to back down from war. In exchange, Fox leaped over half a dozen more senior, more qualified officers to become Deputy Director and run the operations division.

"What's your next move, Gage?"

That was a damned good question.

Much of the answer depended on whether Mercer would go on record.

The CIA fabricating the "proof" about Havana Syndrome was an explosive revelation—it was something on the order of the "Family Jewels," or Watergate.

Fox getting a promotion out of this would be icing, but it wouldn't be the reason he came up with it. I could see that the White House would take it as an opportunity to put out one more fire they didn't need. But the question remained: What was the problem Fox was trying to solve with this plan?

Mercer's hard stare reminded me there was an unanswered question there.

"My next move is to get this information to my client. I promise to keep your name out of it, as we agreed. However, I was wondering if you might be willing to be an anonymous source for her."

Mercer took some time in considering that answer.

"There would have to be conditions," he finally said.

"Of course," I said.

"Are you…all right? You look like you just watched someone kick over a tombstone."

"I always believed the Agency covered Havana up. I mean, I was *there*. I *saw* it used, what it did to people. I wanted this to be more, wanted those lives to be worth more than some bullshit de-escalation to save face."

"What did you think it would be?"

I shrugged. "Some 4D chess move, telling the world it was all made up to lull the Russians into complacency and then wrecking them across the globe? I mean, I knew it wasn't, right? I heard them say the lies. Guess I just hoped it would be for something more."

"My experience, it usually isn't," Mercer said. "Of course, my perspective is calibrated by Iraq."

"I bet you and I hate a lot of the same people, Colonel."

He laughed, short and curt. Because that's about what you can do here. "I bet we do. Good luck, Gage. I think I know you well enough not to tell you to be careful, so just watch your six."

"Thank you. I can't tell you how much I appreciate what you've done here today. I'm grateful."

Colonel Mercer and I shook hands, and I watched him walk north out of the parking lot.

Maybe now was the time to call Danzig and see if I had enough to trade.

Rawlings wanted me arrested for murders I didn't commit, and I had no real proof that I didn't do it. Maybe giving them Fedorov's intel, plus what Mercer just revealed, would be enough to buy an ounce of grace from the feds.

A queer feeling came over me, which I first attributed to the lingering vertigo.

But this was different.

You spend enough time working the streets, the dark corners of the world, you develop a sense of things. An instructor called it a "sixth sense," which I never bought into. More of a survival instinct. Anyway, you have a way of knowing when you're being watched. The world feels off somehow, like the axis tilted half a degree and no one knows it but you.

Turning my head, I saw a black Chevrolet Suburban with blacked-out windows at the far end of the parking lot. Not sure why they bothered with the presumption of secrecy, might as well paint "OBVIOUS FEDS" on the side.

Acting as though I hadn't seen them, I made for the sidewalk. There was a movie theater on the parking lot's west side, so I headed toward that, and once their line of sight was blocked, I dashed into an alley. I could hear the engine roar from here.

Goddamn it, Rawlings.

I guess we're doing this.

32

Why would I run if I planned to turn myself in anyway?

First of all, getting dragged out of a parking lot by some lurking agents wasn't my terms. I'd talk to Rawlings, but only after I'd negotiated a deal and ensured I didn't lose control of Fedorov's intel. He was trying to grab me and take that off the table, which was dirty pool.

I needed to split the pursuit, so I dashed out of the parking lot, between the theater and an apartment complex. There was a tree-lined plaza between several buildings. It was filled with small pockets of people crowded around the few bars or restaurants that spilled out into the open space between buildings. I was a block from the Courthouse Metro entrance.

I was somewhat familiar with this neighborhood, though it'd been a couple years since I'd been here. Improvising an evasion route was difficult but not impossible.

It would get harder if the feds had backup from the local police.

Back in the parking lot, the Suburban screeched to a stop. Doors slammed.

Ignoring that, I kept pressing to the north, toward the Metro. Through the gap in the buildings, I could see Clarendon Boulevard, sporting a stream of cars. I moved quickly, exiting the plaza and ducking to the right when I hit the street.

Metro's tracks were underground in this part of the city. The entrance was in the corner of the building between Clarendon and Wilson. I bolted across Clarendon, darting between cars like I was wearing a force field. Once I'd made the sidewalk, I looked up the street and saw the Suburban speeding through a cross street. Traffic here was one-way, with Clarendon Boulevard handling eastbound traffic and its parallel road, Wilson, westbound. I made the far sidewalk, turned, and bolted up the pavement. I had to make the Metro station before that Suburban rounded the block.

It registered in some part of my brain that I hadn't seen lights or sirens when the Suburban first rolled on me in the parking lot.

Looking back over my shoulder as I ran, I saw an agent in plainclothes clearing the crosswalk at full speed, only he had the benefit of a walk signal, which let him gain ground.

The sound of screaming tires told me the Suburban cleared the corner.

I dipped into the Metro entrance and made for the stairs. I bounded down them, two steps at a time, safety ignored. At the bottom, the hallway split in a T. One branch led to the entrance on the opposite street corner; the other reached into the terminal's dimly lit depths. I mixed with the throng of commuters and joined the flow moving toward the turnstiles. Just before it was my turn, I spotted a secluded and dark hallway leading to a maintenance door. I turned around and saw my pursuer hadn't rounded the corner yet, so I slipped out of line.

This wasn't a perfect hiding spot. In fact, anyone looking down this black alcove would see me immediately. It only worked because if you were in a crowd jostling to get to a Metro card reader on a turnstile, why would you look over here?

I saw the agent from the streets jog into the station and then pad himself for a Metro card. He pulled something out of his wallet and got into the queue. He turned his head to the side, trying to pick a sonic needle out of the din around him.

Someone behind the agent jostled in line, impatient at the stall in forward progress.

The agent turned back to the card reader, paid a fare, and walked through the turnstile.

I stepped out of the alcove and slipped into the caterpillar line of people moving to exit the station. At the end of the hallway, I turned right, taking the long corridor to the opposite side of the street.

I did not stop to look back.

Once I'd returned to street level, I frantically looked for the Suburban. My nerves flared when I didn't see it. I ducked into a wedge-shaped drugstore on the corner. The pharmacy had another exit, which opened to Wilson, and I slipped out that door. There wasn't enough foot traffic that I could truly blend in, so I hugged the wall and walked fast.

I crossed to the next block and dipped into the lobby of an office building, then navigated through it to a parking garage. That led me back to 15th Street, opposite the parking lot where I'd met Colonel Mercer and two blocks from the Metro. I'd just made a huge loop of several blocks. I stayed beneath the shadows of the trees lining the street. If I kept going, this would take me east to Rosslyn. My car was behind me, to the southwest, on a side street beneath the parking lot.

This was all wrong.

There should be Arlington County Police all over this place by now, and certainly more than one vehicle's worth of FBI agents.

Rawlings had given me some shit about a twenty-four-hour limit, which I'd blown past. If he was going to arrest me, they'd have announced themselves as federal agents. But how would they do that in the first place?

I opened my phone to call Danzig. Better to negotiate with her than Rawlings.

There was a new message from Denis. Doing some quick math, it looked like it'd come in while I was on the plane, and maybe the phone just hadn't synced with the server.

Denis Coenen: Matt—do you have a number for Charlie Auer? Sppsd to meet 2day but am running late. He's reached out over email w/ info for story, deets l8r.

What the hell was Denis talking about? Connor had never met Denis, virtually or otherwise. He'd have no reason or way to contact him.

And Connor was still in the hospital.

Which Denis wouldn't know, because I hadn't told him Connor—"Charlie Auer"—was in Zürich with me. I'd only told Denis about Fedorov.

Oh dear God.

The realization cracked my mind with terrible clarity.

Someone pretended to be Charlie Auer, not knowing who he really was, to get to Denis. If they'd been on Fedorov's phone, they could easily have picked up the Auer alias. Connor probably used a cheap mobile phone to communicate with Fedorov, which could easily be spoofed.

This would be two days after someone shot three GRU contract killers.

I called Denis, and it went straight to voicemail. Frantically, I scanned through my contacts for another foundation member. Finding Denis's number two, Lina, I called her, but she didn't pick up. Of course not...it was, what, five in the morning Brussels time?

Someone followed me to this meet, and it wasn't the feds.

How?

The only one who'd known I was here was Jennie, but...

I remember thinking at the time it was odd that she didn't use Signal, but I was so scrambled from the attack and the crash I didn't make the connection that I should have. And I was just so happy to hear from her, I didn't question it. I hadn't been thinking straight, otherwise that would've tripped my internal alarms immediately.

I called Coogan, who did not pick up. Two more attempts, a text and an email, all saying this was an emergency. I also tried the front desk at his firm, and his assistant.

Coogan finally got the message.

"I cannot talk to you, Matt. Not while you're a—"

"Shut up and listen. Jennie's life is in danger." He stammered out a reply, which I just bowled over. "Thomas, damn it, stop talking. The Russians who kidnapped me in your building have compromised Jennie's phone."

"That's paranoid, Matt. I'm hanging up now."

"Thomas. I'm in DC, I just flew here from Switzerland. They sent me texts from Jennie's phone asking where I was and if I had Fedorov's information. Someone tracked me here and just tried to grab me off the street." I screenshotted a picture of the text exchange and sent it to him. "You ask her if she sent these. I know she didn't, now, because she lit me up in our last phone call. I told her when we spoke that Fedorov was dead and Charlie Auer was seriously hurt. Don't you think she'd have mentioned that in her message?"

"This didn't occur to you then?"

"I'd been in a car accident and the Russians shot me with a microwave gun. I was a little slow on the uptake."

Coogan didn't have an answer to that.

"I got away, but I'm not sure how long any of us have."

"Okay. I'll call her right away."

"Goddamn it, do anything *but* that. Aren't you listening? They own her phone. They can read any message you send her and listen in on the phone."

"How—"

"I don't have time to explain. Go to her, right now, show her those messages. Then get her a burner and have her call me on it. Immediately. Can you do that, Thomas? Her life is at stake."

"Shouldn't I call the police?"

"Yes, but after you talk to Jennie. They're making a move on Denis Coenen too. He sent me a message saying Charlie Auer wanted to meet."

"That's Jennie's whistleblower?"

"That's his *alias*. Someone claiming to be him set up a meeting with Denis, and now I can't get ahold of him."

"How do you know it isn't Auer, or whatever his name is?"

"Because he's in the hospital. He was with me. I never told Denis that."

Coogan said, "I'm on my way."

I called Danzig, who did answer. Once I got through the torrent of invective and demands to turn myself in, I explained the situation as best I could.

"I realize Rawlings is trying to do his job, but he's so far off base he's not even in the park. Fedorov is dead. We were in Zürich with a CIA officer named Connor Bishop. He was Burkhardt's source. She didn't and doesn't know Bishop is CIA. He used his dip cover to communicate with her. Some GRU contract killers were tracking Fedorov and got to us. They had the latest version of that microwave weapon. They hit all three of us with it. I got the least of it and am still pretty messed up."

Danzig spoke in flat tones. "Those GRU men, those are the ones who were found executed?"

"Right. I think an SVR black ops team killed them. Probably the same group that got me in LA. That's not all. They hacked Jennie Burkhardt's phone, pretended to be her, and got me to give up my location. They knew when I got to DC and—"

"You're *here*?"

"I'm in Rosslyn. Listen, they've been following me since I landed and just tried to snatch me out of a parking lot in Courthouse. I got away. Before you ask, no, I didn't kill anyone. They also spoofed Bishop's phone and used that to draw the head of the Orpheus Foundation out. I don't know where Denis is and can't reach him."

"Where exactly are you now?" Danzig asked.

"On a side street next to the Arlington County Courthouse. At first, I thought it was you guys, but when I didn't see lights and sirens, I realized it probably wasn't."

"It's not us, Matt. Rawlings thinks you're rabbiting and still in Europe."

What a dick. No benefit of the doubt.

Danzig continued. "You're only a couple miles from the Russian embassy. If they did a snatch job, you'd be gone before anyone would know. I need a couple minutes to get our counterintelligence team engaged. I know some of the people on the Russia squad. Do you have somewhere safe you can go?"

"I think so, yeah. I lost them."

"All right. There's a lot of restaurants in that area and a lot of people. Hopefully, I can get some guys to you in less than an hour."

"Wait," I said.

I was on a dark side street with minimal traffic. A quick glance behind me revealed nothing, though it was getting dark enough now that one car looked the same as the next, and people were just shadows against the gray.

"Clock's ticking, Matt. What?"

"I have Fedorov's documents with me. All of the Projekt Molniya files—

weapons designs, mission reports, and a list of Western companies they were stealing from."

"What are you saying?"

"Before I come in, I need to know we're going to do something with this. It's not just going to get buried somewhere."

"We can talk about that once you're safe."

"I risked my life for this shit. If I did that for nothing, I'm better off on my own. I'll give it to you, not to Rawlings."

"Matt—this isn't my case. I am only involved because you keep dragging me into it!" Danzig didn't say anything for long seconds. "Rawlings is a good cop, but he's going to do what he is told. And he was told to plug a leak. Someone pretty high up is worried about what your reporter friend knows, and who told it to her." I could not believe Danzig was admitting this to me. "For what it's worth, I don't believe Rawlings thinks you broke into that law firm. There's no PC, but your behavior since then hasn't exactly been predictable."

"I mean, it's predictable for me."

"Okay, that's fair. The point is that Rawlings is not going to help you, not until he gets what he's after, which is the name of Burkhardt's source. You're telling me that's this CIA officer? Matt, that's big medicine."

"Connor didn't give her anything classified. That was the point. The person Rawlings is after isn't him."

"Well, Rawlings will demand those files as a show of good faith before he moves on any counterintelligence thing, which he won't take seriously anyway," Danzig said.

"What if I can prove it's a wild goose chase?"

"I don't understand. What the hell is Burkhardt doing in jail if she isn't protecting someone?"

"Oh, she's doing that for sure. She's protecting a whistleblower. But I can prove the CIA lied to Rawlings about the leak. It's a smoke show, something they made up to stop Jennie and Orpheus from exposing what happened," I said.

"What's your proof?" Danzig said.

"Do we have to do this now?" I said, looking around.

"I'll remind you that you started this shit a minute ago. Stay out of sight and keep your phone on. I'll let you know as soon as I've got a team scrambled. When this is all over, you and I are going to have a long goddamn talk, do you understand?"

"What about Jennie? She's in danger."

"Okay. I'll make some calls to the LA field office. They're going to love this. Don't do anything stupid until you hear from me. I want you to promise me that."

"I won't. Do anything stupid, I mean."

Though, in practice, there tended to be some daylight between what I defined as "stupid" and what people in authority did.

The next call I got was going to make it very hard to keep that promise.

I didn't recognize the number, but the voice I knew immediately.

33

"Hello, Matthew." The voice was icy and black, a Siberian highway in winter.

Anton Malyshkin.

"Obviously, my spam blocker doesn't work."

"By now, you've seen the news, yes?"

The son of a bitch timed this.

"I'm a little behind on current events. See, I was just on the phone with the FBI discussing foreign agents in my country."

"Indeed. A bit hypocritical of you to become angry over this, yes? You may want to check your phone. I will wait."

I opened a web browser.

Turned out, I didn't even need to search for it, there was an alert on my news app.

Crusading journalist and founder of Orpheus Foundation, Denis Coenen, found dead in Brussels.

There were no words.

The feeling drained out of my body.

I stared at the words *Coenen found dead*. At some point, I looked away from my phone and I saw their afterimage burned into my view.

My friend was…gone.

The barely accented, serpentine speech coming from my phone broke me out of my trance.

I put the phone back to my ear, words were already slithering out of Malyshkin's mouth.

"...very unfortunate for Mr. Coenen. I also hope you haven't done anything stupid with the information Grigori Fedorov stole from my government."

"I'm going to fucking kill you," I said. I put no bravado in my words. I spoke it like fact, like it was physics.

"Yes, yes, I am sure. Get your idle threats out now, because you have little time. I have a man inside Ms. Burkhardt's building. On my signal, he will go into her flat and put a bullet between her eyes."

"You lay—"

"Shut up, I'm not done." His voice was icy calm. "I also have someone watching Audrey Farre. She's at home now with her family. She will get an emergency phone call that will bring her out of the house, and one of my men will shoot her. Colonel Richard Hicks, he's working late tonight. Unfortunately, this weather is going to be very unpredictable. I fear he's going to get into an accident on his way home from work. Now, are we done with threats? Excellent. Do you have the drive on you?"

"Yes," I said through gritted teeth.

"Excellent. You will get in your rental car and drive across the Key Bridge in Georgetown. Stay in the right lane and make a right turn on M Street. I will give you instructions then. And stay on the line. If you hang up, I start with Farre."

Well, I guess that answered the question of what they did with the files they stole from Coogan's office.

Malyshkin didn't know where I was, or he'd have sent the Suburban back to intercept me. Of course, he might have another reason for wanting me to go into Georgetown.

The sprawling Russian embassy complex was just north of there, in Glover Park.

I turned and started walking back to my car. "I'm a few blocks from my car. Give me a minute," I said. I didn't take a direct route; rather, I zigzagged up through the streets, mindful they might try to ambush me. I put the phone on mute and locked the screen, keeping it in my hand rather than next to my ear so I didn't have to listen to him. There was no way to know that I wasn't being watched, which meant if they saw me texting, it might trigger those consequences anyway.

As I approached my car, a muffled sound came from the phone. I brought it up to my ear, unmuting on the way. "What?"

"I am just making sure you're still with me," Malyshkin said calmly.

"I'm here," I said. I got my backpack out of the trunk, found the AirPods, and put them in. "You got me?"

"Yes."

I started the car and set the phone in the cupholder, which put it out of sight from anyone that wasn't looking directly over my shoulder. There wasn't time for a lengthy explanation over text. Instead, I pulled up my last message to Danzig and toggled the "Location" feature, sending her an electronic flag. Hopefully, she picked up on the meaning. Especially when I didn't answer.

I navigated over to Wilson Avenue and headed east into Rosslyn.

"I'm moving," I said.

"Good. What are you driving?"

"Blue Ford Explorer."

My phone rang with another call as I was driving. I didn't recognize the number, but it was a 323 area code. That would be Jennie calling from the burner I had Coogan get for her. And I couldn't warn her of what was coming. What was in her building right now.

Traffic was heavy, and since I didn't have the radio on, I could hear the boulder crash of thunder above me. Clouds infested the sky, swarmed it and threatened to unleash a torrent of water when they finally collapsed.

Arlington's Rosslyn neighborhood is perched on a steep hill that dives into the Potomac. I followed that down to make a left turn, carrying me over the Key Bridge and into Georgetown. Traffic slowed to the pulsating sludge, like water from a busted sewer pipe. We'd be here for a while.

"What's taking so long?"

"Because you have me going into Georgetown on a Friday night. You're not very good at this," I said.

Danzig called, and as with Jennie's, I ignored it.

It took twenty minutes to cross the bridge, and with each minute I sat on it, I could practically hear Malyshkin's patience draining out of the hourglass.

"I'm turning right onto M Street now," I said.

Georgetown sprawled out to either side. One of DC's most distinctive neighborhoods, a mix of modern architecture and residential buildings predating the Second World War. And since M Street was one of the four major roads into and out of the District, it was a perpetually clogged artery.

Malyshkin said nothing for a few minutes as I drove. Thunder crashed above, and the skies opened up. Trees shook like they'd been slapped. People on the sidewalks popped umbrellas or dove into alcoves, inside whatever shop or restaurant was closest. "Turn right on Wisconsin," Malyshkin said.

Being completely honest, I didn't love that.

The Russian embassy complex was about a mile north in the opposite direction on Wisconsin Avenue. They were sending me further downhill, toward the Potomac and Water Street, which ran parallel with the river. Water was also beneath an elevated road that cut through the southern end of Georgetown, called the Whitehurst Freeway. The buildings that fronted Water Street, all beneath the freeway, gave the impression of being in a slice of Georgetown the rest of the city just forgot about. It didn't require a vivid imagination to picture them stuffing me in the trunk of a car and making a very quick trip up the street to the embassy.

I made the right and descended toward the river. Rain crashed down, smearing the yellow streetlights.

A text from Danzig flashed onto the screen, asking me what the hell I was doing.

Eyes had to be on me now, because Malyshkin's cues to turn right onto Water Street were just in time.

The Whitehurst Freeway, standing atop its gothic girders, loomed above me.

"Turn right," Malyshkin said, and I was expecting that. The few places on Water Street that were open after regular business hours were located in the opposite direction. That's not to say it was empty. Cars lined both sides of the street, parallel parked into spots that spatial reasoning deemed improbable. The metal girders that held the Whitehurst in place looked like relics of the Industrial Age, and they wept yellow light from suspended streetlamps.

I drove forward slowly, away from the traffic and crowds, the rhythmic rumble of traffic above me on Whitehurst distinguishable from the thunder only in its repetitive patter.

Soon, there were no more parked cars.

I'd reached the end of the street, having wrapped all the way back around to the area beneath the bridge. A murky outline of a building beyond the last concrete pillar—if memory served, it was boathouse.

"Stop," Malyshkin said in my ear. As soon as my foot touched the brake pedal, a dark shape slid out of an alley and blocked the road. That Suburban from earlier. "Turn the car off and get out."

Removing the AirPods from my ears, I disconnected the call. Then I grabbed Fedorov's drive and stepped out.

Help was not coming.

And I was unarmed.

The SUV was about thirty feet away. Doors opened, and Russians slithered out. Malyshkin appeared, wearing a dark suit and a smirk that would look good on the sole of my shoe. Another exited out of the front, also in a suit, and he pulled a pistol out of a shoulder holster. I counted at least three more in the Suburban, including the driver. Doors opened on the other side.

"Where are the files?"

Slowly, I rotated my right hand so they could see the drive.

"So you're, what, cleaning up Aleksandr Orlov's mess? That it?"

Even in the dim light, I could see Malyshkin blanch. He recovered quickly, but I saw the shot land.

"Fedorov talk in his sleep?" Malyshkin said.

"You should assume that the FBI knows everything I do. You should also assume they have copies of the files. Amazing, this digital world we live in."

"I very much hope for the sake of the people you dragged into this that isn't true."

"No way for you to know, is there? Not here." I inclined my head for effect. The man opposite me jumped.

"Give me the drive, Gage. You'll be coming with us. The others may live, assuming you haven't done something stupid and told them everything you know. Which, considering your track record..." Malyshkin's shoulders lifted in a nonchalant shrug.

"You really think you can get me to Moscow? Didn't work out so well last time. How's your man, by the way?"

"Moscow? No. You'll leave the embassy, Gage. Just in pieces."

"I doubt you'll leave that place, either. Except in handcuffs. They know you're here. Unless you plan on going back to Moscow in a diplomatic bag, you're not getting out of Washington."

"The odds would suggest otherwise," he said. "Now, give me the drive."

"You'll pay for Denis, Anton."

"Not likely," he said. "Enough of this. Hold your arms out at your sides."

His man stepped forward. Yellow light glinted off the gun in his hand.

I did as instructed. I stood about a foot behind the Explorer's back end.

Thunder exploded above with the afterimage of lightning. That storm was directly overhead. Torrential rain fell in a solid wave, with more oozing through the seams in the aged freeway above.

Malyshkin's man closed to within a step.

"No moves," he said, and made some motion with the pistol in his hand. "Give me drive."

I flashed back to that dank basement beneath the Russian consulate. I smelled my stink, tasted my blood, felt the pain of the beatings and the deeper pain of having failed. The humiliation over being caught, on my home field. The humiliation of breaking, even though I'd been trained to understand the inevitability of it. I remembered the hours of torture—beatings and electrocution.

They'd chased me across half the earth and murdered someone I'd tried to protect.

I was done running.

They'd probably kill me, but I'd make the bastards earn it.

Before the Russian knew what I was doing, I snapped my left arm down in a chop block on his wrist. Then, wrapping my hand around the hard drive, I smashed the knuckles of my other hand into the Russian's nose. Cartilage crunched and blood spurted, warm and dark on the back of my hand. He cried out. I hit him again, driving my first further up his ruined nose.

The Russian screamed.

He staggered, blood pumping out of his mangled face.

The opposition scrambled.

I got both hands on his gun arm—one slamming down on the forearm and the other hitting him in the opposite direction. With his attention on his shattered face, he didn't mount much of a defense, and the gun game loose in my hand. I snapped my elbow back into his trachea, and he fell backward, choking.

I transferred the gun to my right hand and shot him. It was a low hit and probably not lethal.

I hoped it hurt like hell.

Malyshkin's men were running for me, so I fired several rounds at the Suburban. Wasn't really aiming, I just needed to buy some distance.

I didn't know for certain what the pistol's make was, but we'd trained extensively on all of their small arms. My guess was MP-433, a nine millimeter with a seventeen-round magazine that was the Russian equivalent of an M9 Beretta. Combat math said I had thirteen left.

I dove around the Explorer's corner.

Malyshkin shouted across the gap. "Burkhardt dies for that, Gage."

They'd all taken up positions behind the Suburban. To my right, on the Ford's other side, was a park on the riverbank. To my left there were stubby buildings bathed in yellow light and shadow that reached up halfway to the freeway above. Behind them, I knew there was a dirt trail along the old C&O Canal towpath, with foot bridges crossing back into Georgetown.

I didn't know how many men Malyshkin had with him. I figured at least three, counting him.

So far, they hadn't shot back. They were careful about drawing attention, whereas I wanted to make as much noise as possible.

I popped out of cover and sent two rounds downrange at the Suburban.

Then I sprinted for the sidewalk and dove behind a building. They didn't shoot. Malyshkin shouted in Russian for one of his men to find the drive and another to chase after me. Oddly, I could still understand him, while I still couldn't remember a word of German.

I knew that behind these buildings there was a dirt trail running alongside the river. It could take me north, clear into Maryland if I wanted, or link up with the Chain Bridge and into northern Virginia. At night and in this storm, I would be completely invisible.

And the first thing Malyshkin would do is order his man to kill Jennie and the others.

I had to end this.

Breaking into a dead run, I bolted the length of the building and slowed just enough to make the corner. I slipped when I hit a puddle and crashed onto a knee with a bright shock of pain. I was beneath the open sky now, and rain fell in waves. Back on my feet, I raced down the next length of the building. Split the opposition and even the odds. With the one chasing me, I had a few critical seconds to get the drop on the people in the SUV. Really, all I had to do was take out Malyshkin. After that, it didn't matter what happened to me.

My head pounded like a diesel-powered migraine and, all of a sudden, the world was off-kilter. The vertigo came rushing back, and I felt like I was running through a funhouse. My pace slowed, knowing I wasn't running in a straight line.

I rounded the corner.

My head snapped back, and I was violently introduced to colors I didn't know existed.

Somebody flipped the world around, and I was on my back, head bouncing off the concrete.

Ears ringing, water cascading down, everything murky and washed out.

I didn't know if the thunder was above, in my head, or both.

A form of smeared shadow stood over me, laughing. His gun came up, but he didn't shoot. Instead, a dirty chuckle leaked out of his mouth.

I shot my leg out and kicked him in the knee, then scrambled to my feet. He kicked me in the face before I got there. Another painful galaxy burst into view. I tasted blood. My gun was gone, probably went flying when I hit the ground.

Springing forward, I drove my shoulder into his gut and pushed. He brought his pistol down hard on my back, a glancing blow just above the kidney. I went down on a knee. Then he gave me another love tap with the gun, this time upside the head.

I fell backward. Rain fell between the buildings in slow motion, and either there were two attackers, or I was seeing double.

He raised his pistol again.

"Get up."

My right hand slid back. It found metal.

I snapped the pistol up and fired once. The shot landed somewhere in the chest. I caught a snapshot of his face in the half-light. The bastard had the nerve to look surprised. He fell back on his ass, comically.

"Do yourself a favor," I said, climbing to my feet. "Just sit there and bleed."

The Russian didn't move, just hunched over, clutching his bleeding chest. With what strength I could drag up, I kicked him in the head, and he went over backward.

Dangerously off-balance, I fell into the building next to me for support. I knew I was badly injured. One more hit to the head and I wouldn't have gotten back up.

Bracing against the wall, I slinked down its length back toward the street and Anton Malyshkin. He was down two men now, but it was still three-to-one.

I reached the end of the building, steps from the sidewalk. The world was dim yellow light and rain and shadow.

Malyshkin stood behind the Suburban's driver's side. His remaining two men were on either side of my Explorer, looking for Fedorov's drive. Malyshkin had a gun. Thirty feet away, tops. He was looking in the wrong direction.

The world outside faded.

I was back in that dank basement in San Francisco. I smelled wet concrete, ozone, and tasted blood. Malyshkin laughing at me as he asked his questions, then telling one of his lackeys to hit me again with the waterboarding.

Question—water—drowning—repeat.

Then, the shocks.

For hours.

Because I didn't have the answers he was looking for and needed a way to lie.

Him mocking me over Angel Kelly's murder in Nicaragua.

I detached from the building, staggering onto the sidewalk. The world pitched beneath my feet.

Malyshkin didn't see me immediately.

I made the street and caught Malyshkin's notice. His head turned.

He saw me and he knew. It was in his eyes.

Anton Malyshkin knew he'd never bring his weapon around in time.

We locked stares.

My finger closed around the trigger.

Just outside of point-blank, dead to rights.

A new voice. "Federal agent. Drop your weapons and put your hands in the air."

Malyshkin's leering, laughing face imprinted on my nightmares, directing his underlings to hit me again with the water. To shock me, again. Over and over, until I woke up screaming. Every night. I saw that as clearly as I saw him standing there.

There were vague, distant orders for me to drop it. I didn't care.

"Matt." The voice was cold but calm.

Danzig.

She was my friend, and I knew she'd cover for me. She knew what we were up against, what they'd done to me.

Malyshkin's iced, void-black eyes blazed back at me, and he knew fear and I was fucking glad for it.

"Put the gun down, Matt," Danzig said. "You don't need this."

Malyshkin, afraid, eyes darting to this new voice.

I had him.

Just a hair's worth of pressure was all I needed.

Malyshkin couldn't hurt me now, couldn't hurt Jennie. Or Audrey Farre, or Rick Hicks.

There was something else that I still had to do.

And I didn't need another ghost. I let the gun fall from numb fingers. Metal clattered against pavement.

Wherever he was, I hoped Fedorov understood.

34

The next few hours were a barely remembered whirlwind.

Danzig followed the digital breadcrumbs to Water Street, just in time to stop me from shooting Anton Malyshkin in the face.

I remembered Metro PD rolling in hard shortly after she did. Georgetown is one of the most densely populated parts of the city. Lots of college kids, lots of diplomats. When cops come in, they go hard and they go fast. They had the Russians boxed in. The two still standing tried to scramble and didn't get far.

An EMT checked me out while another gave me a dry blanket and pumped me full of something that made the pain go away. Someone tested me with a penlight and pronounced me concussion free. The EMT implored Danzig to get me to a hospital for medical evaluation, and she assured him that she would, after questioning.

I never did see that hospital.

After some perfunctory interviews by MPD, Danzig drove me to the Bureau's DC field office. There, we met Rawlings in a conference room. Danzig offered me a cup of government-flavored coffee. Guess it was going to be one of those nights. Great.

It wasn't an interview room, and it wasn't a cell, so that was something.

We'd scoured everything, scraping the dregs of my memory. What tipped me to Fedorov's flight to Zürich and how I'd guessed right. When and how I'd involved Connor Bishop. I said a silent *I'm sorry* to him when I gave the FBI agents his true name and occupation. I told them, as much as I could recall, about that cafe conversation with Fedorov. About the trip to the bank, clocking the men in the courier van but not really registering who and what they were. Details about the accident didn't really come, and Rawlings suggested perhaps it was because I'd made them up.

With calm and exacting profanity, I described exactly what Rawlings could do with that theory.

Danzig pulled him into the hallway for a bit, and I closed my eyes until they came back.

Rawlings's tone changed after that.

I gave them every detail about tonight. And even though I understood why I needed to debrief while it was fresh, my body had been pushed far beyond its limit. There was nothing left to give.

Danzig stepped out to take a phone call.

Rawlings didn't utter a word while she was gone.

Danzig came back in a few minutes later. "Our SWAT guys in LA just made an arrest at Ms. Burkhardt's building. Perp had a valid California driver's license but was on the watchlist the San Francisco counterintelligence squad put out after Gage's run-in there. He was just hanging out, waiting for orders."

Say this about the Russians, they were not fire-and-forget.

Earlier, the Bureau snagged another operative outside Audrey Farre's Arlington home. Looked like Malyshkin was going to make good on his threat. They also confirmed that Rick Hicks made it home safely.

"Matt, tell Cedric everything you told me on the phone tonight," Danzig said.

I relayed my conversation with Colonel Mercer. For once, I played straight. I told them everything, with one minor modification.

"Mercer only spoke with me because I told him what Joshua McDonough planned, and he wanted to make sure his name was not associated with it." Oh, yeah, I'd given them all the dirt on ol' Josh.

The questioning lasted hours.

The only thing I didn't tell them was that Damon Fox gave the White

House its way out. I referred to the Agency ubiquitously. Danzig watched me, hawkish, as I told this part of it. She probably thought I was protecting old friends.

Old enemies, in truth.

Those were saved for me.

It was enough of a bombshell that the minor nugget of culpability I'd held back made little difference.

When I'd finally finished, Rawlings said nothing more for a long time.

Danzig, finally, erupted.

"Jesus Christ, Cedric, you have to tell him. Or I will."

"Tell me what?" I said.

Rawlings's eyes cut the air between them. His jaw clamped tight, and it was clear he wasn't going to do it.

"The information on Jennie Burkhardt allegedly receiving classified information, that came from the Agency's counterintelligence division," she said, with a side-eye leveled at Rawlings the entire time.

"Let me guess. Damon Fox told the Bureau about it personally," I said.

"We don't know," Rawlings said at length, pinching the bridge of his nose. "You know they won't share sources and methods with us."

"And you didn't think to question them? So, the charge, the probe, it was all bullshit. Fox made it up," I said.

"Matt, the Justice Department wouldn't have opened an investigation just because the CIA told them to. And anyway, domestic counterintelligence is our responsibility," Danzig said. "Maybe they connected the dots with Connor Bishop faster than you thought?"

That was possible, but my hunch was that Jennie's source was somewhere within the ODNI. The Director of National Intelligence was created in 2004, part of the post-9/11 reforms designed to streamline coordination between the eighteen members of the Intelligence Community. ODNI was an administrative and oversight body rather than an operational one. Jennie's reporting suggested a whistleblower within the Intelligence Community; Fox just constructed the appearance of a leak around that and, because it came from "Agency counterintelligence sources," was classified such that no one outside CIA could ever look at it. That existed before she started talking with Connor.

I was in a helpful mood, so I summarized it for them. "Before Jennie's reporting, Havana was effectively dead. Congress held a hearing but said they were convinced by the IC's report. It was out of the public eye. The Agency could do whatever they wanted and on their timetable. Then Jennie starts asking questions, she gets people from two administrations to go on the record so that no one can argue it was politically motivated. The stories start getting momentum, people are asking questions again. Hell, it was even on *60 Minutes*. Now there is talk of a whistleblower, and the Agency brass start panicking because they think Jennie is actually onto something. And they've testified before Congress. If this gets traction, they are in a world of shit. So what do they do? They go after her. They fabricate an intelligence leak and get the DoJ involved. You guys do your thing. Jennie refuses to reveal her source—and before you ask, again, I still don't know who it is. She gets locked up, and the Agency is counting on her making a deal to get out of jail. I know that, because before you decided to shake me down, Fox approached me with an offer for her. I told him to fuck off. He called you and said I was an accomplice, and you arrested me within ten minutes."

Storm clouds crashed behind Cedric Rawlings's eyes, but his face took on an ashen, pallid caste. Of course, I couldn't know exactly what was going through his head at that moment, but I had an idea. He was realizing that he'd been played, lied to, and worse, manipulated into using the law for an outcome other than justice.

The look on Danzig's face suggested that some of this was news to her.

"So, what happens now?" I said.

"It's late. Go get some sleep, Matt. We'll pick this up in the morning," Danzig said.

Danzig arranged for one of the FBI's uniformed police officers to drive me back to my hotel since MPD impounded the rental car.

Sleep didn't come easy, but when it did, it came like an avalanche.

The alarm dropkicked me into consciousness about two days before I wanted it to. But that couldn't be helped, I had one last thing to do.

Well, two things.

The Explorer I'd been driving wasn't getting released from police custody anytime soon, so I had to secure new transportation from a rental agency near the hotel. Thankfully, it wasn't the same one.

For obvious reasons, the government religiously protects the home addresses of intelligence officers. There are ways to find that out, though. The official term is "insider threat," but I liked to think of it as people who owed me favors. Firing someone from the government takes time, I'd actually spent a few weeks at Langley while they were gradually kicking me out, and I'd used that time wisely.

One of the things I did was get Damon Fox's home address.

Should I ever need it.

He lived in a modern, brick two-story that backed into a forest in the city of McLean and not far from headquarters. Debris from the previous night's storm littered the street. At ten o'clock on a Saturday morning, I expected Fox to be home and probably catching up on unclassified paperwork. I parked around the corner and walked up the path to his front door, noting the security service signs and looking for hidden cameras. I assumed I was being recorded. I hit the doorbell and did my best not to look smug.

My whole body hurt, and there was a distant ringing in my ears, like I'd gone to an especially violent rock concert the night before. There was no vertigo, but concentration still took effort.

From the other side of the door, I heard a woman order a kid to answer it. A few moments later, a teenaged girl opened it. Whatever smug countenance I showed had nothing on her. Behind her, I could see the foyer and a staircase leading up to the second floor. Wings extended in both directions, leading deeper into the home.

"Hi. I was wondering if your dad was home. I'm a friend from work."

She cocked her head to the side, clearly confused because she knew her dad's job. That quickly flushed to annoyance that she now had to do a second thing, and she called into the house. About a half a minute later, I saw Fox appear from the left side. He wore a gray Stanford T-shirt, athletic shorts, and glasses.

I folded my arms across my chest.

Check, asshole.

"I'm not sure what you have more of, Gage. Nerve or stupidity."

"That's good, Fox. Piss me off. Give me more of a reason."

That part of my brain responsible for my better judgment, the one I rarely listen to, cautioned against threatening him.

"It should take a security detail seven minutes to get here from HQS. You've got that long."

"You may want to hold off on that phone call. I'm not sure they're going to want to hear what I have to say. I'm talking to you first out of respect for the institution. After this, I go to *The Washington Post* and the FBI. Well, *back* to the FBI. Only this time, I fill in the blanks," I said, and let him ponder the implications of the latter.

We stared each other down for a long, hard second.

Fox broke contact first and looked beyond me to the street. I watched as his eyes scanned it from one side to the other.

"We're not having this conversation here," he said in a warning growl. Fox stepped backward and indicated with his jaw for me to follow him. I stepped inside the home. Fox closed the door behind me and then shouldered past to lead the way into his office. French windows opened onto a perfectly manicured lawn, boxed in by sentinel-like coniferous trees. The office was two massive bookcases, filled with old volumes and mementos of his career at Langley. Flags, pictures, the token piece of warped shrapnel to commemorate a battle he hadn't been in.

There was a long desk with a docked government laptop on it. Fox closed the laptop, and the mirrored screen on his desk went dark. He sat in the chair and didn't offer me one. Fox's expression was one of a person force-fed spoiled milk.

Fox tapped the lock screen on his phone, and the clock appeared.

"You have my attention. I suggest you make the most of it."

"I have all of the Projekt Molniya files. Technical designs. The components they had to steal from Western defense companies to overcome their own limitations and the companies they stole them from, some of which were here in the US. I have mission reports, specifically of their attack against Vienna Station. Hell, I even have a commendation that Colonel

Aleksandr Orlov, the head of Unit 21955, received from the General Staff for the project."

Damon Fox painted the air between us with his glacial stare. Then he said, "So what? We knew Molniya was a legitimate threat ever since Havana."

"Then why did you people tell Dylan West and God knows how many others that they were making it up?"

"Because we didn't have an answer for it. Moscow caught us flat-footed. What I told you before about the rules governing espionage was true. These were practices we both agreed to since the Cold War started. We never believed they'd be so brazen as to attack our embassies like that. Let alone people's homes."

"That doesn't surprise me," I said, though in truth it did.

"Initially, yes, some in the Senior Intelligence Service thought it was a hoax. Or, at most, people were being weak. Then, as the cases mounted, we knew it was a problem. But we couldn't just release all these people into the wild, medically retire them, and have the word get out. Have you any idea the catastrophic impact that would have on what we do here? Christ, it would shut the State Department down. We're talking generational damage to foreign policy and national security."

"I know about the option you offered the White House. I know that the idea for the report was yours and that you came up with it before the 2021 Geneva Summit. I also know about that off-the-record conversation POTUS had with the Kremlin, that he gave them a way out. And I know that CINDER SPIRE was the stick if he did not."

Fox was unreadable.

"You've got a vivid imagination, Matt."

"No, I've got someone who will go on the record and say you made up the report for the purposes of that meeting. This gets out, that will put the CIA Director and the Director of National Intelligence in a very uncomfortable position, because they both testified before Congress that the report was true."

Fox waved a dismissive hand. "We have hundreds of medical experts who contributed to that report."

"The Molniya files conclusively disprove that. And my source's testimony will show you orchestrated the coverup. You told the Director and the White House we weren't attacked, or at least that it was inconclusive enough to be plausibly deniable. I can prove you lied."

"That would be an interesting theory, if literally anyone would believe you, Matt. Let me tell you how this plays out. You're a disgruntled former employee working for a muckraker that traffics in stolen documents. This never sees the light of day."

My temper flared at him calling Jennie a muckraker, but I wrestled it into submission.

"On your list of accomplishments, I might also add you're currently wanted for murder, espionage, smuggling, and burglary. Do you have any idea the problems this caused for the Agency? A former employee being implicated in the break-in of a law office? A practice, which I might add, does significant work defending Guantanamo detainees? Have you any concept of how this is going to look when the media gets their hands on it? Of course you don't, because that would imply that you ever thought more than one step ahead. Jesus Christ, Matt, if you wanted to star in a sequel to Watergate, I'd thank you to leave us the hell out of it. Frankly, I don't care what you claim to have. You are easily discredited. So is Burkhardt."

"Do you know who Denis Coenen is, Damon?"

"No."

"He was the head of the Orpheus Foundation. The Russians murdered him yesterday. Even if you silence Jennie, you can't stop them. And if you think they'll let this go now, you're woefully ignorant. They have copies of the Molniya files, and they have a global reach. This all comes out."

"They can publish a story on a website. No one will care, and no one will hear it."

I lifted the hem of my shirt and enjoyed the grim satisfaction in seeing Fox flinch. He thought I was showing him a pistol. I dragged the shirt up, revealing the burn marks on my rib cage. "The night I was supposedly breaking into Case Ritter to steal Jennie's files—which is the most bullshit story I've ever heard, by the way—I was in the basement of the Russian consulate in San Francisco being tortured for information on Grigori Fedorov." I held my shirt up until Fox was forced to look away.

"I didn't know," he said, and the venom had drained from his words.

"The waterboarding was...bad. They hit me with alligator clips hooked up to a generator, Damon. The one who did it, an SVR officer named Anton Malyshkin, he's now in FBI custody. They arrested him last night in Georgetown. He wanted me to hand over the Molniya files in exchange for not murdering Jennie Burkhardt, a Senate staffer named Audrey Farre, and an Army colonel, Rick Hicks. You see, these were names that were in Burkhardt's files that *they* stole from Case Ritter. They had a hitter in the lobby of Jennie's building. And outside Farre's house. In exchange for the Molniya files, those people would be spared. Not me, though. Malyshkin said I'd be leaving their embassy in pieces."

I was fifty-fifty on whether Fox would know about the arrest. Apprehending Russian operatives in the nation's capital would light up all the wires in the counterintelligence world. However, the Bureau may have held that back for operational concerns, particularly if they thought Malyshkin had more agents in the field.

"Where is Fedorov now?" Fox asked.

"He's dead. We were in Zürich. They hit us with their EM weapon, so I can personally attest that it works. Then they ran Fedorov down. We think that was a GRU contract hit squad. Those three, by the way, turned up dead a day later. Most likely, the SVR was trying to cover tracks and keep the Kremlin clear. Before he died, Fedorov said Orlov contracted a team to use the Molniya weapon on the NATO meeting in Vilnius last year. That's what kicked off Moscow trying to close ranks on this thing."

Fox leaned against his desk, arms folded. Whatever internal deliberation fired in that vault of shadows he had behind his eyes, it was unreadable to me. "I'm sorry about what happened to you. That shouldn't be. And I'm sorry about Fedorov. For what it's worth, we couldn't take him in. It would have tipped our hand to Moscow that we acknowledged the weapon's existence, and its effectiveness. The deception doesn't work if that happens. Even you can appreciate why we didn't think Fedorov was credible." Fox shrugged dismissively. "We didn't think the GRU would be as aggressive as they were. The bit about contractors is news to me, I'll have to look into it. This doesn't change anything."

"Damon, the FBI debriefed me last night after the arrests. Rawlings was there. They know everything. They have the Molniya files too. They know that CIA fabricated the report to give the White House a way out. What they don't have is your name."

A dark light flashed in his eyes. "Ahh, now I see what this is about. You're here to bargain for Burkhardt's freedom. Afraid I can't help you there."

"I am here to trade, but not for that. I will have more depositions with the Bureau shortly, and I'll be under oath. When that happens, I'll tell them everything I *know*. We're here to decide how much I remember. Maybe my memory is a little spotty after Zürich, or maybe it isn't."

"What are you offering?" Fox asked.

"The discovery of the Molniya files lets you retract the report. You've found new information that convinces you the Russians were behind Havana Syndrome. You recognize the victims, get them medical and psychological support. When necessary, you medically retire them. The State Department will follow your lead, I'm sure. You don't need to say anything public, I don't care about that. I'm not here to drag the Agency through the mud. I just want the people you gaslit to receive the care they deserve. If not, the FBI learns you made up the report. And so does Jennie, and so does Orpheus. And so does Congress."

"No."

"Excuse me."

"I said no. The Russians attacked us, yes, and it was clearly an act of war. You have no idea of the dominoes that begin to fall if we admit this. One of your many character defects, Matt, is you are selectively blind to bigger pictures. If we do this, the United States will be forced to respond. Do you really think the American people can stomach another war? Or that we're even prepared to fight one? Sure, the Russians are weak and incompetent, we could defeat them, but not immediately and not with the limited forces in Europe today. We get tied up in Europe, and Beijing decides *that's* the opportune moment to invade Taiwan, which they will do. We can't fight the Russians and defend Taiwan, upon which the global technology industry depends." Fox held up his smartphone as if to remind me of the stakes.

His lip folded in a sneer, smug and dangerous. It was one I knew well. "The chubby psychopath in Pyongyang knows we can't defend all threats too, so maybe he decides that's the time he pushes south. But he's also got atomic artillery, and he thinks everything is a video game. What do you think happens to Seoul? That's nine million lives. How many terrorist groups would see this as their time to shine? Or, for that matter, any of the dozen militias here at home that want to topple our government? We made some deeply unpalatable choices, Matt, but this is the world we live in."

"Your problem, Damon, is that you try to pass cowardice off as grand strategy."

"No," he said with barely restrained fury. "You have no concept of the terrible decisions we make every day. We *all* knew what Havana was when it happened. I briefed the last Director on it. He practically begged me to pin it on anyone but the Russians. And you know why? Because that president couldn't be seen to be weak in front of Moscow. Worse, that White House wouldn't even consider the possibility it was Russia. You know this. We'd minimized reporting of Russian activities in the President's Daily Brief because the White House ordered us to. So, we called it Anomalous Health Incidents, and we went back to hitting the Russians in the shadows."

"That's a great story, Damon, but you had a chance to correct the record with the new administration. It was a new president that went to Geneva."

"And admit to the country, to the world, to them, that the Russians caught us with our pants down? Could attack us wherever and however they chose? But let's just follow your train of thought for a moment. Do you know what this president and his staff thought about Havana? That it was the other guy's fault. Because that's how this town works. They just wanted it to go away so they could focus on what they came to Washington to do. And they wanted to avoid a war they believed their predecessors teed up. I gave them a way to do that, so we could go back to hunting our enemies down. The Russians are broke, they are isolated, and they are blind now, and that's mostly because of us. Their president is in his seventies, and he's in poor health. The same is true in China. If we can keep these two pots from boiling over for just a couple years, nature will handle it."

I would never admit this to Fox, but I couldn't fault his logic about the global chessboard. His assessment of the threat, I believed, was correct. That may explain what they did, but it was far short of justification in my eyes. We put ourselves at risk, in harm's way in this job, and we understand that. Accept it knowingly, willingly. The other side of that pact is they'll take care of us. That was still what this was about. I understood Fox's decisions, could even empathize with it to a degree. Doing that at the cost of Dylan and those like him was not acceptable.

"I know you well enough that you didn't come here to negotiate. You had the outcome you wanted, and if you don't get it, you'll light the world on fire to spite the other side. You want to believe I'm Mephistopheles, fine. You're wrong, I don't need to burn air trying to convince you otherwise."

"Do you agree to the terms or not?"

"Fine, Gage. Have it your way. You do this, and there's no stopping what's coming for Burkhardt."

"If she's received classified information and used it in her reporting, she'll need to face the consequences of that. I'm not here to negotiate a get-out-of-jail-free card. Though, Cedric Rawlings had an interesting theory on that."

Fox's eyes flared, just a touch, but he didn't rise to the bait.

"You should know, I'm not proud of what we did. It was necessary to keep us out of wars we didn't need to be fighting, to mask the actions of a president who couldn't be bothered to lead. I am only too aware of the human cost. I made the best choice I could. When you're gone from here, Matt, I want you to think on what you'd have done differently if the choice had been yours?" Fox paused, and a grim smile of absolute cunning crept up one side of his face. It looked like if the Cheshire Cat sold timeshares in hell. "I've learned something in my years here, which you would do well to take to heart. Deals, agreements...pacts, they have a kind of gravity. Once they are made, the two parties are linked. You are in my orbit now, Matt." Fox opened the door. "I will see you out."

35

The FBI kept me in DC for the next week for intensive debriefing.

But, before that could begin, Danzig got me a thorough evaluation by a neurologist at George Washington University Hospital. He said that I appeared not to have "significant" lasting damage. I'd only taken a glancing shot and was incredibly fortunate. Without some longer-term study, the doc couldn't explain why I'd lost the ability to speak a language, only that he assessed that some of my neurological pathways were destroyed.

The neurologist cleared me for my FBI debriefing, but cautioned them against keeping me there too long and insisted they schedule breaks.

The sessions were thorough, exhausting, and I did my best to keep up. Recalling details was often difficult. Between Minsk, San Francisco, Zürich, and DC, I'd cut a pretty wide swath of chaos across the globe. Not that it was entirely my fault, mind you.

At one point, a senior agent used the term "international mayhem," and honestly, I couldn't tell if he meant it as a compliment.

Understandably, they wanted to focus on how I learned about Grigori Fedorov and why I felt it necessary to extract him from Minsk. I genuinely wanted to protect Connor. He'd acted righteously, in my view, and had tried to compel an organization into overcoming its own foolish intransigence. However, I was now under oath. I hoped that Connor would understand.

Under normal circumstances, I'd be guilty of smuggling Fedorov into Lithuania. However, the debriefers cut me some unexpected slack and intimated that I couldn't know whether it was an official CIA operation at the time. It seemed they were setting Connor up.

On the matter of the SVR officer's death on the train platform, my testimony that Fedorov shot and killed the man was not questioned in the official record. I'd hear no more of it.

I described bringing him to Brussels to meet Denis Coenen and the Orpheus team, and how Fedorov still held information back because he'd learned that was the only coin he had to buy his continued safety.

My debriefers were, naturally, most interested in the SVR operation in California. Recalling my abduction and subsequent torture at Malyshkin's hand was...unpleasant. I noted a distinct softening in Cedric Rawlings's attitude toward me after that. More than one of them remarked at my amazing restraint at not having shot Malyshkin in the face when I had the chance.

Maybe there'd been enough death in this thing and one more body wouldn't balance the scales.

Not even his.

I was not implicated in the San Francisco death. The Bureau told me the SFPD ruled the death as accidental and closed it.

They did share that the fire alarm stunt that the SF field office pulled at the Russian consulate gave the Bureau's counterintelligence team a chance to plant some listening devices inside the building. Odds were, they'd already been discovered by the sweeper team who undoubtedly checked immediately after. The mere fact that they'd been found would have the Russians tied up with paranoid searches for weeks.

The Bureau cleared me of the break-in at Case Ritter and resolved any open questions on my involvement with the LAPD. I did, finally, speak with a detective there who was grateful to close the case. This also meant Case Ritter lifted their prohibition against helping me, so I could get legal representation by someone who at least had an inkling of what in the hell was going on. As a way of apology, Thomas Coogan volunteered. I didn't hold anything Coogan had done against him and accepted his help gratefully.

Once the conversation got to Zürich, things got a little murkier. The agents pressed me on why I'd left the hospital before the legal attaché could interview me. All I could offer was the truth, that based on my conversation with Rawlings, I assumed they'd mistakenly arrest me for the death in Belarus. I justified my actions as best as I could. The SVR's hacking of Jennie's phone underscored my argument that there was a bit of a ticking clock at this point, and had I been detained, she'd almost certainly have been murdered along with Denis.

There was also the matter of medical expenses, which would have to be settled. I put Coogan on that.

There still wasn't a good explanation for why Natalie Harper ran interference for me. I knew she distracted the Swiss cops. The only reason that made any sense was that she was trying to mask the Agency's hand in all this. There wasn't a benefit that I could see in bringing this up, so I left it out. And it meant the Bureau concluded I'd simply outmaneuvered them, which I thought was funny as well.

We spent nearly two full days on the attack.

Ultimately, the Bureau determined that while my actions were highly questionable, roguish, and lacking good judgment, they were largely understandable, if not justifiable, considering the circumstances. I was not charged with anything.

The Bureau's digital forensics experts verified the provenance of Fedorov's documents. They wouldn't tell me how they did it, though I had a good guess. It proved that the information was right, even without Fedorov alive to attest to it. I felt some measure of solace for that.

I agreed to debriefing with the Agency and saw some old friends, and a few old enemies. It was mostly cordial, which, I suspect, was Fox's doing.

The Justice Department ended Jennie's house arrest immediately, or at least as "immediate" as sprawling bureaucracy allowed. In any event, the ankle monitor was off within forty-eight hours. They dropped the espionage charges later in the week. Jennie joined me in Washington for a series of depositions. Given the actions of the Russians, the threat on her life, and Denis's murder, the Justice Department dropped its charges.

At the end of the week, Danzig and I met for a drink at Off the Record. This time, I was less of an asshole.

"I didn't get a chance to say this before, but I'm sorry about your friend," Danzig said over a glass of wine.

"Thank you." Belgian officials confirmed that Denis had been poisoned. There was talk that they wanted to charge Malyshkin with his murder, though I didn't think it likely the US would extradite him. He was too valuable a prisoner.

"This is the second time you've rolled up a spy ring," she said wryly.

"Yeah, I really need to start reconsidering my life choices."

She laughed, and it sounded like soft breaking waves.

"Any idea what you're going to do next?"

I shook my head. "Sleep. The secret is out, but it still doesn't feel like we won. The Agency hasn't acknowledged any of this yet."

"Likely, they won't," Danzig said. I hadn't told her about confronting Fox.

"Well, Jennie's reporting might change that." Once she was out of jail, I learned who Jennie's source really was. It was an attorney in the Office of the Director of National Intelligence's Inspector General. The IG had conducted its own review and concluded the Agency not only suppressed witnesses but that they privately acknowledged Havana Syndrome was the work of a foreign power. The assessment further showed the IC's "report" was written with the intent of manipulating official opinion, that its conclusions were not based on objective, scientific fact. Several high-ranking officials had testified before Congress on this, and there would certainly be a reckoning.

"What's going to happen to Malyshkin?" I asked.

"Not my circus, not my monkey," Danzig said. "But between you and me, he's going into a dark hole."

"He talk?"

"No, but his subordinates did. They don't know much. We're getting some good stuff, though. It'll put Moscow on their heels a bit."

We finished our drinks and hugged and agreed to catch up once the dust settled.

I thanked her for having my back.

"You are my cross to bear for unrepented sins," she said, but with a smile and a light in her eyes that said all was forgiven.

The next day, I flew home.

The George Washington doc connected me with the neurology team at UCLA Medical Center for ongoing care and evaluation. I also got connected with the team at the University of Pennsylvania who'd done the initial research into Havana Syndrome. There would be some flights to Philly in my future.

Jennie had gotten back the day before and asked me to call her as soon as I got in.

I'd been gone nearly three weeks, and there was a lot to sort through. I took the first night to just be in my place, to work through my mail, and to not worry about waking up at the wrong end of a gun. The next night, she treated me to dinner at Shutters on the Beach, an upscale Santa Monica resort. She wore a bright blue shirt and white linen pants, the wide-legged kind that were currently in style.

We had a table on the patio, with a light breeze and an unobstructed view of the sun diving into the Pacific.

The sommelier presented the bottle to her for inspection and went through the ceremony of tasting, pouring, and disappearing.

"What you did." Strangely, Jennie couldn't meet my eyes. She shielded herself with a wineglass and looked out to the ocean, the waves capped with orange light. "I can't ever repay that."

"You don't have to," I said, but she shook a gentle, but resolute, protest.

"Without you...without you going to Europe, getting Fedorov, and then risking your life for the information he had, this story would've dried up."

I smirked. "Jen, you had someone in ODNI's front office. They—"

"Went away when I got arrested. Monica only resurfaced and agreed to go on record when you disclosed the Molniya files. ODNI was trying to spike the report, which was why she came forward to begin with. After I got arrested, she got scared and said she couldn't help. That was why I asked you to carry the investigation forward."

"Why didn't you tell me?"

"For one, to protect her. I trust you, completely, but I didn't want the government to put you in a position where you'd have to make a choice. The other reason was I hoped that Fedorov had something they absolutely could not refute. If it came from outside our government, I thought they'd have no choice but to admit it."

"Well, we did it," I said. We'd "won" and yet, we hadn't. This case, this story, marked its path with lives lost, careers ruined, and damage done that could never, ever be repaired or repaid. More than that, it eroded the last shred of faith and trust I had in Washington, or the Agency to which I'd dedicated much of my life. CIA was the first line of defense in a murky and dangerous world. Sometimes it was the last and only line. But these events would forever tarnish it, at least to me. They crafted a fiction to hide the fact that their old nemesis bested them.

Still, given what I'd learned from Damon Fox, that felt reductive. Possibly even unfair.

When faced with an executive that had a weird opposition to any suggestion that Moscow would attack us, the CIA leadership either tried and failed to convince them, or didn't try at all. What would I have done in Damon's shoes? I didn't have a good answer for that. I only knew I couldn't accept the answer I'd been given.

Our conversation drifted to other things, equally weighty. Denis's legacy, his funeral. And how they were going to manage the wave of worldwide attention the Foundation was now receiving. Orpheus was well known in journalistic circles before; now they were a household name.

"The Foundation asked me to take over for Denis," she said. "I wasn't sure how to tell you."

I didn't need her to finish that sentence and was grateful when she didn't. It meant she'd already accepted the job.

I was able to muster a quiet, "Congratulations." I meant it, and I didn't.

"I don't know that I need to be there full-time, but it's difficult to manage the operation from LA."

"It's quite a time difference," I said. "I'm sure the team is shaken up over Denis's murder. You need to be there for them."

The ghost of a sad smile graced her lips and then was gone.

"The Foundation's lawyers have said we can't work with you any longer. It's too much of a liability."

Normally, this was the part where righteous indignation would spew forth like Pop Rocks in a Coke can, but for once, I couldn't argue.

That FBI agent's comment about "international mayhem" came back to mind.

"We can cover your expenses for this case," she said, leaving her voice to trail off. At this point, I was well into the five figures with so many last-minute plane tickets, many of them international. And that was before my fees.

Jennie rose when the wine and the sun were gone.

Since there was still wine in my glass, I did not stand.

"If you'd have stayed here, would we have had a chance?"

"I'll always love you, Matt."

She broke up with me before we were even officially together. That had to be a first.

To this day, I don't know why she ended it there the way she did. It felt more like running away than the end of a thing's natural life. I couldn't help but draw a parallel to how she ended things when we'd dated in college. It called to mind the observation about our similarities and how our relationship was a mirror for the other person.

Maybe she didn't like what she saw in herself when she looked at me.

For my part, it was too easy to bend the rules in her name.

I'd never admit it to anyone, but part of me was glad she ran. It meant I didn't have to.

36

My wounds, the physical ones at least, faded as the weeks marched on.

I'd been spending a lot less time at Ray's lately, preferring to work out of my home. I'd built a website, started advertising, and, in general, tried to present a more professional image than a guy who had a tiki bar for an office. But that afternoon I found myself at Ray's anyway.

Jennie had left for Brussels two weeks before. She kept her condo and planned to come back to Los Angeles "at some point."

I hadn't picked up any new work yet, though I wasn't quite in the mood to. My bills were current and the surf was fair, so I'd gotten the kayak out and spent a few hours on the water. I'd showered on the beach and changed into my usual off-duty attire—an aloha shirt and Florida Gators ball cap—and wandered into Cosmic Ray's. I ordered a beer, Ray could get Pliny the Elder, sat at the bar, and shot the shit with Ray. It was quiet. Summer was over, and the place was half filled with the usual rotating cast of driftwood regulars.

I drank slowly, and we talked.

At some point, Ray's attention went to the door. I watched his eyes and his face focus on something behind me.

"She's either lost or about to have a really awkward first date," Ray said.

Turning my torso so I could face the opened door, I saw Natalie Harper backlit by the afternoon sun.

"Actually, I think it's somewhere in the middle," I said, sliding off the stool. "I'll catch you later, Ray."

"Vaya con Dios, Matt."

I walked up to her. "How'd you find me?"

"Forget what I do for a living?"

"I mean, what are you doing here?"

"Can we...take a walk?"

I waved to the door and followed her out. Once we were outside, I led her to the oceanfront walk.

"Connor is out of the hospital," she said.

"He going to be okay?"

"In time, maybe. I think they will at least medically retire him. Which is a minor miracle in and of itself."

Not as much as you might think.

"Speaking of, how are you recovering?" Natalie asked.

"Fine, I guess." Which was to say I wasn't sharing the details with her.

I stopped on the path and turned to face Harper. A light offshore wind kicked sand up, slapping us with a gritty breath.

"What do you want, Natalie?"

She exhaled heavily, cross her arms, and turned to face the water.

"The op was Connor's idea, but I authorized it. I was his station chief."

"Wait, what op? There wasn't one, that's why I got involved. And you are station chief in Vilnius?"

"Was. I was recalled and relieved of duty. There will be a board, which I'm sure will be totally fair and objective," she said dryly. "This will mean my career, but it's okay. I can sleep with what I did."

"What *did* you do?"

"Connor tried to recruit Fedorov, that much you know. We ran it up and HQS shot it down, said he was too much of a risk."

"Damon Fox told me they knew Fedorov was a GRU agent and that if they accepted him, it'd tip their hand to Moscow that they know Havana was a weapon."

Harper laughed. "He's so full of shit."

"No argument there," I said.

"I already knew what the prevailing winds were about AHIs and knew we'd never get any traction. That didn't mean I wouldn't try. One of my friends, a Farm classmate, was hit in Vienna. They gaslit her the same as they did everyone else, told her it was stress and that she couldn't handle it. She was never the same."

"*Was* never the same?"

But Harper just shook her head. Whatever that story was, it was staying with her. "Connor read about Burkhardt's series and thought that if the Agency wouldn't act, maybe the best bet was to light it up in the press."

"Why not go to another service? The Brits would've taken him."

"Thought about that. Part of me really wanted to see Fox get scooped by MI6. But I was worried Langley could get involved anyway. It'd be too easy to discredit him or use their influence to bury it. Plus, the Brits don't have a stake in this. None of their people have been hit, far as we know. The other thing you need to know is that we reached out to Burkhardt purposefully. Connor did not know about you."

"I taught him at the Farm, briefly. I was under an alias at the time. My meeting him in Vilnius was a freak coincidence."

"Not as much as you think. I knew that you were working with Burkhardt. Word had gotten around. I told Connor that she had someone who'd probably been an operator working with her. He assumed that meant SOF. It was risky, I admit. I knew Connor hadn't crossed a 'Matt Gage,' but it never occurred to me you'd have been undercover at the Farm."

"Did you help me in Minsk?"

"We did. You were going to get arrested, Matt. Connor used an asset to get you out of that jail. What we didn't count on was Fyodor Vasiliev. Once we got you sprung, we couldn't also distract Vasiliev without burning the asset. However, we didn't count on him following Fedorov all the way to that village. Fedorov…handled it, I suppose. Though not cleanly."

"Your visit in Zürich makes a lot more sense now. I figured you were covering for me. I was just wrong about the reason."

"I assumed you'd realize what was going on, even hurt as you were." Harper stopped and regarded me with wet eyes. "I'm truly sorry for that.

Whatever the treatment costs, whatever isn't covered, I don't care how much it is. I'll take care of it."

"That's not necessary." We walked in silence for a while. People jogged past us in either direction. An afternoon sun set pure golden light down, and the world looked almost clean. "What do you think happens next?"

Harper thought about the question before she answered.

"Hard to say. Word got out fast that senior leadership is trying to figure out how to get new medical evaluations for everyone, especially the ones that are no longer with the Agency. The simple fact that they're going to medically retire Connor says something."

Yeah, like they weren't going to prosecute him.

"Thank you for telling me about Connor. Give him my regards when you see him."

"I will. You deserved to know. It was his plan, I just helped out a little when needed and gave him some top cover. Had it not been for Malyshkin and his squad of crazies, this might have worked. We debated telling you it was an op, but we decided not to. Deniability. And we weren't sure how you'd react."

"No worries," I said.

"And I'm sorry for what I said in the hospital. It was…harsh. I hope you understand what I was doing."

"I do now," I said. "But thank you. I appreciate the apology."

"There's one more thing," she said. There always was. "Fedorov is alive."

That, I was not expecting.

I stared at her, unable to hide the stupid and confused look I knew was there.

Harper continued. "I learned all of this after the fact, and only through Connor. After the crash, you three were rushed to the hospital."

"They told me he was killed, a hit-and-run."

Harper shook her head. "Made up. Swiss intelligence knew about Fedorov already and suspected ties to the Russians. So, because Fedorov is a Swiss citizen, they did not disclose his identity when he was hospitalized and had him under guard. Once Fedorov woke up, they worked out some kind of deal so that he'd dime out the GRU operations in country in exchange for protection, a new identity, and secure relocation. Swiss officials put out word that he'd died in the crash. He took more of a shot than even Connor did. He's in a pretty bad way, as I understand it. He is also painting a nice picture of Russian intelligence operations inside Switzerland."

"How did you find out?"

"He figured out how to contact Connor. Said to say thank you."

Son of a bitch.

A question formed, and I started to ask but stopped. Natalie said, "What is it?"

I was about to ask her if Fedorov was GRU. I knew what he told me, that he'd been recruited. Though it struck me that might be what we needed to hear at the time.

I decided I didn't want to know. If that was his secret, I'd let him keep it.

"Nothing," I said.

Natalie Harper and I shook hands, and she left. I wished her well.

I flew out to see Dylan, and over a few beers in his backyard, I told him the full story. This time, I left nothing out.

"Thank you, Matt. You can't understand what this means."

Actually, I thought I could.

"Nothing has actually happened yet," I said.

"Yet," Dylan said.

"Yet," I agreed.

"It has to start somewhere. And you got us the truth. That matters more than anything else."

I'd tipped over the first domino. Jennie would handle the rest of them. Hopefully, this time, they would fall.

Jennie's series on Havana Syndrome was a global sensation, a spy novel come to life. I would have featured prominently in it, but I asked that she keep my involvement out. Instead, she referred to me only in the abstract, painting me as a relentless, swashbuckling, and anonymous private detective.

She used "dashing" at least once in the story.

Though it would've meant a gold mine of new work, I wanted to keep my name out of it for security reasons as much as for personal ones.

This case was unlike any other, before or since.

Often in my life, I've found myself on the wrong side of power. I've seen governments, ours and others, abuse that power for ignoble ends. This time it was different. It was not just the visceral betrayal of trust, it was the active measures used to not only cover it up but to convince the affected—and the public—nothing ever happened. That they were wrong. That they lied.

I never told Jennie about the deal I'd made with Fox.

She'd never have forgiven me. But I did it for reasons that she couldn't appreciate. She believed that given enough public pressure, the government would be forced to reconcile with the victims. I harbored no such fantasies. Perhaps I'd taken a page from Damon Fox's playbook. When faced with impossible odds, I'd made an improbable choice. One that I would have to live with. The day might come when Jennie would figure out what really happened. If it did, our relationship would be over. I'd have to live with that too.

For my part in this, I'd paid a steep price. The doctors told me to expect occasional, though infrequent and unpredictable, pain and disorientation for the rest of my life.

If what I'd done brought a measure of comfort to those who'd suffered far worse, it was worth it.

My phone rang, and I looked down to see it was Joshua McDonough.

I just let it ring.

Even Gods Bleed
Book 4 in The Gage Files

Someone wants a tech CEO gone. Murder was just the opening move.

Julian Kessler, the visionary CEO of NOVA AI, has pushed the boundaries of artificial intelligence, blurring the lines between human and machine. But progress comes at a price, and Kessler has made enemies—ones closer than he realizes. And when a ruthless smear campaign threatens to destroy his reputation, he turns to ex-CIA officer turned private investigator Matt Gage to uncover who's orchestrating his downfall and why.

Going undercover as a consultant, Gage soon realizes that NOVA AI's boardroom is a nest of hidden agendas. Some of the most powerful figures in the country have a vested interest in Kessler's ruin, and the deeper Gage looks, the more it becomes clear—this is more than just corporate sabotage.

Then the first body drops.

Now, in the crosshairs of a murder investigation, Gage finds himself caught between the police, a killer determined to keep him quiet, and a fight for control over a technology that could reshape the world. With his client's fate—and his own neck—on the line, he'll have to dust off the spycraft skills he thought he left behind. Because in this game, the only way out is to play it better than the rest.

**Get your copy today at
severnriverbooks.com**

AUTHOR'S NOTE

In researching this book, I relied on some excellent and courageous investigative journalism. First and foremost, the courageous work done by the team at *The Insider*, a group of investigative journalists whose primary focus is Russia and upon whom the Orpheus Foundation is partly based. *The Insider* has provided detailed and courageous reporting on the GRU's involvement in Havana Syndrome. Jeff Stein's *Spytalk* Substack was an invaluable source of information on this topic and espionage operations and tradecraft in general. I also relied on several pieces by journalists at CNN, the Associated Press, and *GQ*. Finally, the Vice News podcast series *Havana Syndrome* provided first-hand accounting by several victims.

Now, let's separate fact from fiction. Because I was using actual events as the backdrop for a fictional story, I tried to keep the timeline and locations of Havana Syndrome attacks as close to what was reported in the media. The last reported attack was against the Vienna embassy in 2021, and in July of that year, the US and Russia held a summit in Geneva to reset relations. The "five-minute, off-the-record" conversation was invented for this story. I don't know that Havana Syndrome was discussed at that meeting, but the attacks ceased following it, which I worked into the story. There was one additional attack reported at the NATO meeting in Vilnius in 2023. Curiously, this did not get much media attention at the time.

As for the suspected perpetrators, *The Insider* and others have long reported that Russia's military intelligence agency, the GRU, was responsible, and I have maintained that in the story. The outsourcing of the attacks to paramilitary contractors, as described in this book, was my own invention. I would also not be surprised for that to be proven true. Additionally, the name of the GRU's operation, "Projekt Molniya," was created for this story.

As of this writing (December 2024), neither the United States government as a whole nor the Intelligence Community have officially acknowledged that the "Anomalous Health Incidents" were the work of a foreign power. However, on December 5th of this year, the House's CIA Subcommittee released an unclassified interim report stating that it is "highly likely" that Havana Syndrome was the work of a foreign power. I suspect that between now and this book's publication in October 2025, there will be additional movement on this story.

I've attempted to create a plausible explanation for the Havana Syndrome incidents based on the information available to me. I also wanted to do so in a way that was respectful of the victims. It is to them that I humbly dedicate this work. I hope they receive the support and justice that they deserve.

ABOUT THE AUTHOR

Dale M. Nelson grew up outside of Tampa, Florida. He graduated from the University of Florida's College of Journalism and Communications and went on to serve as an officer in the United States Air Force. Following his military service, Dale worked in the defense, technology and telecommunications sectors before starting his writing career. He currently lives in Washington D.C. with his wife and daughters.

Sign up for the reader list at
severnriverbooks.com

Printed in the United States
by Baker & Taylor Publisher Services